LUCAS FLINT
VILLAIN TOWN
BIG BAD

aethonbooks.com

BIG BAD
©2023 LUCAS FLINT

This book is protected under the copyright laws of the United States of America. No part of this publication may be reproduced, stored in a retrieval system, or transmitted, in any form or by any means, without the prior permission in writing of the publisher, nor be otherwise circulated in any form of binding or cover other than that in which it is published and without a similar condition including this condition being imposed on the subsequent purchaser. Any reproduction or unauthorized use of the material or artwork contained herein is prohibited without the express written permission of the authors.

Aethon Books supports the right to free expression and the value of copyright. The purpose of copyright is to encourage writers and artists to produce the creative works that enrich our culture.

The scanning, uploading, and distribution of this book without permission is a theft of the author's intellectual property. If you would like to use material from the book (other than for review purposes), please contact editor@aethonbooks.com. Thank you for your support of the author's rights.

Aethon Books
www.aethonbooks.com

Print and eBook interior formatting and design by Josh Hayes. Artwork provided by George Patsouras.

Published by Aethon Books LLC.

Aethon Books is not responsible for websites (or their content) that are not owned by the publisher.

This book is a work of fiction. Names, characters, places, and incidents are the product of the author's imagination or are used fictitiously. Any resemblance to actual events, locales, or persons, living or dead is coincidental.

All rights reserved.

ALSO IN SERIES

VILLAIN TOWN

Big Bad

Arch Enemy

Villain

Check out the series here! (tap or scan)

CHAPTER 1

Damn, this attic was dusty. Had it really been *that* long since Mom last cleaned this place out?

Maybe Mom was right. Maybe I should have spent less time playing video games and more time doing actual productive adult things, like cleaning attics.

Of course, "playing video games," as Mom so lovingly put it, was also how I was putting bread on the table. Another productive adult thing that I was supposed to be doing. Not like Mom could work, given her current health problems.

Then again, it was not as though being a professional gamer was an especially lucrative career.

If it was, we would have moved out of this old house *ages* ago, definitely after Dad died.

Thinking about Dad's death made me sad, however, so I decided to get back to work sifting through the seemingly endless amount of boxes, covered furniture, and various random knickknacks that my parents, primarily Mom, had collected over the years. I even found a box of my old toys from when I was a kid, which I thought Mom had thrown out a long time ago.

Embarrassing.

Sighing, I sat down in a creaky chair that must have been at least a hundred years old and looked around. Boxes upon boxes were stacked everywhere I looked, some from our first move to the house before I was even born, others just full of things Mom couldn't bear to give away.

This whole thing was Mom's idea. She figured we could hold a yard sale to earn some money and clean out the house at the same time.

And to be frank, it wasn't a *bad* idea. We needed the money, after all, and we *did* have too much stuff, more stuff than we knew what to do with.

But the problem was that because I was the "young, healthy man," Mom decided that *I* should do all the heavy lifting, sorting through the boxes and carrying down anything in saleable condition from the attic to our front yard.

Given how we were in a two-story house, that was multiple trips up and down a couple flights of stairs.

And did I forget to mention that professional gamers usually don't have the physiques of bodybuilders and superhero movie actors?

But I couldn't complain.

I was a good person. Always the good son to my mom.

It would be cruel of me to make her do all the heavy lifting, given her age and health.

I decided to take a break. My aching muscles deserved it. Mom was probably fast asleep right now, anyway. She couldn't stay awake very long due to her illness.

Actually, a nap wouldn't be out of place right now …

Beep.

My eyes snapped open. Where did that sound come from? Did I imagine it?

Beep.

No. I definitely didn't imagine it, though it was very faint. But where—?

Beep.

My eyes darted over to the left side of the attic, the part I hadn't worked on yet. Light faintly streamed in through the blinds covering the big window at the front of the attic, though I didn't see the source of the beep.

But it was definitely coming from over there and I definitely hadn't imagined it.

Rising from the creaky old chair, I rushed over to the mess I hadn't cleaned yet and started digging through the boxes and junk, tossing things behind me. The beeping sound became louder and louder as I got rid of more stuff, until I finally found it:

A portable ... sewing case?

Sitting on the wooden floor before me was an old plastic case. I'd never seen it before, hence why I thought maybe it was Mom's old portable sewing machine.

What? You didn't know they made portable sewing machines?

Well, you do now. And they are *very* heavy. Ask me how I know.

But portable sewing machines don't beep. At least, Mom's didn't.

I took a closer look at the case and realized pretty quickly it wasn't a sewing machine after all. Aside from the irritating beep, it looked more like one of those old computers from the '70s. A word, *Osbourne*, was labeled on the side of the machine.

Wait ... Osbourne ...

I undid the clasps on either side of the front of the machine and pulled the top off, showing me exactly what it was.

And it definitely *wasn't* a sewing machine.

It was a ... computer? The front part became a clunky plastic keyboard, attached to the main device by some kind of belt or something. The machine didn't even seem to have a screen until I noticed that its "screen" was set in the middle of the device.

I called it a screen but it was about five inches tall, max. This thing made even my mom's old 2022 laptop look like cutting-edge technology. Seriously, it looked like something my grandpa would have owned when he was my age.

And it was *still* beeping, even though the machine didn't seem to be on. I tried lifting it, but the thing weighed like thirty pounds, so that didn't work.

But trying to move it around seemed to knock something loose, because a folded-up piece of paper fell out of the machine. Curious, I picked up the paper and, unfolding it, found this note in very familiar handwriting:

Annoyed by the beeping? So am I. Press Enter.
-RJB

Holy. Crap.

RJB were Grandpa's initials. Short for Robert J. Baker, same name as me, actually, because I was named after him when I was born. It was how he always signed little notes he used to write to me, which were usually riddles he would have me try to solve on my own. Even his voice sounded the same, even though the note was written. I could just hear him saying those very same words to me in that old, professory voice of his.

And it was just like him to acknowledge the problem, agree that it *was* a problem, and then give me vague instructions on how to fix it.

Even more importantly, however, this was absolute proof that this machine wasn't one of Mom's old portable sewing machines, but a personal belonging of my late grandfather. Given how little he left for us after he died, this was an amazing find, because Grandpa died penniless despite having so much wealth when he was alive.

And given how famous Professor Robert J. Baker was, maybe Mom's idea of a yard sale to raise money wasn't such a bad idea after all.

First things first, though: the riddle.

Yes, technically it was not a real "riddle," but that's what Grandpa always called the little intellectual challenges he gave me growing up. Sometimes they were actual riddles, but most of the time they were more like scavenger hunts with obscure clues and hints to get me thinking creatively.

But this was pretty straightforward, as far as Grandpa's riddles went. He was telling me what to do, which was kind of unusual for him. Then again, based on the beeping sound this thing was making, I guessed Grandpa probably wanted me—or someone—to find this note and follow its instructions.

Regardless, "press Enter" seemed pretty self-explanatory.

The keyboard on the old computer, which was obviously what the ancient machine was, had an Enter key. Kind of weird to see an actual physical keyboard after using holo-keyboards my whole life, but vintage stuff is cool, especially vintage stuff owned by Grandpa.

So I pressed the key …

And the keyboard fell apart in my lap. The keys bounced off my lap and scattered across the floor, causing me to panic. I immediately leaned forward to grab all the keys, worried that I had just destroyed a priceless object belonging to Grandpa, only to hear a *thunk* in front of me. I looked down.

Something had fallen out of the keyboard. Another device, this one smaller and rounder. Sleek and black, it reminded me of Mom's old miniature CD player she had when she was a teenager.

Only I immediately realized it wasn't a CD player at all.

It was a personal holo-projector. Pretty common device nowadays. You could record a holographic message of yourself to someone on the device, which could then be played back by said person at a later date. Most personal holo-projectors were big in the 2030s, but fell out of favor when handheld devices like smartphones could take and send them as easily as normal videos and messages. The beeping sound was coming from the projector, not the actual machine.

The outdated tech wasn't what caught my eye. The printed label attached to the top, however, did.

Picking up the projector—which was thankfully lighter than the bulky computer, though much louder now that it wasn't hidden inside the keyboard—I read the label:

Still annoyed by the beeping? Press the power button.
-RBJ

Wow. This was even more straightforward than the last note. There was even an arrow drawn on the note pointing to the black power button right underneath so I wouldn't miss it.

Grandpa *definitely* wanted me to find this device. His riddles were never this easy.

So I pressed the power button.

And a projection of Grandpa suddenly flickered into existence before me.

Startled, I almost dropped the holo-projector. Despite knowing what this machine was and what it did, it'd been ages since I last touched one and I wasn't emotionally prepared to see my long-dead grandfather again.

But it was him, all right. He looked almost exactly the same as I remembered him. Short, slightly stooped from age, with a shock of silvery-white hair that stood up in all directions. His tweed jacket, neatly folded button-up, and brown slacks made him look like the professor of philosophy he was.

But to me, he just looked like Grandpa.

Grandpa smiled. "Bravo, Robby, my boy. If you are watching this hologram, then that means the beeping has stopped and it is no longer annoying you. Congratulations! I hope you did not find the instructions too obscure or difficult to follow. I knew you are a smart man."

I chuckled. Grandpa always liked to give me a hard time. What some people might interpret as sarcasm or unnecessary harshness I knew were just Grandpa's ways of messing with me.

I missed it. Mostly because I missed him. I wiped away the tears in the corners of my eyes.

Grandpa was still talking. "I am sorry for the beeping. I know how annoying it can be, but I didn't know how else to make sure this thing caught your attention enough to make you try to do something about it. Otherwise, you would never have found my hologram. Or perhaps the wrong person would have found it and then … well, let's not dwell on what-ifs, shall we?"

I frowned. "You're talking like you're here."

I didn't know why I said that aloud. It wasn't like Grandpa could hear me. He was dead.

But then Grandpa's hologram looked straight at me and said, "Actually, I am, Robby. This is an interactive holo-message, powered by the miracle of artificial intelligence. Although my reactions are somewhat limited, I can interact with you to some degree in a way like your original grandfather could."

Right. I forgot about the interactive holo-messages, mostly because I'd never seen one in real life.

And as wonderful as it was to hear Grandpa call me "Robby" again, I knew this wasn't my real grandpa. It may have been based on and even programmed by him, but Grandpa died ten years ago. People talk about how far AI has come, but in my opinion, interactive holograms like this one would never be "real" to me.

Not when I knew the truth.

The cold, harsh truth.

But I didn't see any harm in responding to the AI clone of Grandpa, so I said, "Cool. I didn't know Grandpa left me a holo-message. It wasn't in his will."

Grandpa, or the AI pretending to be him, chuckled. "Well, I didn't put a lot of things in my will, as you are about to find out. Such as the remainder of my fabulous wealth, for example."

I looked at Grandpa in confusion. "You are not Grandpa. Don't act like you are."

Grandpa tilted his head to the side. "Excuse me?"

I shook my head. "You're just a message. The real Grandpa died ten years ago. It's just … you're not real."

"Grandpa" tapped his chin. "I suppose. Would it make it more comfortable for you if I spoke of Robert J. Baker in the abstract?"

I pursed my lips. "Not really."

"Then I will continue to act as if I am him," said Grandpa. "It's easier for both of us and more accurate to the message that the 'real' Robert J. Baker left you."

I didn't miss the odd emphasis on the word "real" the projection used, almost as if it disagreed with that characterization of itself.

Weird. Then again, AI had gotten pretty advanced over the years. Even to the point where a lot of people were choosing to live inside video games than face the real world.

Not me. I knew what happened when someone got too comfy in virtual reality. I didn't want to end up like my brother.

Grandpa cleared his throat. "Anyway, as I said, there are many things I didn't put in my will, including the remainder of my wealth."

I frowned. "But Grandpa died without any money. He—you—didn't leave Mom and me anything."

That was true. Although Grandpa was born into a wealthy family, he wasted a lot of it investing in failed ventures into AI and virtual reality. As much as I loved Grandpa, even I couldn't deny that he was kind of an idiot when it came to money.

If he'd had left us money, then maybe I could afford to get Mom into a good hospital to have her treated for her disease.

That was why Mom hated him, by the way. And I couldn't really blame her for that.

Grandpa, however, chuckled again. "It's true that I spent nearly all of my money before my death, but note the word I used: *nearly*. I saved some of it, hid it somewhere no one could find it. No one, that is, but you, Robby, my favorite grandson."

Another inside joke: I was Grandpa's favorite, but so was my older brother, Daniel. Depending on which of us he was talking to, either Daniel or I was the favorite of the moment.

Guess this machine was pretty good. Very lifelike.

But still not him. Never him.

Machines weren't people.

"Exactly how much are we talking about here?" I said. "A few hundred? A few thousand? Ten thousand?"

Grandpa smirked. "More like ten *million*, Robby. Ten million dollars. Enough for anyone to live off of for the rest of their life. And maybe cover a few unexpected medical bills along the way."

My heart nearly stopped when Grandpa said that.

Ten million dollars … I couldn't even imagine that kind of money. I barely cracked $35k a year with my gaming. That, plus Mom's Social Security and my late dad's Social Security, was all that kept us afloat, leaving little for anything else, including Mom's medical expenses that just seemed to mount higher and higher every day.

"I see I got your attention," said Grandpa. "Good. Because I am about to tell you exactly how you can get that ten million dollars. Without needing my will."

I stepped closer to the hologram, my eyes fixed on Grandpa. "How? I'm all ears."

Grandpa smiled. "You will have to do one of your favorite things: play a video game."

I smiled in return. "Play a video game? I do that all the time. Which game? Is it one I've played before?"

Grandpa's smile seemed to turn slightly sinister. "It's not one you've played before, no, at least not to my knowledge. But it is a game you have heard of and know quite well: The world's biggest, most popular virtual reality massively multiple-player role-playing game.

"Also known as Capes Online."

CHAPTER 2

Nope.

I immediately turned off the holo-projector, put it back inside the old laptop, and went downstairs. I closed the attic and even thought about locking it up, but decided against it. It's not like Grandpa's actual ghost was up there. His hologram couldn't follow me as long as I kept the projector it was stored on inside the attic.

I stomped down the hallway, walked into my room, closed the door, and immediately lay down on my bed. Staring at the cracked plaster ceiling of the room I'd lived in since middle school, I scowled.

Capes Online.

Really, Grandpa? *Really?*

Okay, I knew that that projection still wasn't Grandpa. Given how Grandpa had died ten years ago, he couldn't have known about the Blackout.

Or the second Blackout that followed not long after the first.

Or what that fucking game did to my older brother's mind.

But still. Out of all of the games in the world, why did Grandpa have to hide his wealth inside *that* one?

Sorry. I probably should explain why Capes Online was the evilest video game ever created by a power-hungry, profit-driven megacorporation in the entire history of video games.

Capes Online was a VRMMORPG. And not just *any* VRMMORPG,

but the first, biggest, and most popular. Kind of surprising, given how it was a superhero game and not your standard medieval fantasy like so many others.

Probably because, unlike previous attempts at VR games, Capes Online was *real*. Or felt that way. The VR tech used to immerse players inside the game was so lifelike that people said it's impossible to tell the difference between being in the game and in the real world.

And I said "people said" because I'd personally never played the game and never, ever would. Even before the Blackouts, people worried about players losing the ability to tell the difference between real life and virtual reality due to the advanced tech the game used.

Everyone else pooh-poohed those concerns. Even when there were documented cases of what the game did to people's minds.

Like my older brother, for example.

Then everything came to a head last year when the Blackout happened not once, but *twice*.

To sum it up, millions of people all over the world got locked into the game. No one could log in or out. The first time, they were locked in by a Villain NPC named Dark Kosmos, while the second time, it was a so-called glitch referring to itself as Paradox that did it.

And both events happened within the span of roughly a few months of each other.

As you could probably guess, tons of people died after being stuck inside the game for so long. Granted, players inside the game were able to free everyone else from the game pretty quickly, but it was still one of the scariest things ever, in my opinion. Even the people who didn't die logged off forever and needed tons of therapy. Some countries, like China, even outright banned the game, and I didn't blame them.

But here in the United States, Capes Online was still legal to play, even though its parent corporation, SI Games, got into hot water with the federal government over its role in both Blackouts. Last I heard, the game was still online and was being rebranded as a virtual life simulator or something. I'd even heard rumors that you could apparently upload your mind to the game and live there forever.

I didn't know because I didn't pay attention to that.

Even before the Blackouts, though, I knew all too well how

dangerous VR games could be to people. A year before the first Blackout, my older brother, Daniel, … well, I didn't even want to think about what happened to him. We were just lucky we got him to stop playing the game before the Blackouts, otherwise I was almost certain he would have died during one of those awful events.

You might think it weird that a pro gamer like me would want nothing to do with the most popular game in the world, but Capes Online wasn't the only game in town (literally). I preferred playing games that didn't require lying inside a pod and hooking your brain up to a computer, giving everyone *else* with a computer access to your mind.

Seriously, I used to wonder how stupid my parents' generation was for falling for those social media companies who stole your personal data and sold it off to the higher bidder. Given how my generation just jumped into VR games wholeheartedly, though, maybe it wasn't my parents' generation that was dumb. Maybe humanity is stupid in general.

Regardless, all this to say that Grandpa must be either lying or insane to have hidden his wealth in Capes Online and expecting me to go and get it. Even if there was life-changing money in there—and ten million dollars would definitely be life-changing—there was no way in hell I was going to risk my sanity and mental health just for it.

Then again, maybe it wasn't surprising. Before his death, Grandpa had always been interested in VR stuff due to being a philosopher. He'd even written a book on the concept of digital immortality, *Our Virtual Immortal Future*, that was a bestseller for a while in the early to mid-2000s. I never read it, even though we had boxes of copies of it in the attic (another one of the few things Grandpa left for us), because philosophy was boring.

And to be fair, Daniel only lost his mind *after* Grandpa's death, so it wasn't like Grandpa could have known just how dangerous VR would become. He probably only saw the upsides and never considered the downsides.

Grandpa was an optimist. I appreciated that about him, even though I'm more of a pessimist (or realist, depending on your point of view).

My thoughts were interrupted by the sound of glass breaking

down the hall and loud curses just outside my door. Jumping to my feet, I opened the door and rushed into the hallway, heart pounding.

But as it turned out, I didn't have to worry. Mom, who despite being younger than Grandpa when he died looked even older than him, was leaning on the railing built into the hallway's walls. A shattered cup lay on the floor at her feet, the scent of sweet tea vaguely filling the air around us.

"Mom, what are you doing?" I said gently, walking over to her while doing my best to avoid stepping in the tea.

Mom breathed in deeply before answering. "Just trying to get myself a cup of tea. I knew you were working hard in the attic, so I didn't want to bother—"

Mom suddenly broke into a series of incredibly loud coughs. She coughed so hard that she sounded like she was hacking up a lung, forcing me to grab her and say, "It's okay, Mom. If you wanted tea, you should have just asked me to get you some. You need to rest, like the doctor said you should."

Mom, her coughing fit dying down, looked at me with her startlingly green eyes. "You're right, Robby. But you know me and my tea. And I'm just not used to lying in bed all day."

I nodded. Mom used to be a very active woman when she was younger, on her feet all the time, always doing something. She used to regularly participate in triathlons in her youth and was even a personal trainer for a while. Hard to believe when you saw how small, weak, and frail she was now, but I still remembered being taken on runs with her when I was a little kid.

Never did enjoy them, but I also never thought I would miss having that time with my mother so much, either. Guess you never appreciate what you have until it's gone.

I led Mom back to her room and helped her back into bed. Promising to get her a fresh cup of tea, I turned to leave the room, only to catch something white out of the corner of my eye. I glanced to the left and saw an opened envelope on the top of her dresser, barely hidden underneath a book.

"Mom, where did this letter come from?" I said, gesturing at the envelope.

Mom broke into a coughing fit again, although I knew her well enough to tell when she was faking it and she was definitely faking it now. "W-What letter? You know I can't get the mail on my own anymore."

That was definitely a lie. Even though nearly everywhere offered the ability to pay bills online nowadays, Mom was stubbornly old-fashioned and wanted a paper bill anyway for "records." I had set up a pulley system in the hall to let her get the mail that was delivered to the front door every day without having to go down the stairs. That was how Mom could get the mail despite barely ever walking down the stairs herself.

But I wasn't offended. Mom had a tendency to lie whenever she learned bad news she didn't want to share with me, probably because she didn't want to hurt me.

Of course, if this bill was what I thought it was—

I pulled it out from underneath the thick tome and immediately saw that it was from the hospital. Even before pulling the piece of paper out of the envelope and unfolding it, I knew it had to be another bill.

And it was.

Actually, calling it "another bill" was the understatement of the year. It was huge, easily the biggest hospital bill we'd gotten yet.

And that was on *top* of what we already owed the hospital.

"Mom," I said slowly, looking at her, "when did this bill arrive in the mail?"

Mom pursed her lips. "Last week."

"Last week—?" I almost swore. "Mom, you can't hide keep hiding the bills from me like this. Even if you do, you know I can just log into your account with the hospital and see all of our bills online anytime, right? Including this one?"

Mom didn't meet my gaze. "I know, Robby, I know, but I didn't want to stress you out. I just want you to be happy."

I sighed. "Hiding the truth from me doesn't make me happy, Mom. You should know that by now. Anyway, are there any other bills you're hiding from me?"

Mom shook her head. "No. That's the only one."

This time, I could tell she was telling the truth.

With another sigh, I promised to get her the tea again, though not before getting *her* to promise not to leave her bed again without calling me first. I left the room, hospital bill in hand, walking toward the staircase to the kitchen.

Damn it. We owed so much money to the hospital it wasn't even funny. And that was *before* Mom's most recent diagnosis of a particularly deadly form of cancer, which could only be treated with some super-expensive treatment that our meager health insurance couldn't cover.

Oh, and did I forget to mention that we were still back-paying taxes to the IRS that my dad had apparently "forgotten" to pay before his death? It wasn't as much as Mom's hospital bills, but it was still a lot.

I stopped at the top of the stairs, hospital bill in hand, my eyes fixed on the huge number. It wasn't even that big, honestly. It was just knowing that we had yet *another* bill to pay on top of everything else we owed. The straw that broke the camel's back, so to speak.

And professional gaming wasn't bringing in nearly enough to cover that. Frankly, it probably never would, unless one of my online followers dropped a huge donation or a kindly billionaire decided to sponsor my livestreams.

Ha. "Kindly billionaire." I cracked a smile at my own stupid joke.

But I didn't even need a billionaire. Even a kindly millionaire would be nice.

I looked toward the attic. I had had zero intention of talking to that AI pretending to be Grandpa again, much less taking it up on its offer. Maybe I'd sell the holo-projector at the yard sale for a couple hundred bucks and he would be someone else's problem.

A few hundred bucks versus ten million dollars that would pay all our bills and then some ... give or take losing my sanity in Capes Online, of course. And Mom was so sick...

Right then and there, I made a decision. I didn't know if I'd regret it or not. I didn't think I would. I hoped I wouldn't.

Clutching the hospital bill firmly in my right hand, I climbed the stairs to the attic again.

I needed the money. *Mom* needed the money.

And this was our best chance at clawing our way out of the financial hole we'd dug ourselves into.

Even if it meant risking my own comfort—and sanity.

CHAPTER 3

One week later…

"Robby!" Mom called out suddenly, voice slightly muffled by the walls of my room. "There's someone at the door for you!"

Startled, I almost fell out of my gaming chair. Running over to the window of my room, I tore open the red curtains and gazed down at the yard in front of our house.

Mom was right. She must have seen them from the window of her room. A delivery truck was parked in the driveway, the back open. Two big men carried a huge crate between them from within the truck. They seemed to be using one of those floating device thingies that I'd seen laborers use to move heavy crates and boxes around, though it still looked like a lot of physical work.

It was here.

Finally.

I bounded out of my room, down the stairs, and to the front door. Opening the door, I immediately directed the delivery guys to the living room, where I'd spent the last week moving everything out of the way to create a space for the crate "Grandpa" had told me was on the way.

The delivery guys dropped off the crate right where I told them to. They even opened it for me, removing all of the wooden panels and revealing what was inside:

An SI Games GamePod. A Zeus Model, specifically, and not those New Future Models that supposedly let you upload your mind to the game. Big and sleek, it was roughly six feet long and a couple feet wide, more than big enough for the average person to rest inside. It even came with a copy of Capes Online pre-installed.

The delivery guys were even kind enough to hook it up for me and explain how it worked. I already knew, of course, because Daniel had shown me how to use his GamePod once before he totally lost his mind inside the game.

Did I mention that GamePods were kind of like sensory deprivation tanks? And that was partly why so many people who played VR games like Capes Online lost their marbles?

But I didn't share my phobias with the delivery guys, who seemed like a couple of working-class dudes just happy for a job. I didn't even have to pay them for the delivery, mostly because "Grandpa" already had.

Once the delivery guys left, I stood in front of the GamePod. I hadn't opened the lid yet to get inside, mostly because I was having to fight against my own instincts that told me that that was a *bad* idea.

"Worried, Robby?" said Grandpa's voice suddenly behind me. "It's perfectly safe."

I looked over my shoulder to see Grandpa standing in the entryway to the living room. Of course, Grandpa wasn't actually there. It was his AI holo-message. I'd brought the projector down to the living room so I could have him around in case I needed his help figuring out how this damn thing worked or if there was anything else I needed to know before going inside.

"Perfectly safe, huh?" I said with a snort. "Tell that to Daniel—and everyone who got locked in the Blackouts."

Grandpa shrugged. "I have no knowledge of any of that, being an AI. But I wouldn't ask you to do this if I thought it was dangerous. I'm sure of it."

I pursed my lips. That was true. The real Grandpa always looked out for me. He would challenge me, sure, but never put me in any sort of life-threatening situation.

But however much this guy looked and acted like Grandpa, I knew he wasn't.

Grandpa folded his arms in front of his chest. "Besides, I would have expected a 'thank you.' After all, you didn't even have to order it yourself, much less pay for it. I saved you a great financial burden."

That was true. When I went back up to the attic a week ago and told Grandpa I accepted his offer, the holo-projector itself immediately sent out an order to a nearby department store to deliver a GamePod directly to my house. Apparently, it had been pre-set to do so by Grandpa before his death, which included Grandpa prepaying for the whole thing ahead of time, so all I had to do was be present at the house to accept the package and oversee the installation.

And yeah, that set off some alarm bells in my head. It implied that Grandpa had apparently planned this out well in advance of his own death. I mean, the man had been dead for ten years. How could he have known that I would find his holo-projector and activate it, much less that I would accept his offer to go into Capes Online to get his money and need a GamePod to do it?

But I wasn't mad. I'd always known Grandpa was one of the smartest people I knew. I just didn't know *how* smart he was.

Mom, of course, didn't know about Grandpa or the holo-projector. I'd just told her that I'd won an online contest for a free GamePod and that I planned to use it to make money in VR. I even made up a lie about how VR gaming was more lucrative than normal gaming, which was true. VR streamers and gamers DID make a hell of a lot more than your average non-VR streamer or gamer.

I checked.

Although as far as I knew, no streamer or gamer was making ten million dollars.

Mom didn't seem to mind too much, nor did she ask any probing questions. She did ask me if I was worried about becoming "like Daniel," but I'd already told her I was going to take regular breaks from VR to prevent that. According to the mental health professionals I spoke to when Daniel had his breakdown, the best way to avoid the mental health problems associated with VR was to spend no more than two hours in a GamePod at a time and spend lots of time outside and exercising.

Honestly, I didn't plan to spend even one hour in that thing if I could help it.

I licked my lips and gazed at the hologram. "What will I do after I log in?"

Grandpa scratched his chin. "Once you log into Capes Online, you will receive further instructions. I can't say more than that, mostly because my original self didn't program me with more information beyond this point."

"So you're a glorified note, basically," I said.

Grandpa shrugged. "I was designed with a very specific purpose in mind, a purpose I like to think I excel at."

I rolled my eyes. "Right. Well, I guess I should get to it, then. No point in delaying the inevitable."

Taking a deep breath, I popped open the lid of the GamePod. The interior smelled vaguely like a new car and was cushioned with velvet memory foam padding. I hesitated a moment before climbing inside and lying down. The padding was actually really soft and comfortable. I could see why some people even used their GamePods as beds. Certainly more comfortable than my old mattress.

But I didn't fool myself.

This wasn't a bed.

It was more like a yet-to-be-activated mental torture device.

Fortunately, the delivery guys had shown me where the emergency off switch was. It was a small red button underneath the locking mechanism for the lid. It was hidden well enough that I probably wouldn't accidentally hit it during gameplay but would be able to press it if I needed to get out in a hurry for whatever reason.

That comforted me, though not much.

Before closing the lid, however, I looked toward Grandpa, who nodded at me and said, "How does it feel, Robby?"

"Comfy," I replied, "though I don't see why you would care."

Grandpa smiled. "Why wouldn't I care about the comfort of my own grandson?"

I scowled. "For the millionth time, you're not really my—"

Without warning, the lid of the GamePod closed down on top of me and I heard it lock in with a soft *click*. Before I could locate the emergency unlock switch, a VR helmet suddenly fell onto my head, covering my vision.

For a long moment, all I could see was blackness …

And then, without warning, a message popped up in my view:

WELCOME TO YOUR SI GAMES GAMEPOD™, ROBERT! INITIALIZING ... SYNCING GAMEPOD™ WITH BRAIN WAVES ... CONNECTING TO INTERNET ... STANDBY FOR TOTAL IMMERSION ...

I waited for what felt like an eternity for "total immersion," whatever that meant. During that brief yet seemingly endless time, I seriously considered flipping the emergency unlock switch, jumping out of the GamePod, calling up the department store, and demanding a refund. My anxiety was bad enough normally, but the brief sensory deprivation was already making it worse.

Then, without warning, what looked like a movie started playing before me.

Actually, it was more like I was *in* a movie. I hovered in the sky, seemingly of my own free will. Wind whipped through my hair and a sea of clouds spread out around me in every direction.

But my attention was forcibly diverted to the sprawling mega city below me. And by "mega city," I mean *mega*. It was like New York City, Tokyo, and Beijing had an orgy and this was the result of their unholy union. The way it spread out everywhere reminded me a lot of Oklahoma City, my hometown, actually, although it looked much denser than OKC, too.

Nor was the city empty. I could see cars, trains, and people rushing through the streets, giving me the impression I was looking at the blood flowing through the arteries of some kind of gigantic creature.

But the streets weren't the only things full of life. Human beings flew among the massive skyscrapers in colorful costumes, some with majestic capes flowing out behind them, others clad merely in spandex. Those who couldn't fly apparently just jumped from rooftop to rooftop or used other travel methods, like web-slinging, to get around easily.

Wow. This really *did* look like real life.

But I had to remind myself:

It was just a game. A very advanced game, maybe, but a game nonetheless.

A disembodied, somewhat middle-aged, familiar-sounding male voice suddenly blared in my ears, startling me. "Fifty years ago, a significant portion of humans all over the globe developed strange and fantastic abilities, thanks in no small part to the discovery of enigmatic 'Power Crystals' found deep within the Earth's crust. From the United States to Japan and everywhere in between, humans in every country across the planet began leaping skyscrapers in a single bound, lifting cars overhead with one hand, sprouting the wings of mighty falcons or developing other animal-like characteristics, controlling the elements with a thought, and every other superpower once thought to reside only in the domain of comic books and movies."

The camera zoomed in on what looked like the tallest building in the city. A man wearing a hoodie and jacket stood at the very edge of the building's rooftop, looking like he was thinking of jumping. I tried to tell him not to, but for some reason, I couldn't talk, so all I could do was watch as the young man jumped off the roof ...

And floated in the air like a cloud.

The man blinked in disbelief, looked at his hands and feet, and then experimentally started moving in the air. Despite his initial awkward attempts, the man soon got the hang of flying and flew laps around the building. Office workers—maybe his coworkers?—ran to the windows of their offices to see the man flying, pointing and talking excitedly, taking pictures and videos on their phones.

The voice continued speaking. "But not all humans used their Powers for good. Although the emergence of superpowers in people brought about many dramatic changes in humanity, one thing it didn't change was human nature. Many used their newfound powers to hurt others, rob banks, and commit all sorts of heinous crimes. These evil people—called Villains—swept the globe, ushering in an era of crime and lawlessness the likes of which humanity had never seen before. Indeed, human civilization itself began to come undone due to the reckless actions of so many Villains running rampant, governments unable to keep up with the meteoric rise in superpower criminal activity."

The camera shifted again. This time, it showed me the lobby of what appeared to be a bank before the front door blew open and several masked men wielding guns entered, led by a man whose hands smoked like he had just caused the explosion. The man immediately barked silent orders to the gunmen, who began gathering up hostages among the employees and bank customers.

Another scene shift, now showing a dark alley in some big city (maybe the city from before? I couldn't tell), where a young woman was backing away from a man who appeared to be part-crocodile, based on his reptilian features. He grinned wickedly, licking his lips hungrily and clicking his clawed fingers together, while the young woman backed away, trembling with fearful eyes.

Seeing the woman in danger made me angry. I wanted to help her. I knew this was a game and she wasn't real, but I still wanted to help her. Hopefully I wasn't already losing my mind.

"But not all hope was lost," said the voice. "While many people used their Powers for selfish purposes, just as many decided to use their newfound Powers to protect the powerless and weak and uphold truth and justice. These people, called Heroes by the general public, clashed often with the Villains, thus turning back the tide of chaos that threatened to engulf society itself."

The last couple of scenes replayed, only this time with better endings than I expected. In the bank robbery, a man in red and blue tights suddenly broke through the window, landing in front of the explosion man. The explosion man raised a hand, but the Hero punched him in the face, knocking him out in one blow, and sending his Minions running.

Good.

In the other scene, a man in green tights and a tiger mask dropped down from the shadows and fired a punching-bag-tipped arrow at the would-be rapist. The arrow slammed into the back of the rapist's head, knocking him flat onto the ground. The frightened woman rushed into the arms of her rescuer, crying tears of joy while he held her.

Again, I knew this was a video game and none of this was real. But damn … if I had to play this game, I might as well do some good and be a Hero.

"Welcome to the world of Capes Online," the voice finished, "where every choice you make decides your fate. Which side will you choose in the never-ending battle between good and evil? Choose wisely."

I snorted. Who would ever *willingly* choose to be a Villain?

A loud, surprisingly epic orchestral song blared in my ears just then. The bird's-eye view of the mega city appeared before me again, only this time, the title of the game, CAPES ONLINE, was superimposed over my view. The subtitle, in smaller font, appeared below the title, reading, HEROES, VILLAINS & SIDEKICKS.

Sidekicks? Did that mean I could choose to be someone else's Sidekick in the game?

Before I could fully explore the implications of having *Sidekick* in the title, the title screen vanished only to be abruptly replaced by a notification. Set in a blue box with white text, the notification read thus:

Before you begin, please take a moment to adjust your character settings, such as height, skin color, hair color, and more. Although your GamePod^{TM} does its best to accurately translate your physical body in the real world to the world of Capes Online to make your experience as lifelike as possible, we understand if you want to make a few adjustments to your body first.

NOTE: *This will not affect your Costume or Powers, which will be decided once you enter the world of Capes Online itself.*

A full-scale 3D model of myself in the real world appeared on the screen before me. At first, I thought I was looking into a mirror or something, before I realized it was actually the character creation screen.

I didn't know whether to be impressed or horrified by how accurate the 3D model of myself was. It looked almost exactly like me in the real world. Tall, almost lanky, though toned, with short dirty-blond hair. Even my clothes, a bright blue T-shirt and jeans, were exactly what I was wearing in real life right now.

I scrolled through the options available to me. They weren't joking about making a few "adjustments." I could change literally *everything*. Height, skin color, eye color, hair style and color, clothes, musculature ... and I could change it in the most minute of ways, too. I could even remove the acne on my face.

Now I was starting to understand why people became addicted to this game. How many people took full advantage of these options to make a body for themselves that was superior to their real body in every way? And who wouldn't, after playing in said body for a long time, decide to *stay* in that body or prefer it over their real one?

Even to someone like me, who knew the dangers of VR very well, the temptation was hard to ignore. I never was overweight, but I'd always been bullied for being small and skinny at school. There were more than a few things about my physical body I would have liked to change, and I could do it all here with a simple thought.

But it wasn't real. None of this was. "Total immersion" may have been the goal of the game, but my goal was to get in, get Grandpa's money, and get out.

So I decided against changing my body *too* much. Okay, I will admit I did alter things a little bit. I made myself slightly more muscular, for one, and removed my acne. I figured that being a superhero meant I needed more muscle than I currently had, and I hated with a burning passion my adult acne that never went away.

Besides, these were just small things. I didn't make myself look like someone else entirely. I just made myself look a little ... better. Like wearing your Sunday best instead of those sweats that had been in the hamper for a week, for example.

That was a good way to think about it. My VR self was just another change of clothes. It wasn't really me.

Right?

That done, I clicked the Save button with a thought and the character creation screen vanished, replaced by a new notification that came out of nowhere:

> *Body adjustments saved! Now choose your Pain Level. Your Pain Level determines how much and how extreme the pain the Dynamic Environment System (or DES for short) stimulates in your brain. Pain Levels also determine your experience level gain, and certain*

levels are only available to adults and those without preexisting medical conditions!

Choose from the Levels below:
- *Easy*
- *Tough*
- *Difficult*
- *Hard*
- *Real*

WARNING: *Once selected, Pain Levels* **cannot** *be changed except by contacting Capes Online customer service directly or deleting your saved file and starting over. Choose wisely.*

I snorted. "Choose wisely" must have been the game's tagline or something. Bet there was a guy in SI Games' marketing department who felt real pleased with himself when he came up with that. Maybe he even got a bonus for his genius creativity.

But anyway, this was apparently Capes Online's infamous Pain System. Based on the research I'd done ahead of time, "Easy" meant you basically felt no pain except maybe if you stubbed your toe, while "Real" meant you felt what you would feel if you got hurt in real life.

As for why anyone who wasn't totally insane or a masochist (or both) would choose anything other than Easy, that was because, as the game itself alluded, experience gain varied wildly from level to level. Easy basically meant you got the slowest experience gain, while Real meant you got the highest possible gain from encounters and missions, and therefore would level faster than if you were a wuss (or intelligent person) and chose not to subject yourself to real pain.

Someone might wonder why anyone would choose the possibility of feeling real pain in exchange for leveling up your character in a video game.

That same person has probably never meet an actual hardcore gamer in real life. Because I can assure you, I knew one too many gamers willing to go to extreme lengths just for a few measly extra points, up to and including injuring their own bodies.

I wouldn't put *anything* past gamers.

But because I was neither insane nor interested in maximizing my character growth as quickly as possible, I selected "Easy." I doubted it would make much of a difference when it came to getting the money, so there was no need to subject myself to Real Pain and potentially drive myself insane.

A small pop-up appeared when I selected Easy, more or less explaining what I already did about the balance between feeling pain and gaining points. I impatiently clicked Confirm and the Pain Level selection screen vanished and was immediately replaced by the following notification:

> **Congratulations! You are now ready to enter the dynamic and ever-changing world of Capes Online. Before you can truly begin playing, however, you need to go through your Origin Story. Be warned, the decisions you make in your Origin Story will have ramifications you can only begin to comprehend. Each decision you make will determine whether you're a Hero or a Villain. As always, choose wisely.**

Origin Story? Guess it made sense. All superheroes had origin stories, whether they were bitten by a radioactive spider or were the last surviving member of a dying world sent to Earth. I imagined it was probably more like a glorified tutorial or something.

Although I was annoyed at how it kept bringing up "Villain" like that was a valid choice. I knew it was just a game and all, but the very last thing I wanted was to become a Villain. Good people didn't become Villains, after all, even if doing evil things in video games could be fun sometimes.

The notification vanished and the darkness around me evaporated, leaving me standing in a city that highly resembled the mega city I saw in the opening cinematic. The towering buildings looked even taller up close and I felt like I was in a real city.

Then an elderly woman screamed behind me, "Purse thief!"

CHAPTER 4

BEFORE GETTING TO THE PURSE THIEF PART, I WANTED TO SAY HOW *overwhelming* Capes Online's virtual reality system was.

Seriously. The transition from the title screen to the actual game was so smooth I almost felt like I was standing in the real world. The dilapidated buildings around me looked—and smelled—so *real*. The dying rays of the setting sun felt as warm on my skin as the sun did in the real world. The taste of dirt and smoke in the air was real, too, though a little too real for my taste. Even the random city background noises were so believable I almost thought I was standing in the streets of Oklahoma City back in the physical world.

Touching my clothes, I felt the soft, cotton surface of my T-shirt, along with the comparatively rougher (but still quite comfortable) denim of my jeans.

But somehow, things didn't just feel real. They felt *better*. The light was stronger, the colors of the buildings around me more vivid, the city skyline looked sharper than any any video game should have, especially the strange dome-like structure in the distance. The calm evening breeze felt sweeter on the skin. Even the overturned trashcan nearby looked more real than any trashcan I'd seen in the real world. Not to mention my clothes, despite being identical to what I wore in the real world, seemed to fit better and feel more comfortable here, too.

That was the scary part. Not that Capes Online's VR *looked* real, but that it felt even more real than the real world.

I wasn't normally prone to sensory overload, but I was struggling to take everything in at once. The vivid sensations were almost overwhelming, to the point where I seriously considered logging off right away. I had no idea what that would do to my Origin Story, but I almost didn't care. I just needed a break.

Then someone ran into me and knocked me flat off my feet onto the street. I fell on my hands and knees, even scraping my palms against the pavement as I heard the person run past me. I held up my slightly bloody palms, amazed at how lifelike they looked and felt. Even the pain from the scrapes felt more real than it would in the real world, sharper and more tactile. Yet still not quite as painful as it would have been in the real world, if that makes sense, due to my Pain Level being on Easy.

"Young man!" an elderly female voice behind me said sharply. "Are you going to get my purse back from that thief or just stare at your hands all day like an idiot?"

Startled, I looked up to see a guy in street clothes running away from me. He wasn't very fast, probably because he was also really fat.

First, I wanted to see who this lady was. I looked over my shoulder and almost started again.

The oldest, ugliest-looking lady was glaring out at me from under her hood. Seriously, she looked like a stereotypical old witch, minus the green skin but with extra pimples and moles. I wasn't trying to be rude, but wow.

She even wore a black cloak like a witch, her white hair poking out from under her hood. Her eyes were a startling orange, almost red, and she smelled like she showered in onion juice.

I crinkled my nose. "Ew."

"Ew?" the elderly woman repeated. "Didn't your mother ever teach you how to properly talk to a lady, young man? I doubt you have a girlfriend."

"Sorry, ma'am," I said as I rose to my feet. I wasn't sure why I was apologizing to what was probably an NPC. It wasn't like she had actual feelings I was offending. "I'm just not used to, well, this place."

The elderly woman perked up suddenly. "It's been *decades* since anyone called me 'ma'am.' Perhaps you did learn some manners from your mother, after all."

Her abrupt change in demeanor seemed weird to me, but because I didn't want to piss her off again, I pointed at the running guy and said, "Did you say that that guy stole your purse?"

The elderly woman scowled. "He most certainly did! I, a lonely widow, was walking this street outside my humble apartment when this hooligan, who was almost as disrespectful as you, assaulted me, stole my purse, and ran off like the miscreant he is! Can you get my purse back for me?"

I ignored the jab about me being disrespectful. NPC, remember? She was probably programmed by some bored programmer to act this way. Probably thought it made her quirky or interesting, but I thought it just made her a handful.

Even so, I recognized this was part of the game's opening tutorial. I didn't understand Capes Online's "Alignment System," as I heard it was called, entirely well, but it seemed like our Origin Story determined a player's starting Alignment.

And because I wanted to be a Hero, the obvious heroic thing to do in this scenario was to return this woman's stolen purse to her. Stopping a purse thief seemed like a very cliché origin to me, but I guessed it was slightly more creative than foiling a bank robbery or whatever.

Then two notifications popped up in front of me:

MISSION: *Stop the purse thief*

A sweet, innocent old widow was assaulted by a rude hooligan while on her morning walk. Even worse, the disrespectful miscreant stole her purse, which has all of her life savings and precious personal belongings in it.

Although you are an Unaligned Civilian yourself and definitely not a Hero like the kind you see on TV, you feel a powerful urge to help the woman, even if it means putting your own life at risk. You don't know if that man is armed, after all. Or if he belongs to a gang or something.

ALIGNMENT: *Hero*
DIFFICULTY: *Easy*
RARITY: *Common*
SUCCESS: *Retrieving the purse and returning it to its rightful owner*
FAILURE: *Letting the purse thief get away with the purse or stealing it yourself*
REWARDS: *Instant promotion to the Hero Alignment*

ACCEPT? Y/N

My first quest, or "mission," as the game called them. That gelled with the research I did on Capes Online before logging in. Funny how even the game acknowledged that stopping a purse thief was cliché with its *Common* designation for the mission.

Before I accepted the mission, however, sheer curiosity and my desire to avoid missing out on potentially important information drove me to check out the second notification:

MISSION: *Take the purse for yourself*

A weak, annoying old woman evidently didn't realize how dangerous living in the Villain Sector of town was and got robbed outside her home by an enterprising individual who saw an opportunity to enrich himself.

Any half-competent Villain knows when to swoop in and take the rewards after others have done all the hard work. Are you motivated enough to steal the woman's purse from the other thief or are you going to let this perfectly good opportunity to get some quick cash slip you by?

ALIGNMENT: *Villain*
DIFFICULTY: *Easy*
RARITY: *Common*
SUCCESS: *Steal the purse from the thief*

FAILURE: *Let the thief get away with the purse (or worse, return it to the woman, like some kind of disgusting Hero)*
REWARDS: *Instant promotion to the Villain Alignment*

ACCEPT? Y/N

Wow. I guessed the game was serious about giving players a choice between being a Hero or a Villain, but personally, I just saw it as giving me a choice between being a decent human being and an asshole.

And because I wasn't an asshole, I hit "Y" on the Hero mission and the notification vanished from view, replaced by this message:

You have accepted "MISSION: Stop the purse thief"! You are now obligated to see the mission through to the end. If at any time you need a refresher on your mission objectives or any other details about your current mission, go to the MISSIONS menu in your character menu. Good luck!

So I said to the woman, "Yes, ma'am. I'll retrieve your purse for you ASAP."

I turned and ran after the purse thief. Like I said, the purse thief wasn't very fast. He was probably faster than the widow, what with being a lot younger than her and all, but I was in much better shape and I soon caught up to him.

Reaching out with a hand, I grabbed the purse thief's shoulder, saying, "Hey, man. Give that purse back to the—"

The purse thief whirled around and punched me in the face.

The punch sent me staggering back. I couldn't believe it. The last time I got punched in the face was back in high school, and even then, I wasn't been punched that hard. I was completely unprepared for it.

Touching my nose, I even felt blood. And it felt just as real as blood in real life, like everything else in this game. Only the pain was significantly dulled compared to real life, for which I was very grateful. At least it wasn't broken, however much it might hurt.

"Lay off, kid," said the purse thief in what I assumed was supposed to be a very bad Brooklyn accent. He waved the purse in my face. "I stole this purse fair and square. Go steal your own."

Wiping the blood from my nose, I looked at the purse thief and said, "What are you talking about? I don't want to steal—"

I stopped talking when I noticed text hovering above the purse thief's head. It read [PURSE THIEF JOE], and it took me a moment to realize it was the thief's name tag.

Joe, on the other hand, just glared at me like I was an idiot. "What are you staring at?"

I shook my head. Of course. Name tags were common in video games. They helped players identify both other players and characters in-game. I just hadn't been able to see his until now. Did accepting the mission change that somehow—?

Regardless, I held out my hand toward Joe. "As I said, I don't want the purse for myself. I want to return it to its rightful owner, whom you stole it from."

Joe sneered. "Even though you're not in a costume, you sure talk like one of those annoying Heroes."

I scowled. "I'm not a Hero. Just a decent human being who isn't an asshole."

"Call yourself whatever you like," said Joe, stepping away from me, "but I ain't giving up this purse just 'cause you asked nicely. That ain't how things work here in the Villain Sector."

That was the second reference to the "Villain Sector" I'd heard. I had no idea what that meant, but also didn't really care. I just wanted to complete this mission and continue into the main game.

Looked like I was going to have to do things the hard way.

I reached out and grabbed the purse's strap and pulled. Joe, however, redoubled his grip on the purse strap and our struggle quickly devolved into a tug of war. Both of us struggled to rip the purse out of the other's grasp, but we seemed to be equal in strength. If only I was a bit stronger, then I would have been able to get the purse from him no problem.

As if in response to my thoughts, strength filled my arms and I suddenly felt like I could bench press my own body weight. Without another thought, I yanked the purse toward me, effortlessly ripping it out of Joe's hands.

Joe, apparently surprised by my sudden burst of strength, staggered forward slightly from the impact and looked up at me in confusion. "Huh? How did you do that?"

I was about to tell him I didn't know when this notification popped up in front of me:

Power unlocked: Super Strength [Level 1]. *You now have the strength of two mighty men!* **Cost:** *None [Passive].*

Level up your Power further by increasing it with Power Points in your character menu.

I grinned at Joe. "Looks like I just got my first Power. Good night."

Joe frowned in confusion. "Good night? But it's the middle of the—"

I punched Joe square in the face, knocking him flat onto the street. As soon as Joe fell, another notification popped up in my view:

[Purse Thief Joe] has been defeated! Purse Thieves remaining 0/1.

A sense of satisfaction filled me when I read that notification. Even better, my hand didn't hurt when I punched him. Maybe that was due to the Pain Level I had selected, or maybe Super Strength also made my skin and bones tougher.

Either way, punching him out certainly *looked* more painful for him than for me, but given how he was an NPC, I suspected he couldn't feel any pain at all.

Not that I felt any sympathy toward him either way. That's what you got for stealing, pal.

I looked at the purse in my hands. As far as I could tell, Joe hadn't stolen anything from it or even opened it yet. I could probably just return the purse to the widow and gain my reward, which apparently was meant becoming a Hero. Maybe that meant I'd get a cool superhero costume, at least.

So I turned around, intending to go straight back to the widow, only to find myself face to face with the very last person I expected to see here:

Grandpa.

CHAPTER 5

Grandpa looked exactly the same in-game as his holo-message self had in the real world. And because his holo-message self looked pretty much exactly the same as his real self had, it was like I was face to face with my long-dead Grandpa again.

Grandpa clapped slowly. "Good job taking down that purse thief, Robby. One punch, and he was down for the count. Not a very strong thief, was he? Perhaps that is why he targeted elderly women for his crimes."

I was almost at a loss for words. "Grandpa—? What are you—? Wait, you're just another AI, aren't you?"

Grandpa smiled in an odd way. "Close, but I'm not like the holo-message you spoke to. I'm … different."

"Different?" I said. I looked around, trying to figure out where he could have come from, because I definitely hadn't seen him before this moment. "Wait, your other self told me I'd receive further instructions once I entered the game. Did he mean further instructions from *you*?"

Grandpa nodded. "What a brilliant young man you have grown up to be. I couldn't be a prouder grandpa."

I tried not to smile too much at Grandpa's praise, even though I knew this Grandpa was really just another digital recording or something like that. "Thanks, Grandpa. Let me return this woman's purse to her first and then you can tell me how to get the money."

I tried to walk past Grandpa, but he suddenly stepped in my way. An odd, almost malicious light glinted in his eyes. "But that's precisely what I came here to do. Now that you have entered Capes Online, it's time for you to take the next steps toward getting what is rightfully yours."

I frowned. "I know that, Grandpa, but like I said, I need to return the purse first. I'm on a mission, which I am obligated to see through to the end according to the notification, so—"

Grandpa's eyes flicked to the purse. "Why not keep it for yourself?"

I stared at Grandpa in utter confusion. "Keep the purse ... for myself? Weird joke, Grandpa. Really weird."

Grandpa cocked his head to the side. "Robby, do I sound like I am joking? Keep the purse."

I pursed my lips. "Maybe you don't know, but I accepted the Hero mission, which says I need to return the woman's purse back to her. Not the Villain one, where I keep the purse for myself."

Grandpa scowled. "You did what? Damn it, I knew I should have intervened earlier. This ruins everything."

I wasn't sure what I was more shocked by: Grandpa telling me to keep the purse, or him swearing and getting angry because I wouldn't. "What ruins everything?"

Grandpa looked at me again, although his expression had become calm again. "Nothing, nothing. I simply got upset. The situation is still salvageable. You just need to make the right choice."

I lifted up the purse. "You mean returning the woman's purse."

Grandpa scowled again. "Wrong, wrong, *wrong*, Robby. Take the purse. And while you're at it, kill the widow, too."

My eyes widened in shock. "What the—? Kill the widow? Why?"

Grandpa folded his arms behind his back. "What's the matter? You do know this is *just* a game, right? What moral compunctions could you possibly have against murdering a widow and stealing her money in a video game?"

I shook my head. "I mean, I know this is just a game, but still. I don't like doing evil things for no reason."

Grandpa sighed and rubbed his forehead. "That's right. I forgot you still don't know about the Riddles."

"The Riddles?" I said. "You mean like the kind you gave me when I was a kid?"

Grandpa smiled at me, although this time, his expression was definitely not kindly. "Somewhat."

I frowned again. "Not sure I like that word."

Grandpa sighed and began pacing around me in a circle, moving very methodically. And even though I was younger and stronger than he was, I couldn't help but feel like I was being stalked by a predator who would eat me if I made the wrong move at the wrong time.

"You see, when I hid the rest of my wealth in Capes Online, I didn't put it somewhere that just *anyone* could get it," Grandpa continued. "I wanted to make sure that you, Robby, and you alone, had a shot at it. And so I hid my wealth behind three Riddles. They are like the ones I gave you as a child, but far more … complex, both intellectually and morally."

My head turned to follow Grandpa as he walked, which was how I learned that my head can't turn 360 degrees in Capes Online. "Morally?"

Grandpa nodded. "Only, of course, if you think it's morally complicated to murder and steal from video game characters, which I do not."

I tried to follow Grandpa's logic. "Okay. But I'm still doing a Hero mission."

"And?" Grandpa said. "You do know that missions don't lock you into anything in Capes Online, right? The Alignment System overrides any missions you get. You could 'fail' this mission, you know."

I furrowed my eyebrows. "I … I suppose I could, but why?"

"Because I told you to, of course," said Grandpa, "and because it's the first step toward completing the first Riddle. You aren't where I need you to be yet, and the quickest way to get there is by doing exactly what I tell you to."

"I always thought I was supposed to solve your riddles on my own."

"This isn't actually the first Riddle, Robby. The first Riddle will come later, once you are where I need you to be."

I scratched the top of my head. "And where do you need me to be—?"

Grandpa stopped in front of me and smiled again. "You'll find out once you steal the purse and kill the widow."

I pursed my lips. "Can't I just steal the purse and leave the woman alone?"

Grandpa sighed. "That won't get you where you need to go. Killing the widow ought to be enough, if I did my calculations correctly."

I gazed over at the widow, who was standing on the sidewalk where I'd left her. She looked impatient, although she was also standing unnaturally still. "Not sure discussing her murder while she's in earshot is the wisest move."

Grandpa waved a hand dismissively at the widow. "She can't see or hear this, or me, for that matter. I have essentially put your Origin Story on hold long enough for us to have this discussion. Even the game's Dynamic Environment System, or DES, will not register this conversation as having happened at all."

I stared at Grandpa in surprise. "You have that much control over the game? How?"

Grandpa shook his head. "Doesn't matter. The question isn't whether or not it's morally right to kill the fake widow and steal her fake purse, but whether you trust me or not. Do you trust me, Robby? I mean, do you *truly* trust me? Would you do what I say without question?"

I hesitated.

I wanted to say that of course I trusted Grandpa, but Grandpa was acting kind of weird. In the real world, Grandpa never pressured me like this. Even in emergencies, Grandpa would always keep his cool.

But this digital version of Grandpa ... he was acting like the world would end if I didn't believe him and do what he wanted me to do right away and without thinking about it first.

Grandpa pressed his fingers against his temples. "Let me rephrase this. Do you want to get the money to save your mom's life or not?"

I nodded. "I do. Without question, I do."

"Excellent," said Grandpa. "And the only way to do that, Robby, dear boy, is to trust me and do *exactly* what I tell you to do. Got it?"

I bit my lower lip, but nodded again. "All right, Grandpa. I trust you, even if you aren't really Grandpa. I'll ... I'll do it."

Saying that last sentence left a bad taste in my mouth, but I ignored it. Grandpa, or this digital version of him, anyway, was right. Capes Online was just a game. The widow, the purse, even the purse thief ... were all fake. I did bad things in other video games all the time and yet it didn't make me a bad person in real life.

Yeah, Capes Online was probably the most realistic game ever created, but realistic games were still games. It was like all those people who thought video games made you violent or racist. Video games didn't make people bad. They didn't make us do bad things, at least not in real life.

Right?

In the end, it was all for a good reason. Mom needed the money. It was our only hope of treating her cancer and saving her life. Among the many other valid reasons we needed the cash, of course.

Besides, Grandpa wouldn't hurt me or tell me to do something that *would* hurt me. Even an AI version of Grandpa wouldn't. He had to have a good reason for all of this, even if I didn't know what that was yet.

A huge, almost deliriously happy smile crossed Grandpa's face. "Good job, Robby! I knew you would see reason in the end. Just like me, you are able to put aside your feelings long enough to look at the facts and make a smart decision."

"Right," I said. "So how am I supposed to kill the widow? I don't have any weapons on me."

Grandpa pulled a handgun out of his coat and handed it to me. "Take this gun and shoot her. One shot in the head ought to do it."

I stared at the gun. Grandpa never owned guns in real life and, in fact, really hated them. Out of everything I expected Grandpa to have on his person at a given time, a gun was the very last thing.

Grandpa tapped his foot impatiently. "Well? Will you accept the gun ... or not?"

A notification appeared in my view when Grandpa said that:

[PROFESSOR ROBERT J. BAKER] *is offering you a [Handgun].*
Accept gift? Y/N

I gulped, but took the cold, slightly heavy weapon from my

grandpa and hid it in my belt loop behind me. I had never used a gun before in real life, although I figured it shouldn't be hard to point and pull a trigger.

"Good," said Grandpa. He winked at me. "Now you have everything you need to do what needs to be done. The only question is, do you have the willingness to do it? Or the courage to trust me?"

I stood upright. "I do. For both."

Grandpa smiled. "I am so proud of you, my boy. Now I will unfreeze your Origin Story. Do not mention seeing or talking about me to anyone else in the game. If anyone asks why you did what you did, tell them you needed the money more than she did. Good luck."

Before I could ask Grandpa why I couldn't tell anyone else about him, he waved a hand and vanished from view like a ghost.

As soon as Grandpa disappeared, the widow ran up to me, almost out of breath. She stopped in front of me, hands on her knees, panting as she said, "Well? Did you do it?"

Snapped out of my thoughts, I looked at the widow, whose name tag now read [ELDERLY WIDOW MARY]. "Um, yes. I got your purse back, ma'am."

The widow rose to her full height, which wasn't much because she was shorter than me by a solid foot and a half. "Thank you, young man! Please give my purse back. I need to make sure that that awful thief didn't steal anything important from it."

I hesitated. I wanted to give her back the purse, accept my Hero Alignment reward, and move on. Under ordinary circumstances, it would have been the right thing to do.

But these were far from ordinary circumstances. My long-dead Grandpa was telling me I needed to do the exact opposite of the right thing in order to achieve a greater objective. That was hard for me to do, because like I said, I am a good person.

Good people didn't murder widows and steal their purses.

I reminded myself once again, however, that none of this was real. The widow wasn't real. Her purse wasn't real. She was not really in danger of losing her apartment or being unable to pay the bills this month if someone took her purse. Her murder wouldn't have any negative consequences, wouldn't leave her family and friends grieving like it would in real life.

She was just data. All of it was.

This was a glorified video game.

So I might as well act like it.

I held out the purse to Mary. She reached out for it with her almost skeletally thin hands until her fingers wrapped around the straps.

"Thank you, young man," said Mary, her grip tightening on the purse straps. "Now if you will just let it go—"

Bang.

Blood exploded out of Mary's forehead, right where I'd shot her. She didn't even get a chance to finish her sentence. She just stared at me with lifeless eyes before letting go of her purse and falling backward onto the street with a *thunk*.

I still held the gun out toward her, finger depressing the trigger, breathing hard. I couldn't believe it. I actually did it. I murdered her.

A notification appeared in my view:

You have murdered [ELDERLY WIDOW MARY]! By murdering the widow, you have failed your mission.

ALIGNMENT CHANGE: *Because you went the extra step beyond merely stealing the widow's purse, your Alignment has officially changed from [UNALIGNED] to [VILLAIN]. Check your character sheet for further information.*

My eyes widened in shock. I was a Villain now? Grandpa didn't say anything about that. I mean, I guess murdering widows and stealing their money *was* pretty evil, but—

"What the hell, man?" said Joe the purse thief behind me. "What the actual hell?"

I turned around, gun still in hand but finger no longer on the trigger, to face Joe. His nose was clearly broken by my punch, blood gushing down his face, but the look of horror on his face was obvious regardless.

"You ... you fucking *murdered* her, man," said Joe. "That's messed up. Seriously, you straight-up murdered her gangster-style."

My head felt light for some reason. "Well, you ... you stole her purse first."

Joe stared at me in disbelief. "Yeah, but I didn't want to *murder* her. Stealing is easy. I get away with it all the time. Murder, though … that's a great way to get your ass beat by a high-level Hero *and* earn a one-way ticket to a lifetime sentence at the Dome."

"The D-Dome?" I said, my lips trembling. "What is the—"

A shadow suddenly flew by overhead, making me look up, but I didn't see anything. Maybe a large bird flew by? But what sort of major metropolitan city had eagle-sized birds living within its city limits? Perhaps it had been a plane instead.

Bam.

The street shook underneath me, almost making me fall off my feet. Joe, on the other hand, fell flat on his butt, horror in his eyes.

"Crap," said Joe. "You've done it now. We're dead."

"Dead?" I said.

"Villains," said a heroic-sounding voice behind me. "Two of them. My lucky day."

I slowly turned around to face the source of the voice who had spoken and immediately regretted it.

Standing about five hundred yards away from me was Superman. Or, upon closer inspection, a guy who was apparently cosplaying as Superman. He wore a blue-and-yellow spandex costume with a "C" insignia on his chest, a black-and-white cape flowing out behind him. His chiseled jaws and massive muscles gave him a striking resemblance to an old Internet meme I recalled Mom trying to show me once, about some guy called "Chad" or whatever from a couple of decades ago.

But the "C" on this guy's chest obviously didn't stand for Chad. It stood for [HERO CAPEMAN], according to the guy's name tag, although that didn't tell me anything else about him.

"Two Villains?" I said. I gestured at Joe. "Sir, you've got it completely backward. I was retrieving this lady's purse from this purse thief here to return it to her."

Capeman's eyes darted to the dead widow at his feet. "I assume you just accidentally aimed your gun at her point-blank, accidentally pulled the trigger, and proceeded to accidentally murder her in broad daylight, then, since you say you're not a Villain despite your name tag clearly identifying you as one, Villain Robert."

"Villain Robert …?" I looked up at my head but couldn't see my own name tag. It must be visible to everyone but me. "I'm not a Villain. I actually chose the Hero mission, you see, but—"

"How despicable," said Capeman, folding his arms in front of his chest. "Not only did you steal this innocent woman's purse and murder her, but you did it while pretending to be a Hero. That makes you the absolute worst kind of Villain in my book and will definitely earn you a place in the tiniest, most cramped jail cell the Dome has."

What the hell was this "Dome" everyone kept going on about?

But I didn't care. I needed to get Capeman off my tail before he decided to pound me into street paste.

Seriously, *look* at those muscles. Someone definitely decided to change their body before playing the game.

"Look, I wasn't planning to murder her," I said. "Really, I wasn't."

Capeman raised an eyebrow. "So it was a spur-of-the-moment thing? I'm not sure if that makes it better or worse. But one thing it most certainly doesn't *not* make it is murder. And murder is a terrible crime, the worst in my book."

I gulped. "I-I swear. I wasn't planning to murder her."

"Then why did you do it?" Capeman demanded. "Other than because you are obviously a Villain, of course?"

I bit my lower lip. Grandpa's warning about not telling anyone about him or that he told me to do it rang clearly in my ears. Besides, how likely was Capeman to believe that the digital ghost of my long-dead grandpa told me to murder her so I could inherit ten million dollars from him?

Licking my lips nervously, I said, "I … did it for the money."

Capeman's eyes narrowed. "The money?"

I nodded quickly. "Yeah. I need the cash to, uh, pay for my mom's medical bills."

Technically speaking, that *was* the truth. Or part of it. I sincerely doubted that this elderly woman had anywhere close to enough money to pay off Mom's medical bills. She seemed even poorer than me. Besides, she didn't have real money, just whatever currency Capes Online used for its economic system, which I probably couldn't use in real life.

Capeman cocked his head to the side. "For the money, eh? Your mom—assuming she actually exists and isn't just a fiction you came up with on the spot—must be ashamed to have a son like you. I would if I were your mother, which I'm not."

"Thanks for clarifying that," I said dryly. "I was starting to get a little confused."

"Snark won't get you anywhere, Villain Robert," said Capeman. He shrugged his massive shoulders. "As fun as bantering with Villains sometimes is, I'm afraid I am going to have to take you in. But first ..."

Capeman knelt beside the widow, closed his eyes, and muttered something that sounded like a prayer.

Then his eyes snapped open, glowing red, and glared at me.

Crap.

Before I could do anything—even before I could *think* about doing anything—Capeman launched forward and punched me directly in the face with what felt like the force of a piledriver.

And even blunted by Easy, the punch was enough to knock me out.

The last thing I saw, before unconsciousness claimed me, was this notification:

You have been knocked [UNCONSCIOUS[by [Hero Capeman]!

CHAPTER 6

I DISMISSED THAT NOTIFICATION, THOUGH I ALSO BARELY PAID ATTENTION to it, mostly because my face still hurt.

Goddamn. I'd been punched by some pretty big bullies in the past, but the pain from Capeman's punch was a thousand times worse. It was what I imagined getting punched by a very big and very self-righteous gorilla might feel like.

At least I could no longer see anything. I guessed this was what unconsciousness was like. Everything around me was utter blackness, like in the opening of the game. Even the pain in my face was starting to subside now that I was no longer being punched by a Superman cosplayer who went the extra mile and actually got Superman muscles to match his outfit.

A brand new notification abruptly appeared in my vision just then:

MISSION: *Stop the purse thief*
STATUS: *Failed*

You have failed your first mission! Despite having initially started out with good motives, the allure of making a quick buck at the expense of a poor, defenseless widow was impossible to resist. Understandable.

But you didn't stop there. You murdered the widow in the streets in broad daylight, disgusting even the purse thief who stole from her in the first place. And, although you may have gained your first Power, you did not use it for noble purposes, but for selfish, self-seeking reasons.

You have proved once and for all that you have the black heart of a true Villain, ruthlessly seeking power, influence, and possessions at the expense of the lives of the innocent. Crime is a slippery slope and only time will tell what horrific deeds you will commit going forward.

And whether you have what it takes to become the biggest bad guy in all of Capes Online.

REWARDS: *NONE*

PUNISHMENT: *For failing to complete the mission, you have gained the Villain Alignment! Civilians will now view you with hatred and suspicion wherever you go, calling the cops or Heroes to deal with you, even if you aren't actively committing a crime.*

But you don't care. Banished from civilized society, you are now free to build the life you want according to your whims, and to achieve the kind of power that weak people lack the willingness to take for themselves.

Unburdened by the rules of morality, society, culture, and government, there is nothing that can stop you from doing what you want.

Several things crossed my mind when I read that notification.

For example: Mood whiplash.

The first half made it sound like becoming a Villain was a bad thing, but then it ended on a sort of triumphant note? I had read that Capes Online's DES made the game drastically different depending on your Alignment, but this seemed practically schizo to me.

Plus, I thought I had already gained the Villain Alignment back in my Origin Story. Capeman certainly seemed to think so. Maybe this notification just made it official or the game was buggier than I thought.

And I didn't like the sound of being viewed with "hatred and suspicion" wherever I went. It sounded like how most girls treated me in middle school, except now *everyone* would treat me that way, and probably call the cops on me, too.

Again, I know. Video game. Not real. Didn't actually matter.

But I still didn't like the implications.

And I was also mad at Grandpa. He'd said nothing about becoming a Villain. I mean, I guess I should have seen this coming, because murdering a widow and stealing her purse is pretty villainous.

But beyond that, I got hurt by Capeman. Even though Grandpa said I wouldn't.

And now I had no idea what was going to happen next or where I was going to end up. Somehow, I doubted I would end up wherever Grandpa thought I needed to be.

The game had barely started and things were already going off the rails.

The game also acted like I *wanted* to become "the biggest bad guy in all of Capes Online" for some reason. Granted, the DES had no way of knowing my actual motives for playing this damn game, but that still rankled.

Several more freaking notifications popped up in my view before I could get even more rankled than I already was:

Congratulations! You have attained the Villain Alignment! That means you now have access to all Villain Classes, Equipment, Powers, and Stats!

Congratulations! You completed your Origin Story. You are now ready to enter the world of Capes Online as a Villain, albeit as a newbie at the bottom of the totem pole. You probably aren't worried, however. You know that you will climb your way to the top of the pile, taking out any and all threats or rivals to your power, using and discarding allies as needed, and doing whatever it takes to become the biggest bad guy Capes Online has ever seen.

Respawn time: *Instant. You will now immediately respawn in Adventure City. Have fun!*

An instant later, just as the notification promised, I found myself lying on an uncomfortable cot underneath another bed. The cot was lumpy and hard on my back, smelling vaguely of sweat and various other human bodily fluids I didn't want to identify.

The pain from where Capeman punched me was gone. Touching my face, I realized I didn't even have a broken nose. Either Capeman didn't break my nose or maybe the game healed me before dumping me back into the game world. That would be the first nice thing this game had done to me since I started playing. I felt so loved.

Regardless, I had read ahead of time that, after the Origin Story, Capes Online would spawn the player in their first Base if they were a Hero or Hideout if they were a Villain. Which meant this had to be my first Hideout. Seemed … dirty and uncomfortable, but according to the CO players' comments I read online, starting Hideouts were apparently always bad and I could upgrade later if I wanted. Guess I could tolerate it for now.

Taking a deep breath, I sat up and looked around my surroundings to see exactly how bad my first Hideout was.

And immediately realized I *wasn't* in my Hideout.

I was in a prison cell. Several thick iron bars separated my cell from the hallway, where I heard the sounds of other Prisoners arguing and fighting with each other, sneering at the Guards, and more. I also heard a few *thwacks* as Guards slammed their batons into the heads of unruly Prisoners, followed by Guards yelling at them to behave.

I looked down at my clothes and realized I was now wearing an orange jumpsuit. A number, #112023, was pinned to the left front pocket of my jumpsuit, which I assumed was my Prisoner number. That seemed oddly dehumanizing to me. I had a name, after all, yet they didn't bother to put it on my prison uniform.

Honestly, though, I had much bigger problems to worry about than a silly number. The springs of my cot squealed like piglets as I rose to my feet and walked over to the bars. Grabbing the cold, metal bars, I peered outside of my cell into the hallway beyond.

Actually, there wasn't a hallway. Not really. It looked like my cell was on the third level of a pit, built into the walls of said pit, along with hundreds of other identical cells. A long metallic walkway curved along the walls, where a couple of Guards were chatting with each other, leaning on the thin railing that prevented them from falling over into the pit themselves.

The Guards were huge. They were so big that they made Capeman look small. Clad in generic gray prison outfits, [PRISON GUARD MAC] and [PRISON GUARD IKE] reminded me of some of the bullies I'd dealt with in high school, except way more dangerous. They looked about as smart, too

"Hey!" I called out to the Guards, waving a hand through the bars. "Hey, you guys!"

Mac glared at me from underneath his cap, an annoyed look on his face. "What do you want, Prisoner Number 112023?"

I raised an eyebrow. "I have a name, you know."

Ike snorted. "Yeah. And it's Number 112023. That's what your name tag says, don't it? Oh, wait. I forgot. You can't see your own name tag."

Mac laughed hard, slapping his big belly. "Good one, Ike!"

I tried, once again, to look at my own name tag, but I still couldn't see it. Did my name tag really just have my prison number and not my name anymore? That was weird.

Scowling, I said, "Regardless, I shouldn't be here. I'm not a criminal."

Mac gave me a skeptical look. "Not a criminal, huh? Your rap sheet disagrees, buddy."

"Rap sheet …?"

Mac waved his hand and a faintly transparent blue screen appeared in front of me. It had a long list of text on it, with my name, ROBERT BAKER, headlining it.

"Yup," said Mac with a nod. "Theft, murder, resisting arrest, lying to authorities, and tons of other crimes. You were so bad you earned yourself a lifetime sentence down here, buddy."

Ike nodded with Mac. "Yeah. You don't even have a Villain name yet and somehow you were bad enough to end up here with the rest of the scum of the earth. I'd almost be impressed if you weren't such a villainous piece of crap."

"What the hell are you talking about?" I said. "And where exactly *am* I?"

Mac shook his head. "Nice try, Prisoner, but we're not answering any more of your questions. Though if you ask me, I'm pretty sure you got sent down here 'cause the guys up top hate you. You definitely aren't smart enough for this Floor, so I think we can safely say a mastermind, you ain't."

Ike roared with laughter at that distinctly unfunny joke and the two Security Guards walked away, probably going to find more unjustly imprisoned people to laugh at.

I shook my head. This made no sense. My previous research indicated that, even after "failing" my Origin Story, I should have been in whatever the DES decided was going to be my first Hideout. But I was clearly in some sort of prison instead. What in the hell was going on—

"You!" a harsh, yet familiar, voice said behind me suddenly.

I turned around in time to get punched in the face.

Again.

"Ow!" I said, rubbing my face, which hurt more than it did before for some reason. "What was that—"

The guy who punched me in the face pinned me against the bars, wrapping his fingers around my throat. Choking, I looked at the guy and was surprised to see that I recognized him:

It was [PURSE THIEF JOE].

Or, as he was apparently known now, [Prisoner #302098]. Despite wearing a jumpsuit identical to mine, Joe looked much the same as he did on the street. He even smelled the same, like he hadn't showered in a week. Or two. His nose, however, was no longer broken, which I supposed was good for him.

It was not so good for me, though, because right now, he was trying to choke the life out of me.

"You freaking idiot," Joe hissed. "Until I ran into you, I thought I'd avoid prison time. I figured I was always too low-profile for the Heroes to deal with, and of course the cops are incompetent fools half the time, so I thought I'd get by stealing purses from little old widows for the rest of my life."

Joe thrust his face into mine, letting me smell the alcohol and cigar smoke on his breath. "But then *you* came along, ruined my perfect little theft, and attracted the attention of the most insufferably perfect Hero in the entire city at the same time. My luck might be bad, but yours? You're about to find out that it's absolutely *rotten*."

I had a lot of things I would have said to Joe, but because he was currently choking the life out of me, I couldn't say any of them.

A notification suddenly appeared in my view:

Debuff added: *Choking. Lose 1 HP/5 seconds.*

I had no idea how many Health Points my character had in-game, but I'd be damned if I let this fat idiot choke me to death before I had really started playing.

But Joe was still bigger and seemingly stronger than me, despite my Super Strength Power. I tried to rip his hands off my throat but couldn't.

So I did the only thing I could: I kicked him right between the legs where the sun don't shine.

Joe let out a high-pitched girlie whine. More importantly, however, his grip on my neck slackened considerably, letting me rip his hands off my throat and shove him away.

I tried to run away from Joe, put some distance between us, but our cell was very small, and Joe apparently wasn't done with me yet. He lunged at me when I least expected it, forcing me to catch his fists with my hands. I tried to force him back, but even with my Super Strength, I was very nearly on the edge of being overwhelmed for some reason.

That was when another helpful notification popped up in my view:

Debuff added: *Power Negation. While you are in the Dome, all Powers are negated, including passive Powers like Super Strength.*

The Dome? Was that the name of the prison I somehow ended up in?

Somewhere in the back of my mind, I vaguely recalled Joe mentioning a place called the Dome, which made me wonder if this was the same place or not.

Not that I had time to ponder where I was, however. Joe, being both bigger and heavier than me, had me pressed against the bars of my prison cell again, forcing me to re-focus on fighting back.

"There's nowhere to run or hide here, pal," said Joe, his voice slightly strained as he pushed against me. "And since we're in the part of the prison where the worst of the worst go, you can't even count on the Guards helpin' ya. Get ready for the beating of a lifetime, you little—"

A deep rumbling sound suddenly interrupted Joe. At first, I thought it was Joe's stomach, but then I saw Joe's face turn whiter than snow.

He now wore an expression that said, quite clearly, *Oh, crap.*

"What's the problem?" I said, glancing around. "Where did that rumbling sound—"

Joe slapped a hand over my mouth, giving me a taste of his greasy, grimy skin. "Shut up, idiot! Do you want to wake *him* up?"

"Too late," said a deep, yet slightly sleepy, and definitely *not* human voice behind Joe.

Joe froze and looked over his shoulder. I turned my head to follow his gaze, trying to see what Joe was looking at.

Okay. Either there was a miniature T-Rex wearing a paper crown curled up into a ball on the top bunk of my bunk bed or I was going utterly insane.

Points in favor of the T-Rex being real: Joe could apparently see him, too.

Points in favor of the T-Rex *not* being real: Mass hallucinations were a well-established phenomenon in the real world. Given how realistic Capes Online was, I saw no reason why there couldn't be mass hallucinations here, too.

If it was some kind of hallucination, though, it was a very "real" one, at least as real as a video game character could be. It even had a name tag over its head, identifying it as ... no way ... that was a stupid name ... but it clearly said ...

"Sidekick Dinoczar?" I said.

Joe whipped his head toward me, eyes practically bulging out of his skull. "Why did you go and use his name, you idiot? Do you want to be dino-chow?"

"Did someone say Dinoczar?" said the T-Rex. I noticed a hint of a Russian accent under his words. "That is Dinoczar's name."

Dinoczar sat up, the bed springs of the mattress creaking under his weight, while the bed itself swayed slightly beneath his movements. Dinoczar slid off the bed onto the floor and rose to his full, rather considerable height. He wasn't *quite* a full-sized T-Rex, but he was at least two heads taller than either of us, his paper crown practically brushing against the ceiling of the cell. He also was the source of that awful swamp stench I'd noticed earlier, making me wrinkle my nose even more.

"N-No, sir," said Joe in a trembling voice. He immediately let go of me and put his hands behind his back. "No one said your name. You can go back to bed now. Catch up on your beauty sleep."

Dinoczar yawned widely, showing off his frighteningly impressive set of razor-sharp chompers. "Dinoczar can't go back to sleep now that Dinoczar is awake. Dinoczar heard talking and fighting noises." His beady little eyes narrowed. "Who woke up Dinoczar?"

Joe, naturally, pointed at me. "It was him. The idiot."

Even though I knew this was a game, I still didn't like seeing Dinoczar turn his attention toward me. My brief experience in Capes Online so far had shown me that bigger characters were usually stronger than smaller ones.

Dinoczar was *much* bigger than me.

And if what Joe said about the Guards not caring what Prisoners do to each other was true ...

Yeah. I was going to get eaten alive by a Russian dinosaur in a game where I didn't even know that was possible.

Did I tell you how much I love VR?

Because I really do.

CHAPTER 7

Dinoczar sniffed the air before walking toward me slowly. He walked the way I imagined the original T-Rexes in the real world must have moved when hunting their prey: each step carefully calculated, his tiny eyes fixed on me in a way that told me he would notice even the slightest action I took. Drool leaked out of the corners of his mouth, his breathing becoming heavier with each step.

Dinoczar licked his lips. "It has been a long time since Dinoczar has had human flesh. Too long."

I would have tried to move, but I felt paralyzed. I didn't know why until yet another notification popped up in my view:

Debuff added: *Intimidated. Agility decreased by 100%. Duration: 30 seconds.*

Damn it. This Dinoczar guy must have had some sort of Power or Skill that allowed him to intimidate people. Most likely a Skill, since Powers were apparently not allowed here according to the Power Negation debuff I'd received earlier.

Out of the corner of my eye, I spotted Joe—who had retreated to another corner of the cell—watching gleefully as Dinoczar approached me. No doubt the smarmy moron thought he was going to get to watch me, the guy who had accidentally gotten him in jail, end up as dinosaur meat. Jerk.

Dinoczar stopped just a few feet from me, bending his face down until we were eye-level. He sniffed my face, giving me a hint of his breath. And to be fair, I smelled significantly less alcohol and cigarettes on his breath than Joe's, so Dinoczar had that going for him, at least.

But I did smell—however faintly—blood.

Possibly human blood, too, despite what Dinoczar said about not having eaten a human in a while.

Then Dinoczar's eyes widened in recognition and he did the most unexpected thing:

He reached out with his tiny T-Rex arms and hugged me.

"Yay!" said Dinoczar, hugging me tightly. "You are finally here! Dinoczar was wondering when you were going to show up."

Even though Dinoczar's arms were very small, I was still being hugged by a dinosaur, with all of the strength that implied. Felt like I was getting the life get squeezed out of me.

Still, even without my Super Strength, I pushed myself out of his arms and, stepping away from Dinoczar, said, "What the hell are you talking about?"

"Yeah," said Joe, who sounded even angrier than I did. He pointed at me. "That idiot woke you from your nap. Aren't you going to chomp his head off or something like that?"

Dinoczar glared at Joe. "'That idiot' is Dinoczar's Villain, fat man. Shut up."

Dinoczar must have been using whatever he used on me to Intimidate Joe, because Joe instantly shrank to half his size, or seemed to, anyway. Thought he might have peed himself, too, but it was hard to tell because the stench of human bodily fluids was everywhere in this place.

"Wait, wait, wait," I said, holding up my hands. "I'm your Villain? What does that mean?"

Dinoczar looked at me in surprise. "Do you not know about the Sidekick System, sir? Every new Villain gets a Sidekick. And Dinoczar is yours."

Ah. I actually had read up on the Capes Online Sidekick System before playing the game. According to the research I'd done, every new Capes Online player, regardless of Alignment, received a Sidekick, essentially an in-game assistant and support character. The Sidekick was a character in its own right, capable of leveling up, gaining Powers, getting new Equipment, and so on, just like a human player character could, although they grew at only half the rate of the player. That also explained why Dinoczar's name tag had "SIDEKICK" in it, because that was the primary way to identify if a character was a Sidekick or not without resorting to Scan (a Power I currently lacked even outside of prison).

Having said that, I definitely didn't expect to receive a human-sized T-Rex with a Russian accent and paper crown as my Sidekick.

For that matter, I hadn't been expecting to receive a Sidekick at all, given how I had somehow ended up in prison and not my Hideout, where I was supposed to be. My research indicated that new players usually meet their Sidekick in their starting Base/Hideout, depending on Alignment, not in a prison cell.

Something was fishy here and I was already starting to suspect I knew who might be behind it.

"So you are my Sidekick," I said to Dinoczar with a hint of skepticism in my voice.

Dinoczar nodded and held out a stubby hand toward me. "That's right! Dinoczar says you can only fire Dinoczar and replace me with another Sidekick after a week. But Dinoczar knows you would never do that. Right, sir?"

Dinoczar showed every one of his impressively sharp teeth when he said that, prompting me to say, "Of course. I've always wanted a dinosaur friend, anyway."

Dinoczar smiled, which looked chilling on his definitely not human features. "Good. Dinoczar will be your guide to the world of heroism and villainy. Let us shake on it to cement our relationship."

I looked at his short arm and frowned. "You want me to shake your hand."

"Like a civilized being, yes," said Dinoczar without a hint of irony in his voice. "It is only proper, after all."

Deciding I wanted the man-eating dinosaur as my friend rather than my foe, I took his clawed hand and shook it.

Before I could feel appropriately embarrassed by this silly scene, a new notification popped up in my vision:

Sidekick acquired! Dinoczar is now your faithful Sidekick! To check out his Stats, Powers, Alignment, and more, go to the SIDEKICK tab in your menu.

You just unlocked the Sidekick System! Like player characters, Sidekicks can level up, learn new Powers, equip new weapons and armor, and do pretty much everything else players can do. The difference, however, is that you have control over your Sidekick's growth, choosing when and where to invest Stat Points, Power Points, and more under the Sidekick screen in your menu. You can only have one Sidekick at a time. Enjoy your new dinosaur friend!

Letting go of Dinoczar's hand, I gazed up at him in confusion. "Is Dinoczar your actual name? Not, like, a supervillain name or something?"

Dinoczar frowned. "Are you making fun of Dinoczar's name? That is not very civilized of you. You have hurt Dinoczar's feelings."

I held up my hands again. "Sorry, sorry. I don't think your name is ridiculous. I think it's actually very cool and intimidating."

Dinoczar smiled again. "Really?"

I did the smart thing and nodded. "Yes."

Dinoczar stood up a little straighter. "Good. Because Dinoczar is the coolest name ever."

Great. I had a *sensitive* paper-crown-wearing Russian T-Rex as my Sidekick. Fun.

Now that Dinoczar was emotionally placated, however, I did what any good gamer would do in my situation and navigated over to the SIDEKICKS tab. Spotting Dinoczar's stat sheet, I opened it up to see exactly what I'd gotten myself into:

Secret Identity: Dinoczar
Real Identity: Dinoczar
Level: 1
EXP: 0/100
Available Stat Points: 0
Available Power Points: 0

Alignment: *Villain [Sidekick]*
Class: *Bruiser*
Powers: *Super Strength [Level 1], Sprint [Level 1]*
Skills: *Intimidate*
Equipment: *Paper Crown*

Health: *20*
Stamina: *15*
Strength: *25*
Defense: *15*
Charisma: *5*
Intelligence: *9*
Agility: *12*
Evasion: *11*
Accuracy: *3*
Dexterity: *1*
Energy: *1*
Luck: *0*

VILLAIN STATS:
Cunning: *1*
Manipulation: *1*
Infamy: *3*
Terror: *5*
Hatred: *1*

I raised an eyebrow. "Interesting stat spread. You seem to be more focused on brute strength and intimidation than anything."

Dinoczar nodded. "Yes. Dinoczar is a Bruiser. Bruisers specialize in using our brute strength and fearsome looks to commit crimes and intimidate delicious-looking Civilians and Heroes alike."

"I couldn't have guessed that by looking at you," I said sardonically. "Anyway, what's up with your Villain Stats?"

Dinoczar clapped his little hands together. Or tried to, but they simply couldn't reach, so it was more like an awkward little wriggle. "Each Alignment has its own unique Stats that are different from the other Alignments. As you and Dinoczar are Villains, that means we get Villain Stats!"

I pursed my lips. I'd read about how the different Alignments affected gameplay dramatically, even to the point of Heroes and Villains having differing Stats. I dreaded seeing what my own Villain Stats would look like once I accessed my stat sheet.

"What the hell?" said Joe again suddenly, snapping me out of my thoughts. "How did you get Dinoczar as your Sidekick? He was supposed to eat you!"

I looked back to Joe, who seemed to have regained some of his courage now that the situation had calmed down somewhat. "Is that really any of your business?"

Joe scowled. "If we're going to be cellmates for the rest of our freaking lives, then yeah, it is."

Dinoczar licked his lips. "Can I eat the fat one, sir? He does not show you the respect you deserve and seems very rude and mean in general. Plus, fat humans are my favorite. So much meat. Very chewy."

I stroked my chin. I was sorely tempted to have Dinoczar teach Joe a lesson in respect. The Dome's Power Negation debuff did not seem to affect Stats. And although I couldn't see Joe's Stats, something told me that he probably was significantly weaker than Dinoczar. The benefits of having a dinosaur friend were certainly starting to add up.

Yet I hesitated. Joe might have deserved to be taught some respect, but the thought of killing him seemed too far even for me. Yes, I killed a widow, but only because I had to.

Then a strange, yet oddly familiar soft voice in my ear whispered, "Yes, but don't you think Joe deserves it? He stole from the widow in the first place *and* tried to murder you. Turnabout is fair play, yes?"

I looked over my shoulder but didn't see anyone. Had I just been hallucinating that voice or was there someone else in the cell that I was unaware of, aside from Dinoczar and Joe?

Regardless, I felt the voice had a point. Joe *was* a pretty nasty piece of work. Maybe killing him or even maiming him was too far, but he had been nothing but a pain in the ass since I started the game.

And hey, he was just an NPC. His pain wasn't real. Who cared, really, if he got hurt?

So I said to Dinoczar, "Go ahead. Teach him a lesson."

Dinoczar grinned and stalked toward Joe very much like how he had stalked toward me earlier. Only now I could practically *feel* the blood lust radiating off of Dinoczar, perhaps because he was officially my Sidekick now.

Joe backed up against the wall, his eyes wide, but there was nowhere for the little rat to run. It pleased me on a visceral level to see a bully like him so afraid. None of my high school bullies ever looked like that back in the real world.

Then again, I didn't have a dinosaur best friend in the real world, either. Maybe Capes Online wasn't entirely bad after all.

That was when Joe tore his gaze away from Dinoczar to look directly at me. "Wait! Please don't kill me. I'll do anything you want me to. Just get your big stupid dinosaur away from me."

Dinoczar growled. "Dinoczar is not stupid. Dinoczar has IQ of 128. Dinoczar is smarter than the average dinosaur."

"Your big *intelligent* dinosaur, then," Joe corrected. "Please. I'm begging ya."

I cocked my head to the side. "Just why shouldn't I have Dinoczar take a bite out of you? You're obviously a career criminal, unlike me. I'd probably be doing society a favor taking you out."

Joe gulped. "I'll do anything. I'll even become your Minion. Just don't kill me."

I was going to tell Joe where to shove it when a new notification burst into my view, startling me:

[Prisoner #302098] has offered to become your Minion!
Accept? Y/N

Minion? I'd never heard of this mechanic before, so I tapped the highlighted "Minion" and this smaller notification appeared:

A Minion is a loyal subordinate to a Big Bad. Unlike Sidekicks, Minions have no free will of their own, operating purely on the instructions of the Big Bad they serve. Minions also level up at a much slower rate than Sidekicks and can be fired at will. Addition-

ally, Minions count toward a Team. By accepting your first Minion, you will be prompted to create your first Team.

NOTE: Only NPCs can become Minions. Player characters cannot.

Interesting. Did all Villains in Capes Online have the ability to gain Minions or was it only available to "Big Bads"? And did that mean *I* was a Big Bad? I hadn't looked at my own stat sheet yet, so I didn't know what my Class was, but I didn't know how else I could have Minions if I wasn't a Big Bad.

I said this because most of my research prior to entering the game was on the Hero Alignment. I'd barely looked into the Villain Alignment or the Classes associated with it, having assumed ahead of time that I would choose to be a Hero.

Why?

Because I was a good person. I mean, I was not perfect by any means, but I was definitely not an asshole, unlike a certain purse snatcher I knew.

Unfortunately, due to Grandpa's influence, I ended up being a Villain anyway. Looked like I was going to have to learn things on the fly. Or go back and do more research.

Speaking of purse snatchers, Joe's offer to become my Minion was still on the table. I was tempted to reject it and let Dinoczar have his flesh-eating way with Joe, but on the other hand, this offered me a way to keep Joe from trying to kill me without me having killed him.

"A wise choice," said that strange voice in my ear again that I was sure I'd heard somewhere before. "Though if I were you, I would still teach him a lesson. Just so he knows his place."

Once again, I looked over my shoulder but still did not see anyone there. While it was possible I was going insane, I also had a hunch about who it was.

But the voice's idea wasn't bad. Although the notification claimed that Minions were loyal to Big Bads, I couldn't see myself trusting Joe not to stab my back at some point.

Unless I made him fear me first.

So I hit "Y" and this notification showed up:

BIG BAD 61

Congratulations! [Prisoner #302098] has become your first Minion! Go over to the MINIONS tab in your menu to see his Stats, Powers, Equipment, and more!

NOTE: Big Bads can only control up to a certain number of Minions at a time. Your limit is currently 3 Minions. To increase your Minion count, keep leveling up your character.

A second notification popped up almost immediately afterward:

Congratulations! You have created your first Team. Go to the TEAMS tab in your menu to name your Team, see Teammates, and more!

Please be aware that any missions completed while in a Team will result in equal distribution of rewards to all Teammates. Minions and Sidekicks are excluded, however, from earning rewards from completing Team Missions.

That all but confirmed that I was indeed a "Big Bad," whatever that meant. I was also pleased to see that Joe would not get any rewards from any Team Missions we completed, so that was nice.

Dismissing the notification, I looked at Joe again. "All right, Joe. You are now my Minion."

Joe sighed in relief, while Dinoczar pouted. "Does that mean that Dinoczar does not get to feast on human flesh today?"

I shook my head. "No. Bite off his right hand."

Joe gasped. "My right hand? But that's my favorite—"

Even I was shocked at how quickly Dinoczar chomped down on Joe's right hand. Joe screamed in agony as Dinoczar ripped his right hand straight off his arm.

And because Capes Online was so freaking real, I saw it all in glorious detail, complete with blood, bone, and tendons everywhere. My stomach churned at the sight but I kept myself from vomiting.

It was just a game. None of this was real. I was a good person. I was doing this for Mom. Joe deserved it.

Joe lay on the floor in an increasingly large pool of his own blood, while Dinoczar stood above him, happily munching on whatever remained of Joe's hand. A couple of notifications popped up in my view:

[Sidekick Dinoczar] attacked [Prisoner #302098]!

Your Minion, [Prisoner #302098], has lost his right hand and is suffering from the Bleeding debuff. See the MINIONS tab for more information on your Minion's current condition.

Clicking away from the notification, I walked over to Joe and stood over him. I made sure not to step in his blood, however, mostly because I didn't want to get it all over my shoes.
Gazing up at me, Joe said, in a weak voice, "Why …?"
I cocked my head to the side. "To teach you a lesson you will never forget. You used that same hand to steal the widow's purse and to punch me in the face twice. Just be grateful I didn't have Dinoczar eat your head off."
Joe bit his lower lip, but I could tell he was appropriately cowed. He didn't even swear, although I could tell he wanted to. Probably because he was now my loyal Minion. I still didn't see much use for him at the moment, however.
Kneeling close to Joe, I said, "Will you die from that wound?"
Joe bit his lower lip. "Yeah, but I'll also just respawn."
I quirked an eyebrow. "I thought your people couldn't respawn."
By "your people," I meant NPCs. NPCs who died in Capes Online generally couldn't respawn except in special circumstances or if they were Sidekicks. That was what my research about the game told me.
"Prisoners who die in the Dome will respawn very quickly," said Dinoczar, stepping beside me. "That includes non-player Villains and criminals like Joe. Do not worry, however, sir. Once Joe respawns, he will still be your loyal Minion."
That explained why none of the Guards came running, despite Joe's screams of pain. It made me wonder if the other screams I heard from the rest of the prison were other Prisoners dying or getting maimed by their fellow inmates. And it was good to know that Joe's respawn would not free him from my control, if only

because that ensured my safety from any future retaliation on his part.

"I see," I said. Standing up, I looked at Dinoczar again, no longer particularly concerned about Joe's fate. "So where are we again, Dinoczar? You called this place 'the Dome,' but what *is* the Dome, exactly?"

"Excellent question, sir," said Dinoczar. He waved his tiny arms around as if to indicate the general area around us. "The Dome is the largest and most infamous Villain prison in Adventure City. It is where every captured Villain is sent to be imprisoned. Each Villain is sent to one of three Floors within the Dome itself, based on their level and the severity of the crimes they committed."

I nodded, following along easily enough. "Got it. What are the three Floors and what Floor are we currently on?"

Dinoczar cleared his throat. "The first Floor is Minimum Security. It is the Floor closest to the surface and is the easiest Floor to escape from. Indeed, it is so easy to escape that Prisoners regularly walk out of Minimum Security with little opposition from the Guards."

That concerned me. "So you're saying people can just walk out of the Dome anytime they want? That's not a very secure prison."

"Only low-level Villains are ever sent to Minimum Security," Dinoczar explained. "The other two Floors are much more difficult to escape from."

Okay, that was actually kind of comforting. Although I hadn't looked at my stat sheet yet, I knew I had to be a low-level Villain. All players in Capes Online, regardless of Alignment, started out at Level 1. Logically, then, I had to be in Minimum Security.

Perhaps my odds of escaping from here were higher than I thought.

Continuing his explanation, Dinoczar said, "Next is Medium Security. This is where higher-level Villains are usually sent. Medium Security is much more difficult to escape from than Minimum Security, but it is still possible if one is smart like Dinoczar. Medium Security is below Minimum Security, though not too far from the surface."

I nodded. Having already figured I was in Minimum, there wasn't a strictly practical need for me to know about the other two Floors. But Dinoczar seemed to enjoy explaining the game to me, so I decided to let him keep talking. Besides, it never hurt to have more information.

Right?

"And finally, there is the last and final Floor, Maximum Security," Dinoczar finished. "Only the worst of the worst are sent to Maximum Security. It is literally impossible for Prisoners banished to Maximum Security to escape and is located at least a mile below the surface. Also, I forgot to mention that each Floor has ten Sub-Floors within it that have anywhere from ten to one hundred Prisoners each."

I shuddered. "Good thing we aren't there, then. Otherwise, we'd never get out of this place."

Dinoczar looked at me questioningly. "What are you talking about, sir? We *are* on Maximum Security. All three of us. And there is no escape."

CHAPTER 8

I stared at Dinoczar unblinkingly. "I really hope you didn't just say we are in Maximum Security. Maybe you meant to say we're in Minimum Security and can walk out anytime we want."

Dinoczar shook his head. "No. Dinoczar spoke correctly, as Dinoczar always does. We are in Maximum Security. See?"

Dinoczar pointed at the back of the uniform of a Guard who was walking by our cell just then. The words MAXIMUM SECURITY GUARD were emblazoned on the back of the uniform in bright red letters. I also thought I saw the letters F U, but that may have just been my imagination.

"Specifically, we are on Sub-Floor Ten of Maximum Security," Dinoczar continued, "which is the lowest Floor in the Dome and is where the absolute worst of the worst Villains are kept."

I felt a bit woozy when Dinoczar said that. "But … why? I mean, yeah, I murdered a widow and stole her purse, but that shouldn't be bad enough to have gotten me sent here, right? Like, what do you have to do to be sent here?"

Dinoczar considered my question for a moment. "Dinoczar does not know exactly, but usually it is reserved for Villains who are over Level 100 and have committed unforgivable crimes, such as blowing up a city, raping and murdering children on a regular basis, or committing grotesque war crimes and crimes against humanity and nature."

My head spun at this revelation. "But … I haven't done *any* of that. I haven't done anything even close to that."

Joe, still bleeding out on the floor, chuckled. "Guess someone up top must *really* hate you, then."

I kicked Joe in the face, breaking his nose and making him bleed even more. Joe groaned and rolled into a ball again, but I didn't care. I was distraught over being considered as bad as someone who raped children regularly (did people in Capes Online *really* do that? Just what did this game *do* to people?).

"But you are down here," I said to Dinoczar. I gestured at Joe. "And Joe. Unless Joe happens to be Adolf Hitler in disguise or something, I don't think he deserves to be down here, either."

"Dinoczar agrees," said Dinoczar. "Dinoczar's only crime is freeing his fellow experiments from the inhumane experiments that Synth Group scientists inflicted on us. Oh, and eating said scientists and their families alive, plus devouring a lot of Civilians who really didn't have anything to do with said experiments but were quite delicious."

My eyes widened when Dinoczar said that. "You ate innocent people."

Dinoczar licked his lips. "In Dinoczar's defense, he was very hungry and needed to feed his Tribe. Plus, innocent flesh is the best flesh, because it has not yet been corrupted by a person's choices."

As badly as I felt for the Civilians Dinoczar ate, I was also *really* glad he was on my side now.

But then something Dinoczar said caught my attention and I said, "Wait a second, you mentioned scientists and something called 'Synth Group.' Are you a scientific experiment or something?"

Dinoczar nodded. "Yes. Dinoczar was the first—and, in Dinoczar's humble opinion, best—experiment created in a program by Synth Group scientists to resurrect dinosaurs and make them into weapons of war. Using a variety of unethical and legally dubious methods, Synth Group scientists created a Tribe of Dinomen, of which Dinoczar was the first."

I blinked. "That sounds suspiciously similar to the plot of one of the old *Jurassic Park* movies."

"Dinoczar loves *Jurassic Park*!" Dinoczar said with a sigh. "Anyway, one day Dinoczar's superior IQ activated and Dinoczar realized that he and his Dinomen were being unfairly treated by the scientists at Synth Group. So Dinoczar rallied the Dinomen to rise up, overthrow our oppressors, and find the freedom that all sentient beings deserve."

I pursed my lips. "So how did you end up here?"

Dinoczar growled. "After escaping from the laboratory with tummies full of scientists, Dinoczar led the Dinomen Tribe on a rampage through downtown Adventure City, killing every human we could find. But then a Hero named Winter showed up, killed off my fellow Dinomen, and caught me and sent me to the Dome, where Dinoczar has been ever since."

I glanced at the crown on his head. "Is that where the crown came from? To indicate that you were the King of the Dinomen?"

"Exactly," said Dinoczar proudly. "Dinoczar named himself after reading Russian history and learning about the czars of Russia brutally oppressing their own people. Dinoczar also considered calling himself Stalinsaur after another one of Russia's great leaders, but in the end, Dinoczar decided on his current name. As for the crown, Dinoczar took it as a symbol of conquest from one of the scientists' children, who Dinoczar ate alive."

"Wow," I said. "That's dark."

Dinoczar shook his head. "No. Human meat is more like white meat than dark meat."

"I didn't mean—never mind," I said, deciding it best not to argue with an above-average IQ dinosaur. "So you ended up in here after a Hero named Winter caught you?"

Dinoczar hung his head. "Yes. Dinoczar spent many lonely days down here until you arrived, but Dinoczar still yearns for freedom. And vengeance for his people."

It might surprise you to learn that I had actually heard about Winter. He was a Hero player infamous for having been heavily involved in the two Blackouts. I didn't know his exact role in those situations, but he seemed to have played a part in ending both Blackouts and freeing the trapped players.

So personally, I thought he was probably a good guy, but I wasn't going to say that to Dinoczar. Although killing off Dinoczar's friends *did* seem a bit extreme to me, even if they were just bits of data and not actual people.

Regardless, I was now in a very sticky pickle. Not only had I become a Villain, but I was now stuck in a prison specifically designed for Villains, and in the lowest and most secure Floor of said prison, too. If what Dinoczar said was true, then my character was going to be stuck here forever.

And if my character was going to be imprisoned forever, then I could say goodbye to ever attaining Grandpa's vast wealth.

That decided it. I would just have to delete my account and start over. That was the only way to get a new character in Capes Online. Players were only allowed one character per account. It pained me a bit to have to do that, but on the other hand, I had barely started the game, so it wasn't like I was losing a lot of progress or hard work. I knew all too well about the sunk cost fallacy and I certainly wasn't going to sink more of my time and energy into this goddamned game.

"But you are exactly where I want you to be, Robby," said Grandpa's voice behind me. "Deleting your character will just make things harder than they need to be and waste precious time."

I whirled around to see Grandpa—or the digital copy of him, anyway—standing on the other side of the bars of my cell. A quick glance around my cell showed both Dinoczar and Joe frozen in place, similar to what happened during my Origin Story. That meant those two were probably completely unaware of Grandpa or our conversation.

Good.

Because I had a lot to say to Grandpa.

Marching up to the bars, I said, "How did you know what I was thinking?"

Grandpa smiled. "Because I know you so well, Robby. And also because I have some degree of control over Capes Online, including access to your thoughts while you are logged into the game."

My hands flew to my head. "Wait, you mean you can read my thoughts while I am playing Capes Online? Seriously?"

"Don't worry," said Grandpa with a wink. "This particular exploit is not known to SI Games, so you don't have to worry about the company delving into your mind or me controlling you. In fact, the feature is unique to your GamePod, which I had modified before my death. Why else do you think I wanted you to get your GamePod from that specific store and nowhere else?"

"Grandpa, that is incredibly creepy and confirms everything I've ever thought about this horrid game," I said. I looked around. "I want to log out. Where's the menu?"

"You can't access any of your menus or screens while talking to me," said Grandpa calmly. "So you can't log off at the moment. Nor would you want to, unless you really just don't care about your poor mother's health or well-being. But I think you are a better son—no, a better *person*—than that."

Creepy. Grandpa had almost quoted my own words back to me. He really could read my mind while I was in the game.

I scowled. "All right, 'Grandpa,' if that's who you really are. I take it you are the one who sent me to the Dome when I should have respawned in my own Hideout. Right?"

"Correct," said Grandpa. "I'm very impressed that you managed to figure that out. Walk me through your thought process."

I shrugged. "It's the only explanation that makes sense. You've already displayed a degree of influence over the game, plus I've never heard of this happening to any other player in the game. You're also clearly railroading me to some specific purpose and I doubt you'd trap me in an inescapable prison for the scum of the earth if you didn't want me here for some reason."

Grandpa clapped excitedly. "Well done, Robby! Yes indeed, I may have asserted my influence over the game to make sure you ended up here. It was the only way I could ensure you'd meet your Sidekick."

I glanced at Joe. "Was Joe part of your plan, too?"

Grandpa shook his head. "No. He's only here because he got captured at the same time as you. My influence over the game is not always terribly precise, hence why you two ended up in the same cell. Trust me, if I had my way, you two would not be in the same cell together. Oh, and I also changed your Pain Level to 'Real.'"

"What?" I said. "Why?"

"Because I want to make sure nothing prevents you from leveling up and becoming stronger as quickly as possible," Grandpa replied.

"And since 'Real' pain allows for the highest possible experience gain, you should grow very quickly."

I scowled. That explained why Joe's earlier punch hurt more than it did during my Origin Story.

Then Grandpa smiled coldly again. "Regardless, I do approve of you having Dinoczar eat his hand. It should prove a very brutal, if effective, way of keeping him in line. He obviously lacks the courage to stand up to anyone even slightly stronger than him, so I imagine he will be quite the useful Minion for you, don't you agree?"

I threw my hands into the air. "I don't give a damn about having a useful Minion or a Russian dinosaur! Who are you, really? Because I'm not even sure you're my grandpa, or even a recording of him. My real grandfather would never have put me in this kind of situation."

Grandpa stroked his chin. "Technically, you are correct in that I am not 'truly' Professor Robert J. Baker, ethics professor. But I am also not the digital recording who directed you here, either. I am something … in between."

I furrowed my brows. "In between? What does that mean?"

Grandpa began pacing back and forth in front of my cell. "Tell me, Robby, you have heard of digital immortality, yes? Of course you have. I was the one who theorized its endless possibilities at the dawn of the twenty-first century. I saw the way technology, particularly within the virtual reality space, was developing. And I dreamed of the potential that humanity could kill death and live forever."

I folded my arms in front of my chest. "But digital immortality isn't just a theory anymore, right? I've heard lots of people are living in Capes Online now as digital beings. Are you one of those beings?"

"Unfortunately, no," said Grandpa with a bitter sigh. He came to a stop and looked down at his body. "The concept of digital immortality was realized only *after* I died, ironically enough. I invested a lot of money and time into the concept, but I knew I would never live to see it come to fruition. That my billionaire friend, Mark Gene, perished trying to digitize his own mind made me doubt I would live long enough to see the tech perfected."

I cocked my head to the side. "But you are talking to me right now. So you must have *some* form of digital immortality, right?"

Grandpa shook his head. "No. I had to settle for the next best thing. I had the geniuses at SI Games make a copy of my mind and personality just before my death, which they then uploaded to the game. As I said, I am more advanced than the recording you spoke to but less so than my real self."

I scratched the back of my head. "Sounds confusing. And I don't see what this has to do with your money."

"I'm getting there," said Grandpa. He put a hand on his chest. "I am what was then called a Digital Double. By every metric, I am identical to the real Professor Robert J. Baker right before his death. I lack any memories of his time after the upload, but I still remember you, Robby, and everything we ever did together when you were growing up."

"A Digital Double ..." I repeated, trying to wrap my head around the concept. "Sounds weird, but I guess I've seen weirder."

Grandpa glanced at the frozen Dinoczar when I said that. "Perhaps. But in any case, my original self programmed me to guide you to my wealth. That is my primary purpose."

"Okay," I said. I looked around. "So where *is* your wealth? I don't see it here."

Grandpa smiled. "Oh, Robby. I forgot how impatient you were. If you want my wealth, then you'll need to solve my Riddles."

There was that mention of Riddles again. "Uh-huh. By 'Riddles,' I assume you're not referring to a question or statement intentionally phrased so as to require ingenuity to ascertain its answer or meaning, right?"

Grandpa shrugged. "Again, you are correct. The Riddles are a series of tests—or missions, to use Capes Online's terminology—designed to determine if you are worthy of getting my wealth. I designed them specifically for you, Robby. You and you alone are qualified to solve them, and you will need to solve them if you want to gain access to my wealth."

"Right," I said. I looked around at my prison cell. "It's going to be hard to solve your Riddles in an inescapable prison—"

Without warning, a notification appeared in my view just then, partially obscuring Grandpa:

RIDDLE: *Initiate a mass breakout from the Dome*

Well, darn. Looks like you just had to go and get yourself arrested and thrown into jail. And not just any jail, either, but the Dome's Maximum Security Floor, where you are stuck with a talking Russian dinosaur and your least favorite person in the world. Your Villain career is off to a rough start, to say the least.

But you're a clever Villain. What you lack in pure brute strength or power you make up with a strong intellect and ability to control and manipulate others. With just a little bit of charisma, you might be able to build a legion.

They say there's strength in numbers, and who better to tap that strength than the man who will become the biggest baddie in all of Capes Online?

ALIGNMENT: *Villain*
DIFFICULTY: *Suicidal*
RARITY: *Unique*
SUCCESS: *Stage a mass breakout from the Dome's Maximum Security Floor*
FAILURE: *Your breakout is quashed by the Warden and his Guards*
REWARDS: *Another clue to your grandfather's vast wealth and other rewards (based on your performance)*
ACCEPT? Y/N

"What is this?" I said to Grandpa, peering around the notification at him. "This looks like a mission notification, but it says 'Riddle' at the top."

Grandpa nodded. "I altered the Capes Online mission notification system to read that way. Since you are an avid gamer, I figured this would be an excellent way to motivate you and help you keep track of your progress."

I had to admit, Grandpa (technically his Digital Double, but it was just easier to think of him as Grandpa) knew me well. Having the requirements of the Riddle laid out in such a clear-cut, simple-to-understand way made it easier to understand what he wanted me to do. Wasn't a fan of the "Suicidal" Difficulty Level, but even that didn't bother me too much, knowing how serious this mission was.

But I still had questions. Too many, honestly.

With the first being: "You want me to initiate a mass prison breakout from the Dome? Why?"

"For the same reason I had you kill the widow," Grandpa replied. "To test you. To see if you can solve a seemingly impossible challenge."

I frowned. "I don't follow."

Grandpa clapped his hands together. "Think, Robby, think! Back when you were a kid, what were your favorite riddles I gave you? Was it the easy ones, with fairly obvious answers that took you little time to think through? Or was it the hard ones, which forced you to carefully think through the answer and not rush yourself?"

"It was the hard ones, yeah."

"And in video games, I know you always appreciated a good challenge," Grandpa continued. "You never backed down from my difficult riddles, hard school assignments, or challenging video game levels and situations. They say that Maximum Security is impossible to escape from, that no one has ever done it before."

Grandpa walked right up to the bars and stared me straight in the eyes with a shockingly intense look. "Prove them wrong. Show them that you can do anything you put your mind to. And that you are *willing* to do whatever it takes to succeed."

Man, I didn't remember Grandpa ever being this intense before. It was a little scary.

But I would be lying if I said it didn't invigorate me, at least to some extent.

It was true that I always did appreciate a good challenge. Whether in real life or in a game, I never backed down from anything. Not that I would always solve every challenge, but I also never backed down.

Not like Daniel, my brother. He always preferred the easy route. Maybe that's another reason why he lost his mind.

Could I keep my sanity intact while escaping from the supposedly impossible to escape Maximum Security?

And I could finally see, at least partially, why Grandpa wanted me here. He wanted to put my intellect to the test, to see if I was still as clever and talented as I had been back when I was a kid.

Maybe I was. Maybe I wasn't.

But when I thought about how much better our life would be once I got Grandpa's money, I knew I had no choice but to go forward and do it.

Somewhere in the back of my head, a small voice, which I always associated with my conscience, worried about the morality of embracing my Villain Alignment and doing whatever it took to succeed.

But for the millionth time, this was a video game. It had no direct correlation to the real world. I could be as ruthless as I wanted and still be the good person I was in the real world.

That was a freeing thought.

So I immediately hit "Y" and received this notification in response:

You have accepted "RIDDLE: Initiate a mass breakout from the Dome"! You are now obligated to see the Riddle through to the end. If at any time you need a refresher on your Riddle objectives or any other details about your current Riddle, go to the RIDDLE menu in your character menu. Good luck!

A huge smile spread across Grandpa's lips as soon as the notification popped up in my view. "Excellent, Robby. *Most* excellent. I knew you had it in you. I knew I could trust you to do what is necessary to succeed."

I nodded, dismissing the notification at the same time. "Right. I assume you aren't going to tell me *how* to stage a breakout."

"Correct," said Grandpa with a wink. "It wouldn't be much of a Riddle if I gave you all the answers, now would it? But I can give you a hint: You aren't the only person here who wants to be free."

"Yeah," I said, with a hint of sarcasm in my voice. "I'm in a literal prison. I am pretty sure that *everyone* here wants to be free."

Grandpa chuckled. "I wasn't referring to the other Prisoners. But I shouldn't say anything else. It's up to you now, your choices and your decisions, which are entirely your own."

I snorted. "Like how you told me to order Dinoczar to rip off Joe's hand earlier, right?"

Grandpa's smile vanished, replaced by a puzzled frown. "I didn't tell you to order Dinoczar to eat Joe's hand. I thought you did that on your own."

I rubbed the back of my neck. "But I heard a voice whisper in my ear. Thought it sounded kind of like you."

A thoughtful expression appeared on Grandpa's face when I said that. "Hmm ... seems like there's another player I didn't account for." He looked at me abruptly. "I will look into this. In the meantime, I trust that you will figure out a way out of here using that brilliant mind of yours. Once you do, we will talk again and I will have further instructions to share with you. Good luck."

With that, Grandpa blinked out of view, leaving me slightly startled by his abrupt disappearance.

Before I could fully comprehend what Grandpa just said to me, I heard a groan over my shoulder and looked to see Joe still bleeding out on the floor of our cell. His skin was so pale that he looked even closer to death than before.

"May I put him out of his misery, sir?" said Dinoczar, licking his lips in anticipation.

I shook my head. "No, Dinoczar. He'll die on his own soon enough. We have more important things to worry about."

Dinoczar cocked his head to the side. "What is more important than food?"

Turning to fully face both Dinoczar and Joe, I said, "We're going to break out of Maximum Security. And take the rest of the Prisoners with us."

CHAPTER 9

"You're going to break everyone out of Maximum Security," said Joe about half an hour later. He looked like he wanted to laugh at me, but I could tell he also didn't want to lose his other hand. "Not just yourself, not even just the three of us, but *everyone*."

Sitting at the cafeteria table across from the respawned Joe, I stuck a spoon into my bowl of [Slop] and said, "Not so loudly, okay? I don't want the Guards overhearing."

At that precise moment, a huge Prison Guard, with biceps twice as big as my head and the name tag [PRISON GUARD BRICK] floating over his head, walked past our table. He glared at us from underneath his cap, patting his baton in his open palm. Although he didn't use Intimidate on us, I still felt compelled to give him my best innocent smile, even though I knew that none of us were actually innocent. Or that he would ever see us that way.

It was lunchtime in the Dome. Surprisingly, despite having all of the Prisoners locked up in our individual cells isolated from one another, we were still allowed to come out at mealtimes to eat in the same cafeteria.

But there were several restrictions:

First, we were only allowed to eat with our cellmates at designated tables. Our Cell Number was 52, which meant we sat at Table 52. It was literally impossible to go to another table. As soon as we sat down at our table, an electrified barrier sprang up, effectively separating us from the other Prisoners. Only the Prison Guards seemed unaffected by the barriers, which made sense, because otherwise they wouldn't be able to get to us if we were acting up.

This of course was to prevent Prisoners from interacting with each other and planning anything that the Guards didn't want us planning (such as a mass prison break of everyone in Maximum Security, for example). That made sense from the point of view of a jailer trying to keep Prisoners from plotting a breakout.

But it also made it more difficult for me to plan a breakout with only two other people, neither of whom was smart enough to actually plan one themselves.

As well, we were only fed [Slop] at every mealtime. [Slop], as far as I could tell, was an item that met my character's basic nutritional needs but otherwise didn't give any bonuses. In fact, when I took my first bite of the rancid stuff, I got this debuff:

> **Debuff added:** *Bad Taste. Health and Stamina regeneration rate is cut by 90%.* **Duration:** *1 minute for every bite of [Slop].*

Of course, I tried not to eat it, but Dinoczar had informed me that refusing to eat would eventually cause much worse debuffs, such as Starvation, to afflict my character. So I continued eating my horrid [Slop], although I had to appreciate the genius of feeding Prisoners food that technically met their nutritional requirements but also weakened them.

If I had to describe the taste and sensation of the [Slop], it was like eating mud mixed with fresh human pus, boiled in swamp water, with a touch of feces for flavor. This was yet another time where Capes Online's intense realism was almost too much for me, but I didn't want to log out yet. I wanted to gather as much information about the Dome as I could before logging off for the day and this seemed like a good opportunity to do it. I did make a mental note to get some *actual* good food in the real world once I logged off, however.

I had hoped to speak with some of the other Prisoners who had been here longer than me, but unfortunately, the intense segregation meant I couldn't talk to anyone other than Dinoczar and Joe. We didn't even get to stand in line for our food. The Guards had simply directed us to our table, where a very silent drone deposited our bowls of soup and warm tap water in front of us before zipping off to deliver meals—if one could call this crap that—to the other Prisoners.

But I could still see the other Prisoners, and I had to admit they looked like a rough bunch. Some of them looked like normal humans like me, but I also saw a strange lizard-like creature that Dinoczar informed me was called a Dweller, and I was pretty sure I saw a couple of robots or cyborgs as well. There was even a literal bear in a prison jumpsuit at the table next to ours, sitting all by himself and shooting death glares at anyone who stared at him for too long. For some reason I couldn't see his name tag, but I got the impression he was pretty strong.

And, of course, the Prison Guards watched us from every angle. Some of them walked between the tables, searching for any trouble, while others remained on the platforms overhead, watching us from above. Not to mention the dozens of security cameras, each one pointed at a different table, no doubt being viewed by Guards elsewhere in the prison.

The Dome's Maximum Security Floor was hopelessly dehumanizing, depressing, and all-around discouraging. Whoever had designed it was clearly sadistic and took great enjoyment in hurting other people and was probably a certified genius who understood human nature perhaps a little *too* well.

In short, I could respect them for designing what seemed like the perfect prison. And there was probably a whole host of other security measures I wasn't aware of yet.

Looking at Dinoczar, I said, "Making Maximum Security inescapable seems like bad game design to me. What about if players like me end up here?"

Dinoczar, slurping up the last of his [Slop] (which he seemed to genuinely enjoy despite how awful it tasted), looked at me. "Actually, Villain players do not end up in Maximum Security. Dinoczar says even the worst Villain players are kept in Medium Security at most, which is escapable."

I swirled my spoon in my [Slop]. "So I am probably the only Villain player in Maximum Security, then."

"Dinoczar says that is correct," said Dinoczar. His eyes darted to my barely touched bowl of [Slop]. "Are you going to finish that, sir?"

I sighed. "Go ahead."

Without hesitation, Dinoczar snapped up my [Slop], bowl and all, into his mouth. The crunch of plastic filled the air as Dinoczar munched on the inedible soup-like substance. "Mmm ... crunchy *and* soupy!"

I shook my head, partly at Dinoczar's apparent lack of taste buds, but also at the weird way NPCs behaved in Capes Online.

On one hand, most NPCs seemed to act as if they were unaware they were in a game. Sure, they were aware of Levels, Classes, and so on, but they treated these as part of their everyday world much in the same way we real humans treated things like aging in the real world. Using terms like "player" and "NPC" around them often did not register with most of the NPCs I'd spoken to.

On the other hand, Dinoczar seemed to be aware, at least on some level, that he lived in a game and rarely batted an eye at my usage of the terms I just described. Probably had to do with the fact that Sidekicks usually acted as guides to newbie players like me, so they would regularly use video game terms to describe things like a player would without actually being a player themselves.

I knew some people thought NPCs were real, but I didn't. Even so, I was amazed at how realistic they were. Even Dinoczar, despite his very existence being impossible in the real world, felt like a real person to me.

No wonder Daniel lost his mind playing this game. Between the hyper-realistic NPCs and the intense physical sensations, I could easily see how someone might lose their grip on reality if they stayed inside this game for too long. It didn't help that Capes Online had a time dilation feature, where one hour in the real world equaled approximately eight in-game. That made it feel like I'd been here longer than I actually had.

Which made me wonder how long I'd been playing exactly. Fifteen minutes? Half an hour? It felt like a couple of hours at least, but it couldn't have been that long. I'd have to log off at some point, but I figured I'd stay logged in until after lunch. While my in-game character no longer felt hungry, my real body was probably needing some good food right about now.

Plus, you know, I didn't want to risk losing my grip on reality, either.

"Listen, I don't know where you got this idea about a mass prison break from, but it ain't happening," said Joe. He pointed his spoon at us. "No one has ever successfully escaped from Maximum Security. Even during the Blackouts, only Minimum and Medium Security Prisoners managed to escape. Especially given how low-leveled we are, I'd say our odds ain't great."

"How do you know I am low-leveled?" I asked. "I didn't tell you what my Level is."

Joe snorted. "'Cause I can Scan you, duh. Can't you Scan anyone yet? It's a basic Skill that even newbies pick up pretty quickly."

I frowned. "I don't know how to Scan other people yet. I thought I needed a Costume or Power Crystal to get new Powers."

Joe chuckled. "Scan isn't a Power, idiot. It's a Skill. Completely different things."

Dinoczar growled at Joe. "Do not disrespect master or Dinoczar will chomp off your *other* hand."

Joe flinched and, perhaps unconsciously, glanced at his missing right hand. Although Joe had respawned mostly intact after losing more blood than I thought the human body had, his right hand had not regrown and had been replaced with a fingerless stump. Evidently, there were certain injuries that even Capes Online couldn't heal, although Joe claimed we just needed to find a Healer with a Regrow Limbs Power to restore his hand and he'd be all better.

I felt kind of bad about it, but at the same time, Joe was still a disrespectful jerk, so I didn't feel *too* bad about it. Served him right.

Then Dinoczar looked at me. "Despite his blatant disrespect, however, One Hand Joe is correct. Skills are innate abilities that any player can learn, usually through trying them out. Powers, on the other hand, are often only accessed through Costumes or Power Crystals, though one usually gets a new Power every ten Levels congruent with their Class. An important distinction."

I tapped my chin and gazed around the cafeteria. "So if I focus on a particular person, I should be able to learn Scan, right?"

"Yes, sir," said Dinoczar. "It will work on anyone. Also, Skills can be leveled up like Powers, but only through consistent use."

I nodded and looked around the cafeteria for a candidate. I settled on the bear Prisoner earlier, staring at him as hard as I could. It helped that his back was to me, so I didn't have to worry about him seeing me.

I heard a *click* in my head and this notification abruptly appeared in my vision:

> ***New Skill unlocked:*** *Scan Level 1. You can now Scan enemies and items and find out basic information about them. Level up this Skill further to find out more detailed information about the world around you, including information about your fellow Heroes and Villains.*

This was followed by a notification for the bear Prisoner:

> ***Prisoner #379021***
> ***Level:*** *99*
> ***Alignment:*** *Villain*
> ***Class:*** *Bruiser*
> *There is no Scan information on [Prisoner #379021].*

I squinted my eyes. "Why does it say there is no Scan information on that guy? He's right here. Do I need to level up my Skill more or something to find out about him?"

"Dinoczar forgot to mention that the Dome limits what information Scan shows," Dinoczar explained. "Especially at lower levels, Scan will only show you the most basic information about another character."

I scowled. Another irritating limitation, though it made sense. If the Prisoners could Scan, say, the Prison Guards, then that would give us valuable information on exactly how powerful they were, which would make it easier for us to plan how to escape from them.

To test that theory, I scanned [PRISON GUARD IKE] a couple of tables down, earning me this message:

Scan blocked. Unable to retrieve Scan information on [Prison Guard Ike].

I nodded. "Can't even see any of the Prison Guards' Scan information."

"Why would you be able to?" Joe said. He slurped some [Slop] and blanched. "Disgusting. I want a burger."

"Dinoczar wants human flesh," said Dinoczar with a sigh. He eyed Joe's other hand. "Sir, are you *sure* Dinoczar cannot have Joe's left hand, too?"

Joe's face went paler than snow, but I ignored the two to open my character sheet. I had been so busy learning about everything else happening since I ended up in the Dome that I had completely neglected to read my own character sheet, which seemed like a huge oversight to me. In my defense, I had a *lot* on my mind recently.

Navigating over to my menus, I frowned. "Dinoczar, I don't see the tab for my character sheet. Where is it?"

Dinoczar tore his gaze from Joe's scrumptious-looking left hand to look at me again. "Your character sheet should be under your name, sir."

I frowned even more. "Yeah, I don't see a tab with my name on it. Other than an 'UNNAMED' tab, though not sure what that means."

Dinoczar waggled his arms again like he was trying to clap. "Dinoczar forgot! You haven't picked out your Secret Identity yet. Before you can see your character sheet, you'll need to come up with a name for yourself that isn't your normal name."

"I suppose I can't just call myself Robert, then," I said.

Joe chuckled. "Such a menacing name that will most certainly strike fear into the hearts of Heroes and Civilians alike, I'm sure."

I stroked my chin. "Dinoczar, have you ever given thought as to what sauces go best with human flesh?"

A serious expression appeared on Dinoczar's face. "Yes. Dinoczar likes to keep it simple with ketchup, but there is an argument to be made for barbecue sauce and mustard salsa. Why?"

"You might want to discuss it with Joe while I look at my character sheet," I said casually, noticing Joe's skin becoming paler and paler with each passing second. "He might have an opinion."

With that, Dinoczar leaned forward and began trying to have a surprisingly in-depth conversation with Joe about how to properly prepare human flesh for consumption. I tried not to smirk at how terrified Joe looked.

I clicked the "UNNAMED" tab, and a virtual keyboard and a blank space appeared before my vision. But before I could type in anything, a notification appeared in my view:

> **ERROR.** *Unable to choose your name. Dome settings override player-chosen names while player is [Imprisoned]. You are [Prisoner #112023] during your stay in the Dome.*

"Dinoczar," I said slowly. "For some reason, the system isn't letting me pick a name."

Dinoczar paused briefly in his explanation of which sautéed vegetables went well with human flesh to glance at me again. "Dinoczar has never heard of that happening before."

"Easy," said Joe, who, despite still looking absolutely terrified, appeared to have regained some of his courage. He gestured at our name tags. "The Dome is probably just keeping you from picking a name so it doesn't override your Prisoner Number. Very dehumanizing, if you ask me."

For once, I agreed with Joe. It *was* dehumanizing and probably on purpose, too, in order to inflict even more psychological damage on Prisoners like us. Looked like I would just have to wait until I got out of prison before I could pick a proper Villain name for myself. Guess I would think about it in the meantime.

Fortunately, it appeared that I could still access my character sheet, so I flipped over to that to see exactly how powerful I was:

Secret Identity: *Prisoner #112023 (locked by the Dome)*
Real Identity: *Robert John Baker*
Level: *1*
EXP: *0/100*
Available Stat Points: *0*
Available Power Points: *0*
Alignment: *Villain*

Class: *Big Bad*
Reputation: *Unknown*
Powers: *Super Strength [Level 1]*
Skills: *Link [Level 1], Scan [Level 1]*
Equipment: *Prison Jumpsuit*
Minions: *1/3*

Health: *25*
Stamina: *13*
Strength: *10*
Defense: *13*
Charisma: *10*
Intelligence: *19*
Agility: *13*
Evasion: *8*
Accuracy: *11*
Dexterity: *18*
Energy: *14*
Luck: *0*

VILLAIN STATS:
Cunning: *10*
Manipulation: *13*
Infamy: *1*
Terror: *8*
Hatred: *10*

This confirmed a couple of things for me.

One, I was a "Big Bad." Clicking my Class, I found out that Big Bad was a Class focused primarily on controlling and manipulating others to do their bidding and rarely directly intervened themselves unless forced to or necessary. It even showed me how many Minions I controlled, plus my current limit.

All of my Stats were higher than Dinoczar's, or just about, which made sense. My previous research indicated that players always had higher Stats than their Sidekicks.

Oddly, I had *two* Skills: Scan, which I already knew about, and

Link, which I didn't. When did I get that Skill? I clicked on it out of curiosity, only to receive this message:

ERROR. *You cannot use this Skill yet.*

Weird. If I couldn't use that particular Skill yet, then why was it on my character sheet? Eh, I'd worry about it later. I was still trying to make sense of the Capes Online character sheet itself, after all. Wasn't like I was planning to use any of my Skills or Powers right away anyway.

I was disappointed to see that I had no experience, Power Points, or Stat Points, however. Guess that was logical. I'd just started playing the game, after all, so presumably, I'd gain more points in general as time went on.

"So?" said Dinoczar, his voice suddenly snapping me out of my thoughts. "How does your character sheet look, sir?"

Gazing at Dinoczar, I said, "It looks good, though it says I don't have Power Points and Stat Points that I can use to grow my Powers and Stats. How do I gain those?"

"By leveling up, of course," said Dinoczar. "Every time you level up, you get four Stat Points and two Power Points, which can be used, saved, and distributed as needed. Sidekicks like Dinoczar only get half those points at two SPs and one PP respectively."

I rubbed my forehead. "Right. I forgot you Sidekicks level up. Distributing your points sounds like a lot of work."

"You do not have to manually distribute PPs or SPs yourself, sir," Dinoczar explained. "You can set up Dinoczar's character growth to automatic, meaning Dinoczar will distribute his points as he sees fit."

Navigating to the SIDEKICKS tab again, I spotted a tab under Dinoczar's name reading "SIDEKICK GROWTH." Toggling it from MANUAL to AUTO, I said, "Thanks for telling me about that. You just saved me a lot of time."

"Dinoczar is a useful Sidekick," Dinoczar agreed. "Dinoczar will make sure to distribute his points in the most efficient manner possible."

Joe snorted. "Just be careful. Once you spend your points, you can't take 'em back."

Nodding, I suddenly remembered Joe was my Minion, so I toggled over to the MINIONS tab to see how strong he was:

Name: *Joe*
Level: *1*
Class: *Thief [Minion]*
Powers: *Flee [Level 1], Secret Identity [Level 1]*
Skills: *Pick Pocket [Level 1], Scan [Level 1], Stealth [Level 1], Lock Pick [Level 1], Thief Senses [Level 1]*
Equipment: *Prison Jumpsuit*

Health: *10*
Stamina: *7*
Strength: *13*
Defense: *8*
Charisma: *3*
Intelligence: *8*
Agility: *12*
Evasion: *11*
Accuracy: *5*
Dexterity: *15*
Energy: *4*
Luck: *0*

I raised an eyebrow. "Your character sheet is … interesting."

Joe, holding his spoonful of [Slop] halfway to his mouth, gazed at me suspiciously. "What's that supposed to mean?"

"You apparently don't have a Secret Identity, Stat Points, Power Points, or Experience Points," I said. "For that matter, you don't have Villain Stats or an Alignment, either. Your Stats are also pretty low, aside from your Dexterity, and you don't even have any Powers aside from Flee and Secret Identity. Almost like you aren't a full character."

Joe scowled. "Speaking of dehumanizing—"

"Yes," said Dinoczar, speaking over Joe. "Minions do not count as 'characters' in the same sense as Villains and Sidekicks. They level up with you, so they do not need points to grow as a character. Even their Powers and Skills grow with you, which you can also use yourself."

"Wait, I can use Joe's Powers?" I said, suddenly taking much more of an interest in Joe's character sheet.

"Not here," Joe grunted. "Power Negation, remember? But yeah, I guess you can use my Powers and Skills. Not that I have anything worth using here."

Huh. Sounded to me like being a Big Bad came with some neat quirks. My mind spun with the possibilities. Did this mean that I could have access to potentially every Power and Skill in the game, including ones I didn't currently, or maybe *couldn't*, get on my own? That is, as long as one of my Minions had it?

If so, then the Big Bad Class seemed almost OP. Why wasn't every Villain player a Big Bad?

As if reading my mind, Dinoczar said, "Unfortunately, you can only use Minion Powers and Skills while they serve you or are alive. As well, Minions, unlike Sidekicks, do not respawn except in certain situations, so you have to be careful not to lose them before you no longer need them."

I nodded. Made sense. Game balance was an extremely important concept in every video game. Sounded like the developers gave Big Bads this limitation to make sure we weren't overwhelmingly more powerful than the other Classes. My Strength and Defense were rather low as well, which I imagined was another limitation of the Big Bad Class.

I wondered about Joe's Secret Identity Power, though. "Joe, what does Secret Identity let you do?"

"Lets you hide your actual identity from others," said Joe. "I used to use it to hide from people by taking on a different appearance. Sort of like shapeshifting, but not as effective. Mostly, it lets you look like an ordinary Civilian rather than a Villain and can even protect you from being sensed by Heroes or Villains."

That sounded like a really useful Power to me. Unfortunately, much of that use was theoretical at the moment thanks to the Dome's Power Negation System, meaning I wouldn't be able to use it right away. I would have to test it out later, when we escaped from the Dome.

In any case, I had learned a lot about myself, Dinoczar, Joe, the Dome, and the game in general just by sitting here. While I still didn't have a plan for the breakout figured out yet, I was much closer to forming a plan than I had been even five minutes—

Loud alarms suddenly went off, making me, Joe, and Dinoczar jump. The Prisoners at the tables around us also flinched, while the Prison Guards immediately looked around as if trying to spot the source of the danger.

"WARNING!" an automated female voice blared over the alarms. "PRISON BREAK IN PROGRESS! Prisoner NUMBER 10X IS ATTEMPTING TO ESCAPE FROM MAXIMUM SECURITY! LOCK-DOWN ACTIVATED!"

Flinching from the noise, I shouted, "What the hell is going on?"

Joe, his left hand and the stump that had once been his right hand slammed over his ears, shook his head. "Sounds like a Prisoner is making an escape attempt! And probably a stupid one, at that."

A massive explosion erupted from the other side of the cafeteria, easily drowning out the alarms and the automated female voice. Prison Guards rushed over to the explosion, but before they could even get into the smoke cloud, several bodies crashed onto the floor before them, forcing the Prison Guards to stop.

Even from a distance, I could see that the bodies were the decapitated or crushed corpses of several Prison Guards. Given the fearful expressions and body language that the other living Prison Guards word, I guessed they were high-leveled ones, too.

"Holy crap," said Joe, staring at the smoke cloud in alarm. "Maybe this guy isn't so stupid after all."

I struggled to see through the smoke, but it was too thick to tell anything about whoever it was.

That was, until the figure stepped out from the smoke, revealing exactly who it was:

A giant of a man, with skin like stone, emerged from the smoke cloud. The top half of his prison jumpsuit was missing, leaving only the tattered remains of his pants hanging loosely on his legs, while broken chains hung from wrists and ankles. His left hand was behind his back like he was hiding something, though I couldn't even begin to tell what.

And by "giant," I mean *giant*. He had to be at least fifteen feet tall, with hands bigger than boulders. Dark, angry eyes peered out from his rocky face as he gazed out over the assembled Prison Guards, who drew batons or raised their guns at him. The Prison Guards on the higher levels aimed their rifles at him, while the drones buzzed around with their own guns fixed squarely on the escapee.

Despite that, [Prisoner #10X] didn't look even remotely fazed, probably because his rocky skin was covered in the blood of the Prison Guards he'd already killed.

"I count twenty-four, plus a handful of drones," said Prisoner #10X. He snorted. "Is that all?"

"Surrender immediately, Prisoner Number Ten X," said [PRISON GUARD BRICK], the one I'd noticed earlier. "Or we will shoot to kill."

Prisoner #10X chuckled. "Better have good aim, then, unless you want to kill her."

Puzzled looks crossed the faces of the Prison Guards for a moment before Prisoner #10X pulled his left hand out from behind his back and held it up for everyone to see:

It was a female Prison Guard, struggling uselessly against the giant's unbreakable grip.

CHAPTER 10

"Holy. Crap." Joe bent down lower in his seat. "I didn't know *he* was here."

I looked at Joe in confusion. "Wait, you know that guy?"

"Not personally," said Joe in what was obviously a big fat lie. "But he's one of the most infamous Villains in the game: Rock Lord."

"Rock Lord?" I said. "Is that his actual name? What's he infamous for?"

Joe gulped. "He led the Golem Legion, a Villain Legion of rock-themed Villains who specialized in Smash-and-Grab missions. Oh, and assassinations as well. Very bloody, smushy assassinations."

I pursed my lips. "They couldn't have been good at assassination if they are all as big as Rock Lord. Aren't assassins supposed to be stealthy or something?"

Joe shook his head. "You don't need to be sneaky when you're taller than a small house and built like a freaking mountain. Oh, and did I forget to mention that Rock Lord has a special fondness for putting women specifically in danger?"

"This Rock Lord person sounds very rude," Dinoczar remarked. "Unlike Dinoczar, who is a true gentleman dinosaur."

"Listen, we just need to keep our heads down until this situation resolves itself," said Joe, practically hiding under the table now. "No tellin' what Rock Lord will do now that he's somehow freed himself from whatever hole they threw him into."

I shook my head. "No way. This is a great opportunity for us to see what sorts of defenses Maximum Security actually has."

"Watch all you want," said Joe. "I am going to do the sane thing and make sure he doesn't see me. Not because I actually stole from the Golem Legion at one point or have any past history with them in any way, shape, or form. Just basic precautions, you know? Safety first."

I raised a skeptical eyebrow, only to hear the bear Prisoner at the other table growl, "Rock Lord? I thought he was killed by Capeman last month. What is he doing here?"

Gazing at the bear Prisoner, I said, "He was killed?"

The bear Prisoner nodded. "Yes. Or so I heard. I even recall seeing his body being paraded around on TV when that happened."

The bear Prisoner spoke with a distinctly British accent. Combined with Dinoczar's Russian accent, I now wondered if all of the animal-themed Villains had European accents. The Dweller was probably French.

But this was interesting. If Rock Lord was dead, it explained why all of the other Prisoners were surprised to see him. It also explained why he hadn't been eating lunch with the rest of us.

Yet it would not explain how a dead Villain was staging a breakout from Maximum Security at this very moment.

Just out of curiosity, I tried to Scan Rock Lord, only to get this information:

Prisoner #10X
Level: 250
Alignment: Villain
Class: Assassin/Big Bad
There is no Scan information on [Prisoner #10X].

I noticed several odd things about Prisoner #10X, or Rock Lord, at once.

For one, his number was completely different from every other Prisoner on Maximum Security. The rest of us had six-digit numbers, but his was only two digits plus an "X," which, unless he was a '90s kid, probably did not stand for "extreme."

The other thing that stood out was the fact that he seemingly had two Classes at once. He was both a Big Bad, like me, *and* an Assassin at the same time. I had assumed that in-game characters could only have one Class at a time, yet here was someone who was clearly violating that mechanic.

And his Level was easily the highest I'd seen yet. No wonder the Prison Guards looked nervous. Although that may have also had something to do with the fact that he had just slaughtered several of their fellow Guards and was currently holding another one hostage.

Rock Lord waved the female Guard back and forth in front of his face. "Shoot me and your fellow Guard gets it."

The female Prison Guard, whose name tag read [PRISON GUARD ALICE], struggled against Rock Lord's grip, though obviously with no luck. She looked a good deal smaller and slimmer than the male Prison Guards but still way more muscular than the average woman.

"Put Alice down," Brick, who seemed to be the leader of the Prison Guards, said again. "Now. Or else."

Rock Lord took another step forward. "Or what? You will hit me with your toy-like batons? Pop me with your guns? Your weapons are useless against me and you know it. I will happily let the woman go if you would just let me walk out of here."

"Negative," said Brick with a swift shake of his head. "No Prisoner is allowed to leave Maximum Security. For any reason."

Rock Lord sighed. His eyes flicked to the door on the other side of the cafeteria, which was probably the exit. "Then it looks like we will just have to do things the *hard* way." A ghoulish grin crossed his stony lips. "I *love* doing things the hard way."

Without warning, Rock Lord rushed toward the Prison Guards faster than you'd expect a being of his size and weight should be able to. The Prison Guards immediately began firing their guns at him, the blasts of their weapons echoing in the cafeteria.

And not doing one damned thing against Rock Lord.

Rock Lord plowed through the Prison Guards like they weren't even there. One moment, the Prison Guards were firing their guns at him. The next, they were all either very flat on the ground or pulverized into bits of meat and cloth that had once been their uniforms.

The Prison Guards on the higher levels continued to shoot, but their bullets bounced off of Rock Lord's stony skin easily. And I noticed they were playing it safe, aiming for Rock Lord's head and shoulders and not his chest, where Alice was being held.

Not that it mattered one way or another, however, although Rock Lord was apparently pissed off enough to do something about it.

Changing his course slightly, Rock Lord plowed through several nearby tables, crushing several Prisoners and moving through the electrical barriers like he couldn't even feel them. Picking up a couple of tables in one hand, Rock Lord whirled them through the air like Frisbees toward the Prison Guards.

The tables smashed into the Prison Guards hard enough to knock them down. A couple of them even lost their balance and fell to the floor below with a sickening *crunch*.

"Wow," I said, watching Rock Lord's escape attempt in awe. "Are you guys seeing this?"

"Yes," said Dinoczar with a nod. "Dinoczar is quite impressed with Rock Lord's escape attempt so far. It is exactly what Dinoczar would do if he were a giant rock monster with nigh-impenetrable skin and good Frisbee skills."

Joe poked his head out from under the table. "That's nice and all, but do you guys even see *where* Rock Lord is going?"

Dinoczar and I looked at Joe in confusion and I said, "To the exit, obviously—?"

"Idiot," Joe sneered. "He's coming toward *us*!"

Alarmed, I looked up in time to see Rock Lord coming straight toward us. It took me a second to realize that Rock Lord was taking the direct path to the exit, and Table 52—our table—just so happened to be right in the middle of it.

And just like with the Guards, Rock Lord clearly didn't give a damn how many Prisoners he stepped on or crushed on his way to freedom.

Table after table of Prisoners collapsed or got smashed apart entirely under his charge. While some of the Prisoners managed to jump out of his way, most were not quite so lucky. Now the blood of both Prisoners and Guards alike covered Rock Lord's feet and ankles like paint.

Even worse: Rock Lord wasn't stopping. Or even slowing down. If anything, he seemed to be gaining speed somehow and I estimated he would be here in approximately ten seconds.

"Run!" I yelled.

Of course, there was nowhere we could run *to*. The electrical barrier kept us confined within our little circle. Our only hope, as far as I could see, was to stick to the absolute perimeter of the barrier without actually touching it, and hope that Rock Lord wasn't big enough to crush us all like ants anyway.

Soon, Rock Lord reached our table. He was now just outside the barrier, raising his right foot high, about to bring it down directly on our heads ...

Boom.

A lightning bolt lanced out of nowhere and slammed into Rock Lord's chest. Although the electrical barriers had done nothing to Rock Lord, the lightning bolt apparently had, because it knocked him flat off his feet. He staggered backward and fell right on top of the next table, crushing both Table 51 and the Prisoners unfortunate enough to be sitting there when he landed.

My eyes widened. "Was that an act of God or something?"

Joe, who definitely smelled like he'd lost control of his bladder, shuddered. "No idea. But it seems to have pissed him off."

Joe was right. Although Rock Lord was still conscious, his chest had been blackened by the lightning bolt, wisps of smoke rising off it. Clutching his chest, Rock Lord growled and slowly rose to his feet.

"Who dares attack the Rock Lord?" said Rock Lord, gazing around the cafeteria. "Show yourself!"

"That'd be me, boy," said a male voice with a heavy Southern accent. "Though if you ask me, you look more like a Pebble Boy than a Rock Lord."

I whipped my head in the direction of the voice, thinking it probably belonged to some kind of high-level Hero or something.

Instead, I saw a portly, middle-aged black man chomping on a sprinkle-covered chocolate donut.

The black man stood in front of the exit. He wore a uniform similar to what the Prison Guards wore, although his looked a bit nicer. He honestly looked like a stereotypical middle-aged manager guy who had been working in the same job since his twenties and had let himself go, if indeed he ever took care of himself in the first place.

Yet even from a distance, I could smell the ozone wafting off him. I could also see his name tag, [CHIEF WARDEN OLD SPARKY], although it was colored gold rather than the blue of the other Guards' name tags.

Joe sucked in a breath. "Holy crap. That's the Dome Warden. He's in charge of the entire prison."

I tried to Scan Old Sparky, only to get this message:

Scan blocked.

That was it. No other information. Guess the Warden's Scan was blocked just like the Prison Guards'.

Then the Warden's eyes flicked toward me. It was just for a second, long enough that someone else might have mistaken it for the Warden simply looking around the cafeteria at everyone.

But I noticed his eyes lingered on me for a second or two. Did he somehow sense I had Scanned him? That was the only reason I could think as to why he looked at me at all, because I certainly hadn't met him before today.

Old Sparky turned his gaze back to Rock Lord, perhaps deciding (correctly, I might add) that he was the real threat at the moment.

"So the Warden himself decides to appear," said Rock Lord. He cocked his head. "I thought you might be too busy eating donuts to step in and stop me yourself."

Old Sparky took another bite out of his donut. "I do love me some sprinkle-covered chocolate donuts. But do you know what I love even more? Putting down boys like you, whose mothers clearly never taught them any lessons."

Rock Lord sneered. "You are even less impressive than I thought."

"Don't be fooled," said Alice in a strained, yet excited voice. "Old Sparky is the best. You'll never beat—"

Rock Lord tightened his grip on Alice, making her choke and go limp in his hand. "Please shut up, hostage. Your point of view is rather irrelevant here."

Old Sparky's eyes narrowed. "I'm not even going to ask how you broke out of your cell. But I am going to ask that you put down Alice."

Rock Lord cocked his head to the side again. "Why? She is, in Big Bad terms, nothing more than an expendable Minion. There is no reason for you to value her life."

"Every Guard in this prison is valuable to me," Old Sparky replied. He took another bite of his donut. "That's what makes you Villains so sickening to me. You use people like tools and then discard 'em. It's why I took a vow to never let scum like *you* escape, even at the cost of my own life."

Rock Lord chuckled. "You sound too much like the Hero who stopped me in the first place. But enough talk. If you are not going to let me go peacefully, then I will not hesitate to crush you just like how I crushed your fellow Guards."

Rock Lord immediately ran toward Old Sparky, swinging his open fist while keeping Alice close to his chest. That made sense. Rock Lord didn't want to give Old Sparky an open target with his chest, so he decided to put Alice there to discourage Old Sparky from shooting him again.

I had to admit, Rock Lord was pretty smart.

Yet for some reason, Old Sparky didn't look even remotely afraid.

If anything, he just looked annoyed.

Tossing the rest of his donut into his mouth, Old Sparky snapped his fingers.

An electrical rope suddenly shot out of his hands toward Rock Lord. The rope slapped Rock Lord in the face, even burning his stonelike skin. Rock Lord cried out and dropped Alice, who immediately got to her feet and ran away from Rock Lord. Impressive, given how she had been nearly crushed to death earlier. Maybe she was tougher than she looked.

Though when I saw what happened next, I later realized that Alice had known what was going to happen and wanted to get the hell out of Dodge before she accidentally got caught up in it.

Rubbing his face, Rock Lord said, "Is that all you have, Warden? A simple whip? Unimpressive."

Old Sparky smiled. He licked the chocolate off his fingers and said, "Actually, I also have a donut."

Old Sparky clapped his hands together and this notification

suddenly appeared in my view. Based on the startled expressions of the other Prisoners, I guessed they also got it:

[*Chief Warden Old Sparky] is using* **Lightning Donut***!*

Before I could even begin to ask what a "Lightning Donut" was, a ring of electricity suddenly appeared around Rock Lord. The Prisoner looked around in confusion at the ring, which thickened until it bore a close resemblance to a … to a …

"Lightning Donut," I said under my breath in disbelief.

Dinoczar licked his lips. "Sounds delicious!"

Of course, the real "Lightning Donut," which was apparently one of Old Sparky's Powers, probably didn't taste all that good.

And it looked quite a bit painful, too.

A hint of wariness crossing his stony features, Rock Lord still glared at Old Sparky. "You do realize I am Stone Type, yes? Your Lightning Donut won't do a thing to my impenetrable rock-like—"

Rock Lord's boasting was interrupted when the Lightning Donut abruptly exploded around him. Blindingly bright light slammed into me with the force of an tsunami wave, knocking me off my feet. I heard the shouts and screams from all of the other Prisoners around me, including Dinoczar and Joe, but there was nothing I could do about it.

For what seemed like an eternity, my whole world was light, thunder, heat, and ozone.

Then, a second later, the light faded, my sight and hearing slowly coming back into focus.

Blinking rapidly, I sat up, rubbing the back of my head as I looked around. "Is everyone o—?"

I stopped speaking as soon as I looked toward Old Sparky and Rock Lord.

Or rather, where Rock Lord had once stood. There was now nothing except a blackened pit in the floor, right where Rock Lord had been standing. The pit had to be about a foot deep, thick wisps of smoke rising from within.

But the explosion hadn't just destroyed Rock Lord. Several nearby tables of Prisoners had been obliterated in the blast as well, leaving charred corpses of the Prisoners unfortunate enough to be within the vicinity of the explosion when it went off.

Only Old Sparky appeared until unaffected by the attack. His fingertips sparking slightly, he licked the chocolate off his fingers and sighed. "That was a good donut."

A notification appeared in my vision:

[Chief Warden Old Sparky] has killed [Prisoner #10X]!

"Killed" seemed like the understatement of the year to me. It was more like he had *obliterated* Rock Lord from existence. Seriously, there was nothing left of the guy. Not even the chains on his wrists and ankles.

Which was kind of scary when you thought about it. Scan had revealed to me that Rock Lord was Level 250. My research had told me that the maximum Level a character could achieve in Capes Online was 1,000, meaning that Rock Lord was about a fourth of the way to the max Level (although the actual highest Levels most players reached went up to the fifties or sixties, with some reaching 100 and very few going beyond that).

Even better, Rock Lord was a Stone Type, which I assumed meant he had some level of immunity to electrical attacks.

Yet Old Sparky—despite Rock Lord's immense Level and clear Type Advantage—had wiped out Rock Lord in one blow.

How powerful *was* this middle manager?

Old Sparky looked out across the cafeteria. He suddenly wore a very serious expression. "None of you saw anything today. You did not see Rock Lord. You did not see me kill him. Return to your meals."

I blinked. Did Old Sparky really expect us to pretend like we hadn't just seen him wipe out one of the strongest Villains in the game in one hit?

But when I looked around at the other Prisoners, I saw them all sway slightly in their seats. Many nodded in agreement with Old Sparky before returning to their [Slop]. Only Dinoczar and Joe seemed unaffected by whatever spell Old Sparky had put everyone else under, based on their skeptical looks.

With an approving nod, Old Sparky turned and walked out of the cafeteria. He was joined by several Prison Guards, including Alice, who immediately began talking with him in whispered tones. No doubt they were discussing Rock Lord's failed escape attempt.

Yet even as Old Sparky left the cafeteria, he cast one last look over his shoulder at me.

And this time, I could tell he was looking *directly* at me.

Then Old Sparky was gone and the doors closed behind him with a *slam*.

"Well ..." Joe crawled out from underneath our table and looked at me and Dinoczar. "Anyone up for seconds?"

I shook my head. I wasn't at all hungry, not anymore.

Because I now realized that the rest of the Dome's security measures, whatever they were, didn't matter.

Not after I'd finally identified the final boss of the Dome ... who was probably strong enough to wipe out all of Maximum Security by himself.

CHAPTER 11

"Am I the only one who has given up entirely on the idea of escaping from this hellhole after *that* little display?" said Joe about half an hour later, back in our cell. "Because even though I don't like the Dome, I like getting killed by a freaking lightning donut even *less*."

Lunch had ended about half an hour ago and we had been teleported back to our cells. The Dome apparently had some kind of teleportation system in place to allow Prisoners to teleport to and from the cafeteria during mealtimes. Supposedly, the Prison Guards also used the teleportation system to get around the Dome's multiple Floors easily, although I had yet to confirm that myself. It explained how they seemed to be able to move around the place so quickly, however, and added another complication for any would-be prison escapees. Apparently, they also kept our cells unlocked while we were at mealtimes because all of the Prisoners were in the cafeteria rather than in their cells. That explained the soft *click* I heard from the door to our cell when we reappeared here.

Nor was that even on my mind right now. I was sitting on the lower bunk, staring at the floor, unable to get the image of Old Sparky annihilating Rock Lord out of my mind.

"Dinoczar is willing to do whatever master wants to do," said Dinoczar, sitting on the floor nearby. He looked at me. "What do you want to do, sir?"

I sighed and scratched the back of my head. "I still want to break out of this place, but I have to admit, Old Sparky *does* complicate things."

"You think?" Joe snorted. "He's the toughest bastard in the whole Dome. Especially in Maximum Security, where he's damn near unstoppable. Like a force of nature."

I looked up at Joe quickly. "'Especially in Maximum Security'? What do you mean by that?"

Joe grimaced. "The Warden is weaker in Medium Security and weakest in Minimum Security and is apparently *really* weak outside of the Dome. I don't understand the details about it myself, but he's always stronger than the Prisoners, regardless of what Floor he is on, so don't get complacent."

I stroked my chin. While that may not have made sense to Joe, it did make sense to me from a game design point of view.

If Old Sparky was indeed the "boss" of the Dome, then it made sense that Villain players in Minimum and Medium Security might occasionally have to fight him in order to escape. It would be unfair to lower-level players to make Old Sparky as powerful as he was down here, so having his general power level scale depending on where he was fighting was logical.

And having him always be stronger than most Prisoners also made sense from an in-game point of view. It meant that NPC Prisoners—who, as far as I could tell, made up the majority of Maximum Security Prisoners—couldn't escape because Old Sparky would always be more powerful than them.

Again, I found myself impressed by whoever had designed the Dome. They clearly put a lot of thought into it, both from a player and NPC perspective. Guess SI Games had some good designers working for them.

"Tell me more about Old Sparky," I said. "How long has he been the Warden of the Dome? What are his Powers, exactly? Oh, and how do you know so much about him?"

Joe folded his arms in front of his chest, leaning against the wall opposite me. "To answer your last question, this isn't my first time in the Dome, although it's my first time in Maximum Security. Plus, a lot of my ... let's call them business associates have ended up here a few times and shared their experiences with me. So I know a thing or two about the place."

By "business associates," Joe was probably referring to his fellow purse thief friends. I idly wondered if Capes Online had a Purse Thieves Guild before dismissing that idea. Surely even Capes Online wasn't *that* ridiculous.

"Good to know," I said. I put my hands together. "What else?"

Joe glanced through the bars of our cell, as if afraid someone might be eavesdropping. "Firstly, Old Sparky's Powers are primarily Electricity-based, in case you couldn't tell. I'm pretty sure that's his Type, though he also has some Mind-based Powers, too."

"Rock Lord mentioned something about Types, too," I said. I turned toward Dinoczar. "What are Types?"

Dinoczar cleared his throat. "The Type System is another aspect of our world. Many Villains, Heroes, Sidekicks, and other types of characters have a dominant Elemental Power or Type, such as Fire, Water, Electricity, etc. As well, each Prime Type has its own Sub-Types and different Types do better or worse against other Types in match-ups."

I nodded. Seemed like a pretty basic Type System not too dissimilar from other games I'd played that had elemental type match-ups, including a certain monster taming series. "I take it that Rock Types must be strong against Electric Types, then. Yet Old Sparky took out Rock Lord no problem."

"It ain't absolute, genius," Joe said. "Having a superior Type is great, but there are loads of factors that affect how strong a person is. Like being twice the Level of the guy they're fighting and having a maxed-out Ultimate Power, for example."

My heart nearly stopped. "Twice the Level—? Are you saying that Old Sparky is Level Five Hundred? And what's an Ultimate Power?"

"Ultimate Powers are a subset of normal Powers," Dinoczar explained. "They are usually stronger than normal Powers but often take a long time to be used again. You can also redistribute Ultimate Power Points as much as you want, unlike with normal Powers."

"Thanks for the explanation, Dinoczar," I said. "Sounds like I'll need to get me one of those."

Then I turned my gaze to Joe again. "Again, Level Five Hundred?"

Joe held up his left hand palm first. "I ain't saying *nothing*, pal. Truth is, no one other than Old Sparky knows exactly how strong he is. Even the other Prison Guards don't know what his actual Level is. I think he keeps it that way to make it harder to fight him. Probably also why he blocks Scan."

I stroked my chin. "I noticed that. I also noticed how he looked at me when I tried that."

"He did?" said Joe. "Huh. Normally, high-level dudes like Old Sparky don't even notice when a low-level noob like you tries to Scan him. Are you sure he looked at you?"

"Yes," I said. I pointed at my face. "He looked directly at me. I'm sure of it."

Joe gulped. "Uh-oh. That's bad."

"It is?"

"Yeah," said Joe. "It means he's probably going to be keeping an eye on you, which means he will be keeping an eye on us, which is very stressful for me to think about because I am nowhere near strong enough to fight a monster like *him*."

"Dinoczar lives a stress-free life, so Dinoczar does not care," said Dinoczar. "Be like Dinoczar and think about how delicious human flesh is whenever one is tempted to be stressed. It makes life more pleasant."

"Jesus," Joe muttered under his breath. "Maybe Old Sparky would be better."

"If Old Sparky is so powerful, I don't see why he's stuck being the Warden of the Dome," I said. "Why not let him out onto the streets of Adventure City to take out Villains and criminals?"

"Because he is obsessed with guarding the Dome," Joe said. "Seriously, he practically lives here. Even during the Blackouts, the dude didn't leave. He just made sure that no one took advantage of the situation to mount an escape attempt. During the second Blackout, he supposedly killed over 300 Maximum Security Prisoners that tried to join the Paradox Legion. In one blow."

I shuddered. I could buy that, having seen what Old Sparky could do even to high-level Big Bads like Rock Lord.

But this was also good information.

And again, from a gameplay perspective, it made sense.

Old Sparky was very clearly the final boss of the Dome. That made him the last obstacle for any would-be escapees. His scaling Levels meant that he was probably manageable for Minimum and Medium Security players, but for Maximum Security players, he would be damn near impossible to defeat or escape from, which was probably why Villain players were never sent down here (other than me, of course).

Given how I was literally Level 1, I expected Old Sparky could probably sneeze and kill me by accident, with or without an Ultimate Power. No way I could beat him in a direct fight, at least not right now at my current Level.

The question was, how could I get strong enough to defeat Old Sparky if I couldn't level up?

Deciding to think about that later, I said, "But I don't know what my Type is. My character sheet doesn't list it."

"You just need to unlock the Type System," said Dinoczar. "Let Dinoczar help."

A new notification suddenly appeared in my vision:

Congratulations! After listening to a helpful explanation of the Type System from your eternally faithful Sidekick, you can now see your Type, as well as the Types of your Sidekicks and Minions (where applicable)!

NOTE: *You cannot yet view other players' Types until Scan reaches Level 5 or higher.*

I immediately opened my character sheet and frowned. "My Type is ... Water? Seriously?"

Joe chuckled. "You might wanna get comfy, then, 'cause we ain't never getting out of here with a Type match-up like that. Water doesn't conduct electricity very well."

I swiped over to Dinoczar's character sheet. "Dinoczar, I see that you are Rock Type. Makes sense, what with you being a dinosaur and all."

"And Dinoczar loves rock music," Dinoczar added.

Then I glanced at Joe's sheet. "You don't seem to have a Type, Joe."

"Because I don't have any Elemental Powers, idiot," Joe snapped. "And if or until I do, I'll remain Typeless. Got it?"

I nodded again. "Yeah, but I don't have any Elemental Powers, either, and yet for some reason I have a Type. So does Dinoczar, even though he doesn't have Elemental Powers like me."

"Sometimes players can get Types from their Origin Stories depending on their actions," said Dinoczar. "Did you do anything watery in your Origin Story, sir?"

I thought back to my Origin Story. "Not really. I wonder if it's a glitch or something."

Joe shook his head. "Who cares? It's not like you are going to get a chance to practice your new Type. After all, there's no way any of us are getting out of here anytime soon. Not as long as Old Sparky is the boss around here."

As grating as Joe's defeatist attitude was, I had to admit that it wasn't entirely unwarranted. Fact was that even without Old Sparky, the Dome was a formidable prison to escape from. Dozens of high-level Guards, multiple security measures designed to make it impossible for Prisoners to escape, forced isolation of Prisoners from each other to prevent planning, negating Powers and preventing Prisoners from having an easy or convenient way to level up, the multitude of Floors and Sub-Floors making it like a maze … the list went on and on.

And, of course, waiting at the end, like any good final boss, was Old Sparky himself.

Not for the first time, I wondered how Grandpa expected me to solve *this* particular Riddle. I would like to think that Grandpa hadn't given me an unsolvable Riddle, that there was simply something I was overlooking or information I currently didn't have that would turn the tide.

But I also didn't think that Grandpa would hand me a gun and order me to murder a widow and steal her purse, either.

Maybe I really didn't know Grandpa as well as I thought I did. Or his Digital Double was crazy.

That was when another thought occurred to me. "Did either of you notice Rock Lord's weird Prisoner number? It wasn't formatted like ours."

Joe blinked. "That? Oh, yeah. Sorry, but I got nothin' on that."

"Neither does Dinoczar, sir," said Dinoczar with a shrug of his shoulders.

I stroked my chin. "And then there was that weird thing Old Sparky did at the end, where he told the Prisoners no one saw it. Plus, the fact that Rock Lord was supposedly dead, yet was clearly here in the flesh."

"What do you think that means?" said Joe.

I shook my head. "I have no idea. But I think there is more going on inside the Dome than the Warden and the Prison Guards are letting on. That's for sure."

A small *ping* in my ear caused me to glance at a notification in my HUD, but this one was not from Capes Online. It was a reminder of something important happening today that I nearly forgot about.

"Oops," I said, standing up. "Looks like I need to log off for now."

"You're leaving?" said Joe, frowning. "But I thought you were stuck in here with us."

"Master is not leaving," Dinoczar explained. "He is simply going to rest for a while. Right, master?"

It occurred to me that I had no idea what "logging off" looked like or meant to NPCs like Dinoczar and Joe. For them, Capes Online *was* their world. The idea of stepping out of that world, even for a moment, probably sounded as crazy to them as it would to me if someone in real life said they were literally "logging off" for the day.

Whoa. Was I actually looking at things from the perspective of an NPC? Like they were real people?

Maybe this game really was getting to me.

Even so, I sat back down on my cot and said, "Yeah. I've had a long day, so I think I'm going to take a nap."

"All right," said Joe. He gazed at the top bunk and yawned as well. "I, too, am tired. I think I'll just help myself to the top bunk and—"

Dinoczar growled. "No. Dinoczar gets top bunk. You get floor."

Joe winced and said, in a weak voice, "Yes, sir."

Shaking my head at their antics, I lay down on the uncomfortable cot, opened my menus, and navigated to the LOG OFF button.

I pressed the button, my vision slowly turned black, and soon all I could see was this message:

Thank you for playing Capes Online! We hope to see you again soon.

CHAPTER 12

Today was my older brother's birthday.

I knocked on the door to my brother's room and waited.

It always took Daniel a moment to answer. According to his nurse, Daniel spent a lot of time either sleeping, reading superhero comics, or watching superhero movies. He didn't do much else, other than occasionally try to escape from Bright Hope Nursing Home to "save" civilians from supervillains or, on rare occasion, mistake the nurses for evildoers who needed to be punished.

We were still paying court fees on that last lawsuit from a nurse he assaulted.

Finally, after several seconds, I heard Daniel's croaky voice say, "Come in, unless you are a Villain, of course."

Cringing slightly, I opened the door and said, "No, Daniel, it's just me, Robert."

I wrinkled my nose at the scent in Daniel's room. Though not unpleasant, it reminded me strongly of old people, probably because Bright Hope Nursing Home, like most nursing homes, mostly had old people living in it.

The primary exception, of course, was Daniel.

My older brother, who was now twenty-seven, sat on his bed, surrounded by dozens of half-opened superhero comics and graphic novels. Wearing a loose graphic T-shirt with an image of Superman on it, Daniel raised his head from the issue he was reading when I entered and looked straight at me. His face didn't look much like mine, but he did bear a striking resemblance to our father, while I took more after our mother.

"Robby?" said Daniel, slightly lowering the comic book. He smiled. "Good to see a face I can trust around here."

I sighed. "Daniel, you know you can trust the staff here at Bright Hope, right? They just want to help you."

Daniel pursed his lips and looked away. "Some of them, perhaps, but I am almost certain that there are Villains among them. In particular, there is a man I notice outside my room at the same time every day dressed in inconspicuous clothing, mopping the floors."

"That's the janitor," I said, closing the door behind me. "He's just cleaning the floors so they will look nice and people can walk on them without tripping or falling."

Daniel frowned and rubbed his forehead. "Maybe, but you can never be too sure. There are Villains everywhere, you know. Some days, I feel like I can't trust anyone except you and my Sidekick, Nightbird. How is Nightbird doing nowadays, anyway? I haven't seen her in years."

I bit my lower lip. How the hell was I supposed to know how his in-game Sidekick was doing? I didn't have the heart to tell Daniel that we'd deleted his Capes Online profile shortly after we sent him here. That meant that his Sidekick, Nightbird, was probably either a normal Civilian now or had been reassigned to another player, according to the game's rules.

But I didn't tell him that. The last time I tried to explain how we'd deleted his account, Daniel had gotten so upset that it took several of the burlier nurses just to restrain him, and even then, he only calmed down when I lied and said it was a joke.

Perhaps I should note that Daniel is a lot bigger and bulkier than me, so he could definitely take me down if he wanted.

Fortunately, today Daniel seemed to be in one of his good moods, where he was more interested in talking about superheroes than actually being one.

So I said, "She's doing fine. I think she caught some purse thieves recently."

Daniel nodded approvingly. "Tell Nightbird that I will be

returning to duty soon, but not to give up hope and keep fighting the good fight even in my absence."

Daniel's doctors had told us that Daniel should never be allowed anywhere near a VR video game again, whether Capes Online or another. You could probably tell why.

Moving some comic books off of the chair I usually sat on during my visits, I pulled the chair over to Daniel and said, "What have you been reading recently, bro? Anything interesting?"

Daniel sighed and tossed the comic book onto an increasingly large pile of them on the floor. "Just rereading some old favorites. The nurses won't get me any of the new stuff."

Daniel, of course, didn't know that that was another order from the doctor. While 2D media, like comics and movies, were not considered as bad for his mental health as VR games were, the doctor had recommended limiting the amount of superhero content he consumed. The only reason he even had his old comic book collection was because he threw a huge fit if he didn't have it. Mostly we were trying to prevent a psychological relapse.

Having said that, I still wondered if "new" comics were even being published nowadays. I supposed there might still be a few comic book shops around selling those floppies, but it seemed to me that most comic book stores were now hobby stores that sold comics on the side.

Regardless, I said, "Too bad, but hey, rereading old favorites can be fun sometimes."

"I suppose," said Daniel. He looked at me. "What about you? Have you and Mom been safe and well?"

That might have seemed like a weird question to ask, but remember, Daniel thought he was a real superhero. He became convinced at some point that Mom and I were in danger because of the many "archenemies" he had in Capes Online, to the point where he had us promise—in all seriousness—not to tell anyone his secret identity lest his "enemies" find out and use that fact against him.

We thought it was a joke at first.

But then we found out it wasn't. Or rather, Daniel didn't think it was.

"We're fine," I said. "Mom's health isn't that great, but she hasn't gotten worse. Oh, and she wanted me to give you this card for your birthday. We signed it together."

I pulled out a birthday card from my pocket and handed it to Daniel. A big smile crossed Daniel's face as he took the card. Flipping it open, he grinned even more. "Thanks. I forgot today was my birthday."

I smiled weakly. "Too busy fighting supervillains to remember your own birthday, eh?"

Daniel gave me a serious look. "I wish. I've just been thinking about Capes Online a lot recently and wondering how things have changed since I last … since I last played."

I noticed how Daniel deliberately used the word "played," as if he didn't quite agree with it but knew he had no real choice but to use it around me.

That was progress. For the longest time, Daniel wouldn't even acknowledge that Capes Online was a video game at all. Only in the past few months had he started to concede that Capes Online was a game, although he still seemed to think it was real on some level.

But progress was progress.

Of course, *I* knew what had been happening in Capes Online recently. In fact, I just logged out of the game an hour ago, having remembered that I was supposed to visit Daniel for his birthday today. And on the automatic bus ride here, I found myself still thinking about it.

Unlike Daniel, however, I wasn't obsessed with it like it was real life. It was more like I was thinking about a complicated puzzle that had stumped me. Sometimes, putting distance between myself and the problem could make it easier to figure out a solution.

Although I had to admit, the initial awakening from the game was … rough. My Capes Online body was both taller and more muscular than my physical self. The transition from game to real life, while shockingly smooth, was still an adjustment. I even tripped climbing out of the GamePod, though fortunately I didn't get anything worse than a few scrapes and bumps.

Unfortunately, even on the bus ride here, I still hadn't been able to crack Grandpa's Riddle. The Dome was an almost impenetrable prison, both inside and outside, easily the most complicated puzzle Grandpa had ever given me. And, despite what I said about distance, I didn't think spending time with my brother would actually help. I was just doing it because I cared about Daniel and because he was my brother.

Shaking my head, I said, "Eh, not much has changed since you last played as far as I can tell."

Daniel, still holding the birthday card in his hand, whipped his head toward me so fast I worried he'd get whiplash. "You know what's been going on in Capes Online? How? Have you started playing it, too?"

Crap. I let my guard down. I didn't intend to tell Daniel I was playing. The doctor warned me that going along with Daniel's fantasies could get me into trouble.

But Daniel, however delusional he might be, was smart. Even smarter than me, if I was going to be honest, despite his insanity. He was always pretty good at sniffing out lies from other people, so I couldn't just lie and pretend I didn't say what I just said.

So I said, "Yeah, I have. It's … fun."

Daniel smiled even more than before. For a moment, I caught a glimpse of the old, sane Daniel behind that smile.

But then the old, sane Daniel was gone. Insanity glinted in his eyes and his smile became unnaturally wide.

"Isn't it?" said Daniel with a hint of longing in his voice. "It was so real. To be a superhero, fighting supervillains, protecting innocent people, fighting for truth and justice at every turn … it was a lot more real than real life."

"Not really," I said. "I mean, people can't fly around and shoot lasers from their eyes in real life. Nor do we have health bars and levels and all that other video game stuff."

Daniel's shoulders sank. "I'm not talking about that. I'm talking about the … *sensations*. Everything is crisper, clearer. People are bigger, stronger, more beautiful. I felt more alive in Capes Online than I ever have in real life."

The longing in Daniel's voice was undeniable at this point. I could tell he had already left the room and was back in the game, if only in his mind. That wasn't good. I needed to say something to get him back to earth.

Leaning forward, I said, "Have you gotten your birthday cupcake from the nurses yet? I heard they're supposed to give free cupcakes to residents on their birthdays."

Daniel looked at me as if he had forgotten I was sitting there. "Huh? Oh, I tossed it in the trash."

Daniel gestured at a trash can in the corner of the room, where I could see a hint of blue icing peeking out from the rim.

"What?" I said. "Why?"

Daniel stared at me. "I thought it was poisoned by one of my many archenemies. Get me when I am at my most defenseless, in other words. Seems like something a Villain would do."

I shook my head. "That's ridiculous. You don't have any archenemies in real life."

Daniel tapped the side of his head. "That you know of. Besides, I know how Villains think. It's one of the reasons I was such a successful Hero. I could anticipate their actions and stop them before even they knew what they were going to do. A normal person like you could never understand a Villain's thought processes."

I pursed my lips. Daniel didn't know I was a Villain player in Capes Online yet, and frankly, I wasn't sure how to break that news to him or what he would do if he found out. I'd like to think that Daniel would still love me as his brother, but on the other hand, he might also flip out if he found out that his younger brother had gone over to the "dark side," so to speak.

I definitely wasn't going to tell him about the widow I murdered, at least.

Daniel smiled at me again. "Anyway, what caused you to start playing Capes Online? I always thought you didn't like those kinds of … games."

Again, Daniel sounded reluctant to use any word that made Capes Online sound less real than real life, but I was glad he did. It told me that he wasn't entirely lost in his own little world yet.

Sitting back, I said, "Oh, um, I decided I wanted to try branching out into VR games for a change of pace. I even found a good deal on a GamePod, so it didn't cost me much upfront to set it up."

Daniel frowned. "What about my GamePod? Couldn't you have used that?"

That was another thing we hadn't told Daniel. After Daniel's mental breakdown and subsequent placement in Bright Hope two years ago, I sold Daniel's old GamePod, which was harder than you'd think. Since the Blackouts, a lot of people had been skeptical about immersive VR games like Capes Online in general. While they were still legal here in the US, I knew there was a growing movement to hold SI Games and other VR companies accountable for their inability to protect their players from their own games.

Couldn't say I disagreed with that sentiment. Daniel, after all, was living proof of what happened to people who spent too much time in a game that was almost indistinguishable from real life. And that was *before* the Blackouts.

And with luck, I would avoid falling into the same traps he did.

"Your GamePod is kind of old," I said, scratching the back of my head. "I wanted a newer model, plus you're bigger than me, so it would have been kind of an awkward fit."

Daniel nodded. "I see. Well, how has the experience been so far? Have you saved any Civilians yet?"

I nodded. "Oh, yeah. I just started, so I'm still pretty low-level, but I've saved loads of Civilians. Plus, I've met a few other Heroes, including this guy named Capeman, who is—"

"Capeman?" Daniel repeated. He laughed. "That bastard! He and I used to team up all the time. Great guy."

I stared at Daniel in shock. "You mean you know that guy?"

I had to resist saying "that guy who punched me out," mostly because I didn't want Daniel to even suspect I was anything less than a morally pure Hero who always did the right thing out of the kindness of my heart.

And not, you know, someone who was goaded into murdering a widow by a digital ghost of his grandfather.

"Yep," said Daniel. "Like I said, we worked together all the time. A braver defender of justice you will never find anywhere. How's he doing? I haven't spoken to him since … well, in a long time."

"He's fine," I said. "Still fighting Villains, protecting Criminals, and being, er, very strong."

Daniel chuckled. "That's an understatement. Capeman was always stronger than just about anyone else I knew. I figured he could probably lift a building over his head if he wanted, though I never saw him do that."

Vividly remembering how much Capeman's punch to my face hurt, I nodded again. "He sounds like a fascinating guy. I'll mention I'm your brother next time I see him."

"Thanks!" said Daniel. "You should tell Capeman hi from Warman. Tell him I'll be seeing him again soon."

I shook my head. "I doubt that, Daniel. Remember: No VR."

Daniel sighed again. "I guess you're right. But I'm just excited to learn that you know Capeman. He was always encouraging me to spend more time in Capes Online, fighting evil and doing the right thing every day."

I cocked my head to the side. "He was, was he?"

Daniel put his hands on his hips and thrust his chest forward. "Yeah! Said there was always evil to fight, which of course there is. Ah, now I am remembering the good old days when Capeman and I fought side by side every day ..."

Daniel started rambling about the "good old days," though I'd stopped listening closely to what he said.

Before today, Daniel had never mentioned Capeman or any of his fellow players to me. I had always assumed that Daniel's mental breakdown and addiction to Capes Online came about because of the game's intense realism.

Now, however, I wondered if his interactions with other players had influenced his mental condition, too. I could easily see that Capeman moron being just as addicted to Capes Online as Daniel was, if not more so. Addicts feeding other addicts, in other words.

That just gave me another reason to hate Capeman in addition to the fact that he punched me in the face when I didn't really deserve it.

Of course, Capeman wasn't in the Dome with me, but if I ever did run into him again, I would definitely send him a message.

And not Daniel's message, either.

Daniel and I visited for another couple of hours or so, and thankfully, most of the conversation drifted away from Capes Online to other things. Mostly superhero-related—such as Daniel's intense feelings on the entire Justice League Snyder Cut vs. Whedon Cut controversy from, like, twenty years ago.

Before I left, I told Daniel I'd be back next week to visit him again, and Daniel, as usual, warned me not to let my guard down against any Villains.

"Sure thing, bro," I said as I stepped out the door. "Talk to you later."

Right before I left, however, Daniel said, "Robby, wait. I have something I need to tell you."

Pausing in the open doorway, I looked over my shoulder at Daniel. He wore an expression on his face somewhere between somberly serious and encouraging.

"What is it, bro?" I said.

Daniel gave me the thumbs-up. "I am proud of you for entering Capes Online and being a Hero and helping people. Lots of people think being the Villain is more fun, because you can do whatever you want. But a good person knows that the only acceptable path is the path of the Hero. And I am glad you chose it."

I smiled back weakly. "Thanks, bro."

With that, I finally left the room. Closing the door behind me, I paused to let an orderly wheel another one of the nursing home's wheelchair-bound residents past me before heading down the hall to the exit.

Damn. Why did Daniel have to say that? I had hoped that I could have left the room without him mentioning that damn game again. I was too optimistic.

And I felt even worse for lying to Daniel's face. Yet however much progress Daniel had made over the last year or so, I didn't want to risk causing him to revert to his Warman persona. I was lucky today because I got to talk to Daniel, my older brother, and not Warman, the righteous Hero with zero tolerance for injustice.

Or Villains.

Like me.

I shook my head. Daniel's nursing home bills were another bill I needed to pay. Otherwise, they would kick him out and then he'd either be homeless or living with us.

And I was already struggling to take care of Mom and myself. Adding Daniel on top of that would just make it almost impossible.

Unless I solved Grandpa's Riddle and got his money, that is.

More than ever, I was determined to go back into Capes Online and solve Grandpa's Riddle.

Even if I wasn't quite sure how to do that yet.

CHAPTER 13

When I got home that night, I spent a few hours doing a livestream for my online fans of a game I'd been playing recently. After all, I still hadn't found Grandpa's wealth yet, so I still needed to bring in cash somehow.

It also gave me time to think about the Dome and how to escape from it. Unfortunately, despite picking one of the more brainless games I regularly streamed to play last night to give my mind as much time to think as possible, I was still no closer to coming up with a plan to break out of the Dome than I was before.

Nor did it help that my mind kept going back to the mystery of Rock Lord's presence in the Dome. Somehow, I sensed that that would play a very important role in the breakout if I could only crack it.

So I decided to jump back into Capes Online first thing in the morning. I realized I needed more information than I had, particularly about Rock Lord and where, exactly, he had been kept in the prison. I was convinced the Dome had to have *some* kind of weakness I could exploit, because even in real life, the best prisons could still be broken out of.

And since Rock Lord managed to bust out of his cell, that must have meant there was a way to do that, too

Of course, real-life prisons also were not programmed by malicious game designers to be nigh-invulnerable, either. Or run by overweight middle-aged wardens who could fry you with an electric donut.

Thus, when I got up the next morning in the real world, I logged into Capes Online after a quick breakfast with Mom. I woke up in my uncomfortable cot in my cell in the Dome, right where I had logged off for the day previously, feeling every lump in my mattress underneath me. Yawning, I sat up and threw my feet over the side of my bed, accidentally stepping on something soft and squishy on the floor.

"Ow!" came Joe's sharp voice below. "Watch it, pal!"

Startled, I looked down to see Joe lying on the floor in front of my bed, my feet on his stomach. "Oops. Sorry, Joe. Didn't see you there."

Groaning, Joe pushed my feet off his chest and rolled away from me. Dusting off his jumpsuit as he rose to his feet, Joe said, "Well, next time, pay more attention to your surroundings, you son of a—"

"Good morning, master," said Dinoczar, his big head peeking over the side of the top bunk with a smile on his face. "Did you sleep well?"

I rubbed my head. "Yeah. How long was I asleep?"

"Four days," said Dinoczar.

I did the math in my head. One hour in the real world translated to eight in-game, roughly speaking. If I'd been out for a day, then that closely tracked to the time I'd spent in the real world. I'd been gone for about twelve hours in the real world, give or take, which translated to roughly ninety-six hours in-game, or four days.

"Was I really asleep for *that* long?" I said in surprise.

Joe nodded. "Yeah. We thought you were never going to wake up."

I rubbed my forehead. Even though I had been aware of the time dilation effect between Capes Online and the real world, I still found it weird that I apparently had been sleeping in-game for that long. I suppose Capes Online wasn't *that* realistic.

A notification popped up in my view:

Buff added: *Well-Rested! Health and Stamina regeneration x2.*
Duration: *1 second.*

Followed by this notification:

Buff lifted: *Well-Rest. Health and Stamina regeneration have returned to their normal rates.*

I scowled, rubbing my aching back. I guessed that sleeping on the cot in the Dome didn't actually provide long-lasting buffs like it normally would in Capes Online. That was probably another security measure added by whoever designed this hellhole of a prison, just to make sure the Prisoners didn't get any decent buffs from sleeping well.

Dinoczar looked at Joe in confusion. "What do you mean, Joe? Master wasn't asleep for four straight days. He woke up several times to interact with us during that time."

I cocked my head to the side. "I did?"

Dinoczar nodded. "Yes. You did not seem as aware as usual, but you had several conversations with both Dinoczar and Joe during that time."

"What did I say?" I said.

"Nothing much," said Joe. He scowled. "Mostly, you told Dinoczar to chase me around our cell."

Dinoczar chuckled. "What fun! Dinoczar always loves chasing prey."

"Yeah, well, this 'prey' doesn't appreciate being chased," Joe replied.

I wanted to say Dinoczar and Joe were lying to me, but Dinoczar seemed to lack the intelligence or will to lie to me, and Joe seemed genuinely perturbed by whatever I'd told Dinoczar to do to him over the past four days.

If so, that was deeply disturbing. Had someone hacked my account? That couldn't be possible. I had made sure to use the longest, most complicated password my password generator came up with, logged in using a throwaway email, and even activated the game's two-factor authentication just to be absolutely safe. Plus, I'd even written down my log-in information on paper and not on a computer or any sort of Internet-connected device.

But it made no sense. My understanding of Capes Online was that logging off made your character disappear from the game world until you next logged on. That was how all of the reviews and guides I'd read online described it. Either I'd been hacked or there was something else going on I didn't understand.

Clearly, that was not how it worked for me. Maybe it was because I was in the Dome's Maximum Security, so my body stayed in my cot whenever I logged off instead of vanishing like normal. That did not explain, however, how I was apparently interacting with Dinoczar and Joe outside of my logged-in hours, which should not have been possible.

I *really* didn't like those implications.

Nonetheless, it seemed like I hadn't actually done anything during that time, so I decided I would contact Capes Online support about it later. If I'd been hacked, surely support would be able to help me figure out how to secure my account against future hacking attempts.

Shaking my head, I said, "Right. Well, I'm back for real this time, and I've determined that we need to find out where Rock Lord was being kept. I feel like that is the key to figuring out how to escape from this place."

Joe folded his arms in front of his chest. "Good luck with that, boss. I sincerely doubt that any of the Prison Guards will even answer questions about Rock Lord, much less show us his cell."

"Do the Guards ever let Prisoners out of their cells anytime other than mealtimes?" I asked.

Joe laughed. "Of course not! Not unless you're scheduled to be executed, anyway. Otherwise, you get to spend all day every day inside your tiny cramped cell with two annoying cellmates."

Dinoczar tilted his head. "Two? But you are just one person, Joe."

Joe glared at Dinoczar while I contemplated this problem.

However much of an ass Joe might be, he was probably correct about our cells. Thus far during my time in the Dome, I hadn't seen any Prisoners walking freely in the prison. I hadn't even seen any Prisoners being walked out of their cells by the Prison Guards. Indeed, the only Prisoner I'd seen move about freely was Rock Lord, and only because he somehow managed to bust out of whatever cell they put him in.

The problem, of course, was that if I couldn't leave my cell, that made exploring the Dome much more difficult, if not impossible.

Thus, I needed to find a way to leave my prison cell, preferably without the Prison Guards knowing, so I could freely explore the prison on my own. That would make it easier not only to find Rock Lord's prison cell, but also analyze the Dome itself for any potential weaknesses I could exploit.

My first thought was to try to fiddle with the door of our cell, but that would be too obvious. Even if I somehow unlocked our door and got out, the Prison Guards would undoubtedly notice an open cell door. Not to mention they would probably notice if a cell that was supposed to have three Prisoners only had two.

But how else was I supposed to get out of here?

Putting that thought aside for now, I returned my attention to Dinoczar and Joe's conversation:

"… And you made me sleep on the floor!" Joe said, pointing accusingly at Dinoczar. "The cold, hard floor, like some kind of animal!"

"Dinoczar says top bunks are for kings," Dinoczar replied. "Like Dinoczar. Floors are for potential lunch like you."

"Lunch?" Joe repeated. He gestured at the foot of my bed. "I'm not your 'lunch.' Besides, how good could something lying on the floor actually taste? Especially with how cold it is. I mean, I even felt a freaking draft under the bed."

Dinoczar licked his lips. "But food picked off the floor is the superior kind of food! Right, master?"

Ignoring Dinoczar for now, I said to Joe, "Wait. You said you felt a draft from under my cot?"

Joe nodded. "Yeah. Probably just an AC vent, but still. It was really cold."

Curious, I knelt down and stuck my head under the cot. It was hard to see due to the darkness, but I did feel a very light breeze coming from there.

But I didn't see a vent. The breeze seemed to be coming from a portion of the wall that the bed was up against. Crawling under the cot further, I ran a hand along the bottom part of the wall until I felt a cold breeze leaking out from behind part of it. Was there actually a hidden vent there or something?

I tried to pry the panel off, but found it was too awkward to do under the bed. Scooting myself out from underneath the bed, I sat up and said, "Guys, help me move the bunk bed away from the wall."

Joe glanced out the cell doors nervously. "Right now?"

"Yes," I said with a quick nod. "Not all the way, in case a Guard walks by, but just enough so I can get behind it."

With that plan in place, Dinoczar and Joe worked with me to pull out the bed just enough to make it easier to access the panel I'd noticed earlier. I kept an eye on the hallway beyond our cell, but fortunately, no Guards walked by during our little home renovation.

A few seconds later, the panel was much easier to reach. Fiddling with it again, I managed to pry it off, revealing what looked like a small tunnel from which cool wind blew through.

"That don't look like an AC vent to me," said Joe, staring at the tunnel.

I shook my head. "That's because it isn't. Whoever had this cell before us must have made this tunnel, possibly to escape, without the Prison Guards knowing."

Or Grandpa did it, but I didn't say that aloud. Truthfully, I didn't know to what extent Grandpa was still influencing the game in my favor. During our last conversation, Grandpa made it sound like he was not going to influence the game for me anymore and that I'd be on my own from now on.

So I might have just found the first crack in the Dome's almost invulnerable defenses.

I knelt down and peered into the tunnel, but I couldn't see the end of it. It appeared to go on forever into the darkness.

Joe snorted. "That's probably just a dead end. No one has ever escaped from Maximum Security. Might even be a trap created by the Warden."

I stroked my chin. "Not necessarily. Perhaps the Prisoner who dug out this tunnel only managed to make it out of his cell before getting killed. If he hid it well enough, then it's believable that the Prison Guards wouldn't be aware of its existence."

Joe cringed. "That makes it even worse. I can't wait to end up dead like that guy, then."

A notification popped up in my view when Joe said that:

New Skill unlocked: *Perception [Level 1]. You can now notice tiny details that most people would dismiss as unimportant. Level up this Skill further to notice even more things!*

Perception seemed like it would be a useful Skill to have, especially when it came to breaking out of here, though it would not be immediately useful.

Dismissing the notification, I stood up and rolled my shoulders. "All right. I am going to crawl in there and see where it goes. You two stay here and let me know if any Guards are coming this way."

Dinoczar gave me a shocked look. "But master, we cannot allow you to needlessly put yourself in danger like that! What if you get caught or killed or beaten or, even worse, hungry?"

I rolled my eyes. "Thanks for the concern, Dinoczar, but I think I'll be fine on my own. I won't let the Guards find me."

Dinoczar stood in front of the tunnel entrance. "No. Dinoczar will not let you through."

I glared at Dinoczar. "I'm the boss here. You're the Sidekick. Move."

Dinoczar shook his head. "No. Big Bads do not dirty their own hands. You have us, your faithful and loyal servant and lunch, to do your bidding."

I scowled. "Dinoczar, you are way too big and loud to fit into that tunnel. The only other option is Joe, who I do not trust."

"Yeah," said Joe, agreeing with me perhaps a little too quickly. "I'd be a terrible spy. I'd sell you out to the Prison Guards first thing. I definitely do not want to go into a dark, cramped tunnel that might lead nowhere."

Dinoczar frowned. "But master, do you not know that you can manually control your Minions, including Joe, from the Command Interface?"

I frowned in response. "Command Interface?"

Dinoczar nodded. "Yes. Open the Minions tab on your menu."

Slightly annoyed by Dinoczar's unwillingness to move, I nonetheless navigated to the MINIONS tab in my menu. Clicking it, I said, "I don't see anything other than Joe's—"

Without warning, a pop-up screen appeared, reading: *Activate Command Interface? Y/N*

Hesitant yet curious, I clicked Y.

The pop-up disappeared and was immediately replaced by an entirely new display, helpfully titled COMMAND INTERFACE at the top of the screen.

There were quite a few options listed for me, although the majority of them were faded, indicating that I probably couldn't use them yet. This included options such as FORMATION, MINION MAP, and, more interestingly, MINION SACRIFICE, though I had no idea what any of them meant.

"Okay, Dinoczar, I've opened the Command Interface," I said. "What do I do with it, exactly?"

Dinoczar waved his tiny T-rex arms. "You can use it to control your Minions directly, as well as organize them into groups, use special Powers, and so much more! It is an interface exclusive to the Big Bad Class."

"I see," I said with a nod. I noticed that the MINIONS tab had been renamed COMMAND INTERFACE in my menus. "So this interface lets me control my Minions? Can't I control them already?"

"Ah, but sir, this lets you *directly* control them," said Dinoczar. "Or look at things from their point of view, give them orders from a distance, and so on. The more Minions you get, the more possibilities open to you. This interface also is what lets you use your Minions' Powers for yourself."

That explained the MINION POWERS option, although … "How come most of it is faded?"

"It levels up with you," Dinoczar explained. "Every five Levels or so, you will gain access to a new part of the interface, although you can level it up faster if you get more Minions. Dinoczar has also heard rumors that certain sections can be unlocked after completing certain missions, but Dinoczar has not been able to verify that for himself."

I tapped my chin and glanced at Joe. "You mentioned I could look at things from my Minions' point of view if I wanted. How do I do that?"

"Click the MINIONS tab in the Command Interface," Dinoczar said. "Then click Joe's name and there will be Control Options under his name that will let you determine how much control you have over him."

I quickly did as Dinoczar said and found the Control Options. There weren't too many. In fact, the Control Options reminded me of the Sidekick Growth options I had, where I could have my Minions automatically control themselves independently of me or take manual control of their every action.

As fun as it would be to override Joe's free will and make him my literal slave, I decided to select the third option, labeled VIEW, and see what happened.

A video feed suddenly appeared in my view, letting me see myself and Dinoczar, although it was kind of a weird angle. It looked less like I was filming myself and more like …

"I am seeing us from Joe's point of view," I said aloud. "Weird."

Dinoczar tried clapping his hands together but failed because they were too short. "Good job, master! Now you can see what Joe sees."

Joe rubbed his head. "That explains the splitting headache I am experiencing. There's not enough room in the old noggin for two people."

I rolled my eyes, seeing myself do it on the video feed at the same time. "I'm not literally in your head, Joe."

"But you could be," Dinoczar suggested. "Although attaining that level of control over your Minions won't be available to you for several more Levels at least."

"Fine by me," I said. "I don't really want to see what goes on in Joe's head, anyway."

Joe put his left hand on his hip, his right arm hanging by his side. "I am not sure if I should be offended or not."

"Doesn't matter," I said. "So in theory, I could send Joe through the tunnel and, by using this video feed, I could see what he sees?"

"And hear what he hears," Dinoczar said. "You can turn on the audio as well under the video's options."

I did notice three little dots in the lower right-hand corner of the video feed. Hovering my cursor over it, I saw that I could indeed turn on audio and even closed captioning. Gotta make being a Big Bad accessible to everyone, I supposed.

"But how do I tell Joe what to do if we're not in the same room?" I said, gesturing at Joe and myself. "If the tunnel goes far enough, then he might leave my sphere of influence."

"Do not worry, master," said Dinoczar with a wink. "There is a microphone option that will let Joe hear your every command as if you are right next to him shouting in his ear, no matter how far he goes. Try it."

Now that Dinoczar mentioned it, there was indeed a grayed-out microphone icon directly underneath the video feed. I clicked it and it turned red, a universal indicator that the microphone was on.

Unsure of exactly what to do next, I whispered, "Joe, you are a bad person."

Joe suddenly winced, groaning. "Not so loud, damn it!"

"You can also adjust the volume controls on the microphone," Dinoczar explained. He grinned evilly. "If you so desire, master."

As fun as it was to torture Joe, I realized I couldn't risk making him deaf just to prove a point. I adjusted the sound levels on the microphone to a more reasonable level and said, "How does it sound now, Joe?"

Joe slowly relaxed. "Better, although I am still not a fan of having your voice in my ears all the time."

"Get used to it, prey," Dinoczar replied. "You are master's Minion, which means you must do whatever master says."

Got to admit, I was liking how Dinoczar kept referring to me as "master." It felt a bit weird at first—after all, I'd never had servants in the real world—but there was something gratifying about having a man-eating T-Rex at my beck and call who also threatened people I didn't like.

I certainly had nothing like that in real life, anyway.

Regardless, the Command Interface was a useful tool. While I didn't know for sure how it would scale over time as I got more and more Minions, I could easily see it becoming more and more integral to my play style as time went on.

So I looked at Joe with a big grin on my face. "Get ready to squeeze into some dark, tight spots, my friend. Some *very* tight spots."

CHAPTER 14

ONE WOULD THINK THAT JOE, BEING CONSIDERABLY WEIGHTIER THAN ME, would not be able to fit into the relatively slimmer tunnel entrance.

One would be wrong.

As it turned out, Joe fit inside almost perfectly, despite complaining about how dark and cramped it was. I paid his complaints no heed, however, mostly because Joe had no choice in the matter. He could complain about how I treated him as much as he liked, but in the end, I was the Big Bad and he was my Minion, so he always had to do whatever I told him to.

Plus, he was just a video game character. However lifelike Joe might be, he wasn't—and never would be—a real person in my eyes.

Admittedly, bossing people around like this did tickle my conscience slightly, but I dismissed it as my emotions not being able to tell the difference between bossing around real-life people and video game characters. There were clearly ethical reasons not to be a dick to people in real life, but in video games?

There wasn't. Especially with what was at stake here, for me and my family.

Anyway, I took a seat on my cot to make myself comfortable, set up Dinoczar to be the lookout in case any Prison Guards came strolling by our cell, and settled in for the premiere of my new favorite TV show: Joe's View.

Right now, however, Joe's View was pretty boring. The feed was pitch-black and all I could hear were Joe's grunts and swears as he made his way deeper and deeper into the tunnel. It was a pretty sleep-worthy show, if I was going to be honest. I considered singing in Joe's ear to annoy him, but distracting Joe might not be the best idea because I didn't know what he might run into down there or where he would end up.

"Stupid Robert …" I heard Joe mutter under his breath. "Should have let the damned dino eat me … what was I thinking, becoming his Minion … Mom would never approve …"

"What was that, Joe?" I said casually.

"Nothin', except I should have listened to my ma and got an actual career instead of becoming a purse thief," Joe grumbled. "Then I wouldn't have ended up here."

I chuckled. "Your mom sounds like a smart woman. You definitely should have listened to her. Unfortunately, you didn't. Anyway, have you found anything in there yet?"

"What does it freaking look like, you—" Joe caught himself, perhaps afraid of how I might punish him if he kept insulting me. "I mean, no. What you see is what you get, and right now I don't see shit. Not sure this tunnel even has an end. Keeps going on forever."

"Keep going," I said. "Does the breeze feel like it's getting stronger, at least?"

That was one of the unfortunate limits of the Minion View. The only senses I had access to were Joe's vision and hearing. Thus, I couldn't feel what he felt, which was part of the reason I was a lot more comfortable than he was at the moment. Still, it was definitely a limitation, one I hoped I would get past as I leveled up more.

That was another issue: How was I going to level up when the only times I left my cell were to eat? Dinoczar, unfortunately, seemed to have no advice in that regard. Joe had said that the Dome was designed to prevent Prisoners from leveling up, which meant I was going to be Level 1 for a while, it seemed.

But that was a problem for another time. Right now, I needed to focus on what Joe was seeing, as I suspected whatever he found in the tunnel would be integral to figuring out how to get out of here.

Finally, a faint light appeared in the distance on the video feed.

"A light," I said.

"Maybe your Villain name should be Captain Obvious," Joe grunted, "since that seems to be your real superpower."

I ignored Joe's barb as he continued to crawl further and further toward the light.

Then, without warning, Joe gasped and suddenly screamed. I slammed my hands over my ears as Joe yelled at the top of his lungs, the light growing closer and closer, until, without warning, Joe passed through the light and landed roughly on a floor somewhere. He groaned painfully.

"Joe, what happened?" I said, leaning toward the video feed.

Joe groaned again. "The tunnel suddenly turned into the world's worst slide. That's what happened."

I checked Joe's stat sheet. "You're still at full Health. Stop being such a baby and get up."

"I'm not a baby," Joe muttered, though he nonetheless rose to his feet and looked around at his new surroundings.

Based on what Joe was showing me, it looked like Joe had ended up in a locker room of all places. Row upon row of metal lockers lined the middle of the room. Prison Guard uniforms hung on hooks along the walls, while empty showers stood off to the side.

"Looks like the locker rooms for the Prison Guards," said Joe. He sniffed and cringed. "Smells like it, too. Don't see anyone, though."

"Interesting," I said. "I didn't know the Prison Guards had locker rooms."

"What, did you think they actually wear those damn uniforms all the time?" said Joe. "What a stupid thing to think."

I scowled but said nothing to that. I suppose I'd thought that the Prison Guards were like Guards in other video games and had no real life or free will outside of their jobs as obstacles for the player to overcome or sneak past. The locker room's existence implied that the Prison Guards had lives beyond the walls of this prison.

Lucky them.

The sound of a door opening and slamming shut startled Joe, making him jump and look around. I then heard voices through Minion View, two gruff voices most likely belonging to a couple of Prison Guards.

"Crap," said Joe, looking around in alarm. "A couple of Guards just entered. What do I do?"

"Hide," I suggested. "No, wait. Grab a uniform and put it on."

I could tell that Joe thought that was a stupid suggestion, but since he had no choice but to obey me, he grabbed the nearest Prison Guard uniform and darted into a nearby stall. Quickly throwing the uniform on over his jumpsuit, Joe finished just in time for a couple of burly Prison Guards coming around the corner. According to their name tags, these guys were [PRISON GUARD TED] and [PRISON GUARD JORGE].

"… I'm telling ya, man, the Warden is still pissed about 10X's escape earlier," said Jorge as they walked. "Saw him zap a Minnie just 'cause he looked at him the wrong way."

"Minnie?" I whisper in Joe's ears. "Like Minnie Mouse?"

"Prison Guard slang for Minimum Security Prisoners," Joe whispered back furiously. "Now shut up. Don't want them seeing me talking to myself."

"Hey, you!" cried out Ted suddenly. "Why are you talkin' to yourself?"

Oops.

I saw Joe freeze in front of "his" locker before slowly turning around to face Ted and Jorge, arms folded behind his back, probably to hide his missing right hand. I couldn't see Joe's face, but I could just imagine him wearing the fakest friendly smile he could muster. "Talking to myself? Whatever do you mean, my good compatriot?"

"Compatriot?" Ted repeated incredulously. He elbowed Jorge. "Get a load of this noob, using fancy words like that."

Truthfully, I agreed with Ted. "Compatriot" hardly seemed like the word that a Prison Guard would use, plus I didn't know Joe knew that word, either. Perhaps he was better educated than he seemed.

Joe cleared his throat and said, in a much gruffer voice than before, "I mean, I was just joking with you knuckleheads. Makin' fun of them intellectual types, like all those Big Bads who think they're hot stuff because they can boss their Minions around without taking their feelings into consideration."

Passive-aggression, thy name was [PURSE THIEF JOE].

Fortunately, neither of the Prison Guards seemed familiar with that particular concept, because Jorge said, in a heavy Mexican accent, "Aye! I hate Big Bads the most. Wish I could twist their spines into fun shapes sometimes."

"Who doesn't?" Ted said, patting Jorge on the back sympathetically. He eyed Joe suspiciously. "Anyway, you don't look familiar. You new around here … Joe?"

I breathed a sigh of relief. It seemed like the Prison Guards could not see Joe's actual Prisoner name tag, which meant they were unlikely to stumble upon Joe's real identity. So long as Joe didn't give them reason to be suspicious, then this could turn out to be a useful thing for us.

Although I wondered *what* they saw if not his prison name tag. I'd have to ask Joe that later.

"Uh, yeah," said Joe quickly. He patted his uniform. "Just started today. That's why my uniform don't fit perfectly, you know. They haven't gotten my size in yet."

Ted growled. "Let me guess, did the Warden say it's 'cause we have no money? 'Cause we *never* have money, it seems."

"Unless the Warden wants more donuts and cake," Jorge said. "Or throw a pizza party … for himself."

I raised an eyebrow. It seemed like not all of the Prison Guards were loyal to the Warden. At the very least, there was some discontent among them, which I noted down for future reference.

Joe seemed to pick up on it, too, because he asked, "Is the Warden really that bad?"

Ted snorted. He walked over to what was presumably his locker and slammed it open harder than he probably should have. "He's even worse. Bastard just sits in his office all day eating donuts and watching TV while us Guards do the *real* work."

Jorge nodded. He sat down on a bench, hands on his knees. "Yeah. Far as I can tell, the Warden's never worked a day in his life."

Joe cocked his head to the side. "But what about the escapee from earlier? Not that I personally witnessed it or anything, but I heard that a particularly strong inmate staged a breakout during lunch and got killed by the Warden in one hit. It was very explosive, or so I heard."

Ted glanced over his shoulder at Joe. "That's why the Warden's never had to work. He's just naturally powerful, a real force of nature in his own right."

Jorge shook his head. "That's why he thinks he can boss the rest of us around and leave the real dirty work to us. Doesn't want to dirty his precious little hands."

Ted growled and slammed his locker door closed. "Sometimes, it feels like this damned prison is more like a prison for *us* than for the Prisoners. We never get to go anywhere, do anything. Just work, work, and more work, even if it is fun to bust some Villain skulls open whenever an uppity Prisoner tries to escape."

Hearing Ted's complaints reminded me of something Grandpa's Digital Double told me not long ago, about how the Prisoners were not the only ones imprisoned here.

At the time, I dismissed it as Grandpa being unhelpful and vague, but now I wondered if Grandpa had been trying to hint to me that I needed to approach the breakout from a different perspective.

Maybe the Prisoners were not the only ones who needed to be freed. And perhaps the Prison Guards didn't have lives outside of the prison after all, despite the presence of the locker room.

"Sounds like just about every bad boss I've ever had," said Joe in a surprisingly sympathetic voice. "I'm going to hate it here, aren't I?"

"It's not all bad," Jorge said with a shrug. "Sometimes you get free food. Much better than the slop they serve the Prisoners. But yeah, you are probably going to hate it."

"Not that you'll be able to leave," Ted said. He closed his locker shut and turned to face Joe, leaning against the locker. "Prison Guards live here all the time. Can't quit unless the Warden fires you. And you have to do something extra bad to get fired by the Warden."

"Like help Prisoners escape," Jorge offered.

Ted snorted. "And then end up in prison yourself, probably in the same cell as the guys you helped escape."

Joe laughed nervously. "Well, good thing I am not planning to help any of those Prisoner scum escape, then. That would be very unfortunate."

I understood Joe's nervousness. Though neither Ted nor Jorge seemed to be suspicious of Joe, he was definitely walking on thin ice with them here. One wrong word and he could blow his whole cover.

Fortunately, Joe seemed pretty good at thinking on his feet, so I figured we were safe for the time being.

Which was good. Joe seemed to be building some degree of camaraderie with Ted and Jorge, which meant they might be able to answer some of my questions, specifically about Rock Lord.

"Ask them about Rock Lord," I whispered. "Like, where he was being kept before the breakout."

"So ... about that escapee from earlier," Joe ventured. "Rumor has it that it was the infamous Rock Lord, even though he was supposedly killed outside the prison a month ago."

Ted and Jorge both went very still. They shared tense looks with each other before Ted said, "We can't tell you about that."

"Why not?" said Joe carefully. "I'm just asking if the rumors are true. Not asking you to spill all the Dome's secrets to me."

"Because you're still new around here," said Ted. "And newbies like you have to prove yourselves first before we can tell you anything."

Jorge, on the other hand, rested his chin in his hands. "I don't know, Ted. If the Warden assigned him to Maximum Security, then he must be more trustworthy than he looks. Kind of surprised he doesn't already know about it, though, given how every Maximum Security Guard knows about it."

"Guess they forgot to mention 'it' during the job interview," Joe said. "Er, whatever 'it' is."

Ted sighed. "Fine. But if the Warden asks, pretend like you've never seen us, got it? 'Cause Old Sparky doesn't like it when we Guards talk about him behind his back."

Joe crossed a hand over his heart. "Cross my heart, I won't tell Old Sparky anything. In fact, I don't even know who you are."

Ted chuckled. "Good. Then I guess we can tell you about—"

"Master!" Dinoczar said in my ear suddenly. "Guards!"

Snapped out of my focus, I quickly dismissed my Minion View screen, which meant I also could not hear Joe's audio anymore. That was frustrating, because it seemed like Ted was just about to reveal exactly where Rock Lord had been imprisoned and why.

Turning around in my cot, I heard footsteps outside our cell. It did sound like Prison Guards were coming to check on us, although I also caught a hint of ozone in the air. A scent that was perhaps a little too familiar, given what I'd seen in the cafeteria earlier.

Sure enough, a couple of Prison Guards appeared on the other side of the bars and came to a stop. They were not, however, alone.

Because standing between them, munching on a chocolate donut, was none other than Old Sparky himself.

CHAPTER 15

"So …" Old Sparky munched on his donut. "How do you like your accommodations so far, Robert?"

I sat across from Old Sparky in his office. Thick steel chains were clasped around my wrists and ankles, which in turn connected to a metal collar around my neck. It might have looked like a simple set-up to the uninitiated, but when the Prison Guards who escorted me here placed the chains on me, I received a ton of debuffs to my Agility and Stamina, leaving me even weaker than I already was.

And I could believe it. I felt as slow as molasses with these heavy chains, leaving me feeling exhausted.

But not too exhausted to have a conversation with Old Sparky.

Nor did it help that I was sitting on what had to be the least comfortable wooden chair I'd ever had the displeasure of sitting on in my life. The wooden chair creaked dangerously, threatening to fall apart underneath me if I moved too much or in the wrong way.

"They're not great," I said.

Old Sparky lowered his donut, smiling at me, showing me his chocolate-stained teeth. He gestured at the plate of donuts on the table between us. "Want a donut? Go ahead. Take one … if you want."

I glanced at the donuts. I'd Scanned them when I entered the room earlier only to find out nothing much except what flavors and toppings they had. "I'm not hungry, thanks."

Old Sparky nodded. "Smart man. You never know what's in a donut. Could be delicious raspberry jam … or poison."

I raised an eyebrow. "Are you saying you poisoned those donuts?"

"Only one way to find out, isn't there?" said Old Sparky. "But don't worry. If you won't eat 'em, I'll make sure they go to a good cause. Namely, my stomach."

Old Sparky rubbed his stomach when he said that. I would have said it was disgusting, but one, Old Sparky could fry me in an instant if I pissed him off, and two, I didn't know if the donuts actually were poisoned or not. Given how Old Sparky still hadn't picked any of them up himself, it was wise to assume that the donuts were unsafe to eat. Although I gotta admit, it was tempting, if only because the only food I'd had so far in-game had been the Dome's trademark mystery [Slop].

Shifting slightly in my chair, I said, "Is this the reason you had your Guards march me up here? To have donuts and chat about our lives? You could have just asked, you know."

I glanced over my shoulder when I said that. Two Prison Guards, named Butch and George, stood on either side of the only exit in and out of the office. There were no windows or any other ways out that I could see, meaning that if I wanted to get out of here, I would have to go through them. And a preliminary Scan had already shown me that those two alone were over Level 100 each.

And that was assuming Old Sparky wouldn't just zap me if I tried anything funny.

All in all, things were not looking great, to put it mildly.

Oh, and did I forget that Old Sparky's office smelled a lot like donuts? And not fresh donuts, either, but stale donuts. It made me wonder how many donuts Old Sparky had eaten in here over the years and if he ever cleaned his office at all.

Old Sparky leaned back in his office chair, which squeaked under his weight but certainly did not look like it was in danger of falling apart. "I'm not one to socialize with Prisoners like you, Robert. My philosophy on Prisoners in general is that you deserve to be here for all the crimes you've committed and spend the rest of your sorry life rotting away like you deserve."

I raised an eyebrow. "My crimes, eh? Such as—?"

Old Sparky tapped the air and a holographic headshot of me, with a wall of text to the right of the image, appeared between us suddenly. "Theft and murder, along with resisting arrest."

I grimaced. "Okay, so I'm not exactly innocent. But I'm not as bad as some of the other Prisoners. I've heard there are some pretty awful people being held here. People who deserve worse."

Old Sparky cocked his head to the side. "True. I've seen the worst of the worst during my twenty-odd years running this place. You're nothing special."

Then Old Sparky slammed his feet on the floor and leaned toward me, his dark eyes fixed firmly on his face. Sparks of electricity danced around his eyes as he glared at me.

"But I saw you looking at me earlier," said Old Sparky. "Back in the cafeteria."

I gulped, but said, "Only because you were looking at me. But like you said, I'm nothing special."

Old Sparky chuckled. He sat back in his chair, a grin splitting his face cleanly in two. "Ha! I like you, Robert, and I can't say that about most of the scum here. I mean, sure, if you tried to escape, I'd zap you without a second thought, but you're clever. A fast thinker. And, despite what I said, not quite like the other Prisoners."

I pursed my lips. I thought about bringing up Rock Lord, but since Old Sparky had made it clear to everyone that Rock Lord did not exist, I decided not to try my luck. "Thanks. If this is all you wanted to talk with me about, then maybe you could send me back to my—"

Old Sparky snapped his fingers and an electric jolt went through my body. A quick glance at my Health bar showed me that I'd lost just one HP from that, but I was still startled by how real it felt. Capes Online was too real sometimes.

"No," said Old Sparky with a shake of his head. "See, I wanted to speak with you in private because I can tell you're smart. And the fact that you, as a Prisoner, can do things here even I, the Warden, can't do."

I raised an eyebrow. "Such as—?"

Old Sparky took another bite of his chocolate donut, chewed it thoughtfully for a second, and then swallowed. "Such as uncovering a conspiracy among the other Maxies to break out of here, among other things."

I tensed, but tried not to show it. Did Old Sparky somehow know about my plan to stage a mass breakout of the Dome? If so, then he might already know about Joe, which meant he was in even worse danger than I thought.

Despite my best attempts to hide it, however, Old Sparky apparently picked up on my nervousness, because he said, "What's the matter, Robert? You look like you need a delicious donut."

Taking a deep breath, I said, "I just didn't know anyone was planning to break out of here. This place seems pretty ... impenetrable."

Old Sparky sighed. "It is. In over twenty years, not a single Prisoner from Maximum Security has ever escaped. But that doesn't mean they haven't tried. The Blackouts were the worst. Lots of dumb Prisoners thought Dark Kosmos or Paradox would come to their aid, free them from their cells, and usher in a new era of Villains or some such nonsense. Unfortunately for them, that turned out to not be the case."

I recalled Joe telling me about how Old Sparky killed more than 300 Maximum Security Prisoners in one go during the Blackouts. Guess that hadn't just been a rumor after all, then.

"But recently, my Guards have caught wind of another conspiracy brewing among the Prisoners," Old Sparky continued. "Seems like a certain group of Prisoners have gotten together to plan a breakout. Unfortunately, my Guards and I, despite interrogating the suspects, haven't been able to get to the bottom of these rumors, nor figure out how they could be conspiring with each other despite being in separate cells."

"I take it that the other Prisoners are not really interested in talking to you or the Guards," I said.

Old Sparky nodded. "Exactly. In the Dome, there is a strict division between the Prisoners and the Prison Guards. That division is normally useful, as it keeps the Prisoners in line, but it also means that getting the Prisoners to talk can be a challenge even for me."

I shifted my weight again, hearing the chair creak under my weight. "Sorry to hear that. Wish there was something I could do to help."

Old Sparky flashed me a chocolate-stained smile. "But there *is* something you can do to help. You can infiltrate this group, figure out exactly what they are planning, and then report back to me. Then my Guards and I will come up with a counter plan and we can end this breakout before it even begins."

A notification suddenly popped up in my view when Old Sparky finished talking:

MISSION: *None dare call it … conspiracy*

The Warden of the Dome, Old Sparky, suspects a breakout is being planned among the Maxies, or Prisoners of Maximum Security. Unfortunately, Old Sparky and his Prison Guards have been unable to identify exactly who is a part of the conspiracy, when the breakout will happen, and other crucial details to the success of the plan.

But you are a Maxie yourself. Old Sparky wants you to infiltrate this conspiracy, learn its aims and mission, and report back to him with this information for the good of the Dome and Adventure City as a whole.

Whether you choose to accept this mission is, of course, up to you. But remember the old prison parable: Snitches get stitches.

ALIGNMENT: *Villain*
DIFFICULTY: *Hard*
RARITY: *Unique*
SUCCESS: *Infiltrate the group and report your findings back to Old Sparky*
FAILURE: *Fail to infiltrate the group or refuse to share your findings with Old Sparky*
REWARDS: *1,000 EXP, and an upgrade to Sub-Floor 1 of Maximum Security*
ACCEPT? Y/N

I frowned. "The Rewards are a bit … lackluster."

Old Sparky frowned back. "Are you sure? For a Level 1 Villain such as yourself, an extra thousand experience points ought to level you up quite a bit. And Sub-Floor 1 is much closer to the surface than any other Sub-Floor. You're practically free at that point."

I shifted again in my chair. "I guess, but still seems pretty paltry compared to—"

Another zap up my spine made me sit up straight and caused the chair to creak dangerously underneath me. I lost another HP.

Old Sparky, his eyes glowing slightly blue with electricity, said, "I would consider your next words *very* carefully, young man. And the consequences of said words, of course."

I said nothing to that, mostly because Old Sparky's advice seemed reasonable.

It was clear as day that Old Sparky did not intend to let me turn down this mission for any reason. That seemed distinctly unfair to me, but then again, this entire situation was unfair from a greater point of view. Grandpa would probably tell me to stop whining and apply my "brilliant" mind to this problem.

On one hand, this was a good opportunity to potentially explore the Dome more, as well as meet other Prisoners who might be helpful in plotting my own breakout. And if the other Prisoners already had a good plan, then I could probably just join them in that. Plus, at least Old Sparky seemed unaware of my own plans to escape, so that was a huge relief.

On the other hand, as the mission notification itself stated in simple folk terms, snitches did indeed get stitches. If it became common knowledge among the other inmates that I was a snitch, that would make it even harder for me to organize any sort of breakout myself. As well, I didn't like Old Sparky or the Prison Guards one bit and wasn't inclined to naturally help them for any reason.

Still, this was such a good opportunity that I really couldn't pass it up.

And like Old Sparky said, I was clever. I didn't mind acknowledging that fact. Probably cleverer than him. I could tell Old Sparky thought he was pretty smart for offering me such paltry rewards for such an important mission. If I had to guess, Old Sparky probably thought I was as desperate as anyone else here, that I had no loyalty to anyone but myself, and that I'd gladly sell out my fellow Prisoners to benefit myself.

Old Sparky was right about a couple of those things.

I *was* desperate to escape.

And I certainly wasn't loyal to anyone but myself.

But if he really thought I'd help him put down a breakout, rather than join or even hijack it for my own use … well, then he was even dumber than I thought.

I hit "Y" on the mission notification screen and the notification vanished. "Fair enough. I accept."

Old Sparky smiled even more. "Smart choice, kid. I knew I could count on you to do the right thing."

I nodded. "Well, it's every man for himself down here, isn't it? I doubt any of the other Prisoners would have done anything differently in my shoes."

Old Sparky laughed. "Spoken like a true heartless, pragmatic Villain! Man, am I glad we got *you* off the streets early. You'd make a very scary Big Bad for sure."

I didn't know if I should have been insulted by that or not, but I didn't get a chance to choose before Butch and George hauled me off the chair and out of the room. I caught a glimpse of Old Sparky over my shoulder before we left the room, seeing him already talking on the phone to someone.

And he was smiling like he had already ended the breakout himself.

CHAPTER 16

"Master!" said Dinoczar the second I was thrown back into our cell, the door slamming shut behind me with a *clang*. "Dinoczar was so worried when they took you away. Dinoczar even thought they were going to execute you."

Panting, I sat up, dusting off my jumpsuit as I looked up at Dinoczar. My Sidekick was perched on the top bunk of the bed again, gazing down at me with his beady T-Rex eyes. "I'm fine, Dinoczar. The Warden just wanted to talk."

Dinoczar sighed in relief. He then balled up a piece of paper in his hands before tossing it into his mouth. "That is good. Dinoczar was just writing your obituary, but Dinoczar got stuck because Dinoczar does not know how to spell 'Robert.'"

I sighed as I stood up. I was starting to question Dinoczar's loyalty if he thought I was never going to come back. "Well, the good news is that I wasn't executed. The bad news is—wait, where is Joe? Is he back yet?"

Dinoczar shook his head. "Nyet. Joe is still gone, sir."

I rushed over to the bunk bed and crawled across my bed to see that the tunnel, thankfully, was still blocked. "None of the Prison Guards checked our cell while I was gone?"

"None whatsoever," said Dinoczar proudly. "They did, however, ask where Joe was."

Coldness settled in my chest. "What did you tell them?"

Dinoczar's head peeked over the top of his bunk. "Dinoczar said he ate Joe for being disrespectful to master. Dinoczar told them that Joe will respawn soon, at which point Dinoczar will eat him again. They seemed to accept that explanation and left."

I sighed again, this time in relief. Dinoczar's explanation was actually pretty clever, I had to admit. "Good. Anyway, I'm going to reconnect to Joe. If you see anyone coming, let me know, okay?"

Dinoczar nodded while I sat back down on my bed. Clicking over to the MINIONS tab, I found Joe's View and hit CONNECT.

Unfortunately, I got this error message as soon as I hit that button: *ERROR. MINION VIEW is currently down.*

"What?" I said. "Minion View is currently down—? The hell does that mean? Does that mean Joe is dead?"

"It probably just means it hasn't reconnected with Joe yet," said Dinoczar. "Or maybe Joe is outside of your range."

I raised an eyebrow. "Outside of my range? You mean it's possible for Minions to go outside a Big Bad's range of control?"

"Certainly," said Dinoczar. "If they do, they usually try to get back in range, but not always."

I scowled. Joe made no secret that he resented being my Minion. If he had somehow gotten far enough outside of my range that I could no longer directly control him, then he would be more or less free. I could see the little bastard snitching on me to the Prison Guards now that I couldn't see or hear anything he was seeing or hearing.

And yes, I knew it was quite hypocritical of me to call Joe a snitch when I'd just agreed to be a snitch for the Warden, but this was different. I had actual good reasons for doing what I did, while Joe was just selfish and shortsighted. Such traits made him a good Minion but not a good ally.

Either way, this was bad. Whether Joe had gone rogue or not, I'd lost an important resource in him. At least Joe was capable of passing as a Prison Guard in the right clothes. Dinoczar, however loyal he might have been, never could, if only because all of the Prison Guards appeared to be normal humans (not counting Old Sparky, of course).

Just as I tried to figure out what my next move should be, I heard a soft knocking sound at the tunnel entrance and a muffled voice saying, "Open up! It's me, Joe. I'm dyin' in here."

Jumping off the bed, I immediately removed the tunnel entrance covering. Joe crawled out, back in his prison jumpsuit, wheezing and coughing as I closed the tunnel entrance back up.

"Lunch is back!" said Dinoczar, peering over the side of the top bunk again. "Yay! Hopefully he did not betray us."

Joe coughed harshly. "I did *not* betray us. Not that I could have even if I wanted to. Being a Minion means I feel undying loyalty to Robert for some stupid reason."

Sitting back down on my bunk, I said, "For once in my life, I'm glad to see you, Joe. I was worried your cover might have gotten blown and you would have ended up in trouble."

Joe sat up, rubbing his back. "No, but it took me ages to climb back up that slide. Seriously, I felt like an elephant trying to fit inside a three-inch PVC pipe. Whoever designed that tunnel must have been a scrawny little thing, like you."

I rolled my eyes. "Sure thing, Joe. Anyway, I cut off Minion View because the Warden came by to talk to me. What did you find out from the other—"

"The Warden came by?" Joe repeated in alarm. He looked toward the cell bars. "Did he notice I was missing?"

"Dinoczar already told the Guards that Dinoczar ate you," Dinoczar explained. He winked. "Foolish Prison Guards never suspected a thing."

"I'm depressed that they consider that a rational and believable explanation for my disappearance," said Joe.

Dinoczar smiled. "You do have a lot of fat on you. They probably think you look delicious, too."

I waved a hand dismissively. "I'll fill you in on my talk with the Warden later. Last I saw before I left, one of the Prison Guards was going to tell you about where Rock Lord was imprisoned."

Joe gulped. "Oh, yeah. He did tell me. Although frankly, I'm not sure you want to know."

I leaned forward, brows furrowed. "Of course I want to know. That's why I sent you down there in the first place."

Joe pursed his lips. "Fine. But don't say I didn't warn you. First, though, I have something important to show you ..."

Joe pulled a rolled-up piece of paper out of his back pocket and handed it to me. "I got this for you. Merry Christmas."

I raised an eyebrow in confusion. "But it's January."

"Eastern Orthodox Christmas is in January," Dinoczar reminded me.

"So you're religiously Russian, too?" I said, glancing at Dinoczar.

Dinoczar shook his head. "No, but Dinoczar loves Russian history and culture. Plus, Dinoczar loves Christmas because of the bright and shiny lights. So pretty."

Deciding not to get into a religious debate with a talking dinosaur, I took the rolled-up paper from Joe. As I did so, this notification appeared in my vision:

[MINION JOE] gave you a [Map of the Dome]!

My jaw fell when I read that notification and I looked at the paper again. "This is a map of the Dome? As in, of the entire prison?"

Joe nodded, a smirk on his face. "That's right. Jorge gave it to me when I said I was new and didn't know my way around the place. Open it up."

Eagerly, I unfurled the Map, only for it to disappear in my hands. "Huh—?"

A second later, however, a 3D, holographic map of the Dome appeared in my vision. Slightly taken aback by the model, I said, "How did that paper map turn into a hologram?"

"That's how all maps work in Capes Online," said Dinoczar. "Seems like the most natural thing in the world to Dinoczar."

Ah. Translating Dinoczar's comment into terms people from the real world could understand, I took it to mean that the physical map was merely an in-game representation of the actual map the player could access at any time from their menu. Still felt a bit weird to me, but I'd seen way worse examples of this sort of thing in other games before, so it wasn't that bad.

Anyway, I eagerly studied the Map of the Dome before me.

Just as Joe and Dinoczar had explained previously, the Dome was comprised of three Floors, each divided into ten Sub-Floors. I even got to see the naming scheme for the different Sub-Floors. For example, MI-SF#1 stood for Minimum Security Sub-Floor #1, the Sub-Floor of Minimum Security closest to the surface. The prefixes for Medium and Maximum Security seemed to be MD and MX respectively. The Map also outlined the Teleportation Pads that allowed travel between Floors and Sub-Floors; there were no stairs, elevators, or any other way of traveling between the different Floors as far as I could tell.

Each Sub-Floor had at least two Teleportation Pads, one at the beginning, another at the end, the Pads preprogrammed to take the user directly to or from the next Sub-Floor. Only the very highest and lowest Sub-Floors had Pads programmed to transport the user to the next full Floors. Interestingly, the actual Sub-Floors were connected to each other by stairs.

Minimum Security was at the top, practically on the surface. In fact, some of the higher MS Sub-Floors actually *were* on the surface. I also noticed that the Dome had an actual domed roof, which explained the name of the place. I'd figured it had just been chosen because it sounded ominous.

Below Minimum Security, of course, was Medium Security. Sandwiched directly between Minimum and Maximum Security, Medium Security was deeper beneath the surface than Minimum but still much closer to the surface than Maximum. I didn't see much there, other than that was apparently where the prison kitchen was located and where all of the meals for each Floor were prepared.

And finally, right at the bottom, was Maximum Security, where we were.

What I found most helpful about this Map was that it even seemed to show where the other Prison Guards and Warden were at any one time. The Prison Guards were represented by dozens, if not hundreds, of orange dots, while Old Sparky himself was represented by a bright red dot that stood out sharply on the bluish hologram.

It looked like Old Sparky's office was on MX-SF#1, meaning it was close enough to the surface that Old Sparky could keep an eye on the upper Floors while also maintaining his presence in Maximum Security, where he was probably more needed due to how strong the Prisoners down here were.

That was when I noticed a *fourth* Floor directly underneath Maximum Security.

This Floor was largely blank and appeared to have only one Sub-Floor entirely. The Map didn't show much about it, other than its name: Top Secret.

"Joe …" I said slowly. "Why does the Map show that there is a Floor underneath us called Top Secret? Isn't Maximum Security supposed to be the lowest Floor?"

Joe bit his lower lip. "That was the news I was going to tell you about. Turns out the Dome is bigger than it appears."

"How far down does Top Secret go?" I said, glancing at it. "It looks like it only has one Sub-Floor."

Joe shrugged. "Ike and Jorge didn't know. In fact, neither of them had even been down there before. Apparently, only a handful of prison personnel even have the credentials necessary to access Top Secret. For example, the Warden definitely does, but they didn't know who else has access to that Floor."

I stroked my chin. "A secret Floor that only a few have access to … interesting. Who do they keep down there, exactly?"

Joe grimaced. "The worst of the absolute worst, according to Ike. He didn't name any names, but he made it pretty clear that Rock Lord was probably the weakest Prisoner down there. It also has the fewest Prisoners of any Floor at about ten, although each and every one is a powerful Villain in their own right. Far too powerful to keep even in Maximum Security."

I scratched the back of my head. "I wonder what you have to do to get sent down there."

Joe glanced at the floor. "Given how Rock Lord was the head of an assassin's guild that regularly robbed and killed people for the fun of it, I don't even want to think about how bad *those* guys are."

I nodded, although the existence of Top Secret got me thinking.

According to the Map, we were on Sub-Floor 10, meaning we were on the absolute lowest Sub-Floor of Maximum Security. That put us closer to Top Secret than just about anyone else in the prison, including the Prison Guards and the Warden.

At first glance, this sure looked like a coincidence. But then I realized that nothing in this game was truly coincidental, other than Joe's presence in our cell. Had Grandpa known about Top Secret and put me here so I could gain access to it?

As for why I would need access to it … well, if Joe's report was true, the Prisoners in Top Secret might have been the strongest guys here. Strong enough, perhaps, to even challenge Old Sparky, who was easily the biggest threat in the entire Dome.

And then I remembered how easily Old Sparky fried Rock Lord, despite the latter's Type advantage, and realized even freeing the Top Secret Prisoners would not guarantee our escape.

Of course it wouldn't. Nothing was ever that easy. Grandpa made that clear to me whenever I did his riddles in the real world back when I was a kid.

But I also didn't think Grandpa, as out of character as his Digital Double might have been acting recently, would give me an impossible Riddle to solve.

Not to mention I was also still supposed to be working for Old Sparky to uncover a conspiracy among the other Maximum Security Prisoners to break out of the prison. Another thread. Or puzzle piece, really.

I had a lot of pieces floating around in my head, pieces I still couldn't fit together quite snugly yet because I didn't know what the final picture looked like.

But I could see them slowly coming together in my mind's eye. And a plan to fit them together was forming even as I sat on my old, lumpy cot.

"What about you?" said Joe, his voice snapping me out of my thoughts. "You mentioned the Warden came by to talk."

"He did," Dinoczar agreed. "Dinoczar thought the Warden was going to execute Robert, but fortunately, he did not."

I nodded. "Old Sparky thinks there is a conspiracy among the Prisoners to break out of here. He wants me to infiltrate and uncover it and rat them out to him."

Joe gulped. "Does he know about, er, our little plan?"

I shook my head. "No. Even though Old Sparky is probably the most powerful person in the Dome, he's not nearly as smart or clever as he likes to think he is. He just thinks that I'm like the other Prisoners: willing to rat out my fellow Villains for a few nice perks."

Joe sighed. "Whew. That's good. And frankly, that sounds like an easy mission to me. All you need to do is name a few random names and leave the rest to the Warden and the Prison Guards. I doubt they'll even try to verify your information. Bunch of sadists."

I shook my head again. "No. I am going to uncover this conspiracy, but I'm not telling the Warden. I'm going to hijack it instead."

Joe stared at me in disbelief. "Hijack it? Do you want to end up like Rock Lord?"

"That's why I'm going to be careful," I said. "Old Sparky won't suspect a thing. And we need allies. Badly. Because if there's one thing I do know about this place, it's that we won't be able to stage a breakout on our own."

"Dinoczar agrees," said Dinoczar, his head hanging over the side of the bed. "Dinoczar thinks that everyone should serve master. Dinoczar even thinks you should form your own Legion."

I frowned. According to my research prior to playing Capes Online, a "Legion" was a Team of at least 100 Villain players, which apparently came with their own bonuses and everything. "I'm not sure about that. Personally, I just want to free everyone, not lead them."

Joe snorted. "Yeah, what would you even call it, anyway? The Robert Legion? Sounds almost as scary as the Villain Robert."

"We could call it the Dinoczar Legion instead," Dinoczar suggested. "Dinoczar thinks that sounds appropriately villainous and intimidating."

I rubbed my forehead. "One step at a time, guys. First things first: The breakout conspiracy. I need to find out who is behind it and how I can make myself a part of it."

"Exactly how do you intend to do that, fearless leader?" Joe asked. "Remember, no one's allowed to interact with anyone else in the Dome, at least if we are Prisoners. Old Sparky obviously didn't consider that when he hired you to do his dirty work."

I thought about that. It was true that, as Joe said, the Dome had clearly been designed to prevent Prisoners from interacting with other Prisoners other than their cellmates.

Yet I didn't think Old Sparky was sending me on a snipe hunt, either. I felt that he really did believe that a group of Maxies, as he called them, were plotting a breakout. He just needed me to ferret them out.

That was when I heard a *ping* in my ear and got a notification that I had a new message in my inbox. Clicking over to the Capes Online messaging system, I found a message from ...

"Old Sparky?" I said under my breath.

Guess I wasn't quiet enough, because Joe said, "What about him?"

Cocking my head to the side, I said, "He sent me a message. Actually, now that I think about it, he seemed to have sent *all* of the Prisoners a message, because it's addressed to everyone."

"What does it say, sir?" said Dinoczar.

I shrugged. "Dunno. Haven't opened it yet."

"Then open it, genius," said Joe.

Since I was going to do that anyway, with or without Joe's helpful encouragement, I clicked on the message's subject line, which read "RE: Changes ..." and started reading.

And the more I read, the more shocked I became.

"Oh," I said. "So that's how Old Sparky expects me to do it."

"What?" said Joe. "What does the message say?"

I looked at Joe and Dinoczar. "I think Old Sparky might be cleverer than I thought."

CHAPTER 17

To the Maximum Security Prisoners of the Dome:

Warden Old Sparky and the prison administration have decided to make changes to the daily mealtimes in the cafeteria.

Rather than keeping all Prisoners confined to their tables during mealtimes where they can interact only with their own cellmates, the prison administration has decided to lower the electric barriers, allowing Prisoners to freely interact with Prisoners from other cells and tables as they see fit.

This change is part of an ongoing program to improve rehabilitation rates for Prisoners of the Dome. A multitude of recent scientific studies suggest that people who have regular social interaction with other human beings are far less likely to be overly aggressive, suffer from anxiety or depression, kill themselves, or act out in other criminal and antisocial ways.

This change will be tested for one week only. If the results are unsatisfactory, then the change will be reverted. Therefore, the prison administration recommends that the Prisoners of Maximum Security enjoy this freedom while they can and to not abuse it to do criminal or evil things.

Thank you,
Old Sparky
Warden of the Dome
Prison Administrator

"The prison has an administration?" I said, sitting at our table at lunchtime with Joe and Dinoczar, a hot steaming bowl of [Slop] sitting before me. "Seemed like a one-person show to me when I spoke with Old Sparky."

Joe shrugged. "Technically, I guess Old Sparky *is* the prison administration. He probably just calls it 'prison administration' to make himself sound more official than he actually is."

"Dinoczar does not understand why you both are not taking the prison administration more seriously," said Dinoczar. "In Dinoczar's opinion, the prison administration is a genuine threat and must be treated as such."

I rolled my eyes. "Yes, I'm sure their paperwork is as terrifying as it is boring to fill out. Regardless, this change can only benefit us."

Joe sipped his cup of lukewarm water, raising a quizzical eyebrow at me. "How?"

I looked around at the cafeteria. "Now I can actually interact with the other Prisoners."

Aside from the lack of electrical barriers around each table, everything else about the cafeteria looked about normal. No one had yet moved from their table to even attempt talking to other Prisoners outside of their cell, not even to the ones directly next to theirs. I assumed it was because no one really believed they could actually interact with other Prisoners freely just yet, which made sense. The Dome seemed to have been designed to mess with your mind and Old Sparky, in particular, seemed to take great pleasure in gaslighting Prisoners.

It didn't help that the Prison Guards seemed to be watching us even more closely than before. More Guards walked up and down the aisles between the tables than during the last lunch period I participated in, while several more snipers stood with guns at the ready on the upper levels, and both exits had five or six Guards standing in front of them now. Even the floating drones overhead appeared to be watching us carefully, as if trying to make sure no one tried to take advantage of the temporary freedom so graciously bestowed upon us by our prison administrator.

Joe cocked his head to the side. "I didn't peg you as a social butterfly."

"I'm not," I said with a shake of my head. "But Old Sparky obviously changed the cafeteria rules to make it easier for me to complete the mission he gave me."

"And you know that how?" said Joe.

I gestured at the other tables. "Don't you think it's too much of a coincidence that Old Sparky would give me the job of ferreting out the conspirators in the breakout and then change mealtimes regulations at the exact same time? Old Sparky obviously wants me to take advantage of this change to fulfill my obligations to him."

"Suppose that makes sense," said Joe. He took a bite of his [Slop] and winced. "Guess he decided that would be easier than improving the crap they call food here."

"Does that mean you will abandon us, master?" asked Dinoczar, staring at me with worried eyes.

I shook my head again. "No. But I think I will go and introduce myself to some of our neighbors."

Joe glanced around the cafeteria. "Everyone around here sure looks real neighborly, don't they?"

Joe's sarcasm was obvious, but he had a point. None of the other Prisoners appeared even remotely approachable. In fact, more than a few were already glaring at me even though I hadn't even done anything yet. While I doubted the Prison Guards would allow a fight to break out, I would definitely have to rely on my Charisma Stat a lot in order to convince them to talk to me.

"It doesn't matter," I said. "This is my best chance to find out who is behind the conspiracy. I'll have to try my best."

Dinoczar gulped down his [Slop]. "As smart as Dinoczar thinks master's idea is, Dinoczar does not understand how master will figure out who is part of the conspiracy. Master cannot read minds, after all. Seems to Dinoczar like anyone could be part of the plot."

I pursed my lips. "Good point, but I'm sure I'll be able to find someone here who is part of the conspiracy. If I have to go from table to table until I find someone willing to talk, then I will."

Joe snorted. "Good luck with that. Me, I'm going to do the safe and sane thing and eat my [Slop] at my table like a good Prisoner."

I cocked my head to the side. "What are you so afraid of? I know you stole from Rock Lord, but he's not here, so—"

Suddenly, several shadows fell over us, making me look up.

Six other Prisoners stood around our table. While they varied considerably in size and appearance, ranging from a Villain who looked like an evil Hobbit to a woman with snakelike hair, one thing was pretty obvious about all of them:

They were all stronger than us, and looked very pissed off.

"Hi there, Joe," said the woman, standing closer to Joe than to me. She leaned against the table, her name tag identifying her as [Prisoner #419993], the snakes on her head hissing slightly. "What a coincidence seeing *you* here. I thought I recognized you, but wasn't sure, hence why I wanted to get ... up close and personal with you, if you catch my drift."

Joe gulped, leaning away from Prisoner #419993 as if she reeked of dirty gym socks. "Why, hello there, Miss Hiss. I didn't realize you were down here, too. How are your Jeff and Marty?"

Miss Hiss, which was apparently the woman's actual name, flashed her snakelike fangs at Joe. "Terrible. My babies aren't allowed the care they need to thrive. Like the rest of us, they are given only this yucky [Slop] to eat, when what they really need is flesh. Preferably fatty human flesh."

The snakes on her head, apparently named Jeff and Marty, hissed at Joe, showing fangs similar to Miss Hiss's. Joe's face became as pale as snow and he seemed to be at a loss for words.

"Yeah, Joe," said the evil Hobbit, [Prisoner #765801], who wore an eye patch over his right eye. He sat on Joe's other side, resting his chin on his hand. He smelled vaguely of cigarettes. "You look as fat, stupid, and ugly as ever. What did you do to end up down here? Or did you just miss us so much you got yourself arrested?"

The other Prisoners laughed, causing Joe to shrink even more.

Then an absolute giant of a man, who had two heads with one eye each, rested his hands on Joe's shoulders, making Joe look up at him.

Both of [Prisoner #120983]'s heads smiled down evilly at Joe. "What's the matter, Joe? Cat got your tongue? Or just surprised to see your old marks?"

"Marks?" I repeated. I looked at Joe in confusion. "Joe, who are these people and why are they all acting like they know you?"

Miss Hiss gave me an unimpressed look. "The real question, kid, is who are *you* and why do you care about Joe's history with us?"

The evil Hobbit leaned toward me with a smirk. "What she said. I'd recommend staying out of this, kid. It's none of your business."

My temper flared. "Actually, anyone messing with one of my Minions *is* my business."

"Minion?" the two-headed Prisoner repeated. He gazed down at Joe with both sets of eyes. "Don't tell me you've been demoted to this loser's *Minion*, Joe."

The evil Hobbit chuckled. "And here I thought you had more pride than that."

The other Prisoners laughed derisively at Joe, while Joe just sank deeper into his seat. Out of the corner of my eye, I noticed a Prison Guard watching us carefully, though he did not seem likely to intervene unless a fight broke out.

And however much I may have disliked Joe, I liked seeing the other Prisoners bully him even less.

"Loser?" Dinoczar said. "Master is no loser. Show some respect."

"Shut it, dino-face," the evil Hobbit snapped. "No one cares how much you want to gargle your master's cock."

Another round of derisive laughter, with plenty of back-patting and high-fives for everyone. This was starting to feel eerily like high school to me.

And I *hated* high school.

Nonetheless, I couldn't let my temper get me in trouble. Something told me that the Prison Guards would not appreciate having a brawl break out in the cafeteria. I needed to remain calm and collected.

Taking a deep breath, I said, "What exactly is your problem with Joe, if I may ask?"

Miss Hiss sneered at me. "Your Minion has quite the history of stealing from all of us. For example, he stole my golden snake idol and sold it to a collector."

"He stole my glasses," the two-headed Prisoner growled, his grip on Joe's shoulders visibly tightening.

"And he robbed my whole gang," the evil Hobbit said. "And *then* sold us out to the police, thus indirectly helping me end up here."

The other three Prisoners did not share their experiences with Joe, but based on their expressions, I could tell Joe had probably done similar things to them as well.

Couldn't say I was surprised, honestly. It seemed like Joe had a history of ripping off other Villains. And given how Villains were generally, well, villainous, it was even more understandable why Joe did his best to avoid running into or even being seen by the other Prisoners.

But frankly, I had expected Joe to have more sense than to steal from a bunch of high-level Maxies.

Even so, Joe was my Minion, and I didn't want to lose him just yet. He was still useful to me, and besides, I hated bullies.

"I'm sorry that my … Minion was so rude to you guys," I said, "but I would ask that you leave him alone. Killing him now wouldn't accomplish anything or get you back whatever he stole from you."

"What would you know, Level One loser?" the evil Hobbit sneered. "And don't look so surprised. I Scanned you. You're just Level One. I could crush you without even thinking about it."

I scowled and Scanned the evil Hobbit, only to find out that he was Level 100. A quick Scan of the other Prisoners surrounding the table showed me that they were all close to him in Level, including Miss Hiss, who was a respectable Level 120.

This wasn't good. There was no way in hell that Dinoczar, Joe, and I could defeat these six in a fight. Granted, the Prison Guards would probably step in if a fight broke out in the cafeteria. Maybe the other Prisoners didn't know that.

I smiled at the evil Hobbit. "Go ahead. Pick a fight with us. I'm sure the Guards will be very happy to crack some Prisoner skulls. They look pretty bored."

The evil Hobbit held up a couple of fingers. "First, it wouldn't even be a real fight. More like a one-sided slaughter. And two, you must be even more naive than you look if you think the Prison Guards care if we kill each other or not."

Miss Hiss nodded, her snakes also nodding with her. "Indeed. I've been here for over a year and have never seen the Prison Guards break up a fight before."

I gulped. "What? But don't they care about keeping order here?"

The two-headed Prisoner chuckled darkly. "Why would the Guards care if we kill each other or not? We'll just respawn in our cells."

"Bi-Clops is right," said the evil Hobbit with a nod. "The Guards don't care what we do to each other. As long as we don't try to escape from the Dome or our cells, we can treat each other however we like."

As the evil Hobbit said that, his right hand had been slowly moving toward Joe. Just when he finished his sentence, he grabbed Joe's left hand and quickly snapped his index finger like a twig. Joe cried out in pain as I received this notification:

[Minion Joe] has received a [Broken Finger]! -1 HP.

There *had* to be a way to minimize these fairly useless notifications.

The other Prisoners laughed as Joe pulled his finger back to his chest. I glanced at the Prison Guards to see if any of them would react, but none of them did. The nearest Guards looked too busy chatting with each other to pay any attention to us, and even the snipers and drones overhead seemed more focused on the cafeteria as a whole rather than our table.

"See?" said the evil Hobbit, gesturing at the apathetic Prison Guards. "They don't care what we do to each other."

Bi-Clops nodded both of his heads, his grip visibly tightening on Joe's shoulders. "Shorty is right. Although I see you've already taken advantage of that yourself."

Bi-Clops was undoubtedly referring to the stump where Joe's right hand had once been. I did wonder why none of the Guards had inquired about his injury or tried to punish me for it when I did that.

Now, I knew:

The Prison Guards just didn't care.

Which meant we were on our own against six Prisoners who had about 600 Levels between them and had every reason to hate or kill us.

Maybe I was wrong.

Maybe Old Sparky hadn't changed the cafeteria rules to help me.

Maybe he changed the cafeteria rules to get me killed.

CHAPTER 18

"Master, what are we going to do?" Dinoczar whispered to me, fearfully looking around at the high-level Prisoners standing around us. "Even Dinoczar's Intimidate isn't working on them."

"I'm thinking," I replied quietly to Dinoczar, hoping the other Prisoners wouldn't overhear what I said.

Unfortunately, Shorty—which was apparently the actual name of the evil Hobbit—seemingly heard me, because he said, "You do that while we mess up your Minion even more."

"You don't mind that, do you?" said Bi-Clops. His grip on Joe's shoulders tightened, an audible *crack* emitting from his knuckles. "After all, you can always get more Minions. One of the perks of being a Big Bad."

Miss Hiss smirked. "Good luck trying to convince anyone else here to serve a Level One loser like you, though."

Miss Hiss was right. During the four in-game days I was logged off, I'd done some research on the Big Bad Class to learn exactly what I was capable of. My understanding was that Big Bads couldn't have Minions who were at a higher level than they were. Or, if it were possible, it was very difficult to get Minions higher-leveled than you and required a great deal of Cunning just to control them. Evidently, unless you somehow got a particularly loyal Minion, controlling powerful Minions always put you in danger of betrayal.

Of course, perhaps I shouldn't have been worried. Even if they killed Joe outright, he'd just respawn in our cell eventually no worse for the wear unless they permanently damaged him in some way. Technically speaking, I wouldn't suffer in any way if they killed Joe unless they decided to come after me next.

Which, given how cruel they were, seemed like a real possibility to me.

But I also hated how dismissively they treated me and my allies, as if we posed no threat to them whatsoever. I especially hated being called a "Level 1 loser," because it reminded me of the bullies back in my school days who regularly called me a loser (and far worse).

A cold voice breathed along the back of my neck, whispering, "Are you seriously going to sit back and let these impudent fools disrespect you? You are a Big Bad. Act like it."

That voice. It was the same voice that had ordered me to tell Dinoczar to eat Joe's right hand, the same one I had wrongly assumed belonged to Grandpa, the same one who Grandpa told me he was going to investigate.

This time, I could tell it definitely wasn't Grandpa. It sounded far older, for one, and higher pitched, closer to a woman's voice than a man's, oddly enough.

Yet it still sounded familiar to me, even though I was pretty sure I had never met the owner of the voice before. It was as though I'd heard her voice somewhere else before, but I couldn't place where right now.

I was tempted to talk back to her and ask her who she was, but somehow, I sensed she would not respond to anything I said.

She was watching my every move to see if I was going to sit back and let these "impudent fools" boss me around and assault my Minion.

Of course, I had no intention of doing that.

Standing up from my seat, I looked Miss Hiss directly in the eyes and said, "A Level One loser, huh? You really have no idea who I am, do you?"

Miss Hiss narrowed her eyes. "A delusional, arrogant kid who thinks that having one Minion makes him a serious Big Bad."

I chuckled. "Delusional? Miss Hiss, if you knew who I really am, or who I was outside the walls of this prison, you wouldn't even look at me funny without feeling a chill of fear in your heart."

I had no idea where any of those words were coming from. They just seemed to flow out of me as if I'd spent months memorizing them, even though I'd never spoken anything like this before to anyone.

Even so, I meant every word I said.

And they seemed to be working. The Prisoners had shifted their attention from Joe to me, including Bi-Clops, who gazed at me with a skeptical look on both of his one-eyed faces.

"You're just another Prisoner like the rest of us, kid," said Shorty with a snort. "Everyone can see your Level. We know you're just an ant."

I raised an eyebrow. "Did it ever occur to any of you that I might be hiding my *real* Level from you?"

Another comment I couldn't quite explain the origin of. I supposed I had been thinking about saying something like that, but that comment was far more eloquent than how I normally spoke.

Although it was a good idea and I could already see where I was going with it.

The other Prisoners exchanged puzzled looks. They clearly didn't quite know how to react to what I just said.

Finally, Miss Hiss said, "Impossible. Even if you had a Power that allowed you to hide your real Level from us, it wouldn't work here. Everyone knows that the Powers of Prisoners don't work in the Dome, after all."

I put my hands into the pockets of my jumpsuit. "Only if you are a weak-minded fool, I suppose."

Miss Hiss glared at me, her snakes hissing on her head. "Weak-minded fool? I hope you weren't referring to me, newbie. That would not be very ... respectful."

I eyed Miss Hiss with another raised eyebrow. "Why would I respect a woman as vain, superficial, and ugly as you clearly are?"

Miss Hiss's eyes widened as she rose to her full height, which was when I realized she was actually a good deal taller than any of the other Prisoners. Her long, thin, snakelike body twisted in ways that would make even Olympic gymnasts jealous. "You want to say that again to my face, loser?"

"Don't fall for the brat's tricks, Hiss," said Bi-Clops in his usual deep, calming voice. "Anyone can see that he's bullshitting us."

"Yeah," Shorty piped up. "If he really was some sort of powerful Villain in disguise, he'd be able to prove it. But I can guarantee you he can't."

Damn it. As annoying as Shorty was, he was also right. If I tried to perform some kind of display of power in front of them, I'd look like a total fraud. Maybe this plan was not as brilliant as I thought it was.

Then the cold, feminine voice in my ear, completely unlike Miss Hiss's voice, whispered, "They say that only because they fear you, fear *us*. Use my power to show them why you are a threat to be reckoned with."

A notification appeared in my view:

[???] wants to Link with you. ***Accept?*** *Y/N*

I had no idea what "Linking" meant, although it seemed to be related to that mysterious Skill I had noticed on my character sheet earlier. And creepily enough, there wasn't even a prompt I could click to see what the in-game explanation was.

But at the same time, the female voice's offer to use her "Power," whatever it was, to intimidate the Prisoners was tempting. It would certainly solve my short-term, immediate problems.

On the other hand, since I had no idea what Linking did or meant, nor did I even know who this woman was, it was entirely possible I was going to make a bad decision that I would come to regret in the long term.

But then I remembered what was at stake here. I had no legitimate way of Leveling up, easily gaining Powers and Skills, or anything else right now. And until I could escape the Dome, then I needed every advantage I could get, regardless of where, or perhaps *who*, it came from.

Besides, it was just a game. It wasn't like I was signing my soul over to the Devil, after all.

So I clicked "Y," causing the previous notification to disappear. It was replaced by this notification, which read:

Congratulations! You have Linked with [???]. You now have access to the Powers, Stats, Skills, and other aspects of [???] for the next ten (10) minutes.

"Excellent," said the female voice in my ear. "Now show these fools why they shouldn't cross you. Show them why you are a Big Bad, the most fearsome Class in all of Capes Online. And why soon, every man, woman, and child in this world will fear the name of Maelstrom."

I didn't respond to the voice, but I was definitely going to take her advice. Especially with that ten-minute timer ticking in the upper right corner of my HUD, which meant I had no time to waste.

But Maelstrom … that was an interesting choice for a name. It was a name I'd used in other video games, including several of the ones I was currently streaming to my audience. I'd always liked the name because of the connotations of strength and power it carried.

It was certainly a more villainous name than Robert, anyway.

Although I did wonder how she knew about it. Could have been a coincidence, maybe, but something told me it wasn't.

"You want a demonstration of the might of Maelstrom, Shorty?" I said. "Be careful, otherwise you might just get what you wish for."

"Maelstrom?" Bi-Clops repeated in confusion. "Who is Maelstrom?"

I jerked a thumb at my chest. "Me. I'm the Big Bad known as Maelstrom. I'm one of the most dangerous Villains in Capes Online."

Shorty sneered. "None of us have ever heard of a 'Maelstrom.' And since we're all high-level Villains with deep connections in the Villain community, I'd say you're lying."

I smiled. "How long have you all been down here?"

The Prisoners once again exchanged puzzled looks before Bi-Clops suddenly spoke up. "Two years."

"Two and a half," said Shorty without meeting my gaze.

"Three," Miss Hiss admitted.

The other three didn't speak up, but I could tell they had probably spent around the same amount of time in here.

I raised my hands. "So you've all been here for two or three years, presumably with little to no contact with the outside world during that entire time, right?"

Shorty nodded. "Yeah. Other than the Blackouts, that is, although everyone knew about those."

"The Guards don't give us any news about what is happening beyond the walls of the Dome," Bi-Clops said with more than a hint of bitterness in his tone. "They want to keep us ignorant."

Miss Hiss glared up at the snipers. "We can't even rely on word from new Prisoners, since everyone is so tightly segregated down here in our little cells. Makes it impossible to talk to or even meet anyone new."

My smile may or may not have turned into a smirk. "Then I guess you didn't hear about the rise of Maelstrom over the last year or so. Perhaps you are fortunate. My rise to power was … very bloody, to put it mildly."

"Extremely bloody," Dinoczar added enthusiastically. "So much blood. And death. Yummy, yummy death."

I glared at Dinoczar to shut up, although maybe I shouldn't have, because the other Prisoners looked genuinely afraid when Dinoczar said that. Even Miss Hiss, Bi-Clops, and Shorty appeared more interested now, though still quite skeptical.

"But then you got caught and ended up here like the rest of us," Shorty pointed out. "Some up-and-comer *you* are."

I shrugged. "I agree that it is very unfortunate that I ended up in a place as disgraceful as the Dome. Such accommodations may be appropriate for average Villains like you lot, but for a rising Big Bad like me, it's very shameful indeed."

Bi-Clops growled. "Average? You really have no idea who you are talking to, do you, kid?"

I put my hands on my hips. "I could say the same to you."

Shorty sneered. "Don't mock us, brat. We can see your Level and you're—Wait, *what*?"

I blinked and looked around. "What happened? Did the Warden just show up shooting sparks or something?"

Shorty shook his head. "No. Your Level … it's insane."

"My Level—?" I quickly caught myself. "I mean, yes. My Level. It's, um, very high. Much higher than any of yours."

Miss Hiss rolled her eyes. "I'm sorry, but I am pretty sure that Level One is the absolute lowest level a person can have."

Shorty, his face now whiter than chalk, shook his head. "But he's not Level One anymore. Now it says … now it says he's … he's …"

"Spit it out, Shorty," Miss Hiss growled. "We don't have all day."

"No need for that," said Bi-Clops. He gestured at his two heads. "We all have Scan here. We can see his Level for ourselves."

The other Prisoners glared at me again, which made me feel a bit nervous. Despite being as powerful as I was, I still didn't like having so many powerful Villains all staring at me like that.

Then they had the most unexpected reactions:

Fear appeared on the faces of every Prisoner around our table. Even Dinoczar and Joe looked astonished, perhaps using their own Scan on me.

"Impossible," Bi-Clops said. "How did you gain so many Levels so quickly?"

I was tempted to open my character sheet and see exactly what my Level was, but since I didn't have time for that, I just puffed out my chest and said, "I didn't. I was just hiding my true power, like I said before. Did you think I was lying or something?"

"It … it must be another trick," said Miss Hiss, her voice slightly hesitant, her snakes hissing uncertainly around her head. "He found some way to inflate his Level, but he can't be nearly that strong. Right?"

The other Prisoners looked far less sure about that than Miss Hiss. One of them, a bald man with skin as white as snow, even made to step back a little bit, like he was thinking of running away.

Bi-Clops, however, still seemed unimpressed. "Definitely a trick. Not sure how he's doing it here, but that doesn't mean anything. There are a lot of ways he could be faking his Level."

I cocked my head to the side. "Even if I was faking my Level, which you can't prove, doesn't it strike you as at least a little bit alarming that I can do that in the Dome? As Miss Hiss said, our

Powers are supposed to be negated here. At least, they are for the weaker Villains, anyway."

My argument seemed to be convincing the other Prisoners. Even Shorty looked less smug now, glancing between me and Bi-Clops as if he wasn't sure who to believe. Miss Hiss continued to glare at me, but I sensed she was too worried about the possibility of me being the real deal to even think about testing my claims.

Bi-Clops, on the other hand, still didn't seem convinced. He shoved the table aside and out of his way, causing both Joe and Dinoczar to tumble to the floor rather ungraciously.

Bi-Clops then walked straight up to me until we were less than half a foot apart. He was about a foot taller than me and twice as wide. I could feel his Intimidation Skill trying to work on me, make me afraid.

And perhaps it would have worked if not for [???], because I got this notification which said:

You have resisted an [Intimidation] check thanks to your Link with [???]!

The eyes on both of Bi-Clop's heads widened, perhaps reading a notification telling him that his Intimidation check had failed.

Even so, he said, "If you're really as strong as you say you are, then prove it."

I cocked my head to the side. "How, exactly?"

Bi-Clops slammed his fist into his other hand. "Punch me. Right in the chest."

I shook my head. "And cause a scene? I'm not going to get myself in trouble with the Prison Guards just to prove a—"

Bi-Clops didn't let me finish my sentence before taking a swing directly at my face. His fist flew too fast for me to dodge or even block.

Or so I thought. But as Bi-Clops's fist shot toward my face like a bullet, my own hand rose up and caught it like a baseball.

And just like that, Bi-Clops's fist stopped cold, as if he had punched a brick wall rather than a human being.

Both of Bi-Clops's eyes widened in shock. "What the hell? How … did you … catch … my … fist?"

Frankly, I was as shocked as Bi-Clops. There was no way I should have been able to stop him. Especially since he was clearly putting his all into the punch, meaning I should have been the one with a broken hand here. Yet I didn't feel as if I was even trying to hold him back.

"What are you waiting for?" the female voice in my ear hissed. "Finish him. Use my power. Show him why he should never have challenged the might of Maelstrom."

With a grunt, I looked directly into Bi-Clops's twin eyes and said, "Fun. Now my turn."

I tightened my grip on Bi-Clops's fist. I heard—and, more morbidly, felt—the bones in his hand crumble like paper under my grip. He screamed in pain as I tightened my grip more and more. I got a notification informing me that I'd broken Bi-Clops's hand but ignored it to focus on crushing it even more.

"Stop …" Bi-Clops pleaded, his voice breaking. "Please … stop …"

I raised an eyebrow. "I wouldn't be a very good Villain if I showed you *mercy*, now would I? But very well. I'm getting bored with you, anyway. Bye."

With that, I shoved Bi-Clops backward.

I *intended* to shove him to the ground, then maybe step on his chest and go all David and Goliath on him, but I guess I didn't know my own strength, because Bi-Clops went flying backward across the cafeteria. Screaming at the top of his lungs, Bi-Clops smashed into the wall on the other side of the room and collapsed to the floor, leaving a large Bi-Clops-shaped dent where he'd fallen.

As soon as Bi-Clops fell, dozens of security drones flew around him and started tasing him. I wasn't sure why, given how weak and defenseless Bi-Clops was at this point, but I wasn't about to complain. At least they weren't tasing me.

Unfortunately, now every eye in the cafeteria—Prisoner and Prison Guard alike—was on me, including Bi-Clops's friends, Dinoczar, and Joe.

With a shake of my head, I glared at everyone else. "You see that?

That is the fate that awaits everyone who challenges the might of Maelstrom!"

It sounded really cheesy when I said that aloud, but apparently no one wanted to say that, because Shorty and the other Prisoners quickly scrambled away from me while the rest of the Prisoners simply returned to their meals.

A couple of notifications suddenly showed up in my view:

[Prisoner #120983] has learned not to mess with you! Your relationship with [Prisoner #120983] has decreased from 'Neutral' to 'Hated.'

Because you defeated [Prisoner #120983] before the entire Floor, the rest of the Maxies have learned to respect your Villain creds. Your reputation with the Prisoners of Maximum Security has risen from 'Unknown' to 'Feared.' This will affect your reputation with the other Maxies and potentially have other unknown effects in the future.

"Excellent job, Maelstrom ..." said the female voice in my ear. "I suspect our alliance will be truly ... fruitful. I cannot wait to meet you *very* soon ..."

I looked over my shoulder, but still did not see the mysterious woman.

So why did I feel like she was standing right beside me, watching my every move?

CHAPTER 19

———

"Maelstrom, huh?" said Joe five minutes later, sitting across from me at our table. "Is that going to be your Villain name now?"

I shrugged. "Seems appropriately villainous, no?"

"Dinoczar thinks it's the coolest name ever," said Dinoczar, seated beside me, a big smile on his face. "It reminds Dinoczar of the sea, which Dinoczar has tragically never seen. But he likes it nonetheless."

"Where did you even come up with that name, anyway?" said Joe. "I thought you didn't have a Villain name yet."

"Maybe not officially," I said. "But I dunno, I feel like 'Villain Robert' just isn't intimidating enough. I need something cool, like Dark Kosmos or Paradox or whatever. Something that makes me sound like a real badass."

Joe glanced around the cafeteria. "Well, everyone definitely knows it now. Look at how scared the others are of you."

Joe, of course, was correct. After my little display of power and might, the other Prisoners were now clearly ignoring us. Not because they hated us, but rather because they feared us, if the notifications I received after beating Bi-Clops were indicative of my reputation with them. I could sense that no one else wanted to mess with me, which was fine by me. It meant I wouldn't have to worry about accidentally getting into trouble with any other Prisoners who had a bone to pick with me or Joe.

Speaking of, I looked at Dinoczar. "When I knocked out Bi-Clops, I received two notifications. One said that my relationship with Bi-Clops went down to Hated, while my reputation with the other Prisoners went to 'Feared.' What does that mean?"

"You have discovered the Reputation and Relationship Systems!" Dinoczar again tried to clap but failed due to his tragically tiny arms. "Both affect how others treat you. Your Reputation decides how a group of people looks at you while your Relationship applies to your relationships with individuals."

I stroked my chin. "So being 'Feared' by the Maxies means no one is gonna mess with me, while Bi-Clops hating me means, well, he hates me. Do I have that right?"

Joe chuckled. "You got it, boss."

That was interesting. I could already see the ways I could take advantage of both my Reputation and Relationships with the other Prisoners and even the Prison Guards to pull off my escape plan. Another useful nugget of information for the future.

Speaking of the Prison Guards, exactly none of them even reprimanded me for what I did to Bi-Clops, even though I'd indirectly damaged part of the cafeteria while taking him out. And not because the Prison Guards were also afraid of me, either, as I hadn't seen my Reputation rise or lower with them. They simply took Bi-Clops out of the cafeteria—presumably back to his cell—and put up some tape around the damaged wall to prevent other Prisoners from causing more damage. They didn't even look at me, almost like I didn't exist to them.

Either Bi-Clops was correct and the Prison Guards really didn't care if we beat the shit out of each other or the Prison Guards knew about my role as the Warden's mole and had been given orders by Old Sparky not to punish me even if I damaged the facility. Both seemed highly likely to me, but I didn't really care which was true because it made my job easier regardless.

Then Joe leaned across the table toward me, a curious expression on his face. "But what's up with the stupidly high Level and strength? I thought you were a newbie. You been holding out on us?"

I debated with myself whether or not to tell Joe and Dinoczar about [???] and my ability to Link with her, which was a mechanic I still didn't fully understand myself.

On one hand, Dinoczar and Joe were about the only people I even remotely trusted in this place. They deserved to know where my newfound powers and abilities came from, even if no one else did.

On the other hand, I was still unsure about this whole [???] business myself. Although she had been helpful so far, I wanted to wait until I had a better understanding of who she was before I went around telling everyone about her.

So I shrugged innocently and said, "Frankly, I don't know. I suspect the Warden may have given me a power boost to make it easier for me to complete the mission he gave me, but I can't consciously access or activate it whenever I want. What does my Level look like now? Wait, I'll look myself."

I pulled up my character sheet but was disappointed when I saw that I was still Level 1. "It says I am Level One again."

Joe snorted. "Must have been a pretty temporary power boost, then, even if it was helpful."

I scratched the back of my head. "Everyone was freaking out when they Scanned me earlier, but I didn't look at what it said my Level was. What did it say?"

"It said you were Level Six Hundred, sir," said Dinoczar.

I started. "Level Six Hundred? But that would have made me stronger than Old Sparky."

"Not necessarily," Joe pointed out. "Remember, Old Sparky's Level changes depending on who he is fighting, at least while he's in the Dome. If he fought you, his Level would have been even higher than what it was when he fought Rock Lord."

I cocked my head to the side. "So not only does Old Sparky's Level scale depending on the Dome Level he's on, but it even changes depending on who he is specifically fighting at any one time? And you didn't see fit to tell me this information earlier because—?"

Joe rested his chin on his hand and grinned. "You didn't ask."

It took a lot of willpower on my part not to punch Joe in the face for that. I just reminded myself that Joe was my resentful Minion who cared more about scoring points against me than anything else, even if it was in the most passive-aggressive way possible.

Anyway, that was useful information to know indeed. While I hoped to break out of the Dome without having to fight Old Sparky directly, the odds were definitely not in my favor. Old Sparky was the final boss of the Dome, and if I knew anything about video games, it was that skipping the final boss was rarely possible.

"Still, that is a useful ability to have, sir," said Dinoczar. "Dinoczar especially enjoyed seeing you put that two-eyed idiot in his place. Of course, Dinoczar enjoys brutal violence in general, so Dinoczar is happy regardless."

I shook my head. "I wouldn't exactly call what I did to Bi-Clops 'brutal,' per se, although I was perfectly willing to brutalize him if necessary."

Dinoczar winked at me. "Regardless, Dinoczar hopes to see a lot of brutal violence under your leadership well into the future."

I sighed and rubbed my forehead. "In any case, that little scuffle didn't do anything except waste time I could have spent networking with the other Prisoners. And lunchtime is almost over, meaning I might have to wait until tomorrow to complete Old Sparky's mission."

"Plus, it sure looks like none of the other Prisoners are exactly eager to start chattin' with ya," said Joe, gesturing at the other tables. "Think you might have intimidated them a little *too* well."

Joe had a point. Before, the other Prisoners had simply looked antisocial. But after I beat Bi-Clops, they now looked quite afraid of me, which I also knew from the system notification I had received earlier. There was no telling how they might react if I tried to go over and introduce myself.

Maybe I should have just let Bi-Clops and his gang kill Joe. At least that would not have made it any more difficult for me to speak with the other Prisoners and finish this mission.

That was when a huge shadow fell over me and a familiar-sounding, deep British voice said, "Maelstrom, was it?"

I looked over my shoulder, half-expecting to see Bi-Clops again, even though neither he nor anyone in his little gang had a British accent.

Instead, I found myself staring into the face of [Prisoner #379021], the giant British bear from the last lunchtime. He stood behind me, towering over me, Joe, and even Dinoczar. He smelled vaguely of wet animal hair, although based on his rather dark eyes, I decided not to mention that.

"It is," I said, raising an eyebrow defiantly. "And you?"

Prisoner #379021 flashed me a huge ursine grin, showing off every last one of his long, dagger-like teeth to me. "Call me Ursal."

"Ursal?" I repeated. "That is … an interesting name for a bear."

Ursal scowled. "I am not a bear. I may look like one, but only because of an unfortunate accident I participated in a few years ago."

"Uh-huh," I said. "What do you want? Do you want to challenge me like Bi-Clops, too?"

Ursal chuckled. "No, no, mate. I actually wanted to congratulate you on knocking that huge oaf out. Bi-Clops and I have a history together, so it always pleases me whenever I see someone put him in his place."

I shrugged. "What can I say? I don't like bullies. And Bi-Clops is definitely a bully."

Ursal folded his arms in front of his chest. "He was also one of the top dogs in this place, if indeed there are any top dogs among the Prisoners. That's why everyone else, other than me, is too scared to approach you."

I raised an eyebrow. "And you aren't afraid of me because—?"

Ursal grinned. "Because I sense a kinship with you. Despite your clear and overwhelming power, I can tell you are a man who values intellect and deep thought rather than senseless violence."

"But Dinoczar loves senseless violence," said Dinoczar with a frown. "Dinoczar says it is fun."

I waved a hand at Dinoczar to shut him up, which Dinoczar did. I had an inkling that talking to Ursal might be important, so I didn't want Dinoczar's weirdness to scare him off.

I said to Ursal, "You're right. Normally, as a Big Bad, I am more of a master planner than a master fighter. Although I am surprised that you value planning and thinking more than muscle, given your, well—"

Ursal flexed his muscles. "Physically intimidating form? Yes, there is a time and place for brute strength, but as I told you, I wasn't always like this. My real strength lies in my brain, not in my muscles."

I nodded. I was liking Ursal more and more, despite the oddness of hearing the voice of a British man coming out of a walking, talking bear. Not like I could be too critical of that, however, because I had a Russian dinosaur for a friend.

"Thanks," I said. "If that's all you wanted to talk about, then you can leave. Lunchtime is almost over."

Ursal's eyes narrowed. "Actually, Maelstrom, there was something else I wanted to talk with you about. Something far more important than mere social niceties. An offer, if you'd like."

I raised a single eyebrow. "An offer? Of what?"

Ursal suddenly shoved Joe off the table onto the floor and took his place across from him. I heard Joe curse Ursal, but I ignored Joe's suffering to focus on Ursal, who sat across from me with both his paws on the table. He kept his eyes glued to mine, as if he wanted to make sure I did not sneak away from him.

"Let me get straight to the point," said Ursal, leaning forward. "Several other Prisoners and I are planning to escape from this hellhole. And we'd like to extend an invitation to you and your Minions to join us."

I kept a cool face, although deep down, I was shocked. This must have been the conspiracy Old Sparky had told me about. Guess it was real, after all. "Are you sure this is something we should be talking about in the open like this?"

Ursal smiled mysteriously. "The Prison Guards couldn't hear us even if they wanted to right now."

I furrowed my eyebrows and gazed around the cafeteria. It was true that neither the Prison Guards nor the snipers overhead appeared to be paying us the slightest bit of attention. Even the security cameras and drones were trained away from us. "This your doing?"

"A friend of mine, actually, who has found a way around the Power Negation that the Dome enforces on all of its Prisoners," said Ursal. "But it's a small loophole that could be easily patched if someone found out about it. Hence why we have no time to waste."

Wow. I hadn't known it was possible to get around the Dome's Power Negation field, although it sounded like a fragile loophole that Ursal's friend had found. I'd definitely have to ask about that later. I still didn't know how the Power Negation system here worked. Any intel I could get would be great.

Sipping my water cup, I said, "Gotcha. So you're planning a breakout of the Maximum Security Prisoners?"

Ursal nodded. "Yes. We've been planning this for months now and the plan is nearly finished. And fortunately, we've managed to plot out the whole thing without that old Warden or his Guards being the wiser."

That was obviously not true because Old Sparky had warned me about this exact thing. Either Old Sparky had better intel than he let on or he was just so paranoid of the Prisoners that he always thought they were planning a breakout.

And in his defense, he was probably correct in that assumption. Even if he didn't quite know *who* was planning a breakout at any one time.

"Impressive," I said. I took a bite of my slimy [Slop] and tried not to grimace at the taste. "If your plan is nearly complete, then why do you need me?"

"We don't," said Ursal simply. "However, we are currently lacking in raw strength. Although our plan is hinged on avoiding Old Sparky entirely, we will need a way to stop him in case we do have the misfortune of running into him. And since you are Level Six Hundred —despite what your Scan data currently says—you would be the best candidate to hold your own against him in a direct fight."

I pursed my lips. "Seems logical, although what about Old Sparky's level scaling?"

"You needn't defeat him," Ursal told me. "In fact, if all goes well, you wouldn't even have to fight him. But should you need to, you only need to distract him long enough for us to escape."

"What about me?" I said. "Am I just to be a sacrificial lamb or something like that?"

Ursal laughed. "No, no, chap. You have a Sidekick and a Minion, don't you? *They* are the sacrificial lamb. You, on the other hand, are the Big Bad who will escape with the rest of us."

I could tell Ursal was bullshitting me. Although he was nowhere near as aggressive or rude as Bi-Clops had been, it was still pretty clear to me that Ursal thought I would be easy to manipulate into sacrificing myself to allow himself and his compatriots time to escape. Normally, that would offend me, as I tended to think of myself as a smart guy, but I decided to play along with Ursal's demands. However intelligent he might have thought he was, Ursal most certainly wasn't the smartest bear in the room. That would be me.

"Interesting," I said. "When will this breakout happen, if you don't mind me asking?"

"Tomorrow night," Ursal replied. "But tonight, we are going to hold a final meeting to work out the last-minute details, which would be a great opportunity for you to meet the rest of us. Would you like to join?"

A notification popped up in my vision:

[Prisoner #379021] has asked you to join [Team Breakout]!
Accept? Y/N

It looked like Ursal had formed a Team with the other potential escapees. That made sense. In Capes Online, Teams were alliances of two or more players of the same or similar Alignment. Teams could see each other's Health bars easily, send messages in a private group chat, take on Team Missions, and do a lot of other things that solo players couldn't do on their own. Setting up a Team to plot a breakout was a simple, yet logical, solution to the problem of planning an escape without worrying about the Prison Guards being aware of it.

Naturally, I hit "Y" and got this notification:

Congratulations! You are now a member of [Team Breakout]. Go to the TEAMS tab in your menu to see your status in the team, along with the names of your fellow Teammates, current Team Missions and Level, and more!

Eagerly, I flipped over to the TEAMS tab, only to discover that the names of my other Teammates were ... a bunch of Prisoner numbers that made no sense to me.

Ursal, apparently knowing what I was doing, winked at me. "Now, now, Maelstrom, you'll have to wait until tonight to properly meet the rest of your Teammates. I will inform them of your presence at the meeting, so you needn't worry about that."

I nodded, closing my menu, because there was no point in checking Team Breakout's Stats when it wasn't going to last much longer anyway. "Sure. When and where will the meeting take place?"

"I will let you know in a private message after lunch," said Ursal. "Due to how strictly communications are watched here, we have to be careful about deciding the time and place of our meeting. Just keep an eye on your inbox for a message from me with the details. Until then, see you tonight and welcome to the Team."

With that, Ursal rose to his feet and walked away from the table. I watched him go back to his table where he sat alone. Glancing around, I noticed that the Guards, snipers, drones, and cameras had returned to normal, which probably meant that Ursal's friend, whoever he was, had stopped blocking them.

Joe, crawling back onto his seat at the table, dusted his jumpsuit off with his left hand. "That guy was rude as hell. Seriously, he didn't even ask me to get up. Just took my seat without asking."

I looked at Joe incredulously. "You do realize that Ursal is a Villain, right? Villains aren't exactly known for their politeness."

"Yeah, but still," said Joe. He glanced at Ursal's table, where the bear was now sitting again. "Are you sure you trust him?"

I shook my head. "Not even slightly. It's obvious, actually, that Ursal is planning to betray me at the last possible moment."

Dinoczar gasped. "Then why did you join his Team, sir? You are putting your life in danger."

"Because this is exactly what I've been waiting for," I said. I jerked a thumb at Ursal. "I now have an in on the breakout conspiracy. And besides, Ursal doesn't know that I know what he's really planning, so I think it should work out for me."

Joe shook his head. "Whatever you say, boss. But personally, if you want my opinion—"

"I don't," I said. "Thanks."

Joe closed his mouth, looking as offended as ever, but truthfully, I didn't care about his feelings. Aside from the fact that he was just a Minion, he was also not even real. None of this was, in fact.

That was when a *ping* suddenly echoed in my ear and a notification—this one not from Capes Online—popped up in my view. Curious, I opened the notification and, with a start, muttered, "Crap."

Dinoczar looked at me with a worried expression. "What's the matter, master?"

"I need to leave," I said. "Now." I looked at Dinoczar. "Will I be all right if I log off right now?"

"Sure," said Dinoczar with a nod. "Joe and Dinoczar will make sure you get back to your cell."

I frowned. I still didn't know if Dinoczar was aware that he was in a game or not, but he rarely found my usage of game terminology confusing, so I decided to roll with it. "Okay. I'll be back before tonight. See you guys soon."

Opening my menu, I clicked the LOG OFF button in the upper right corner and everything faded to black, with this message being the last thing I saw in the game:

Thank you for playing Capes Online! We hope you return to play again soon.

CHAPTER 20

The transition from the world of Capes Online to reality was smoother than one might think. As soon as the log-off message disappeared, I woke up in the real world, lying on the memory foam–lined interior of my GamePod, staring up at the ceiling of the living room through the glass lid. The lid then slowly lifted up as the GamePod powered down with a very soft hum.

Well … maybe it wasn't quite that smooth. Going from my strong, athletic Capes Online body back to my real, far less in-shape body was always awkward. Just climbing out of the GamePod and standing up felt odd and clumsy, far odder and clumsier than it would have in the game. I almost cursed my real body before catching myself.

No. This was my real body. Not my Capes Online body, which was just a change of clothes I wore while there. However much stronger, more attractive, and more athletic my Capes Online body might have been than my physical body, it wasn't real. It never would be real.

Daniel couldn't accept that and look at what happened to him. I could accept that. It was the only way to make sure I kept my sanity intact.

Although when I remembered the reminder I'd received in-game before logging off, I realized I had far more important things than my body to worry about at the moment.

After spending a couple of seconds adjusting to the change, I ran out of the living room, past the holo-projector containing the recording of Grandpa, and up the stairs two at a time. Reaching the landing, I rushed down the hall and burst into Mom's room, saying, "Mom! I'm sorry. I almost forgot that it's time for you to take your medicine."

Mom, who was lying upright in bed reading something on her old ereader, gazed up at me and coughed. "It's fine, Robby. You're not too late. But I probably should take my meds now. Don't need the doctor lecturing me about not taking them again."

Sighing, I looked at the clock on Mom's wall. It looked like I wasn't too late, after all. Which was a relief. Mom's doctor had made it very clear to me at our last appointment that Mom needed to take her medicine on a regular schedule, otherwise her already poor health would just get even poorer. It didn't help that Mom's memory was starting to go, which was why she usually needed me to check on her and make sure she was still taking her medicine when she was supposed to.

That was why I had to log off Capes Online in such a hurry. I'd set a reminder for myself to help Mom with her medicine—and a good thing too, because I had gotten so absorbed in the game that I had nearly forgotten about it.

Although the idea that I got *that* absorbed in the game was … disconcerting, to say the least. This was how Daniel started, forgetting small obligations and details here and there, until soon he forgot about the real world entirely. Was I already starting to slip, despite having spent far less time in the game than Daniel?

I didn't know. But I did know I would need to be even more careful with how I spent my time in Capes Online going forward.

Shaking my head, I walked into Mom's bathroom, which smelled vaguely of hand sanitizer and her favorite rose-scented perfume, and grabbed her meds from the medicine cabinet. Rushing back to Mom's side, I popped open the first of six bottles and started giving her her meds. Fortunately, although Mom sometimes forgot to take her meds, she still knew how to take them, so I didn't need to do much after giving her the first pill. So I sat down and watched her take the rest of them.

While Mom ingested her pills, I hated to admit it, but my attention did wander a bit. Part of my mind was still in Capes Online, thinking about how much closer I was to completing the Riddle of Grandpa's Challenge, and therefore how much closer I was to getting the money I needed to pay for Mom's and Daniel's care and everything else we need to pay for.

And maybe it was because I was thinking about Grandpa or maybe it was something else, but my eye caught a glimpse of one of the books on Mom's bookshelf. It was the spine of *Our Virtual Immortal Future*, the book my Grandpa wrote a long time ago.

As I said before, I'd never actually read Grandpa's book, even though it had been a huge bestseller when it came out and was even available in Capes Online, or so I'd heard. You might think it weird that I wouldn't care enough about my own grandfather's ideas about digital immortality to read his book, but it was due partly to Daniel's negative experiences with the game and partly because I wasn't a reader. Mom loved her books, naturally, but I never did. Always more into video games.

And, I guess, after Grandpa's death, I couldn't bring myself to read it. I was afraid that reading his book would just remind me of his absence. Grandpa's death had hit me pretty hard, to the point where I'd had to go to therapy for a few months. The therapist even recommended that I avoid reading Grandpa's book until I was in a better head space.

But that was ten years ago. Now that I was directly interacting with Grandpa—or, at least, a version of Grandpa—with little trauma, I wondered if maybe I *should* read it. Not only would it help me understand the concept of digital immortality better, but it might also deepen my understanding of Grandpa himself, which might make it easier for me to solve my current Riddle and perhaps even predict what his Digital Double might throw at me next.

Suddenly, I was very much interested in reading that book.

"Robby?" Mom's voice broke me out of my thoughts. "What are you looking at?"

Turning my attention back to Mom, I said, "Er, nothing. Did you finish taking all your pills?"

Mom nodded, gesturing at the six plastic bottles on her bedside table. "Yes. I was just worried about you because you looked like you were thinking about something. I recognize that face. You can't hide it from me."

I grinned sheepishly. Mom was right. She knew me better than anyone except maybe Daniel. I couldn't lie to her or hide much of anything from her. She might not have been as quick-witted as she was in her younger years, but she was also far from senile just yet. "I was just ... just thinking about Grandpa, I guess."

Mom's expression darkened. "Oh? What made you think about him?"

I shifted in the old wooden chair I sat in beside her bed, feeling the soft cushion comfortably supporting me. "I just saw you had a copy of his book over on the bookshelf over there and realized I'd never read it myself."

Mom frowned and harrumphed. "I wouldn't bother. You won't learn much, other than how brilliant and 'visionary' your grandfather was."

I pursed my lips. I'd known for a while now that Mom and Grandpa didn't have the best relationship, but this was the first time since the funeral I'd heard her speak of him so disparagingly. "I don't know. Grandpa and I never talked about his views on digital immortality or anything like that when he was still alive. And seeing how important those ideas were to him, I feel like I never got to learn about that aspect of him."

Mom snorted. "Yes. I suppose trying to live forever was very important to him. More important to him than his wife, and taking care of his family."

"Mom, that's pretty harsh," I said carefully. "I know Grandpa wasn't perfect, but—"

Mom laughed harshly, an unusual sound coming from her. "He certainly thought he was. And he thought I wasn't. Hence why he spent all of our family's money on harebrained schemes to make 'digital immortality' a thing and left nothing for us."

I suppose I should explain that my family, the Bakers, actually used to be the Oklahoma equivalent of old money. My great-great-great-grandfather, Robert Joseph Baker, was one of the Boomers who settled in Oklahoma just before the Land Run of 1889 and struck oil early on.

Thus, my family got a lot of our money from the oil and gas industry. And while the push to green energy in the early part of the twenty-first century did hurt us somewhat, it was really Grandpa's investing in various tech companies promising hyper-real VR that never took off that hurt us. He'd even sold off a lot of our oil shares and wells just to have more money to invest in these companies, none of whom panned out except SI Games, the company behind Capes Online. And Grandpa was far from the biggest investor in SI Games, so even that deal didn't work out for him or us.

Perhaps if things had been different, Mom and I would already have the money we need to pay for her and Daniel's care from our family's oilfields. But that wasn't how Grandpa did it and that was how we ended up in our current financial position.

"He probably wasn't *trying* to hurt us," I said. "Back then, everyone was trying to get in on the VR industry. He probably thought we could make our money there instead of in oil and gas. Everyone thought oil and gas were on the way out, after all. Nothing wrong with diversifying."

Mom chuckled. "Robby, dear, I appreciate you trying to look for the best in people, but not everyone has sympathetic motives for what they do. Grandpa wasn't a good husband, he wasn't a good father, and he most certainly was not a good person."

I gulped. "Surely he wasn't that bad. I mean, I agree that maybe he didn't invest our money wisely, but—"

"If that was all he did, I wouldn't—" Mom took a deep breath. "I would have had a much better relationship with him. He regularly cheated on Grandma with his younger female students and treated me like I didn't even exist until I had Daniel and you, at which point he finally became interested in his one and only daughter. He was a bastard through and through. I just wish I'd realized it sooner than I did."

I shifted uncomfortably in my seat. "I didn't know about the affairs."

"No one did, other than me and Grandma," said Mom. "He was

such a respected public and academic intellectual with friends in very high places, friends who also cheated on their wives."

I gulped again. "Was he a—?"

Mom shook her head. "He didn't rape anyone. All of his affairs were consensual. Not that it stopped Grandma from suffering from depression. She was probably relieved when she died first, although I bet Grandpa was even more relieved, knowing he wouldn't have to keep pretending to love her anymore."

My jaw fell open. "Pretending to love her? That seems a little harsh, Mom."

Mom gave me a hard look. "If he really loved her, he wouldn't have slept with his students."

I couldn't really argue with that, so I said, "If Grandpa was so bad, why did you name him after me? Why even involve him in my life at all?"

Mom looked down at her hands and sighed. "Because he was still *my* dad and, despite how awfully he treated me and Mom, I thought your birth might be a way to repair our relationship. It did get a little better after I had Daniel, so I hoped it would continue when you came along. He seemed genuinely interested in you and Daniel and your welfare. I thought that naming you after him would make him want to be more involved in your life, to be a better grandfather than he was an actual father to me."

I twiddled my thumbs together. "Did it work?"

Mom sighed again. "What do you think?"

"I think ..." I hesitated. "I think he was a good Grandpa, although I wish I'd known about the other things he'd done."

"I'm glad he was a good grandfather to you," said Mom. She stared bitterly at the wall on the other side of the room. "But even then, he still didn't leave us anything when he died. He wasted our family wealth on stupid video games and VR that did nothing. So maybe he didn't care about you as much as you think."

I bit my lower lip. Mom still didn't know about the Riddle or about the digital recording Grandpa left me. I had intended to tell her when I completed the first Riddle, but now, I was less sure. Given how much Mom disliked, if not outright hated, Grandpa, I doubted she would be very happy to know that I was following his last will at the moment.

Then Mom looked at me and smiled apologetically. "I'm sorry, Robby. It's not good for my health to dwell on the past. We have enough to worry about in the present as is."

I shook my head. "It's fine, Mom. I shouldn't have brought up Grandpa."

Mom reached out and stroked my cheek with her cold left hand. "It's not your fault. Besides, even though your grandfather was not a good person, you are. You are a much better person than your grandpa ever was, Robby, and I don't say that lightly."

I gulped. "Mom, you're embarrassing me."

Mom shook her head. "No, I mean it. You're kind, humble, and helpful. Between taking care of me and Daniel, I know you are so overworked. I don't think I can ever thank you enough for being such a good son and a good person."

Normally, I liked it when Mom complimented me, but for some reason, I felt extremely guilty when she called me a good person. I kept thinking about how I murdered that poor widow in Capes Online, along with the various other immoral or morally questionable actions I'd undertaken since playing the game. I still hadn't told Mom I was a Villain in-game.

I mean, why should I? It wasn't like I was a Villain in real life. I should just agree with Mom. I might not have been a *perfect* person, but I was a good person. No matter what kind of character I played in a stupid game about superheroes.

"Thanks, Mom," I said. I rose from my chair. "Are you hungry? I can make lunch for us if you want."

Mom yawned and put the last of her pill bottles on the table next to her bed. "Thanks for the offer, but frankly, I am exhausted after taking all of my medicine. Go ahead and make lunch for yourself. I think I will do what most old, sick people do and nap."

I nodded. "Okay. But if you need anything, let me know, all right?"

Mom nodded in response, although I could tell she was already drifting off. She closed her eyes and pulled the blankets up to her chin, breathing softly as she fell asleep.

I carefully made my way to the exit, intending to make myself a quick lunch before tonight's meeting in-game with Ursal and the other conspirators in Team Breakout.

But I did stop by Mom's bookshelf to pick up her copy of *Our Immortal Digital Future*, tucking it safely under my arm as I turned off the light in her room and stepped outside.

Should make for some interesting lunchtime reading, if nothing else.

CHAPTER 21

I ate a quick lunch of leftover pizza and water. Not exactly the healthiest meal, maybe, but knowing how quickly time moved in Capes Online versus in the real world, it wasn't like I had much of a choice. The more time I spent in the real world, the less time I had in Capes Online. I was afraid of missing tonight's meeting for Team Breakout, which I suspected would be vital in my own plans to break out of the Dome.

While I ate, however, I started reading Grandpa's book. Although not a thick tome by any means, it was still a hefty 300 or so pages, which was longer than most books I'd read.

I made it as far as the second chapter—titled "The Coming Revolution in Virtual Reality and Artificial Intelligence"—before I realized I needed to log back into Capes Online soon. Closing the book, I sighed and quickly cleaned up lunch while thinking about what I'd read so far.

I learned a surprising amount just from reading the first chapter of the book. It appeared that Grandpa had foreseen, with scary accuracy, just how advanced VR technology would get. Even though Capes Online didn't come out until twenty years after the book, it read like Grandpa had already played the game and was simply describing it to his contemporaries.

More interestingly, however, was how Grandpa explored the morality and ethics of VR. Granted, this was just the first chapter, so he didn't delve too deeply into it. He did bring up some philosophical questions, such as whether NPCs would ever be advanced enough to be considered real human beings with rights like us, but he spent most of the first chapter introducing himself, his thesis, and briefly describing the history of VR up to that point.

And Grandpa's thesis?

I still wasn't sure. Even though *Our Immortal Digital Future* was written for a popular audience, Grandpa wasn't exactly the clearest or most concise writer in the world. If anything, it seemed to me like he had yet to form his final thesis on VR and was merely experimenting with ideas. In particular, Grandpa brought up the possibility of a future where healthcare as we know it might not be necessary anymore because we could just upload our minds to the game world and not need to worry about our physical bodies.

I will admit, a lot of it flew over my head. But what stood out to me was where he discussed whether we'd get to the point where morality in VR would matter as much as it did in the real world. He pointed out how, in most video games, morality was largely unnecessary because of the false nature of video games. He then brought up how, in a digital future, our actions would be as subject to moral scrutiny in the games we played as in the real world.

That made me uncomfortable, to say the least. After all, during my brief time in Capes Online so far, I'd done my fair share of morally questionable, even outright immoral, actions. I was a Villain, for God's sake. What did that say about me, according to Grandpa's philosophy?

More importantly, however, what did that say about Grandpa's Digital Double deliberately pushing me toward the Villain Alignment? How did the Riddle square with Grandpa's own views on digital immortality and the ethics thereof? Grandpa had been a philosophy and ethics professor before his death. He, more than anyone, should have thought this through.

Maybe I would get the answers to those questions later on in the book.

Anyway, I also noticed that the book was dedicated to Daniel and me. The dedication simply read, *To my two grandsons. I hope you both will live long enough to see the future I only dreamed of.*

The dedication caught me off-guard because Mom never told me about it, nor did Grandpa mention it to me at any point. All it did was make me feel even worse about not reading it until now, however, because it was clear that Grandpa had been thinking about his grandsons when he wrote this book.

Yet reading that dedication did not fill me with as much happiness as it normally would have. Mom's words about Grandpa being a "bastard" echoed through my mind as I read the book.

Was Mom right? I didn't know. I hadn't know about Grandpa's many apparent affairs until today, nor that Grandma had suffered depression or that Mom had felt neglected as a child herself. Perhaps Mom and Grandpa just had clashing personalities and they never got along.

Then again, Mom was one of the kindest, least judgmental people I knew. If even *she* was willing to badmouth her own father, then either Mom was a pettier person than I thought she was …

Or she was right and Grandpa was not a good person.

And if Grandpa was not a good person, then perhaps I should not listen to him.

I shook my head as I turned on the kitchen faucet, letting hot water flow over my dirty dishes. Who knew that playing a video game would unearth family secrets and drama that I didn't even know about? What other hidden facts about Grandpa and my family would I learn as I progressed through Capes Online?

I was almost afraid to find out. Almost, because I saw Mom's latest hospital bill on the dining room table and realized that, regardless of Grandpa's morality, regardless of how he treated Mom or Grandma, regardless of anything, I needed his wealth if I was going to keep my family afloat.

And I could only get his money if I continued to play Capes Online and solve his Riddle.

So, less than an hour after I logged out of Capes Online earlier, I logged back into the game. As usual, the mind-to-game process was smoother than peanut butter and I woke up inside Cell 52 in Maximum Security of the Dome, lying on my cot.

"Looks like sleeping beauty has awakened," said Joe, who was sitting on the floor against the wall on the opposite side of the cell, arms folded in front of his chest.

Dinoczar peered over the top of the bunk down at me, an eager expression on his face. "Welcome back, master! How was your nap?"

Rubbing the back of my head, which ached for some reason, I said, "Restful. How long was I asleep and did anything happen while I was gone that I should know about?"

Joe shook his head. "You were asleep for a few hours. And no, nothing particularly interesting happened, unless you count Dinoczar threatening to eat my other hand during an argument as interesting."

I frowned and looked up at Dinoczar. "What's this about an argument?"

Dinoczar cocked his head to the side. "Joe and Dinoczar had a polite disagreement over the nature of these 'Team Breakout' fellows. Joe says you can't trust them while Dinoczar has faith that you will get the better of them yet."

Frowning even more, I looked back to Joe. "You think my agreeing to go to their meeting tonight is a mistake."

Joe snorted. "Yeah. I didn't recognize that Ursal guy at first, but after thinking about it, I realized he was a member of the Ninja Guild for a while before he got arrested."

"The Ninja Guild?" I said. I held up my hands. "Wait a second, let me guess: The Ninja Guild is where all the ninjas are trained, right?"

"How did you guess, sir?" said Dinoczar in amazement. "Dinoczar would not have been able to guess such esoteric facts just by hearing the name."

Joe rolled his eyes. "More or less. The Ninja Guild, which is based here in Adventure City, by the way, is basically the premier ninja organization in the world. Not only do they train up new ninjas, but they also regulate the conduct of their members and act as an assassination guild for people willing to pay them."

I furrowed my brow. "Are they Villains or Heroes?"

"Both," Joe replied. "They don't discriminate based on Alignment, so you'll find members of both Alignments among them. Ursal, for example, was a ninja, although from my understanding, he got kicked out for trying to assassinate the Grandmaster. That's probably also what got him arrested."

"You mean Ursal was a ninja bear?" I said incredulously. "He can't have been that great of a ninja. Bears are not exactly known for their stealth, after all."

"He was apparently stealthier than you might think," said Joe. "Anyway, it doesn't really matter except that I think he is probably not trustworthy. This could be a trap."

I gave Joe an incredulous look. "A trap? Since when did you care about my well-being? Don't you resent me or something like that?"

Joe nodded. "I do, actually, but you are also the only thing keeping the other Prisoners here from kicking my ass. So it's in my best interests to make sure you stay alive, at least for now. Plus, as your one and only Minion so far, I feel an irrational level of loyalty to you, meaning I couldn't betray you even if I wanted to."

I eyed Joe skeptically. "Even so, this is my best bet at completing the mission Old Sparky gave me, as well as gaining more valuable intel on the Dome itself. If Ursal and his Team are already planning to do their breakout tomorrow night, then I think it's safe to say that they have something figured out already."

Joe shrugged. "Fine. You're the Big Bad, after all. I am but a humble Minion. You can do what you want. Not like I actually care."

I sighed and rubbed my forehead. Glancing at my inbox, I said, "But all this talk about Ursal does remind me that he hasn't messaged me yet. I assume you two haven't heard from him yet, either."

Dinoczar shook his head. "No. Dinoczar has only heard the Prison Guards beating some of the other Prisoners to death mercilessly. Otherwise, it has been rather quiet around here."

My interest was piqued at Dinoczar's words. "What do you mean, the Prison Guards have been beating other Prisoners to death?"

Dinoczar clacked his teeth together. "Just the usual prison brutality, sir. No one cares about the Prisoners, so the Prison Guards just do whatever they want to us."

"Right," I said. I stroked my chin. "Anyway, Joe, I may have a mission for you later. The tunnel that connects our cell to the Guards' locker room is still open, right?"

Joe glanced under my cot. "Yes. Why?"

"I'm probably going to need you to get some more intel on the

Dome and the Prison Guards at some point," I said. "Build on the relationships you built with Ike and Jorge, for example. Or—"

A *ping* in my ear interrupted me. Looking at my inbox again, I smiled when I saw a message from Ursal with the subject line "RE: Tonight ..."

Opening the message, I read it:

Maelstrom,

This is Ursal. This message has been sent on an encrypted line that the Warden and the Guards do not have access to, although only for the next ten minutes after you open this. I highly recommend deleting this message once you are done to avoid having it discovered by the Guards.

Anyway, Team Breakout's final meeting will be at midnight tonight. Stay in your cell. Someone will come by to pick you up, but only *you. To avoid potential detection from the Guards, your Sidekick and Minion must remain in your cell.*

See you soon,
Ursal

"Weird message," I said.

"What did it say?" said Joe.

I looked at Joe. "Said I don't even have to leave my cell, that someone would come to pick me up for the meeting tonight. It also said that you two have to stay here, probably because it would be harder to sneak around with a big group rather than one or two people."

Dinoczar's jaw fell as he leaned even further over the top bunk, the bed creaking ominously under his weight. "What? But sir, Dinoczar is your loyal Sidekick who must follow you wherever you go. Dinoczar must come with you."

I shook my head. "Sorry, Dinoczar, but I agree with Ursal's message here. Given how neither Ursal nor his Teammates know about my real reason for going to their meeting tonight, I think it would be safer for us all if I simply follow their instructions to the letter."

Joe snorted. "Your funeral. Me, I'm pretty happy staying in our cell. Definitely safer here than it is out there."

I sighed again and rubbed my forehead. "In any case, tonight should be a very informative night, one way or another. Let's see how it goes."

CHAPTER 22

"Wake up!" an unfamiliar male voice yelled at me. "Time to get up, Prisoner!"

Startled, I sat upright in my cot, wiping the sleep out of my eyes as I looked blearily around my cell. It was difficult to tell what time it was in the Dome due to the lack of access to the sun or clocks, but my HUD did inform me that it was midnight in-game.

That surprised me. After I received Ursal's message telling me to wait until tonight, I decided to nap for a bit. Napping inside a video game might have seemed like a weird thing to do, but given how quickly time passed in Capes Online versus the real world, I couldn't afford to log off for very long and risk missing the meeting entirely. Plus, I'd read that napping in-game supposedly gave your characters temporary Stat buffs, which seemed like something that could be helpful to me since I still couldn't level up in the Dome.

So I plopped down on my cot, ordered Dinoczar and Joe not to kill each other while I was asleep, and then closed my eyes. I only intended to rest for a couple of hours in-game, until just before midnight or so, but I guess I must have been sleepier than I realized. Either that or time moved even faster in Capes Online than I thought.

In any case, I woke up with this notification in my view:

Buff added: *Partially Rested. +5% to Health and Stamina regeneration, +1% to Intelligence. Duration: 1 hour(s).*

Swiping the notification out of my view, I sat up and rubbed the sleep out of my eyes as the male voice continued to shout, "What are you waiting for, Prisoner? Wake up!"

With a soft yawn, I looked toward the sound of the voice. A Prison Guard I didn't recognize, his name tag reading [PRISON GUARD ADAM], stood on the other side of the bars of our cell. He was by himself, which seemed a bit odd to me given how the Prison Guards always appeared to travel in pairs, but maybe the others were asleep or something.

"What do you want?" I said with a slight yawn.

Adam glared at me from underneath the brim of his hat. He jerked a thumb over his shoulder. "The Warden wants to see you, Prisoner. He sent me to escort you to his office."

I frowned. "The Warden wants to see me? In the middle of the night?"

That made no sense, in case you couldn't tell by my bewildered reaction. Did Old Sparky want an update on the mission already? Given how closely the Guards monitored the Prisoners, Old Sparky must have known that my progress on the mission had been slow so far. After all, despite being invited to the meeting, I still didn't have enough proof of the breakout to present to him yet.

Granted, I did consider telling Old Sparky I was part of Team Breakout, but even that wasn't hard proof of anything. What Old Sparky seemed to have wanted during our meeting was a list of names of the Prisoners involved in the conspiracy, which I didn't have. Because despite being on Team Breakout, I still couldn't see the names of my other Teammates or even how many members were on our Team, even when I looked at Team Breakout under the TEAMS tab in my menu.

And like I just said, it was the middle of the freaking night. Maybe Old Sparky really *did* live in the Dome like everyone said he did. Although at this point, I had to question whether Old Sparky even slept.

"Yes," said Adam brusquely. "Now are you coming out or not?"

I yawned again. "I don't know. This all seems pretty suspicious to me."

Adam grinned at me. "If you resist, I have full authority from Old Sparky himself to beat you into submission."

I grimaced and glanced at Dinoczar and Joe. Oddly, the two of them were still fast asleep as far as I could tell. Maybe they were even deeper sleepers than I was.

Regardless, I knew that resisting a Prison Guard for any length of time was unwise, so I got out of bed and walked over to the door to our cell. Adam unlocked it with a wave of his hand. As soon as I stepped out, Adam clasped two steel cuffs around my wrists, giving me this notification:

Debuff added: *Handcuffed. -50% in Dexterity. Duration: Indefinite.*

I grimaced. My Dexterity was already not very high, although I supposed the debuff made sense. It was difficult to be dexterous when one was handcuffed, after all.

Adam wrapped a hand as thick as a sausage around my upper arm and shoved me forward. "Start walking, Prisoner scum."

Stumbling over my own feet, I then got my balance and started marching obediently down the walkway to wherever we were going, passing by the cells of several other Prisoners on our way. "I'm walking, I'm walking."

"You'd better," said Adam, prodding my back with what felt like a baton. "The boss doesn't like it when his guests are late."

I scowled. "The boss, huh? What could possibly be so urgent that it required waking me up in the middle of the freaking night for? Couldn't it have waited until morning, or maybe tomorrow afternoon?"

Adam chuckled behind me. I suddenly felt his breath on my ear as he said, "Because then you'd miss tonight's meeting, Maelstrom."

I almost stopped walking when Adam used my Villain name. "Did you just call me—"

Adam shoved me forward again and snapped, "Keep moving, scumbag! Don't make me beat you to a pulp, even though you obviously deserve it for your crimes against humanity. Your kind makes me sick."

Okay, this was starting to get *very* weird, but I decided to keep walking. Eventually, we reached the end of the walkway, where a mysterious glowing blue platform sat. Scanning the platform, I learned this about it:

Dome Teleportation Pad
Materials: *Metal and other unknown materials*

Part of the Dome's teleportation network, this Pad allows Prison Guards to travel from one Floor of the Dome to another easily and quickly. Supposedly unhackable, the Dome's Teleportation Pads are a Synth Group^{TM} product and are compatible with other Synth Group^{TM} products and services.

The advertisement for Synth Group products—the same group that made Dinoczar, if I recalled correctly—was strange, but the Pad itself was interesting. This was the first time I'd seen one of the Dome's alleged Teleportation Pads myself, which confirmed the rumors that this was how the Prison Guards traveled around the Dome.

More interestingly, however, was the mention of the Dome's teleportation network. That may have just been a fancy name for the system, but the use of the word "network" implied to me that the Pads did more than just teleport you from floor to floor. Useful information for later … assuming my meeting with the Warden went well.

Adam and I walked onto the slightly elevated platform. As soon as both of us were on it, Adam tapped a few buttons on a nearby holographic console and then the Pad glowed a brilliant blue color. The light obscured my vision entirely and I felt the world around me shift even though I wasn't moving at all. The sensation was rather nauseating, making my stomach do enough gymnastics to make even an Olympian gymnast jealous.

Fortunately, the sensation didn't last more than a second or two before the blue light faded. Blinking rapidly, I looked around at my surroundings.

We stood inside a dark room that was entirely unfamiliar to me. The concrete walls, floor, and ceiling indicated we were still somewhere in the Dome, but it didn't look like the cafeteria, the cells, or anywhere else I'd been so far. Along the barren walls were faded or ripped wanted posters, barely illuminated by the glow from the Teleportation Pad, while the air smelled rather stale, as if this room hadn't been used in a while. The room was illuminated mostly by the light from the Teleportation Pad we stood upon, leaving the rest of it in absolute shadow.

"Finally," said Adam behind me, his voice slightly slurred. "I can take *this* off."

Looking over my shoulder, I saw something straight out of my nightmares.

Adam's skin was literally melting off his body. No, that wasn't quite it. His entire body was melting into an amorphous green blob that stank of swamp water. His hat, clothes, and everything else vanished inside the blob.

Two red eyes then opened on the surface of the blob and a toothy grin appeared just below the eyes. Its name tag now read [Prisoner #987102], although I barely paid attention to that because I was too shocked by the sudden appearance of the creature before me.

"What ... what *are* you?" I stammered. I tried to break the cuffs around my wrists but failed.

The blob grinned. "A Villain. Just like you. And a Prisoner. Just like you, too."

The blob suddenly sloshed toward me, getting some of its icky green goop on my shoes. Getting a little too close, the blob seemed to scan me, an unimpressed look on its features that apparently passed for a face.

"You're the infamous Maelstrom?" said the blob. He sniffed me. "You smell weak to me."

I gulped. "I take it you're another member of Team Breakout?"

The blob grinned again. "That's right. Apologies for not properly introducing myself earlier. I'm Glob."

"Glob," I repeated. "Just Glob?"

Glob nodded, or at least did his general approximation of a nod, seeing as he technically didn't have a head or neck. "Yes. I like keeping things simple. Never been one for big plans or subtlety, myself. Certainly nothing as pretentious as *Maelstrom*."

Glob sounded quite disapproving when he used my Villain name, prompting me to snap, "Sorry for being 'pretentious.' I just wanted something slightly more creative than Glob."

Glob's eyes narrowed. "Why, you little—"

"That is enough, Glob," said Ursal's refined British voice somewhere in the shadows around us. "Please do not manhandle the newest member of our Team."

Without warning, lights flipped on, causing both me and Glob to close our eyes to avoid getting blinded. Blinking, I looked around again, now actually able to see our surroundings properly thanks to the overhead LED lights.

The room was much bigger than I originally thought. It looked like it had once been a conference room at some point. Shaped like a circle, it was dominated by a dusty wooden table, which was covered in maps and other documents that seemed to be related to the Dome.

Seated around the table were who I assumed were the other Prisoners. Ursal sat at the head of the table, his massive arms folded in front of his chest. He gave me a polite wave when I looked at him, though otherwise said nothing.

Two other Prisoners sat on either side of the table. One appeared to be a zombie in a top hat, of all things, while the other was a bald woman whose skin was snow white and whose eyes were pure black. Those two—[Prisoner #235910] and [Prisoner #778904], respectively—looked at me with interest.

Glob frowned. "I was just having a little fun with the newbie, boss. I wasn't going to hurt him."

The zombie Prisoner rolled his eyes. "Please, Glob. We all know you are very insecure about your name. It's the whole reason you ended up here, remember?"

Glob scowled. "Let's not poke at each other's insecurities, Skin. Or do you want me to remind you how *you* got here?"

"Stop your bickering," Ursal ordered. "I have called this meeting to go over the plan one last time, as well as introduce the Team to Maelstrom, our newest member. Maelstrom, Glob, please take your seats."

Grumbling under his breath about how he hated being bossed around by a bear, Glob slid over to a chair near the bald woman, while I took a seat at the end of the table closest to me. Raising my handcuffs, I said, "Are these really necessary?"

"You're right," said Ursal. He glanced at Glob. "Glob, give Maelstrom the key to his cuffs. We want to keep our newest Teammate comfortable."

Glob rolled his eyes and spat a key out of his mouth at me. The slimy key landed right in front of me and, while I disliked the idea of touching anything that had been inside Glob's mouth or body, I also didn't want to be handcuffed anymore.

A second later, the handcuffs lay in front of me next to the key. Rubbing my wrists, I said, "Thanks, but I wonder if the whole fake Prison Guard shtick was even necessary in the first place."

Ursal shrugged. "You know how tight security around here is. It's not like Glob could have just walked up to your cell in his normal form and let you out without alerting the entire prison to the fact that we have found a way to break out of our cells and use our Powers."

I perked up when Ursal said that. "I was wondering how Glob did that. I assume his ability to mimic the appearance of a Prison Guard is one of his Powers."

Glob nodded, sending ripples through his body. "Yes. It's a Power called Shapeshifting. Exclusive to the Blob Monster Sub-Class of the Monster Class. Lets me mimic the appearance of just about anyone for a certain period of time, though it's a fragile illusion so I try to avoid getting hit while I am using it."

I nodded. "That sounds like a really useful Power. But how are you able to use it through the Dome's Power Negation Field?"

"We will get to that shortly," said Ursal. "First, introductions are in order, I think. You obviously have met me before and Glob has already introduced himself. Allow me to introduce the last two members of our Team whom you haven't met yet."

The zombie man held up a hand. "No need for that, Ursal. We can introduce ourselves just fine, thank you very much."

The zombie man looked at me. "Call me Skin and Bones, or Skin for short. In case you couldn't tell, I am a zombie."

I blinked. "I can see that, yes. Are you a special kind of zombie or—?"

"And I am Snow," said the pale woman, interrupting me like I hadn't been talking. She gazed at me with her black eyes. "And I can see into your soul."

I frowned. "Um, what?"

"What Snow means is that she has the ability to see into a person's soul and determine their true Alignment," said Ursal, "among many other Powers and Skills, of course."

Snow nodded in agreement. I still didn't quite understand what Snow could do, but at the same time, I supposed it didn't matter that much.

"So this is it?" I said, looking around the table. "Just the five of us?"

Skin narrowed his eyes. "You don't want too many people in on a conspiracy. Otherwise, it's not really a conspiracy anymore. Not a secret one, by any means."

"Which is why we find it very curious that Ursal has recruited you so late into the game," said Snow. She cast a suspicious glance in Ursal's direction. "Very curious, indeed."

Ursal grinned, displaying each one of his long, dagger-like teeth. "You all saw what he did in the cafeteria at lunch, didn't you? The one thing our little group is lacking is raw, brute strength, which I have reason to believe Maelstrom has in spades."

Skin pushed up the brim of his hat, looking me up and down with an unimpressed gaze that was all too familiar to me by this point. "I fail to see how a Level One newbie could possibly provide us with the muscle needed to make it past the Medium Security Guards, much less the Maximum Security Guards, or even worse, the Warden himself."

"I'm stronger than I look," I replied. I locked eyes with Skin. "Want to try me?"

"Settle down, you two," said Ursal. "I know we are all Villains here with our own distinct agendas, but for now we must put aside our differences to escape this hellhole. Unless you all wish to rot away in the Dome for the rest of your life, of course."

The other three members of the Team clearly still looked unconvinced that I should be here, but they also didn't look like they were going to fight with Ursal about it. Either Ursal was stronger than them or maybe his logic was so sound that even they couldn't argue with it. I benefited either way, seeing as this made it easier for me to infiltrate their group.

Putting my hands on the table, I said, "Now that everyone is here and knows each other, are we going to start going over the plan?"

Ursal nodded. "Certainly. Let me show you—"

The Teleportation Pad behind us suddenly flashed a blue light that briefly cast a sapphire shade over everything in the room. Startled, I looked over my shoulder, wondering who had decided to show up now.

But no one was there. The Teleportation Pad was empty.

Scratching the top of my head, I looked back toward Ursal and the others, saying, "Was I the only one who saw that flash of light or am I going crazy?"

Two clawed hands landed on my shoulders and a voice overhead said, "If you're crazy, I'm insane."

Freezing in my chair, I looked up to find myself staring face-to-face with a demon.

CHAPTER 23

THE FIGURE STANDING ABOVE ME RESEMBLED A STEREOTYPICAL DEPICTION of Satan. Dark red skin covered his face and neck, with curling ram horns growing out from his head. Glowing yellow eyes peered down at me unnaturally from his demonic features, his eyes blinking at a far slower rate than they should have been. He even smelled like fire and brimstone, another pleasant stench in a place full of them.

And his grip was *strong*. I felt like my shoulders were going to collapse in on themselves if he tightened his grip even slightly. I certainly couldn't break his grip even if I wanted to.

Which, I mean, I did. But I also didn't want to have my shoulders broken into itty bitty little pieces, even if this was a video game where the injuries and pain were not real and I healed far faster than I did in the real world.

"Ah, Abaddon," said Ursal with zero surprise in his voice. "I was wondering when you would show up."

Abaddon looked up at Ursal, his yellow eyes still not blinking when they should. "Sorry for being late. I slept in."

Abaddon let go of my shoulders and sat down a few seats from me. He didn't even walk. He seemed to slide across the floor until he reached a chair, and then he was suddenly sitting in it. His entire presence felt wrong to me, like he wasn't supposed to be here. None of the others seemed to feel that way, though. They just seemed annoyed at him being late.

Ursal gestured at Abaddon. "Maelstrom, this is Abaddon. The actual final member of the Team."

Abaddon twisted his head toward me and cocked his head, his neck making snapping sounds as he did so. "Maelstrom, eh? The same Maelstrom who beat Bi-Clops? I missed that whole thing, but everyone was talking about it earlier."

"You missed it?" I said. "But how? Weren't you there at the cafeteria at lunch like everyone else? Everyone saw it."

Abaddon yawned. "Yeah, but I fell asleep in my food, so I missed the action. Had to have my cellmates fill me in on the details later."

I frowned. "You fell asleep? In your food?"

"Abaddon likes to sleep," said Snow with more than a hint of judgment in her voice. "It's a miracle he made it tonight."

Abaddon flashed Snow a grin. "I'd never miss an opportunity to be in the presence of such a beautiful woman, babe. Maybe once we break out of this joint, you and I can spend some quality time together in a shady motel. Just the two of us."

Snow grunted. "I'd rather spend the rest of my life in Maximum Security than spend even five seconds alone with you."

Abaddon chuckled. "Touché. But if you ever change your mind, you know where to find me. Most women do take a while to realize they're in love with me, after all."

Snow grunted again and turned her black eyes away from Abaddon. Glob just snickered while Skin rolled his eyes, which was a lot creepier than you'd think because his eyes made a disgusting squelching sound when he did that.

This was certainly not the serious group of Villains I expected to be in charge of the breakout. In fact, they struck me as being more than a little dysfunctional, which I supposed made a certain amount of sense, although I didn't see how they thought they could escape if they barely tolerated each other's existence.

"Anyway," said Ursal, sounding more than a little disgruntled by the antics of his Teammates, "now that the whole Team is here, we can finally start the meeting."

Ursal clapped his hands and a holographic map of the Dome appeared in the center of the table. Similar to my map, it showed all three Floors of the Dome and was covered in red pins, which I assumed were points of interest marked out for the purposes of the plan.

Oddly enough, however, their map was missing the Top Secret Floor, the one directly below Maximum Security. It made me wonder where Ursal had gotten this map from. Were there multiple maps of the Dome floating around that showed different parts of the Dome? Did some maps not show Top Secret? That was logical if Top Secret was supposed to be, well, secret, but it still struck me as odd.

"This is the Dome," said Ursal, gesturing at the map. "As you can see, we are currently on Maximum Security, the lowest Floor in the prison."

"I was going to ask about that," I said. I looked around the room we sat in. "This doesn't look like a prison cell or like the Warden's office or anywhere else in the Dome I've been recently."

"That's because it is neither of those things," said Ursal. "The room we are currently using was once a conference room for the Prison Guards. It is located directly underneath Sub-Floor 10, but was abandoned shortly after the construction of the Dome due to reports of supernatural happenings that scared the administration. No one has used it for years."

I raised an eyebrow. "Supernatural happenings? As in—?"

Abaddon slouched in his chair, a strange grin on his face. "The Ghost of the Dome. According to legend, the Dome was built on the graveyard of a witch who got hanged for performing witchcraft back in the colonial era. Supposedly, her spirit still haunts the Dome, particularly Maximum Security, which is the part of the Dome closest to her burial place."

I folded my arms in front of my chest. "What exactly did this 'Ghost of the Dome' do that forced the prison administration to abandon this place?"

Glob leaned forward. "Rumor has it that the Ghost drove most of 'em insane. And those she couldn't turn crazy, she killed in brutal, bloody ways."

Glob said "brutal, bloody ways" in the same way that one might describe fine food as "yummy and tasty." In other words, I decided to keep a careful distance from Glob for the remainder of this mission.

Skin scoffed. "The Ghost isn't real. It's just propaganda created by the Warden and the Prison Guards to scare us into submission and keep us from trying to escape."

I gave Skin a skeptical look. "The zombie says ghosts don't exist?"

Skin shook his head. "I'm not saying *ghosts* don't exist. I'm saying that *the* Ghost doesn't exist. Like I said, Old Sparky probably made it up just to scare us. I've been in Maximum Security for over a decade and haven't seen any evidence or proof of this alleged Ghost's existence."

Glob snickered. "Pretending something doesn't exist won't make it go away, Skin."

Skin tapped the table with a pen irritably, glaring at Glob. "No one's seen the Ghost. No one's heard the Ghost. No one, that is, other than Old Sparky, and does anyone trust what that fat ass says? I certainly don't."

"But if the Ghost doesn't exist, then explain why this conference room was abandoned by the prison admins," Glob said, his gelatinous form visibly rippling. "Or is that part of your little conspiracy, too?"

While Skin and Glob argued about the reality of the Ghost, I kept quiet. Not because I had a firm opinion one way or another, but because I was thinking about the legend of the Ghost of the Dome.

Was the female voice I had Linked with—which I still needed to either ask Dinoczar about or research online—the Ghost?

That would explain a lot. After all, I always heard it in my head and it sounded like a woman, yet I never saw a woman anywhere near me. Given how she was constantly goading me into doing evil things, that would fit with the legend describing how she drove her victims insane.

Had the Ghost of the Dome, assuming she even really existed, decided to make me her next target? Was the Ghost even real or just propaganda created by Old Sparky to keep the Maxies in line? Or was there another explanation for the mysterious disembodied female voice in my head that had empowered me that I didn't know yet?

One thing was clear about the Dome: There was more—a lot more—going on here than met the eye.

Ursal clapped his hands together loudly, causing Glob and Skin to stop talking. "Regardless of the veracity of the Ghost myth, we have no control over whether she exists. Besides, took the Ghost's potential existence into consideration when we were putting the plan together, so there is no point in worrying about something over which we have no control. Thus, we should focus on what we can control: namely, our breakout plan."

Both Skin and Glob fell silent, as did everyone else in the room. It seemed like they, too, were more interested in talking about the breakout rather than arguing over ghosts that may or may not exist. I could tell, however, that neither had changed their opinions on the subject.

I didn't know what Snow or Abaddon thought about the Ghost. Snow simply rolled her eyes, while Abaddon chuckled. They were a bit harder to read than Skin or Glob, which made it more challenging for me to guess what was going on in their heads.

Although I supposed it didn't matter. We had far more important things to worry about, after all, just as Ursal said.

I raised a hand, causing Ursal to look at me. "I agree about discussing the plan and all, but I think you forgot that I am still in the dark about how you've managed to put together this team. For example, Glob used a Power, Shapeshifting, to sneak me out of my cell, even though the Dome has a Power Negation System in effect that prevents Prisoners from using our Powers. How did you do that?"

Glob chuckled. "It's easier than you'd think. Snow did it."

I looked at Snow, frowning. "You're the reason why Glob can use his Powers?"

Snow nodded. "Yes. When I was arrested, I was stripped and searched just like every other Prisoner who is brought here."

I grimaced. "They strip and search new Prisoners?"

Skin gave me a puzzled look. "Why wouldn't you know that? Didn't they strip and search you when you were brought in?"

I gulped. "Um, I was unconscious when I got arrested, so no, I don't remember."

Snow scowled. "Lucky. It is not a pleasant experience, especially for a woman. But anyway, the Prison Guards weren't as thorough as they liked to think they are. They didn't find this."

Snow pulled a necklace out from the front of her jumpsuit.

Dangling at the end of the necklace was a glowing green gem cut in the shape of a heart.

"This is the Emerald Heart," said Snow, "an ancient gem that was hidden in the mountains of Peru. It was supposedly made by a tribe of devil worshipers who sacrificed their own children to make it."

I eyed the Emerald Heart skeptically. Scanning it, I got this information:

The Emerald Heart
Materials: *Stone and other unknown properties*

Description: *The Emerald Heart is a long-lost piece of Peruvian jewelry from before the Spanish Empire's arrival in the New World. Its exact origins and powers are unknown, though some say it was designed by demon worshipers who sought the power of Satan himself, while others claim it was simply the jewelry of some long-forgotten monarch who ruled over the Peruvians thousands of years ago.*

Either way, the Emerald Heart is not a piece of jewelry to be trifled with.

I nodded. The Scan description wasn't exactly helpful in determining what the Emerald Heart actually was, but it lined up with Snow's explanation, anyway. I wondered if it had other powers aside from protecting the user from the Dome's Power Negation System.

"And how did you get the Emerald Heart?" I asked. "It looks—and sounds—very valuable."

Snow gave me the stink eye. "How I got the Emerald Heart is none of your business. What matters is that the Emerald Heart is unaffected by the Dome's Power Negation System."

Ursal nodded. "Although we don't understand why, it seems to cast a protective field over the user which allows them to use their Powers even inside the Dome."

I eyed the Emerald Heart with far more interest when Ursal said that. If the Emerald Heart really did grant the user protection from the Dome's Power Negation System, then that might be something I could use for my own escape plan later.

But that just brought another question to my mind. "If the Emerald Heart only protects the user, then how was Glob able to use his Powers earlier when he picked me up? He's not wearing it."

"I never said it *only* protects the user," Snow said with a huff. She waved a hand at Glob. "I can also cast its protective charms over other individuals who I choose to share it with. Unfortunately, it only lasts for an hour, maybe an hour and a half, on someone who is not me."

Ursal grinned. "Which should be more than enough time for us to escape from the Dome, if everything goes according to plan."

"Big 'if,'" said Skin, skulking in his chair. "I'm still not convinced this plan will work."

"It will," Ursal insisted. "Old Sparky still foolishly believes that we are all too divided to work together. Once we put my—I mean, our—brilliant plan into action, the donut-eating fool won't know what hit him."

Wow. And here I thought Ursal was actually smart. Guess he underestimated Old Sparky, although I couldn't blame him too much. Old Sparky did seem pretty silly, but if he was onto their plan without even them knowing, then he was much smarter than I first assumed.

Which did not bode well for my own breakout plan, to put it lightly.

Ursal put his hands on the table, the blue light from the holographic map of the Dome reflecting off his dark pupils. "Anyway, the Emerald Heart is truly the key to getting out of here. By using the Emerald Heart's power, we can use our Powers freely, which neither the Warden nor the Prison Guards will expect."

Abaddon cracked his knuckles. "Finally. I've been meaning to teach those Guards a very painful lesson they won't forget for a while now."

Glob nodded and licked his lips. "Yeah. Can't wait to see the looks on their faces when we start using our Powers left and right. It will be glorious."

"So is that the plan?" I said. "Use the Emerald Heart so we can use our Powers to beat up the Prison Guards and escape?"

Abaddon gave me a surprised look. "You're smarter than you look, kid. You figured out our plan even before anyone explained it to you."

Ursal cleared his throat. "Actually, there is a lot more to the plan than just brutalizing the Prison Guards. As I told you when we first met, Maelstrom, we are currently lacking in raw brute strength. Abaddon was probably the strongest member before you joined, and he's not particularly powerful as Villains go."

Abaddon raised his hands. "What can I say? I'm a lover, not a fighter."

I frowned. "Is that why you call yourself Abaddon? A word literally meaning destruction?"

Abaddon flashed me a smile. "Eh, it's not an entirely inappropriate name. And not one I chose for myself, either, but we play the hand we are dealt in this world, so no point in getting upset over it."

Ursal cleared his throat again. "Anyway, Maelstrom, as you can see, the biggest obstacle to escaping the Dome is Maximum Security itself. So long as we remain on this Floor of the Dome, our odds of escape are … low, to put it mildly."

Skin shook his head. "More like impossible."

I put the tips of my fingers together, thinking about Ursal's statement. "It's because of the Warden's level scaling ability, isn't it?"

Ursal nodded. "Partly, but also because of the Prison Guards and various other security systems designed to keep us Maxies in line. After all, Maximum Security was built specifically to be impossible to escape from, unlike Minimum or even Medium Security, which regularly suffer breakouts."

Glob licked his lips. "So the plan is that we're gonna try to reach at least Medium Security. 'Cause if we can get that far, the rest of the prison ought to be a walk in the park."

"Precisely," said Ursal. "That is why the Warden is so keen on making sure no one makes it past MX-Sub-Floor 1. Both Minimum and Medium Security are designed to contain much weaker Prisoners than us. Thus, if we make it to Sub-Floor 10 of Medium Security, then we will essentially be home free even if we haven't escaped the Dome's walls yet."

A blinking yellow dot appeared on MD-SF #10, which was short for Medium Security Sub-Floor 10, assuming the other Floors used the same naming scheme as Maximum Security did for its Sub-Floors. That seemed like a safe assumption to make, because it would be very inefficient to make up a new naming scheme for every Floor, in my opinion.

Leaning forward, I frowned. "Going from MX-SF#10 to MD-SF#10 looks really long. That means getting past ten Sub-Floors of high-level Prison Guards and drones, plus whatever other security measures are in place to prevent us from going that far. And that's assuming we don't run into the Warden at some point, which seems likely to me."

Ursal glanced at Skin. "That is where Skin comes in. Right, Skin?"

Skin held up a gleaming plastic key card I hadn't realized he was holding. "Yep. This is the Emergency Access Key that Old Sparky uses to get around the Dome when the Teleportation System isn't working."

"But doesn't the Teleportation System always work?" I said, scratching the top of my head.

Skin flipped the key card over in his hands. "That's why it's called the Emergency Access Key. Should the Teleportation System fail, there is a secret series of stairs hidden in the walls of the Dome to allow the Warden and the Guards to travel between Sub-Floors without issue."

Glancing at the map again, I said, "But I don't see the stairs—"

Without warning, the map shimmered and then a series of stairs within the walls of the prison appeared on the right side. The stairs did indeed seem to connect the various Sub-Floors together, and even appeared to connect the Floors themselves together, though it was hard to tell how.

"Oh," I said. I looked at Ursal. "How did you do that? Make the stairs appear, that is?"

Ursal smirked. "Because I have a high Cartographer Skill, which means I can find secret details on blueprints and maps that are meant for certain eyes only. That is how I've been able to learn so many of the Dome's secrets."

Other than Top Secret, apparently, but I kept my mouth shut about that. Not because I wanted the plan to fail—well, okay, I kind of did, seeing as that was the whole point of my mission and all—but because I didn't want to let these guys know about it yet. Until I could figure out how to enter Top Secret myself, it was going to remain my little secret.

"So the stairs are meant to provide emergency access to the Sub-Floors if the Teleportation System breaks," I said, stroking my chin as I studied the holographic map more closely. "Makes sense. Tech does have an unfortunate habit of breaking, so having a backup in place is logical."

"It is," Ursal agreed. "Plus, we suspect that the Teleportation System might automatically turn off in the event of a breakout, which we do not want to risk."

"Or the Warden might just shut it off manually," said Snow. "We know that he has control over it because of the intel we've gathered. If we try to break out but are confined to whatever Sub-Floor we find ourselves on, then we might as well not have escaped at all."

My thighs were already shuddering at the thought of having to climb all those stairs, but at the same time, I couldn't disagree with the logic behind using them. "Okay. So what's the plan, exactly?"

Ursal gestured at everyone sitting around the table. "Tomorrow night at midnight, Glob will come around in disguise as a Prison Guard to free each one of us from our cells. He will give us a cloaking device to hide ourselves until we all meet up at the entrance to the stairs."

A glowing yellow dot appeared on the map near the entrance to the stairs. I was relieved to see that the entrance wasn't far from my cell, which meant that I should be able to access it relatively easily.

Ursal continued his explanation of the plan. "Once all of us are at the entrance, Skin will open it and we will climb the stairs to Medium Security."

"Preferably, without the Warden or the Prison Guards being aware," said Snow with a snort.

Ursal nodded. "They shouldn't be, seeing as I have hacked into the Dome's scheduling system. I am going to make some last-minute changes to the Guards' nightly rotations tonight so we won't have to risk accidentally running into them during our escape attempt."

"You hacked into the Dome's scheduling system?" I said in surprise. "How?"

Ursal pulled out a small watch-like device from his jumpsuit and waved it at me. "This is a Prison Guard Watch, which they use to communicate with each other across Floors, check their work schedules, and more. I had Glob nick one off of the Guards earlier and, using my brilliant hacking skills, now have access to the Dome's scheduler."

I whistled. "Didn't realize you were a hacker as well as a cartographer."

"I have many talents," Ursal replied.

Glob grinned at me. "And if either the Warden or the Guards do somehow run into us, then you gotta deal with 'em, newbie. Got it?"

I nodded. The plan seemed simple enough. Assuming everything worked as they explained it to me, it sure seemed like a foolproof plan.

Unfortunately, these fools had not counted on me being a spy sent by Old Sparky to put an end to this plan before it even began.

Speaking of fools ...

I raised another hand. "What about my Sidekick, Dinoczar? And my Minion, Joe? Can I bring them with me?"

Ursal sighed. "I suppose so. As long as they do not get in the way of our plan, I see no reason why they can't tag along."

"They might make useful cannon fodder," Abaddon said, tapping his chin thoughtfully.

I said nothing to that, aside from finding it amusing how even Team Breakout thought that Joe was more useful as cannon fodder than anything else.

Then Ursal looked around the table at the Team, a serious expression on his face. "This will be the first serious breakout attempt of Maxies since the Blackouts. We will all need to do our best to pull this off. If even one of us fails to play their part, then we will *all* suffer. Got it?"

Everyone nodded in agreement, including me. It made me glad that neither Ursal nor anyone else on Team Breakout had any telepathic Powers.

Otherwise, they would have all known just how screwed they were.

CHAPTER 24

AFTER THE MEETING, GLOB, USING HIS PRISON GUARD DISGUISE AGAIN, escorted me back to my cell. As soon as I returned, Dinoczar and Joe both demanded to know about the contents of the meeting, so I filled them in on the plan very briefly. I mentioned they could join us but left out the part where Abaddon called them cannon fodder, mostly because I didn't need to deal with Joe throwing a temper tantrum or showing his insecurities again.

As soon as I finished telling them about the meeting, I sent a message to Old Sparky via the Capes Online Personal Messaging System. Apparently, the PM system was mainly used by players to communicate with each other privately, but even NPCs like Old Sparky had access to it. Old Sparky did not seem particularly perturbed by receiving a message from me like this, but then again, the characters in Capes Online did seem to have different expectations for what was natural and unnatural than we did in the real world, so I guessed that wasn't a surprise.

But I didn't tell Old Sparky to bust Team Breakout just yet. Instead, I sent him a brief idea for what I thought would be the most efficient way for him to destroy the Team and foil their plan before they could escape, which did not involve punishing them now or breaking up their Team right away.

To my surprise, Old Sparky actually agreed to my plan. He even told me that it was better than any plan he could have come up with and that it was "quite brilliant."

One might wonder why I didn't want Old Sparky to immediately bust my Teammates. It had nothing to do with loyalty to the Team—of which I felt very little—and everything to do with the existence of the Emerald Heart.

My plan was to take advantage of the chaos that Old Sparky and the Prison Guards would inevitably create when they confronted Team Breakout to steal the Emerald Heart from Snow without Old Sparky knowing. Honestly, that was probably the best part of Ursal's so-called plan, because the inability to use our Powers was one of the main things keeping the Maxies from being able to fight back against the Guards, much less attempt to escape.

Of course, I'd have to be smart about it. I did mention to Old Sparky that Team Breakout had access to an "item" that allowed them to use their Powers even within the walls of the prison, but I did not mention what that item was specifically, pretending that they had not told me what it was. I was hoping to pull a switcheroo during the inevitable clash between Team Breakout and the Prison Guards without anyone being the wiser.

Because the breakout attempt would not happen until the following night, I decided to take a break from the game and log off for the next few hours. While I was logged off, I made myself dinner, went for a walk around the block, chatted with Mom, streamed a new video game to my fans and followers online, and read more of Grandpa's book.

I got a bit farther into the book this time, getting through most of Chapter 2, which dealt with existing VR tech at the time the book was written, extrapolating from the early 2000s as to how the tech might develop in the future. As usual, Grandpa was pretty spot on, although he seemed to think the idea of digital immortality would be a lot more popular (and less controversial) than it had turned out to be so far.

Even though the chapter was primarily about the existing tech at the time the book was written, Grandpa also addressed some ethical objections to the idea of digital immortality, including the possibility of forced digitization of people. He even speculated on how the legal system would change to accommodate the existence and rights of "digital beings." Grandpa seemed to think that the legal system *would* eventually recognize digital beings as equal to physical beings, although I noticed the language he used to discuss digital beings made it sound like he himself wasn't sure if they were "real" human beings or not.

That was interesting. Ever since the second Blackout, which was when people learned that digital immortality was possible and that some Capes Online players had already done it, I'd been seeing people talking about "digital civil rights" all over the Internet. Some even argued that this was the next civil rights frontier:

The rights of humans who digitally downloaded their minds into Capes Online and other video games in an effort to avoid death.

What did I think about that?

I thought it was scary as hell.

The idea of escaping death was not necessarily a bad one, per se. The problem I had was that digital immortality was not true immortality. It seemed to me that a person whose mind ended up in Capes Online or some other similar video game simply made themselves dependent on the company that owned and ran the game. Deletion, after all, was still a real possibility, as was termination, which went a step further than deletion and actually got rid of a character's data entirely.

Plus, I still couldn't forget about Daniel. There was no doubt in my mind that my brother would have jumped at the chance of digital immortality if the feature had been available when he'd been playing the game. Not because he feared death or anything, but because he liked the world of Capes Online so much more than the real world.

In other words, to me, there wasn't that much of a difference between digital immortality and death, even if one allowed you to talk to the person who was no longer in the physical world. It was another form of loss.

And I couldn't stand to lose my brother even more than I already had.

Having said that, though, it was possible I was wrong. Maybe Grandpa's book would delve deeper into that and explain why digital immortality wasn't as scary as I thought. It was a bit dense for me, despite having been written for a general audience. But I had plenty of motivation to keep reading it and try to make sense of it to the best of my ability. It was probably the best way I could understand Grandpa's motivations for having me play Capes Online because I didn't know how to contact his Digital Double.

In fact, I found it so engrossing that the next few hours passed by without me even realizing it until the timer I set for myself on my phone beeped. Panicking at the thought of missing the breakout attempt, I rushed back over to my GamePod and logged back into Capes Online.

A second later, I found myself lying on my lumpy cot in my cell. I immediately swung my legs over the side of my cot and stood up, looking around in alarm as I said, "Am I late? Did I miss Glob? Did I miss the breakout?"

Joe, who was lying on the floor, started when I got up and looked at me in annoyance. "No, you didn't miss anything. You did, however, ruin my sleep."

I scowled at Joe. "When did I say you could sleep? You two are coming with me as well, you know."

Rubbing the back of his neck, Joe sat up, annoyance clearly plastered all over his features. "Because you told us we could rest a few hours ago. Right, Dinoczar?"

Dinoczar hopped off of the top bunk, landing beside me with a crash, cracking the concrete floor under his feet. "Joe is correct for once in his life! Master told Dinoczar and Joe to rest for the breakout tonight, so Dinoczar and Joe did."

I frowned. "I don't remember—wait, I told you guys that a few hours ago?"

Joe nodded. "Yep. Surprised you don't remember it. You were really insistent that we catch up on our sleep so we'd be all energized and ready for the breakout."

I stroked my chin thoughtfully.

There was definitely something weird going on here. And unfortunately, I had gotten too caught up in Grandpa's book in the real world to investigate either this or the Linking mechanic, which meant that I would have to think about it later.

For now, I was just happy that I hadn't missed the breakout

attempt. "Have you guys seen or heard anything from Team Breakout or the Prison Guards while I was out?"

Joe shook his head. "Nope. It's been pretty quiet tonight. Almost unnaturally quiet, now that I think about it."

"Dinoczar agrees," said Dinoczar. He gestured at the prison bars with his short arms. "Dinoczar has not seen even one Prison Guard pass by our cell tonight, which is unusual because Dinoczar usually sees at least one."

I nodded. "That must be Ursal. Last night, he said he had access to the Prison Guards' schedule. If I had to guess, he probably hacked the schedule to put Glob on it, just to make sure we don't run into any Prison Guards."

It was a pretty brilliant move, and under any other circumstance, probably would have guaranteed the success of our breakout.

Of course, the real reason for the absence of Prison Guards was that this was a trap that Old Sparky and the Prison Guards had laid for Team Breakout. Old Sparky told me that he would leave the hole in the scheduling system unpatched so that Ursal would think he had outsmarted him. Thus, Old Sparky was probably monitoring everything Ursal and the other members of Team Breakout were doing even now, thus completely taking the element of surprise away from them.

Unfortunately for Ursal and the others, however, they would not find out that particular fact until it was too late for them to do anything about it.

My thoughts were interrupted by the sound of footsteps outside of the cell. A second later, the familiar fake face of Glob, in the guise of [PRISON GUARD ADAM], appeared on the other side of the bars, clutching a billy club in his hand.

"Hey, you awake, newbie?" Glob whispered, his voice much deeper in his Prison Guard disguise. He tapped the bars softly with his club. "Everyone else is waiting."

I nodded. "We're ready to leave this place."

Glob smiled. "Good to hear. Let me work this lock first …"

A second later, Glob, Dinoczar, Joe, and I were walking down the hallway outside our cell. My cellmates and I held our arms behind our backs to pretend like we were cuffed. Although I was pretty sure that none of the other Prisoners were awake, Glob did not want to risk any of them seeing us and possibly raising noise that would give away our position. I pretended to agree, although I knew that the plan was destined to fail from the start.

We eventually reached the end of the hall, which ended in a blank stone wall. It sure looked like a dead end to me, but Glob walked over to the wall to our right and swiped the Emergency Access Key in front of it. The wall shuddered and slid aside silently, allowing all four of us to step inside. Then the wall slid back into place behind us, giving us nowhere else to go but forward.

We had emerged inside a wide-open stairwell. It was almost as wide as the abandoned conference room. A series of metal stairs went straight up into the darkness overhead, going so high up that I couldn't see where it ended. The room was stuffier and dustier than the rest of the prison, which made me wonder when the last time was this place had been used.

As Glob had said, the rest of Team Breakout was indeed waiting for us already. Abaddon sat by himself on the foot of the first staircase, while Ursal, Snow, and Skin stood a few feet away from him quietly talking among themselves.

But as soon as they saw us, Ursal broke off from the other two and strode toward us. "Finally. I was wondering when you four would get here."

"Sorry," Glob said, his Prison Guard disguise melting off his body, revealing his normal blob-like appearance. "We had a bit of a delay with the T-Rex."

"It is not Dinoczar's fault that Dinoczar can't move very fast," Dinoczar said defensively. He yawned. "Although Dinoczar would not mind taking a nap right now."

"You can nap later outside of the prison once we escape," said Ursal. "I assume you weren't seen?"

I nodded again. "We got here without waking up any of the other Prisoners and we didn't see any other Prison Guards on our way down, either."

"Excellent," said Ursal, rubbing his paws together evilly. "Then the plan is still on schedule. In fact, I'd say it's gone off without a hitch so far." He pointed at the stairs. "All we need to do is take these stairs until we reach Medium Security, at which point we will practically be free."

Glob sighed. "Finally. I can't wait to say goodbye to this godforsaken hellhole of a pri—"

The stench of ozone in the air—along with the buzz of electricity—was the only warning any of us got before a thunderbolt struck Glob from above.

The thunderbolt exploded, the blast sending us all flying. I crashed onto the floor, covering my head with my hands, my whole world turning white. I couldn't see or hear anything other than the crackling of electricity and the white glare of the blast. The metallic taste of ozone filled my mouth and I thought I smelled smoke somewhere nearby, possibly from my own clothes.

A couple of seconds later, however, the white glare faded, allowing me to lower my hands from my head and turn my head toward Glob.

Or rather, toward the spot where Glob had been standing. Now there was nothing left of him other than a blackened crater, the metal floor panels still hissing and melting, smoke rising in wispy columns. Even from a distance, the heat from the blast made sweat break out across my forehead.

"Glob?" said Ursal, sitting on the opposite side of the room from me. His fur was singed slightly around the edges but he otherwise looked uninjured. "What happened to Glob?"

A groan to my left made me look in that direction. Snow lay on the floor nearby. Even though she hadn't taken the brunt of the blast, she had still somehow lost her leg, which was bleeding out profusely. Skin, being the lightest of us, had been thrown into the wall by the explosion, his eye twitching.

The only member of the Team who seemed unharmed was Abaddon, still sitting on the foot of the stairs, a slightly puzzled expression on his face. He turned his gaze upward and frowned. "Looks like we have company, Team."

Although Glob's death notification had already informed me—and presumably the rest of the Team—who Glob's killer was, we nonetheless looked up the stairs to see who Abaddon was talking about.

Standing on the landing to the ninth Sub-Floor, surrounded by a dozen heavily armed Prison Guards, was Old Sparky himself. His eyes glowed an electrifying blue while sparks danced along his fingertips.

"Now, who let *you* dogs out of your cages?" Old Sparky said, cocking his head to the side. He cracked his knuckles, sending more sparks flying. "Time to teach you what happens to naughty Prisoners under my watch."

CHAPTER 25

Damn. Although I knew that I was safe from Old Sparky's wrath, even I was chilled by that display of power. This was not the first time I'd seen him one-shot a Villain far stronger than me, but it still reminded me of just how vast the power differences were between him and me. Made me glad I wasn't going to have to fight him just yet, although it did make me dread our inevitable confrontation later on even more than I already did.

Everyone else was staring at Old Sparky, too. Skin had pried himself out of the wall, dusting off his suit, though keeping his eyes on the Warden. Even Snow had stopped groaning about her missing leg long enough to gaze in horror at Old Sparky. Abaddon was also looking at Old Sparky, though he appeared to be more irritated than afraid, unlike the others.

Ursal, on the other hand, looked like his absolute worst nightmare had just come true right in front of his eyes.

"How …" Ursal's voice trailed off. "How is this even possible? We were so careful … so careful to avoid letting anyone outside of our Team know …"

Old Sparky chuckled. "There's no honor among thieves, or Villains, as the case may be. You might want to ask who among your 'friends' would benefit from betraying the group."

Ursal's eyes immediately darted around the rest of us. He rested his eyes on each member of the Team before locking on me. I tried not to look too guilty, but I may have accidentally shot him a brief smirk. Ursal's eyes widened even more and he snarled, "Why, you—!"

"Before you start ripping each other apart, give me one good reason why I shouldn't utterly *smite* all of you right now," said Old Sparky. He raised his hands, bands of electricity bouncing between his fingers.

Skin hesitated. "Um, because we will just respawn in our—"

Boom.

Skin was gone, replaced by another smoking crater. All that remained of him were the tattered remains of his top hat, slowly turning to ash.

"Wrong answer," said Old Sparky. "The truth is, there's no reason for me to show you sons of bitches mercy. The only thing you deserve is death."

Old Sparky pointed a fingertip at Ursal and fired a lightning bolt at him. Ursal rose to his feet, but he was clearly too slow to dodge and definitely not powerful enough to deflect the attack.

That was when a giant wall of dark flame erupted between Ursal and the lightning bolt. I expected the lightning bolt to just go straight through the barrier, but instead, it bounced off and ricocheted off into another wall, sending chunks of concrete and metal falling down toward us. Dinoczar and I leaped out of the way to avoid getting our skulls caved in, but Joe wasn't so lucky. A particularly thick chunk of concrete slammed straight into his skull and he collapsed instantly, with a notification telling me that he had died.

Dismissing the useless notification, I looked around for the source of the fire barrier that protected Ursal until I spotted Abaddon.

The demon-like Villain had not moved an inch from his spot at the foot of the stairs, other than to raise his right hand. Sighing in frustration, Abaddon gazed up at Old Sparky again. "And here I was hoping that I wouldn't actually have to *do* anything. Should have known things would go to hell, and not in the fun way, either."

Old Sparky scowled. "Abaddon. You are the very last Prisoner I would have expected to try something as stupid as attempting to break out of Maximum Security."

Abaddon shrugged and rose to his feet. "I surprise even myself sometimes. But hey, what's life without a little risk and danger?"

Old Sparky shook his head. "Such a fool. Men, open fire!"

The Prison Guards dutifully took aim with their guns at Abaddon and fired. At the same time, however, Abaddon's eyes flashed red.

And instead of shooting bullets or lasers or whatever, the Prison Guards' guns literally exploded in their hands. The Prison Guards screamed and yelled as their own weapons blew up in their faces. Many of the Guards staggered backward, clutching their faces or dropping the remains of their weapons while shaking their injured hands, but a few fell down the stairs and landed at Abaddon's feet with sickening *thuds*. Based on their groans, however, it was clear that those Guards were not dead yet.

I blinked. "What just happened?"

Abaddon scratched the top of his head. "I dunno. I guess they must have just gotten ... *unlucky*."

Old Sparky, who seemed completely unharmed by the exploding guns despite standing right in the middle of the Prison Guards, dusted gunpowder off his shoulder. "Don't play dumb. Everyone knows about your Powers, Lord of Evil."

I looked at Abaddon in alarm. "Lord of Evil? Why did he call you that?"

Dinoczar gasped. "Dinoczar recognizes Abaddon now! Abaddon was an infamous Villain who led a legion of demons to destroy Capes Online during the Demon Day event."

I gave Dinoczar a questioning look. "And how do you know this?"

"Because Dinoczar did his research on your Teammates while you slept," said Dinoczar.

Abaddon chuckled. "No one's called me the Lord of Evil in a long time, although it's not inappropriate. It definitely got me a lot of attention from the ladies." He winked at me. "Women love bad boys, and I was the baddest of them all."

Old Sparky scowled. "You are indeed bad, Prisoner, but not in the way you think. You are guilty of every crime of which you were accused, and then some, as decreed by our justice system."

Abaddon raised his hands. "I don't remember having my day in court, but then again, I also don't deny all of the awful, yet fun, things I did while I was free."

I furrowed my brow. "So what *are* your Powers, exactly?"

Abaddon smiled at me. "Luck manipulation, primarily, along with various demonic Powers like that nifty fire wall I created. How else do you think Ursal's breakout plan managed to get this far? Without my help, it would have fallen apart ages ago."

"Your luck has just run out, Prisoner," said Old Sparky. He pointed his index finger at Abaddon, electricity curling around it, making his finger look like a drill bit. "Die!"

Old Sparky shot a lightning bolt that spiraled like a drill toward Abaddon. This attack came even faster than the last one, and I felt there was no way that Abaddon would survive.

But Abaddon bent over, grabbed the half-dead Prison Guards at his feet, and ripped a strange white, silvery substance out of their bodies. His hands moving at the speed of light, Abaddon soon formed an ethereal, clear white barrier in front of him.

Just in the nick of time, too, because Old Sparky's spiral bolt slammed into the barrier at the exact moment Abaddon finished creating it. Lightning arced around the barrier, yet surprisingly, the barrier held.

Old Sparky's eyes widened, which was the first time I'd ever seen the Warden show fear. "You bastard. Using the souls of my Guards to protect yourself … I now see why everyone called you the Lord of Evil."

Abaddon grinned devilishly. "And this isn't even my best trick. Observe."

Abaddon did those strange hand movements again, his hands a blur. The barrier quickly collapsed, the spiritual energy sinking into the floor underneath us.

That was when I got this notification:

[Prisoner #299012] is using **Demonic Call**!

Demonic Call …? Based on the emphasis the DES put on the Power's name, it had to be some sort of Ultimate Power.

The floor cracked before Abaddon, the cracks growing wider and wider until they blew wide open, causing the bodies of the dead Prison Guards to fall within. Two giant, clawed hands reached out and grabbed the side of the hole it was in, pulling itself up until a new creature I'd never seen before stood in our midst.

It was a literal demon. It had to be. At about twenty feet tall, the demon towered over Abaddon and was nearly level with Old Sparky and his Guards. Its horns were twisted and cracked, while its hands ended in thick claws that appeared to be stained with blood. It smelled strongly of sulfur, making me wrinkle my nose, while the heat from its body raised the temperature of the emergency stairs by at least ten degrees.

I immediately Scanned the demon:

Demon Giant
Level: *300*
Alignment: *Villain*
Type: *Fire*
Description: *Considered monsters even in the underworld, Demon Giants thrive on the pain and suffering of mortals. It is said that only a demon or half-demon can hope to successfully control them once they are summoned, and even then, their independent personalities have spelled defeat for the summoner as much as they have assured them victory. They are only as loyal to their summoners as their summoners are able to feed them fresh, delicious human souls.*

Abaddon grinned. "Old Sparky, meet Ralph. He's friendlier than he looks."

Ralph the Demon Giant roared and swiped a claw at Old Sparky and the Prison Guards. Old Sparky leaped into the air, avoiding the claw, but the remaining Prison Guards were not so lucky. Ralph's claw smashed through both the concrete stairs and the Prison Guards as easily as if they were made of sand. It quickly turned its attention to Old Sparky, who was now flying around its head like some kind of annoying fly.

Old Sparky grunted. "A Demon Giant, eh? You just gave me a bigger target is all."

Old Sparky shot another spiral bolt at Ralph, striking it in the head. Rather than die instantly, however, Ralph just staggered a step or two back, shook its head, and slashed at a surprised-looking Old Sparky, who barely avoided the attack by diving to the right.

Abaddon tsked. "I think you forgot that a Demon Giant's actual Power is determined by the Level of the Summoner. And since I have a high Level, you're going to have to do a lot more than that if you want to kill Ralph."

Ralph roared, seemingly in agreement, and resumed attacking Old Sparky. The Warden flew wildly around the Demon Giant, dodging the attacks, which were now coming hard and fast.

I'll admit it, I was impressed. This was the first time I'd seen Old Sparky on defense. It upped my respect for Abaddon quite a bit, because now I knew he was a lot more than the lazy ladies' man he first appeared to be.

On the other hand, Old Sparky still had his level scaling ability in play. There was no doubt in my mind that Old Sparky would get back on the offense soon. Once he did, I bet neither Abaddon nor Ralph would last very long.

But Abaddon did provide me with an excellent distraction. It meant that now was the perfect time to loot Snow's Emerald Heart off of her, before Old Sparky saw me.

Rising to our feet, Dinoczar and I rushed over to Snow. Her stump of a leg was still bleeding profusely, making a small puddle of blood that I was careful to avoid stepping in. Her normally pale skin was even paler than before and her Health bar was dropping precipitously even as we watched.

"Maelstrom …" Snow breathed out hard. "Get me a Health Drink."

I furrowed my brow. "A Health Drink? What is that? Like a healing potion?"

Snow rolled her eyes. "Of course it's like a healing potion, you—! Never mind. Just get me one. It will heal my injury."

I eyed her missing leg skeptically. "Are you sure about that? Because that injury looks pretty bad."

"Health Drinks can heal anything, master," said Dinoczar. "They can even regrow missing limbs, if drunk right away."

I knew this was a video game and all, but I still thought that sounded utterly ridiculous. In my mind's eye, I saw Snow's missing leg regrowing like a lizard tail, which just added to the absurdity of the idea.

"But I don't have a Health Drink," I said.

Snow gestured at her jumpsuit. "I have a few in my jumpsuit pockets but I can't reach them myself. My hands ..."

Ouch. I just noticed that her hands had been largely blown off, too, leaving a few stumps here and there that barely resembled fingers.

I smiled, though not for the reasons Snow likely thought. If Snow was allowing me to rifle through her pockets for stuff, then I could also take the Emerald Heart.

Scratch that. The Emerald Heart was hanging off her neck, meaning I wouldn't have to dig through her pockets after all.

Grinning, I reached toward her neck and wrapped my fingers around the Emerald Heart, feeling the cool surface of the gemstone in my grasp.

Snow looked at me in surprise. "What are you doing? That's not a ... not a Health Drink."

I shot her a wicked grin. "Sorry, Snow, but I'm afraid I'm not going to be helping you. I'm just going to take this necklace of yours and—Ow!"

As soon as I tried to pull the necklace off her neck, the Emerald Heart heated up like it had been in the oven. Yanking my hand back, I got this notification:

Debuff added: Burned Hand. -1% in Dexterity. Duration: 30 seconds.

"What the—?" I said, staring at the notification in disbelief. "Why couldn't I take the necklace?"

"Because the Emerald Heart belongs to me, dipshit," Snow snapped, gesturing at the glowing necklace around her neck. "It's Soul-Bound, meaning I won't lose it unless I die or am killed."

Damn it. I'd never heard of "Soul-Bound," which seemed like an utterly random ability to have in a superhero-based video game, but I guessed it didn't matter. It just meant I'd have to kill Snow, which should be relatively easy, because she was already—

A grunt and a snarl was the only warning I got before a furry fist flew toward my face. I ducked and rolled out of the way to the side, stopping several feet away even as I heard a loud *crack* break the air. Looking over my shoulder, I grimaced at the sight before me.

Dinoczar, who had been standing behind me when the fist appeared, now lay on the floor, his head jerked unnaturally to the side. Despite that, however, he was apparently still alive, although he had only a small sliver of Health left.

Standing over him, his claws balled into tight fists, was Ursal. His chest heaved up and down with every breath, his normally cool, intelligent eyes now glaring at me with bestial wrath. His fur even seemed to be smoking, like he was about to burst into flames.

"Quick reflexes," said Ursal, "although I suppose if you are a traitor, you will need them to avoid getting ripped to shreds by your former Teammates."

As soon as Ursal said that, a new Skill notification popped up informing me I now had the Skill called Dodge. But I quickly swiped it away and rose to my feet, having no time to worry about my Skills at the moment.

"So you figured it out, eh?" I said, cracking my neck. "That's right. I sold you guys out to Old Sparky. That was always the plan."

Ursal growled. "I thought it was suspicious how quickly you accepted my invitation to join the Team, but I just assumed you were as desperate as the rest of us to escape this hellhole. Now, however, I see that you were simply trying to destroy the group from within on Old Sparky's orders."

I folded my arms in front of my chest. "I'm not sure why you are surprised. We're all Villains here, aren't we? That makes us automatically untrustworthy."

Ursal sighed in frustration. "It is exactly that sort of thinking that has let Old Sparky control us. He uses our very nature as Villains to pit us against each other, knowing that if we were united, even he would not be able to stop us."

I hesitated. Ursal actually had a good point there. It was obvious that Old Sparky was indeed playing the Prisoners against each other, appealing to our individual self-interest to prevent successful breakouts. I'd made a similar observation myself not long ago. It was something I would need to take into account for my own breakout plan later.

Rolling my shoulders, I said, "Even so, what are you going to do about it? Kill me? What would that accomplish, exactly?"

Ursal rumbled. "Nothing, really. But do you know my origin story?"

I shook my head. "No. And I'm not sure I really want to."

Ursal cracked his neck. "I was once a normal bear until a Mad Scientist gave me human-level intelligence through a series of cruel experiments. The Mad Scientist in question sought to raise up an army of intelligent bears and other big animals to take over the world."

I raised an eyebrow. Ursal's origin story sounded very similar to Dinoczar's. "I assumed it didn't work."

Ursal grinned, showing every one of his dagger-like teeth. "It didn't even get off the ground. I killed my creator and quickly found my place in the Ninja Guild, where I learned the art of stealth and assassination, which only made me stronger."

"And you are going to use that against me how?" I said. "After all, you don't exactly have the element of surprise, buddy."

Ursal's eyes glimmered dangerously. "I'm not going to use my Ninja training to kill you. I'm going to use the abilities that my dear 'father' unintentionally gave me when he increased my intelligence."

Ursal grunted and shuddered. His body expanded rapidly, mountains of muscle and fur erupting from his relatively small normal self. His jumpsuit tore into pieces as his body grew, leaving little more than tatter patches of orange cloth hanging loosely on his body. His claws grew in length until they were like short swords.

Soon, Ursal towered above me. He looked like a normal bear on steroids, his eyes now glowing red. This notification helpfully explained what just happened:

*[Prisoner #379021] used **Nature Unleashed**!*

CHAPTER 26

Crap. I really needed to get my own Ultimate Power at some point. I was starting to feel left out.

Nonetheless, I Scanned Ursal, only to get this message:

Scan [Blocked].

Ursal grinned even more, showing his massive teeth to me. "Tried to Scan me? I'm not stupid. I already let you Scan me once. Knowledge is power, and power is the last thing I want you to have."

I gulped. Although I didn't know exactly how powerful Ursal was now, I could guess he'd at least doubled his Level, and with it, his Stats. He probably still wasn't a match for Old Sparky, but at this point, I think he was more concerned with killing me than with killing Old Sparky.

Even worse, I didn't have anyone to help me. Joe was dead, probably already respawned in our cell where he was stuck, while Dinoczar was in no shape to fight Ursal.

I was completely on my own. And that was pretty scary.

Of course, I wasn't *completely* on my own. I did have access to the Skills and Powers of the woman who I assumed was the Ghost of the Dome, after all. Then again, I still didn't know how to consciously access said Skills and Powers, or if it was even possible to do so on command.

"Ghost," I said under my breath frantically, "now would be a *really* good time to give me a power boost. Like with Bi-Clops."

No response. Of course. Maybe the Ghost had decided to outsource her supernatural killings to Ursal.

"Who are you talking to?" Ursal demanded.

I returned my attention to Ursal. "No one. I was just trying to figure out how I am going to beat your ass into submission."

Ursal chuckled. "I think you have it wrong, Maelstrom. It is *I* who will be beating *your* ass into submission."

I grimaced. "That sounded both wrong *and* threatening coming from you. Good job on that."

Ursal snarled and roared at me.

His roar slammed into me with the force of a tornado. But instead of knocking me over, my muscles locked up, my heart started beating faster than it ever had, and I found I couldn't take my eyes off Ursal.

I had no idea why my body refused to respond to my commands until this notification popped up in my view:

Debuff added: *Paralyzing Fear. -100% in Agility. Duration: 5 minute(s).*

Five minutes—? Ursal must have somehow put a debuff on me that made it impossible for me to move. Not a separate Power, but one of the effects of his Ultimate Power, most likely.

Which meant I was definitely going to die. And it wouldn't even take five minutes for Ursal to do it.

Ursal licked his lips. "Normally, I am not one to devour my enemies. But I think I will *enjoy* crunching your traitorous little bones in my mouth."

I would have given a witty response to that, but unfortunately, the Paralyzing Fear debuff made speaking impossible. Even my eyeballs could barely move.

Ursal clawed at the floor for a moment before lunging at me, mouth wide open, claws held out before him. He flew super-fast despite his bulk, practically sailing through the air like a jet plane.

Stupid body.

Act.

Move.
Do something.
Anything.
No dice.
My body didn't do a damned thing.

I was going to die and it was going to be in the most painful way possible.

Then, without warning, a new notification popped up in my view:

Link activated! [???] has shared her Skills, Stats, and Powers with you! Accept? Y/N

I hit "Y," hoping against hope that [???] had something useful for me.

Instantly, I felt the fear in my bones and muscles melt away. Raw power and strength filled my body, giving me a high unlike anything I'd felt before. It was similar to how I'd felt when I punched out Bi-Clops, only a thousand times stronger.

Unfortunately, I didn't have time to revel in my newfound feeling of power, because Ursal was now less than ten feet away from me.

But I was faster than Ursal.

I reached out with both hands and caught Ursal's mouth with my hands. This brought Ursal to an abrupt halt, the bear-like Villain digging his claws into the floor to avoid crashing into me. His eyes widened in shock and confusion as he looked down at me, clearly unprepared for what I'd just done.

And he was *definitely* going to be unprepared for what I was going to do next.

With a grunt, I lifted Ursal over my head and hurled him across the room. Ursal slammed into the wall with a loud *boom* that shook the entire room, leaving a bear-shaped imprint where he crashed. He slid off the wall and landed on his stomach on the floor, blood leaking out of the corners of his mouth.

Unfortunately, Ursal wasn't dead. With a grunt, he rose unsteadily to his feet and turned to face me. This time, however, I saw fear—bestial fear—in his eyes.

The sort of fear a predator likely felt when it finally ran into something that considered *it* prey.

"That was ... impressive," said Ursal. He wiped blood from his mouth. "You even made me bleed."

I cracked my knuckles. "You said I was supposed to be the Team's muscle, right? This is the muscle you asked for, after all. I'm just giving you what you wanted."

Ursal snarled, yet I could sense the fear flowing through him like a river now. I wasn't sure how, given how I wasn't able to so easily pick up on the emotions of others before. Another Power or Skill from the Ghost, perhaps?

"Because he knows you are his superior now," whispered the voice of the woman in my ear. "The weak fear the strong, and right now, Ursal is very weak. We feast on the weak. It is *our* right."

I raised an eyebrow. "Who are you, lady?"

A soft, ladylike chuckle. "You know that already, young man. All you need to do now is show this pathetic cub why you are a Big Bad."

"You're the Ghost of the Dome?" I whispered back.

Another chuckle, this one far more condescending. "Close. Perhaps if you kill this annoying one, I will give you more hints. Although I believe I've given you enough already. You are a smart one. Figure it out yourself."

Frankly, I felt like I needed more hints before I could figure out her real identity. But I also could tell that the Ghost wasn't going to be giving me any more hints or information about her identity, so there was no point in continuing to ask her about it.

Besides, she had a good point:

I did need to put this uppity bear in his place.

"Who are you talking to?" Ursal demanded.

I shook my head. "That really isn't any of your business. You should focus more on how I am going to give you the beating of a lifetime, you stupid bastard."

Ursal scowled. "You dare to call me stupid? Why, I'll tell you—"

I didn't bother to listen to what he was going to say.

Mostly because I rushed over to him and slammed my fist into his lower jaw.

A sickening *crack* echoed in the air as Ursal staggered from the blow. I followed it up with another punch, then another, each one striking harder and faster than the last. I gave him no time to respond. I wasn't even thinking. I was just letting my body take advantage of the Ghost's power boost to teach Ursal respect.

With a final punch, Ursal fell to my feet with a *thud*. I didn't stop, however. I jumped on top of him and, slamming my foot on his chest, gazed down upon him mercilessly.

Ursal looked absolutely awful. He was missing most of his teeth, one of his eyes was swollen, and his fur was matted with blood. I caught a whiff of blood mixed with wet animal hair, which was not exactly the best smell, although it was a good reminder of the work I'd just done on him.

Ursal gazed up at me, trembling under my foot. "P-Please, Maelstrom, I didn't mean all that awful stuff I said about you earlier. W-We could still be a good team—"

I smashed his face in with my foot. Ursal's head exploded under my boot, sending blood and brains flying everywhere. Some of it even got onto me, but I didn't care. Ursal was getting on my nerves. So I showed him what I thought about his pathetic pleas for life.

A notification popped up in my view:

You killed [Prisoner #379021]! +5,000 EXP.

Your relationship with [Prisoner #379021] has decreased from 'Trusted' to 'Hated'! Now you and [Prisoner #379021] will be enemies for the rest of your lives. Only time will tell how this will affect your future.

Huh. I found it interesting that the experience points didn't actually let me Level up. I assumed that was because I was still Linked with the Ghost, meaning I had her Levels, Stats, Skills, and Powers for the time being. Maybe the DES didn't treat the experience points as my own, which was kind of annoying, although I supposed it didn't matter at the moment. Or perhaps the Dome was still interfering with my ability to level up.

Nor did I care about destroying my relationship with Ursal. It wasn't like it was going to be that important going forward. I didn't need Ursal's help to escape from the Dome. I didn't even like him that much in the first place, so I didn't see this as a loss.

"Brutal," said Abaddon's voice behind me. "Although I can't say it's undeserved."

I turned to face Abaddon. The so-called Lord of Evil stood a few feet away from me, hands in the pockets of his jumpsuit. Behind him, Ralph was still fighting Old Sparky, slashing at the air, only to get blasted in the face by Old Sparky's electricity.

I cocked my head to the side. "You didn't like Ursal, either?"

Abaddon chuckled. "Let's just say I am not a fan of animals that don't know their place and leave it at that. Truth be told, I only joined this Team because I thought it would be fun. And man, has it exceeded my expectations, thanks mostly to you."

I furrowed my brow. "I don't understand. Aren't you angry that I betrayed the Team?"

Abaddon laughed. "You said it yourself. What place does loyalty have among Villains? We're all destined to keep backstabbing each other for short-term profit, even if it hurts us in the long run. If we were capable of much else, none of us would be here, right?"

I shrugged. "Can't argue with that. I guess evil really is stupid."

Abaddon stroked his chin. "Not necessarily. You seem smart, despite being a Villain. Smarter than Ursal, anyway, although given how he was a bear, I guess that isn't saying much."

I stared at Abaddon. "So is that the whole reason you joined the Team? Just to have fun?"

Abaddon nodded. "Sure. Life in Maximum Security is boring as hell. Actually, that's an insult to hell, because hell is at least interesting."

"You sound like you've been there yourself."

Abaddon smiled mysteriously. "In a way, although still nowhere near close to the real thing."

I raised an eyebrow and glanced at the fight between Ralph and Old Sparky. "And the reason you're talking to me instead of helping your demon fight Old Sparky—?"

Abaddon shrugged. "We can't beat Old Sparky. I knew right from the start that this plan would fail. Sooner or later, Old Sparky will land a killing blow on Ralph, and then I'll be next."

I frowned. "You don't sound terribly upset by that."

"I'm kind of a Stoic, in case you couldn't tell," said Abaddon. He smiled. "With a hint of absurdism tossed in for good measure."

"Interesting mixture of philosophies there," I said. "Although you also strike me as a bit nihilistic."

Abaddon spread his arms. "You've seen Old Sparky's power. Dude could probably vaporize every single Maxie at once if he wanted to. Even if everyone teamed up to beat him, Old Sparky would just zap us and that would be that."

"So you think it's impossible to escape from Maximum Security, then," I said.

"I didn't say that," said Abaddon. He winked at me. "If anyone *can* escape from Maximum Security, I'd bet good money it would be you."

I put a hand on my chest. "Me? Why me?"

Abaddon tapped the side of his head. "Because you're smarter than just about anyone else on this Floor, including Ursal and even Old Sparky. You can see a bigger picture than any of us. You have a long-term vision, whereas the rest of us only see our short-term profit and amusement."

I folded my arms in front of my chest. "Thanks for the compliments, I guess."

Abaddon gave me the thumbs-up. "No, thank *you*, Maelstrom, for giving me such a fun night tonight. Should you ever decide you want to try to break out of here yourself ... well, that will be fun to watch, too. See ya."

I blinked. "See ya—? But you're standing right—"

Boom.

A smoking crater had replaced Abaddon, prompting this notification to appear in my vision:

[Warden Old Sparky] killed [Prisoner #299012]!

"That's enough of that, I'm afraid," said Old Sparky's voice overhead.

Looking up, I saw Old Sparky floating in the air, slowly descending toward me. He landed right behind the smoking crater that had once been Abaddon and wrinkled his nose. "Ugh. Forgot how nasty burned demon flesh smells."

Old Sparky had a point. Abaddon's crater did smell like sulfur and brimstone, although I barely paid attention to that because I was still shocked by how quickly Old Sparky had taken out Abaddon. A quick glance toward the stairs showed me Ralph's corpse lying on the stairs, a star-shaped hole burnt straight through his chest. And everyone else was dead already as well, except for Dinoczar, although he was pretty much out for the count as far as I could tell.

Dusting off his hands, Old Sparky looked at me with a smile. "Let's go back to my office. We have a lot to talk about."

CHAPTER 27

Old Sparky's office smelled just like donuts when we entered. As usual, Old Sparky took his seat behind the desk, while I had to sit on the most uncomfortable wooden chair in the world. As soon as I sat down, four thick steel chains wrapped around my arms and legs, giving me those debuffs from my previous visit that would make it difficult for me to attack Old Sparky if I wanted to.

Which I didn't.

Not yet, at least.

Chomping on a donut covered with blue frosting, Old Sparky said, "Good job, kid! Thanks to your efforts, my team and I were able to end the breakout before it even got off the ground. Here are your rewards."

Old Sparky waved his hand in the air and a notification popped up in front of me:

Congratulations! You just completed "MISSION: None dare call it … conspiracy"! +1,000 EXP!

Congratulations! You leveled up to Level 5. +8 Power Points and +16 Stat Points! Continue to level up in order to gain more Power and Stat Points!

Your relationship with [Warden Old Sparky] has increased from

'Distrusted' to 'Liked'! Continue to improve your relationship with [Warden Old Sparky] to gain further benefits.

That second notification, while nice, did not surprise me. After Old Sparky violently slaughtered Team Breakout, I'd received a notification informing me that my Link with the Ghost had been deactivated. I wasn't entirely sure of what that meant other than I apparently no longer had access to her Powers, Skills, etc. That was probably why I was allowed to level up now, since I no longer had her Level.

Although that third notification was interesting. I guess Old Sparky really did like me, after all. I wasn't sure if that was a good thing or a bad thing, however, so I decided to interpret it as a good thing.

"And don't worry about your Sub-Floor promotion," said Old Sparky with a wink. "Once you leave this room, I will have the Prison Guards escort you to your new cell on Sub Floor One. Your Sidekick and Minion are already there."

I nodded, though truth be told, I wasn't happy.

Yes, I'd completed the mission. Yes, I'd leveled up, which was nice. And yes, I'd even gotten promoted to the nicest cell in Maximum Security, which would surely make it easier for me to escape from the Dome when the time came for me to try.

But I felt empty because I had failed to get the one reward I actually wanted: the Emerald Heart.

See, while Abaddon and I had our discussion, Snow had died of blood loss and had probably respawned in her cell by now. And since her Emerald Heart was Soul-Bound, I assumed it had most likely respawned with her.

Without Snow's Emerald Heart, I wasn't at all sure how I'd break out of here. Even Linking with the Ghost only increased my Stats and did not give me access to her actual Powers due to the Dome's Power Negation System. That was a problem, because without being able to use my Powers (or rather, the Ghost's Powers), my odds of escape were lower than I would have liked.

And I needed all the power I could get if I was going to beat Old Sparky.

"So is that it?" I said, gazing at Old Sparky. "Now that the breakout has been thwarted, am I just going to go back to my cell?"

Old Sparky nodded. "Sure. What more do you want? A donut? You can have a donut, if you want."

My stomach growled at the smell of the donuts on the plate on the desk between us, but I still didn't trust them. "No. I was just curious about what would happen to the rest of the members of Team Breakout."

"The conspirators?" Old Sparky said. He shrugged. "They're back in their cells. Duh."

I blinked. "You mean you aren't going to punish them further? I guess that makes sense. They're already in Maximum Security, which is a punishment in itself. It's not like it can get any worse, right?"

Old Sparky laughed. He laughed so hard that he doubled over, slamming his fist on the table, rattling the donut plate and causing a couple of the less secure ones to tumble off onto the papers covering the desk. He didn't stop laughing for a *very* long time, uncomfortably long, making me feel like he was laughing at some super-funny private in-joke that I didn't know anything about.

Finally, after a solid minute of hearty, derisive laughter, Old Sparky calmed down, though he still giggled. "Can't get any worse … good one, kid. Nearly choked on my donut. Congrats, by the way. You came closer to killing me than any other Maxie in the history of this prison."

I grimaced. "What's so funny? Is anything I said wrong? Maximum Security is the lowest Floor in the Dome. There's nowhere else they could go."

Of course, even I knew that was a lie. There was Top Secret, after all, but because I was pretty sure that was supposed to be, well, secret, I did not mention it to Old Sparky. The last thing I needed was to make him more suspicious of me, especially after improving my Relationship with him.

Old Sparky giggled and nibbled on his donut. "I guess no one's told you about the Black Room, huh?"

I blinked. "The Black Room? What's that?"

Old Sparky snapped his free hand.

A holographic screen appeared on the desk in front of me, directly over the donut plate. The screen was pitch-black.

I frowned. "Did you forget to press play on the video you wanted to show me or—"

Old Sparky held a finger up to his lips. "Shh. This is the good part."

I was about to ask Old Sparky what was so "good" about a blank TV screen when a door opened on the screen. Light spilled in from the hallway outside, just enough for me to see the concrete floor of the room but not much else.

Ursal was unceremoniously tossed into the room by an unseen figure outside. Landing roughly on the floor, Ursal rose to his feet and dashed back to the door.

Unfortunately for him, however, the door slammed shut with a *bang*, plunging the room back into pitch-black darkness. That also made it impossible for us to actually see Ursal, leaving the screen dark again.

But I could still hear Ursal just fine. Banging his fists on the door, Ursal shouted, "Let me out of here, you insolent Prison Guards! I do not belong in this place. Let me out *now* or I'll—"

A low rumble, which I belatedly identified as the hungry growl of an unseen animal, interrupted Ursal. I heard his fists stop beating against the door and, in my mind's eye, imagined him turning toward the direction of the growl.

"What was that?" said Ursal, a hint of fear in his voice. Then he suddenly coughed and said, in a far more confident voice, "I don't care what kind of monster you threw in here with me. If, indeed, there is a monster in here at all. Perhaps it is actually a recording of a monster growling, meant to scare me, yet another mental trick meant to torture me. Yes, that is the most likely—"

The growl turned into a tiger-like roar and Ursal screamed. His screams ended abruptly, however, replaced by the sound of teeth chomping into skin, claws ripping apart flesh, and other bestial sounds that made me grateful the screen was black.

A second later, even those sounds died down, and we were left with a silent, black screen once more.

"Is ... is that it?" I said hesitatingly.

Old Sparky grinned. "Watch."

A second later, Ursal's voice came from the shadows loud and clear again. "What … what was that? What happened? Why am I still here? Shouldn't I have respawned in my cell? What the hell is going on—"

That same tiger roar from before. More chomping and slashing. More screams from Ursal.

Then more silence.

Another second or two passed. Ursal's voice again, more panicky than before. "What? Why am I back *here*, of all places? This is inhumane. This is torture. This is—"

The monster roared again, this time far louder than before, and then Ursal screamed.

The holo-screen vanished in an instant, causing me to start. My heart pounding out of my chest, I looked at Old Sparky, who looked like he had just finished watching the greatest horror movie ever.

"That, my son, was the Black Room," said Old Sparky, leaning back in his chair, arms folded in front of his chest. "A torture chamber reserved only for those who try to escape Maximum Security."

I gulped. "I … I don't understand. How does it work?"

Old Sparky smiled. "I think you can figure that out. You're smart. You got enough clues. Use that big brain of yours to find the answer."

Taking a deep breath, I thought back to the video and audio. "It seems like you are feeding Prisoners to some kind of monster. But when the Prisoner dies, they don't respawn in their cell like they normally would. They instantly respawn in the Black Room, presumably because their respawn point is locked there, only to be instantly killed by the monster again. I assume this cycle happens for a long time before the Prisoner is taken out of the Black Room and returned to their cell."

Old Sparky rested his cheek on his fist. "Close. The Prisoner is subjected to the Black Room for three hundred full cycles before they can go back to their cell."

My eyes widened. "Three hundred times—? Does it get any easier?"

Old Sparky barked a laugh. "Of course not! That would defeat the point, which is to utterly crush their spirits and prevent them from even *thinking* about breaking out again."

I gulped. As much as I disliked the other Prisoners and knew that none of them were real human beings, I still thought that was too much. "Is that even legal? I thought torturing Prisoners was outlawed."

Old Sparky tapped the desk with his fingers. "Not here. In the Dome, I have complete and total control over the fate and condition of the Prisoners. The only reason I haven't subjected *all* of those bastards to the Black Room is because I found it's not necessary. Once a Prisoner goes through the Black Room, they usually don't even want to leave their cell, much less Maximum Security, or the Dome itself."

"It still seems cruel to me, though," I said. "And not just because I am a Prisoner or a Villain, either. That just seems to violate basic human decency."

Old Sparky stood up abruptly, shoving his chair back, which fell onto the floor behind him with a *bang*.

Not that Old Sparky seemed to notice or care. He glared at me with the most hateful eyes I'd ever seen on another human being. Sparks of electricity shot off his body, including toward me, but I didn't move because I suspected Old Sparky would annihilate me on the spot if I so much as blinked.

"What gives *you* the right to talk about 'violating basic human decency'?" Old Sparky demanded. He spread his arms wide. "Do you even remember where you are? This is the Dome, a prison specifically designed to contain Villains. And Villains *aren't* good. They certainly don't give a damn about violating the 'basic human decency' of others, yet here you are, preaching to me like I am a sinner in need of repentance."

Old Sparky leaned forward and slammed his fists on the desk hard enough for an audible *crack* to fill the air. He made eye contact with me and, for the life of me, I couldn't break it.

"Here, I am no sinner," Old Sparky said, his voice low. "I am the judge, jury, and executioner. I bring *justice* where there is none. I punish the wicked and reward the righteous. I make sure that no bad guy is allowed to hurt innocent people—especially children—ever again. You know what that makes me, kid?"

I gulped. I couldn't say anything. Even though I knew Old Sparky was just a video game character, right now he seemed like a real person almost.

Old Sparky cracked a grin. "A damn good prison warden, that's what. Any questions?"

I shook my head. I really just wanted to get out of here as soon as possible and not have to worry about Old Sparky losing his mind and smiting me like the god he clearly thought he was.

Old Sparky nodded once. "Good. Again, I must thank you for your cooperation in this important matter, Maelstrom. Should I ever need your services again, I will be sure to call you."

Two Prison Guards suddenly entered the room, undid the chains around my arms and legs, and marched me out of the office.

As we stepped through the doorway, I didn't even bother to cast one last look over my shoulder at Old Sparky.

Mostly because I didn't want him to see how badly he had actually scared me.

CHAPTER 28

"Master!" said Dinoczar about ten minutes later as my Prison Guard escorts shoved me into our new cell. He rolled off the top bunk and, landing on the floor, ran over and hugged me. "Dinoczar missed you so much, master! Dinoczar was worried that you might be in danger."

"I wasn't," said Joe, who was sitting on the floor opposite the bunk bed, paging through what looked like a magazine. "I figured you were getting your 'reward' from Old Sparky for being such a good little snitch, if you catch my drift."

Pulling myself out of Dinoczar's tiny arms, I glared at Joe. "You have a really dirty mind, you know that?"

Joe looked up from his magazine at me, unimpressed. "What? You don't think something like that isn't going on in this hellhole all the time? Or do you think, every time you hear a Prisoner scream, it's because the Prison Guards hit them with their *actual* sticks?"

I grimaced, thinking back to the footage of Ursal being tortured in the Black Room. "There are worse things than that happening in this prison."

Joe rolled his eyes. "So spooky. So ominous. You're only Level Five and you're talking like a Big Bad already. There may be hope for you yet, sir."

Dinoczar gasped. "Joe is right! Master *is* Level Five. So is Dinoczar.

Well, actually, Dinoczar is only Level Three due to only receiving half as many experience points as master, but—"

"That's nice, Dinoczar," I said, interrupting Dinoczar before he could keep talking. I looked around the cell and frowned. "Are you guys sure this is our new cell? It looks exactly the same as our old one."

Joe gave me another deadpan look. "Every cell in this Godforsaken prison is exactly the same. The only thing that's different is the cell number and our relative closeness to the surface. Other than that, same old, same old."

"Dinoczar has already claimed the top bunk as his territory," Dinoczar informed me, "although master may take it if master likes."

I shook my head. "No, Dinoczar, you go ahead. Top bunk is all yours, buddy."

Dinoczar smiled. "Yay! This makes Dinoczar happy."

Joe sighed and looked at the floor. "And I still have the same concrete bed as before. The more things change, the more they stay the same."

I rubbed my forehead and sat down on the bumpy mattress of the second bunk. "Maybe not, but—Wait, the tunnel!"

I looked underneath the bunk bed, but did not feel any air flowing. "Crap. We don't have access to the Prison Guards' locker room anymore."

Joe shuddered. "Good. It smells like the body odor of a thousand sweaty men down there. It should count as torture to send anyone in there who isn't a Prison Guard, in my humble opinion."

"Idiot," I snapped as I stood up, dusting off my jumpsuit. "The Prison Guard locker room gave us a way *out* of our cell that even Old Sparky doesn't know about. Now that we're up here, however, we're even more stuck than we already were."

Joe shrugged. "Then I guess our 'promotion' really wasn't, huh?"

I scowled, but Joe had a point. Old Sparky had unintentionally made it harder for me and my cellmates to scout out the prison and escape. I didn't know if I just had bad luck or if I was outright cursed at this point. Maybe I should have just helped Team Breakout escape and not sold them out to the Warden. At least then I might have escaped Maximum Security.

Sighing, I sat back down on the bed. "Damn it. First we fail to retrieve the Emerald Heart, then we lose access to our only exit to the rest of the prison. If things can get worse, I don't see how."

"I don't know," said Joe, flipping through his magazine. "At least I have entertainment, if nothing else."

I looked up at Joe, frowning. "I was going to ask about that. What magazine is that?"

Joe held up the magazine, showing a picture of a scantily clad woman on the cover. "*Hot Damn!* magazine, of course. It's an adult magazine for mature individuals such as myself."

I gave Joe a deadpan look. "Very mature. I'm sure the pictures are quite entertaining."

Joe snorted. "I don't look at it for the pictures, but rather for the thought-provoking articles. The pictures just make it more ... interesting."

Joe licked his lips when he said 'interesting,' which would have made me shudder. But frankly I'd seen creepier behavior from the Prisoners already, so I wasn't surprised to learn that Joe was something of a degenerate.

Even so, I said, "Why did they give us a magazine? I thought we weren't allowed entertainment."

Joe looked up from the magazine again, annoyance on his face. "I actually got it from Ike and Jorge before we got moved up here. They gave it to me because they consider me a friend now."

I raised an eyebrow. "You made friends with a couple of the Prison Guards? Seriously?"

Joe nodded. "Don't look at me like that. I might be a snarky bastard, but I can be charming and friendly when I want to be, too, you know. Before we got transferred to this cell, I went down to the locker room again, ran into Ike and Jorge, and talked with them some more."

I narrowed my eyes. "I don't remember telling you to go to the locker room again. Did you go while I was asleep?"

"Yep," said Joe. "In fact, I went down on your orders. Are you sure you don't remember that?"

I scowled, but truth was, I didn't. I was still baffled by how my character seemingly came alive of its own free will whenever I logged off and interacted with Dinoczar and Joe. I hadn't realized, however, that my other self was apparently even giving them direct orders while I wasn't around.

I wondered what else my other self did while I was logged off that Dinoczar and Joe hadn't mentioned to me yet.

Not that it really mattered at the moment. Sighing, I rested my head on my hand. "I'd rather have the Emerald Heart than smut at this point. Unfortunately, Snow was still wearing it when she died and I wasn't able to get it off of her before she died."

Dinoczar looked down at me in surprise. "What are you talking about, master? Dinoczar has the Emerald Heart."

I looked up at Dinoczar, almost giving myself whiplash from how fast I looked up at him. "You do? Where?"

Dinoczar held up one of his tiny hands as if to tell me to be patient. "Hold on, sir. Let Dinoczar get it."

Dinoczar gulped and made choking noises. He then fell onto the floor and rolled on his back, kicking his feet wildly in the air, his eyes bugging out of his skull. His Health bar even started to deplete as a notification popped up informing me that Dinoczar had the Choking debuff and was slowly losing HP as a result.

"Dinoczar?" I said, rising to my feet in concern. "Dinoczar, are you okay? Dinoczar?"

Joe rolled his eyes, turning the page of his magazine over. "Drama queen."

Before I could snap at Joe for his insensitivity, Dinoczar hocked once, twice, three times …

And then the Emerald Heart flew out of his mouth.

The Emerald Heart clattered to a stop at my feet. The jewel glistened under the light on the ceiling of our cell, covered in Dinoczar's saliva and whatever other bodily fluids that I did not even want to try to identify right now. It smelled vaguely like the cafeteria's [Slop], too.

Rolling over onto his side, Dinoczar said, in a hoarse voice, "See … master? I … got … the … Emerald Heart …"

Dinoczar coughed and hacked even more, this time helpfully vomiting all over the floor. I wrinkled my nose at the stench.

Fortunately, Dinoczar had made sure to turn around and vomit all over Joe's shoes at the last second, so my shoes did not get dirty.

"Gross!" said Joe, looking down at his shoes. "Why did you have to vomit all over *me*, jackass?"

Dinoczar, licking the vomit off his lips, said, "Because Dinoczar certainly could not vomit all over master. That would simply be disrespectful."

Trying to hide a grin, I bent over to get a better look at the Emerald Heart. "Amazing. Where did you get this? I thought Snow was still wearing it when she died."

Dinoczar rolled around to face me, a proud expression on his face. "Dinoczar stole it while you were fighting Ursal but before Old Sparky noticed. Dinoczar only had enough time to swallow the Emerald Heart before anyone could see it, however, because Dinoczar knew how much master needed this item for our plans."

I scratched my chin. "And the reason you swallowed it rather than, say, hide it in your jumpsuit is—?"

Dinoczar waggled his short arms toward me. "Dinoczar's arms are too short to hide anything anywhere. Plus, there was no time to hide it elsewhere. And Dinoczar can think of no place safer for important objects than his stomach. It is where Dinoczar hides all of his valuables, after all."

I furrowed my brows. "You hide all of your valuables in your stomach."

Dinoczar nodded. "Yes. That includes Dinoczar's ID, wallet, and even a shiny penny Dinoczar found on the floor a few days ago. T-Rex stomachs are well-known for their privacy and security. After all, no one has ever stolen anything from a T-Rex stomach before, right?"

I was pretty sure T-Rex stomachs didn't work even remotely like that, but at the same time, I was also pretty sure Dinoczar wasn't like most T-Rexes. And hey, he was technically correct. I certainly had never heard of anyone performing a heist on a dinosaur tummy and probably never would.

Joe held up a hand. "Hey, Dinoczar wasn't the only one who stole something. I stole this from that Glob guy when he wasn't looking."

Joe fished out a key card from his pocket and held it up for me to see.

I narrowed my eyes. "Isn't that the Emergency Access Key?"

Joe flashed me a smirk. "Sure is. Nicked it off Glob when he wasn't looking. Not an observant one, that one."

I stroked my chin. "Well, I can't complain about that. Good job, man. I suspect that that will be very useful when we do our own breakout later. Don't lose it."

Joe put the Emergency Access Key back into his jumpsuit. Patting the pocket where he'd put the Key, Joe said, "Don't worry about me, boss. I won't let it out of my sight."

I nodded. I hadn't realized how useful Joe's thieving Skills were until now. I made a mental note to think of other ways to use his Skills in the future. They could be useful.

But for now, I had a more important item to worry about: the Emerald Heart.

Gingerly picking up the jewel, I suddenly received this notification:

The original owner of the Emerald Heart perished while not wearing this item on their person! Would you like to Claim the Emerald Heart as your own and bind it to your soul? **Y/N**

Curious, I said, "It's asking me if I want to 'Claim' the Emerald Heart."

"That's how you get it bound to your soul, idiot," said Joe irritably. "Unless you want either me or Dinoczar to have it, you'll have to Claim it yourself."

Deciding to ignore Joe's insults, I clicked "Y" and the notification was replaced by this:

Congratulations! You have successfully Claimed the Emerald Heart! The Emerald Heart is now bound to your soul, meaning it will respawn with you even if you die, although only while you are wearing it or it is in your inventory. Check out more information about the Emerald Heart in your inventory!

Eager, I opened my menu and tabbed over to my item inventory, where I found the Emerald Heart listed. I clicked its name on the list, and it showed me the Emerald Heart's properties. Most of it was stuff

I'd already seen when I'd had a chance to Scan it earlier, but the description now included this key phrase:

Protects the wearer and nearby allies from Power Negation Fields.

I grinned. Now Dinoczar, Joe, and I could use our Powers as freely as the Warden or the Prison Guards. That would be *very* helpful for planning our own breakout.

Of course, the problem was that none of us really had any Powers to speak of. Even so, I was still Linked with the Ghost, which meant that I could now use her Powers, whatever they might be.

Thinking of the Ghost, I looked at Dinoczar and said, "Dinoczar, I have a question for you. What is Linking?"

Dinoczar perked up when I asked that question. "Linking, sir?"

I nodded. "Yeah. It's a term I came across in my, uh, research, but I don't know what it means."

Of course, I didn't want to tell Dinoczar or Joe about my Link with the Ghost just yet. Even though Dinoczar and Joe were literally my only allies in the Dome (minus possibly Abaddon, although I had no idea where he was), I still didn't trust them quite enough to tell them about the Ghost or even just my suspicions about it. I needed more information before I could start telling them that I thought a ghost lady was giving me enough power to make me stronger than most of the other Prisoners.

Although another thought occurred to me: Wasn't keeping secrets from your Minions something that an actual Big Bad would do? It certainly seemed like a stereotypical supervillain thing to me. How many supervillains refused to divulge important information to their Minions because they just didn't trust them for some reason? And how often did that lead to their untimely yet poetically just demise?

Maybe I really was becoming a Big Bad after all. Or maybe I was just overthinking things again.

My thoughts were interrupted when Dinoczar said, "Linking is a very rare ability, sir, one even Dinoczar knows little about. But Dinoczar does know that certain Heroes and Villains can Link with other Heroes or Villains to gain temporary access to their Powers, Skills, Stats, and so on."

I nodded. "Is this ability available to all players or just certain ones?"

Dinoczar shook his head quickly. "It is available only to a select few, sir. Only players with the Link Skill can do it."

Hmm. Back when I first started playing the game, I noticed I had a Skill called 'Link' on my character sheet. I hadn't thought much about it at the time, thinking it was just another useless Skill, but if what Dinoczar said was true, then I really was lucky.

Maybe not lucky, though. Maybe a certain grandfather of mine rigged the game so I'd start with that Skill. Grandpa had interfered with everything else so far. Why wouldn't he give me that particular advantage, too?

In any case, I said aloud, "Then I guess I must be really lucky, because I happen to have that Skill on my character sheet."

Dinoczar gasped. "You do, sir? Amazing! Have you tried Linking with anyone yet?"

I shook my head, perhaps a little too quickly. "Uh, no. I haven't tried Linking with anyone yet. How do I do that?"

Dinoczar waved his tiny hands together. "You can only Link with other people who you have a strong affinity with already."

I pursed my lips. "A strong affinity? What does that mean?"

A thoughtful expression crossed Dinoczar's face. "Let us see if Dinoczar can explain … You can only Link with other people who have the same Class as you, generally speaking, or me, your Sidekick. As a Big Bad, therefore, you can only Link with other Big Bads."

"Of which there seem to be very few in this place," I noted.

Joe chuckled. "Big Bads are one of the rarer Villain Classes out there, mostly because they tend to be the most overpowering. That's probably why we haven't run into too many of them here yet. I imagine the more dangerous ones are probably in Top Secret."

I nodded. "Right. We still need to figure out how to get down there."

Joe gave me a quizzical look. "Why? We don't even know how to get down there. Shouldn't we focus on escaping this place, like we originally planned?"

I gingerly picked up the Emerald Heart off the floor by its chain, causing the green gem hanging from it to swivel in the air. "If there's one thing Team Breakout's plan did teach me, it was that we won't be able to break out of here on our own. We'll need allies, preferably ones strong enough to take on Old Sparky, and I suspect we'll find them in Top Secret."

Joe snorted again. "You mean like Rock Lord? Who got one-shotted by Old Sparky? Those Top Secret guys have had an excellent track run against the Warden so far."

"Because Rock Lord was still affected by the Dome's Power Negation System," I pointed out. "And because Old Sparky's level scaling ability means he's effectively invincible. If we can get some of the powerhouses down in Top Secret to help us, however, I could give them their Powers back with the Emerald Heart."

"And then they could provide useful distractions for us while we run away!" Dinoczar said. He gave me a knowing look. "You really are so clever, master. Makes Dinoczar proud to be your Sidekick."

I shook my head. "No. We can't just use them as pawns, as useful as that might be for our own ends. If we are really going to break out of here, we're going to need a Team that won't fall apart at a moment's notice or is susceptible to bribes and external pressures."

Joe gave me a disbelieving look. "You do realize that every single Prisoner in here is a Villain, right? And Villains, by our very nature, are self-centered assholes who are always looking out for number one. That's just how we are."

I rose to my feet. "But is it how we are *supposed* to be? Is it how we *should* be? I'm not saying we should become Heroes, which is probably impossible. But if we can form an effective, functional Team that can stand united against Old Sparky and the Prison Guards, then we might just be able to break out of this place."

"That idea sounds as ridiculous as the Tooth Fairy, sir," said Dinoczar. He smiled. "But Dinoczar trusts master, so count Dinoczar in."

Joe sighed. "It's not like I have much of a choice, but fine. We'll see if we can form a Villain Team that doesn't inevitably fall apart due to backstabbing and stupid drama. Your funeral. And probably mine, too, now that I think about it, but don't say I didn't tell you so."

I nodded in understanding.

Truth be told, I didn't need either Dinoczar's or Joe's support. As their Big Bad, they were obligated to follow my commands, no matter how much they might disagree with them.

Having said that, though, it was nice to know that I had their support. It would make things a lot easier for me, that was for sure.

In actuality, however, I was thinking about my conversation with Abaddon when I said all of that. Abaddon, despite his pessimistic description of Villains, had given me an important clue to breaking out of here: that was the generally, well, villainous nature of Villains and learning to factor that into my own plans.

In order to break out of here, however, I was going to need more allies, hopefully allies I could trust. Powerful allies, too, who might be able to stand a chance against Old Sparky.

Hence why I wanted to enter Top Secret. I'd been meaning to try to go there for a while, but now more than ever, I was convinced of the necessity of figuring out the mystery of that Floor.

But first, I had just leveled up.

And what did you do whenever you leveled up your character in a video game and got points to distribute?

Why, you immediately used them up in the most efficient and logical way, of course.

CHAPTER 29

WHAT, DID YOU THINK I WAS JUST GOING TO LEAVE THE POINTS UNUSED because I wasn't sure how and where to distribute them? That would be weird. What sort of real gamer leaves PPs and SPs unspent just because they weren't sure where to put them and they had no external pressure preventing them from using them?

That would just be silly.

Sitting back down on my bed, I opened my spreadsheet to see where my character currently stood:

Secret Identity: *Prisoner #112023 (locked by the Dome)*
Real Identity: *Robert John Baker*
Level: *5*
EXP: *6/1,789*
Available Stat Points: *16*
Available Power Points: *8*
Alignment: *Villain*
Class: *Big Bad*
Type: *Water*
Reputation: *Unknown*
Powers: *Super Strength [Level 1]*
Skills: *Link [Level 1], Scan [Level 1], Perception [Level 1], Dodge [Level 1],*
Equipment: *Prison Jumpsuit*

Minions: 1/5

Health: 25
Stamina: 13
Strength: 10
Defense: 13
Charisma: 10
Intelligence: 19
Agility: 13
Evasion: 8
Accuracy: 11
Dexterity: 18
Energy: 14
Luck: 0

VILLAIN STATS:
Cunning: 10
Manipulation: 13
Infamy: 1
Terror: 8
Hatred: 10

Good to see that my Minion count had increased, from 3 to 5. Based on how many Minions I gained in comparison to the number of times I leveled up, it seemed like I gained the ability to control one more new Minion every two Levels or so. Easy enough to understand, although unfortunately not immediately applicable to me right now before of my current lack of access to Minions other than Joe.

But I had plenty of Stat and Power Points to spend. I decided to spend my Power Points first, dumping all of them into Super Strength. That may have seemed a bit risky—putting all of your eggs in one basket generally was—but I also had no choice, seeing as I didn't have any other Powers at the moment and there was no telling when I would get another, seeing as Power Crystals were in short supply for me at the moment. Looked like I just needed to spend two more PPs to get Super Strength to Level 2, which I would definitely do the next time I leveled up.

As for my Stat Points, that was a bit more difficult. I had sixteen of those bad boys and a much greater variety of Stats than Powers, meaning I had way more options for how to spend my SPs than I did for my PPs.

But in the end, the choice was obvious: I dumped six of my SPs into Intelligence and ten into Charisma, bringing them up to twenty-five and twenty, respectively.

You might be wondering why I decided to put all of my SPs into just those two Stats, rather than spread them around a bit more evenly. That idea might have made sense under different circumstances, but knowing what I did now about how the Big Bad Class worked, as well as what I'd need for the breakout, these were actually the two most logical Stats to min-max.

Big Bads, from my understanding, were focused less on physical or even Energy-based combat and more on controlling, manipulating, and directing others, especially their Minions. While I didn't know if the Intelligence Stat actually raised my IQ or not, I assumed it made it easier for me to control my Minions and strategize and plan.

As for Charisma, like I said before, I would need as many allies as I could get if we were going to have a chance in hell of escaping Maximum Security and the Dome alive. The Charisma Stat seemed to influence how well you persuaded others to support or help you. And while I wasn't the most charismatic individual in the real world, I could at least be more charming in-game, where it mattered a lot more. That was why I put slightly more SPs into Charisma than Intelligence, as I felt it would be a more immediately useful Stat than Intelligence.

With that out of the way, I closed my character sheet. I considered looking at Dinoczar and Joe's character sheets, but given how they both auto-leveled on their own, I saw no reason to worry about them. I would worry about them later, when and if I needed to.

Standing up, I said, "All right. I just finished adjusting my character sheet. I'm all set."

"Good for you," said Joe. He sighed and looked into the air, as if seeing something I couldn't. "Meanwhile, I, as a Minion, have zero control over my Stats. All I can do is watch as I level up and everything follows your Stats except weaker."

"Dinoczar also finished adjusting his Stats," Dinoczar said proudly. "Dinoczar is ready for whatever the world has to throw at Dinoczar now."

I nodded. "Appreciate the confidence, Dinoczar, but I think the next step of my plan will require me to go alone."

Dinoczar frowned. "Go alone? Where?"

"Where else?" I said. I pointed down at the floor. "Top Secret, of course."

Joe scowled. "You keep saying that, but you also haven't explained how you even plan to get down there. Ike and Jorge made it sound like only a handful of people in the Dome have access to Top Secret, so unless you're going to try stealing a key from the Warden, then I don't see how we're going to pull this off."

I stroked my chin. Joe raised a valid point. Given how Top Secret was, well, top secret, it wasn't like I would be able to just waltz on in. And, of course, we were still stuck in our cell, too, meaning yet another obstacle to overcome.

I needed to escape my cell first, as well as identify who had a key to Top Secret in the first place.

Old Sparky definitely had one, but like Joe said, stealing from him would be … challenging, to put it lightly. As well, I'd need to break into his office, which was probably protected by various security measures, too.

Yet I saw no other option for me than to sneak into Old Sparky's office, steal a key to Top Secret, and leave before he knew it was missing.

And then there was locating the entrance to the Floor itself. However, I wasn't as worried about that as I was about other things, because I still had the Map of the Dome, which showed where Top Secret was. Presumably, if I inspected the Map more closely, I'd learn where the entrance to Top Secret was, too. I wondered if inspecting the Map would also give me that Cartography Skill that Ursal mentioned having.

Tapping my chin, I said, "You know, Joe, that's actually a good idea."

"What?" said Joe. "Stealing from the Warden? Are you crazy or just stupid?"

I shook my head. "It's neither. It makes a lot of sense. Old Sparky is probably the only person with a key to Top Secret. Therefore, if I want to get down there, I'll need to steal from him first."

Joe shook his head. "Utter insanity, unless getting fried like chicken is on your bucket list for some reason."

Dinoczar licked his lips. "It has been a long time since Dinoczar has had fried chicken. That will be the first thing Dinoczar eats after he gets out of here."

I looked at Dinoczar. "You have a bucket list of food you want to eat when we escape from the Dome?"

Dinoczar nodded eagerly. "Yes! Fried chicken is at the very top. After that is bacon, pizza, spaghetti, curry, and, perhaps the most important, the legendary Elvis sandwich, named after a legendary king from long ago whose musical talents are said to be like those of the gods."

"You mean Elvis Presley?" said Joe.

Dinoczar shrugged. "Dinoczar does not know the king's name, but Dinoczar figures that any sandwich made by a king must be fit for a king. And seeing as Dinoczar is the king of dinosaurs, it is only right that Dinoczar eat a sandwich fit for a king."

"Good to have goals, buddy," I said, patting Dinoczar on the shoulder. "And honestly, an Elvis sounds a lot better than any amount of [Slop] they serve here."

"We're kind of getting off-topic, though," said Joe. "You know? The topic about how you are going to get yourself killed and/or tortured by stealing from Old Sparky?"

I stroked my chin again. "Not necessarily. Joe, you still have the Secret Identity Power, right? Plus Stealth, Pick Pocket, and Lock Pick?"

Joe nodded slowly. "Yeah. What are you getting at?"

I smiled. "Think I am going to put your Powers and Skills to good use. I am going to put them to *very* good use."

Joe gulped. "Not sure I like the way you said *very*."

I winked at Joe. "Don't worry, Joe. If everything works out the way I think it will, then none of us will get hurt. Gather around and listen to my plan, because if we're going to pull this heist off, then we really only have one chance to do it …"

CHAPTER 30

"Ugh," said Joe the next day at lunchtime, staring at the steaming bowl of [Slop] set before him. He rubbed his stomach. "I'm not sure my stomach can handle another day of more slop."

Dinoczar slurped up the contents of his bowl instantly and licked his lips. "While it is not the tastiest food Dinoczar has ever had, Dinoczar does not see any problem with it. What about you, master? Master?"

Snapped out of my thoughts, I looked at Dinoczar in confusion. "Huh? What? Oh, I agree with Joe. This food is terrible."

Joe smirked at Dinoczar. "See? Even the boss agrees with me that this crap is crap."

Dinoczar pouted. "Well, Dinoczar still likes it. Can Dinoczar have yours?"

"Would you two stop arguing about food?" I said, keeping my voice low. "We need to remain aware of our surroundings if we are going to pull off this plan."

Joe gave me a harsh look. "Why? Old Sparky isn't here. I doubt he'll show up. He's probably still holed up in his office, gorging himself on donuts and beating his meat to videos of Prisoners getting tortured in the Black Room like the fat bastard he is."

Joe had a point. The cafeteria, although heavily patrolled by Prison Guards and Drones alike, was noticeably absent of Old Sparky himself. I did see the other Prisoners sitting around us, however, although many of the closest tables to ours had been vacated for some reason. That included Ursal, who had moved from his table to one where he sat with a couple of other Prisoners I didn't recognize but who I assumed were his cellmates.

Ursal looked rough. Not physically, since he looked normal physically. It was the way he sat. Hunched over his bowl of [Slop], eyes practically bulging out of his skull, Ursal hadn't actually touched his food as far as I could tell. He just shook silently, his eyes staring into the distance, as if gazing at something only he could see.

Nor was Ursal the only Prisoner who looked traumatized. Snow, Skin, and Glob, who sat pretty far away from us, had similar expressions and body languages as Ursal. Only Abaddon, who sat by himself at a table in the corner, looked unconcerned, calmly eating his [Slop] and drinking his lukewarm water as if he hadn't been killed and forcibly respawned over three hundred times in a row just last night.

Man, Abaddon was hardcore.

"Why is everyone avoiding us, anyway?" I said, looking around the cafeteria. "We're not that scary, are we?"

Joe held up two fingers. "Two reasons. One, everyone still remembers—and fears—how you took down Bi-Clops. And two, I'm pretty sure everyone knows you're the one who snitched on Team Breakout by now."

"What?" I said in alarm. "How? I didn't tell anyone."

"Old Sparky apparently did," said Joe. "Or did you not notice the message everyone received after Old Sparky killed Team Breakout?"

"Message …?" I opened my inbox and, after scrolling through several messages from Capes Online Customer Support regarding updates and patches to the game's code made recently, finally found a message from Old Sparky dated the night before.

The subject line was "RE: Failed breakout" and read thusly:

Prisoners of the Dome,

At midnight last night, a Team of Maxies calling themselves Team Breakout attempted to escape from Maximum Security behind our backs. Fortunately, thanks to help from Prisoner #112023, or Mael-

strom, as you might know him, the prison administration was able to put an end to the breakout before the Prisoners could escape.

Please find attached video and audio recordings of the fates of the failed escapees in the Black Room for your viewing information.

Old Sparky
Prison Warden and Administrator

Indeed, attached to the message were several video files showing the torture of the Team Breakout members in the Black Room. Granted, perhaps "showing" wasn't the right word, seeing as the video was mostly black, but you could hear the screams of the tortured Prisoners and the noises made by the monster as it killed them over and over again just fine.

Dismissing my inbox before the sounds of torture could make me lose my lunch, I said, "Damn it. That bastard."

"Who, Old Sparky?" said Joe with a snort. "Looks like your plan to form a Team of Prisoners to break out of the Dome is going to be harder than you thought."

My hands balled into fists on the table. "It's fine. I was always planning to get the Prisoners of Top Secret on my side. I don't need the other Maxies. At least, I don't need most of them."

Joe shrugged, pushing his bowl of [Slop] toward Dinoczar, who ate it happily. "If you say so. I'm just saying that there's a reason no one wants to associate with us. Even Villains don't like snitches."

I scowled. Joe's mention of snitches reminded me of the mission notification I'd received when Old Sparky first offered me the mission to uncover the breakout conspiracy. It had said that "snitches get stitches," but as far as I could tell, that only happened if the other Prisoners were not deathly afraid of you for some reason.

Shaking my head, I said, "This still doesn't change the plan."

Joe, tapping the table with one finger, raised an eyebrow. "You mean the one where we start a riot in the cafeteria that forces the Warden to show up so you can steal his key to Top Secret? That plan?"

I held up a finger to my lips to shush Joe. "Shhh! Do you want the Guards to overhear us?"

Joe, in a much softer tone than before, said, "Sorry. I just wanted to make sure I knew how stupid our plan was."

"It's not stupid," I said. "It makes perfect sense. The last time Old Sparky showed up in the cafeteria was when Rock Lord appeared. I think if we can start a riot so bad that even the Prison Guards can't handle it, it will force Old Sparky to come out of his office to stop it. Then I can snatch the key from his person and use it to enter Top Secret."

Joe continued to tap the table with the fingers of his left hand. "And I am telling you that your plan has all sorts of holes in it. First off, what if Old Sparky doesn't show up? Second, even if you do steal his key, how are you going to get down to Top Secret and use it? That's assuming he doesn't even feel you nicking the key off his person in the first place, which I wouldn't put past him."

I scowled. "And I already answered your objections, but if you'd like a repeat: First, Old Sparky is obsessed with order and hates any chaos or riots happening under his watch in the Dome, so he'll definitely show up. As for getting to Top Secret, that's why you are going to pretend to be me using Secret Identity. That way, no one will notice my absence when I sneak out of the cafeteria. After all, the cafeteria is on the lowest Sub-Floor of Maximum Security, so Top Secret should be nearby."

Joe frowned. "I forgot about the part where I'm supposed to pretend to be you. That definitely isn't risky."

I sighed. "Remember, the idea is that we will start a really chaotic riot. You will 'die' during it, which will explain *your* absence, while I will be using your Powers to craft a fake Prison Guard identity so I can sneak out and about the halls of Maximum Security unseen. So long as you act like me, it should work."

"Dinoczar trusts in master's plan," said Dinoczar. "What is Dinoczar's role again?"

I patted Dinoczar on the shoulder. "Make sure that Joe doesn't get killed during the riot. If he dies and respawns in our cell, he won't look like me anymore, which will alert the Prison Guards that I am no longer in my cell."

"But what if I don't respawn?" said Joe. "Won't they notice if I don't respawn in my cell?"

I shook my head. "They shouldn't. The riot will be so bad that they won't be paying attention to our prison cells. And by the time they are, I will have returned to our cell, pretending to be Joe, and no one will suspect a thing. As I said, the plan is foolproof."

"Exactly how will you get to our cell before we do?" said Joe.

I gave Joe a long-suffering look. "Every cell in Maximum Security is unlocked during mealtimes because no one is inside them. I don't even need a key. As long as I get there before you guys—which, thanks to the Emergency Access Key you gave me, I should be able to do—we should be fine."

Dinoczar nodded. "You are so smart, master! Dinoczar wishes he could be as smart as you."

Joe glared at Dinoczar. "Only because yours is the easy part. Mine is probably going to get me killed."

"It shouldn't, if Dinoczar does his part," I said. I gestured toward Bi-Clops's table on the other side of the cafeteria. "Now go over to Bi-Clops. You know what to do next."

Joe sighed heavily, but rose from his seat at our table and walked over to Bi-Clops's table, where Miss Hiss, Shorty, and the other Prisoners also sat, eating and laughing. As Joe walked, I distinctly heard him mutter under his breath, "I should have just let Dinoczar eat me … being a Minion is so stupid …"

One might wonder why I sent Joe over to Bi-Clops and the other Prisoners. That was simple.

In order to start the riot, I needed to find a way to inflame the emotions of the other Prisoners. Given how everyone was too afraid of me to cross me, however, I knew I would struggle to provoke anyone. Even if I walked up to Ursal and socked him in the face and called his mother a whore right to his face, Ursal and the other former members of Team Breakout were simply too traumatized to fight back.

Joe, on the other hand, lacked my Infamy among the Prisoners. Or rather, he had a different sort of Infamy. In his previous life, Joe had apparently stolen from and double-crossed a surprisingly large number of Maxies. That included Bi-Clops and his clique, but I suspected there were other Maxies who probably had similar motivations for hating Joe.

I was also betting on the generally dysfunctional nature of Villains to rear its head. Tension was running high in the Dome and especially among the Maxies, who probably felt like caged animals. I could easily see some of the Maxies deciding to take advantage of the chaos to attack the Prison Guards under the delusional belief that they might be able to escape from here.

But I knew there were other Villains here who didn't really need a reason to riot. Brutes and thugs who looked for any excuse to get violent, even if that excuse was paper thin.

And, of course, I fully expected the Prison Guards to get involved. They would undoubtedly try to put down the riot, which would serve only to inflame it. Once it got out of control, then Old Sparky would have to make an appearance to end it, at which point I could do my part of the plan.

In my mind's eye, I saw the plan like a line of neatly placed dominoes. Once you tipped over the first one, the rest of the dominoes would naturally have to fall.

Joe soon reached Bi-Clops's table. Though Joe was too far away for me to hear, I accessed the Command Interface in my menu, letting me see and hear what Joe saw and heard far more efficiently and clearly.

"What do you want, shrimp?" Bi-Clops demanded in his usual gravelly tone, although I noticed that he didn't raise his hands or try to do anything intimidating. Probably still remembered how I punched him out not long ago.

Joe folded his arms in front of his chest. "I just wanted to say that you have a face that only a mother could love."

Bi-Clops narrowed his eyes. "I killed my mom. Your point?"

I grimaced, as did Joe, who said, "I guess you're not winning any Son of the Year awards, then."

Bi-Clops growled, but still did not attack Joe. "If you came over here just to troll me, then don't bother. I know the only reason you feel safe is because you know that your boyfriend is gonna keep you safe."

Joe raised an eyebrow. "*My* boyfriend? Don't sound so jealous. You can have him if you want. I'm sure you'd make a great bot—"

Bi-Clops's fist flew through the air and slammed into Joe. The blow sent Joe flying into the next table, causing it to collapse under the impact. The other Prisoners who had been sitting around that table quickly scurried away, including a particularly large man whose biceps seemed to be bigger than his head.

"Huh?" said the bulky man, staring at Joe lying on the table before him. "Where did you come from?"

Joe, miraculously still alive, coughed and pointed at Bi-Clops. "He threw me over here because he thinks you're fat and stupid."

The bulky man growled and glared at Bi-Clops. "You think I'm fat, huh? Why don't you come over here and say that to my face, you idiot?"

Bi-Clops rose from the table, cracking his knuckles. "My fight isn't with you, moron. It's with that little shrimp I threw at your—"

Bi-Clops never got to finish his sentence before the bulky man roared and rushed toward him. The bulky man body-slammed Bi-Clops, sending the two-headed Prisoner crashing into his table, getting [Slop] all over him.

In a flash, Shorty, who had jumped away from the table along with the other members of Bi-Clops's clique, drew a knife from nowhere and stabbed the bulky Prisoner. The bulky Prisoner roared in pain as Bi-Clops rose to his feet, both of his massive eyes glaring at the bulky Prisoner angrily.

Good. The riot was almost started, but I knew it needed something a bit more just to make sure it happened.

So I opened my item inventory, selected the Emerald Heart, and activated its ability to protect the user and others from the Power Negation System. I selected myself, Joe, Dinoczar, Bi-Clops, and the bulky Prisoner as the targets.

As you might have guessed, I had spent some time fiddling with the Emerald Heart between last night's failed breakout and lunch today. I learned that I could apparently share the Emerald Heart's protection with up to five other people at once.

And even better: I didn't need to be physically near them for the Emerald Heart's protection to work.

Unfortunately, it did activate a timer of about an hour and a half, which began ticking down as soon as I activated the Emerald Heart's ability.

But it was worth it, because in the next instant, Bi-Clops's eyes glowed red and he launched two laser beams from his eyes at the bulky Prisoner. The laser beams shot straight through the bulky Prisoner's heart, making him gasp in pain before collapsing onto the ground, dead as a doornail.

And then the cafeteria fell silent as every eye in the room—Prisoner and Prison Guard alike—turned to focus on Bi-Clops. Even Bi-Clops looked shocked, staring in disbelief at the smoking corpse of the bulky Prisoner. Given how Bi-Clops didn't know about the Emerald Heart, I could well understand where his confusion was coming from.

Then the silence was broken by a Prison Guard raising a gun and shouting, "Get down!"

And then all hell broke loose.

The Prison Guard started shooting at Bi-Clops, who somehow managed to leap out of the way of the bullets before they could hit him. As soon as the Prison Guard started shooting, however, a Maxie sitting at a nearby table suddenly threw a bowl of [Slop] at him. The bowl nailed the Prison Guard in the head, causing him to turn his gun on that Maxie, only for another Maxie to jump him from behind and struggle with him for his gun.

Naturally, this prompted the other Prison Guards to rush over to help their fellow Guard, only for more Maxies to rise up from their tables and join the fray. Some attacked the Prison Guards, while others took advantage of the chaos to settle some grudges they had with other Prisoners. There were already bodies on the floor, mostly Prisoners at this point, but I expected the ratio between Guards and Prisoners to even out soon.

All in all, things were going swimmingly.

As for myself, I hid under our table with Dinoczar. You might be surprised to learn that the underside of the cafeteria tables were surprisingly spacious, so I didn't feel too cramped with Dinoczar by my side.

"So much chaos, sir," said Dinoczar, glancing around the room. "Dinoczar wants to join in on the fun!"

I pointed ahead. "Go ahead. Joe needs your help. Remember, your job is to make sure he doesn't get killed, okay?"

Dinoczar nodded. "Yes, sir! Dinoczar will not disappoint you, master. Good luck!"

With that, Dinoczar jumped out from under the table, roared at the top of his lungs, and plunged into the riot. I watched as Dinoczar bit and clawed his way through the increasingly rowdy riot toward Joe, who had also taken shelter underneath one of the tables.

Sighing in relief, I knew that now, all I needed to do was wait for Old Sparky to show up. And once he appeared, I could sneak the Top Secret key from him.

Actually …

I opened my character sheet, ignoring the sheer chaos going on all around me, and toggled over to the MINIONS tab, where I clicked the MINIONS POWER tab. Once again, I was shown a list of Minions I currently controlled, which of course was just Joe.

Still, I clicked Joe's name and this notification came up:

Do you want to use this Minion's Powers and Skills? **Y/N**

Smiling, I clicked "Y" and this notification appeared:

Congratulations! You can now use all of your Minion's Powers and Skills yourself! Go to your character sheet to activate each Power.

Toggling back to my character sheet, I saw that I did indeed have Joe's Powers and Skills listed under my own. They were clearly labeled "Minion Powers" and "Minion Skills," probably to help me distinguish them from my own Powers and Skills.

The one I was most interested in, however, was Secret Identity. Clicking on that, I received this notification:

You have activated Secret Identity! Choose your Secret Identity from the list below:

- Prison Guard Mike
- Polite Young Man Joseph

- Definitely Not a Purse Thief Mitchell

I raised an eyebrow at the last two. Were those previous fake identities that Joe had used in the past? Probably. Wouldn't put it past him.

But Prison Guard Mike seemed like the most useful to me, so I picked that. Then this notification showed up:

Confirm choosing [Prison Guard Mike] as your Secret Identity? **Y/N**

I hit "Y" without thinking and then the notification disappeared.

And then ... nothing happened.

Seriously. My body didn't change shape. I didn't even feel any different. Looking down at myself, I looked and felt just the same as I always did. Did the Power not work or something? If not, then we were going to be in *big* trouble and I was going to have to abort the entire—

"Mike!" a nearby voice yelled. "The hell are you doing under that table?"

Startled, I looked out from under the table to see another Prison Guard—this one named [PRISON GUARD HOWARD]—standing not far from me. Clutching a gun, Howard glared at me like I was sitting around doing nothing.

"Uh, um," I stuttered. "I was taking a ... tactical position? To shoot the Prisoners from a safe distance?"

Howard scowled. "Get out from under that table and stop acting like this is some kind of video game! We have a riot to put down and if we don't stop it before Old Sparky gets here, then we'll *all* die. Got it?"

Before I could tell Howard that I understood, a Maxie with a chainsaw for a head rushed toward Howard and tackled him. Howard screamed in terror as they both disappeared into the rioting happening all around me, although I could hear the splatter of blood and the sound of steel teeth ripped through flesh well enough. Howard's key ring flew off his person and landed with a clatter in front of me. I quickly grabbed it, thinking it might be useful to have for later.

Interesting. Even though I looked and felt the same to me, I apparently must have looked like a Prison Guard to everyone else. That was good. It meant that Secret Identity was working.

Unfortunately, I couldn't just hide under the table forever. I needed to get somewhere safer, at least until Old Sparky arrived. Based on Howard's comments, it sounded like Old Sparky was on the way already.

Crawling out from underneath the table, I spotted an opening through the riot and rushed toward it. Ducking to avoid flying bullets from the Prison Guards, I kept my eyes on the cafeteria exit. If I could just reach it in time, then maybe I could—

Without warning, I tripped over something soft and slimy and landed on my hands and knees. Looking over my shoulder, I saw that a familiar green slime was wrapped around my ankle.

And holding the other end, a wicked grin on his face, was Glob.

"Where do you think you're going, Guard?" said Glob, licking his lips. "The fun has just started. Let's play."

CHAPTER 31

CRAP. I COULDN'T LET MYSELF GET DISTRACTED FIGHTING GLOB. OLD Sparky would be here any minute and I needed to be in the perfect position to steal from him if I was going to pull off my plan.

"Let go of me, you stupid Prisoner," I growled in my best fake Prison Guard voice.

Glob cocked his head to the side. "Why should I? I don't know if this riot will lead to a breakout, but it gives me a great excuse to get some good old-fashioned vengeance on you Prison Guards who have been nothing but mean to us. So I'll take advantage of it as much as I can."

Glob's slimy form was already rising up my leg. I pulled as hard as I could but I couldn't escape. Even though Glob was probably the weakest member of Team Breakout, I had to remember that he was still much higher leveled than me. He wouldn't be in Maximum Security otherwise. That meant that escaping him would be very difficult.

That was when I noticed a fallen gun from one of the other Prison Guards lying underneath a table nearby. I reached out to grab it, only for Glob to yank me back, pulling me out of the reach of the gun.

"No guns for you," said Glob, shaking his head, sending bits of his blobby form flying everywhere. "We're going to do things nice and easy. And by 'nice and easy,' I mean I am going to suffocate you with my slime."

I bit my lower lip. I didn't fancy getting suffocated by Glob, but it was starting to look like that was going to be my fate. I tried to reach out to the Ghost for help, but she was stubbornly silent.

That was when Abaddon appeared out of nowhere and slammed his fists into Glob's head. Glob's head exploded, sending even more slime and crap flying everywhere. The rest of Glob's body collapsed into a heap of slime that spread out all over the floor.

The slime that had been attached to my leg also dissipated, allowing me to scramble to my feet. Turning to face Abaddon, I said, "Why did you help me, uh, Prisoner?"

Abaddon winked. "Just consider that a favor. You can pay me back later."

With that, Abaddon turned and dove back into the fray, cackling like a madman and leaving me with too many questions. Did Abaddon somehow see through my Secret Identity? Maybe he saw me transform and knew who I was. Now I was worried that other people might have seen me change my identity, which would complicate my plan if they decided to tell the Warden about it.

Either way, Abaddon had saved me from Glob, so I doubted he was trying to stop me from escaping. I remembered what Abaddon had said earlier, about how he wanted to help me stage a breakout, and realized that that was what he must have been doing. He was trying to help me.

Regardless, I still needed to keep moving, so I turned and resumed running to the doors.

And right when I got there, both of the doors swung wide open, almost hitting me. Coming to an abrupt stop, I stepped backward and stared at the figure standing in the doorway:

It was Old Sparky. His eyes glowing blue with electricity, sparks dancing along his fingers, Old Sparky looked more pissed than anything.

"What on God's green earth is going on here?" Old Sparky demanded, gazing around the cafeteria. He seemed to notice me for the first time and pointed a sparking finger at me. "You! Why is there a riot going on in *my* prison?"

Startled, I said, "Uh, a couple of stupid Prisoners got into a fight and it got out of control. Now there's a huge riot going on."

Old Sparky scowled. "I knew it. Should have kept them all separated in their electrical cages. But thank you for the update. I will go and put an end to this riot right now."

Old Sparky stalked past me, forcing me to step aside. As he did so, however, I noticed several card keys hanging off his belt, one of which almost certainly had to be the key to Top Secret.

Unfortunately, I had no time to Scan each card key individually to figure out which one was the key. So I activated Joe's Thief Senses Skill.

In short, Thief Senses was a Skill that let the user "sense" how valuable or important an item was. According to Joe, it was a Skill exclusive to the Thief Class and was how Thieves determined what to steal from potential targets. At higher Levels, it even let you see exactly how valuable a specific item was.

But at Level 1, it just let you know that your mark was wearing something valuable on their person and where it was.

Thus, my eyes zeroed in on the last key on Old Sparky's belt. It looked no different from the others, but my Thief Senses were telling me that it was very important.

In a flash, I switched out Old Sparky's Top Secret key for a key I'd nicked off of Howard earlier. The key I'd stolen from Howard was identical to Old Sparky's Top Secret key in appearance, so hopefully Old Sparky wouldn't notice when he looked at his key ring later.

And I did it without Old Sparky even feeling anything. In fact, Old Sparky just kept stomping forward, so focused on ending the riot that I probably could have punched him in the face and he wouldn't have noticed or cared. Even I was surprised by my Dexterity, although I credited that to Joe's Dexterity, which I, as his Big Bad, had access to.

Clutching the Top Secret key in my hands, I Scanned it, getting this information:

Name: *Top Secret Key*
Materials: *Plastic*
Description: *A key card that gives the user access to the Top Secret Floor. Only a handful of members of the prison administration have one, much less know that it or the Floor that it allows access to exists.*

I grinned. This was excellent. I'd snatched the right key. Now all I needed to do was get to Top Secret before Old Sparky ended the riot.

Unfortunately, I suspected that Old Sparky would end it sooner rather than later, which was why I opened Emerald Heart again, altered who was included in its protections and who wasn't, and then left.

As I left the cafeteria, I heard the familiar roar of Ralph the Demon Giant behind me, along with the cackling of Abaddon and Old Sparky's foul swearing.

That should keep that old fat Warden occupied for a while, along with the other surprises I left for him.

CHAPTER 32

THE HALLS OF MAXIMUM SECURITY SUB-FLOOR TEN WERE EERILY QUIET in comparison to the rioting coming from the cafeteria. In fact, as soon as the doors closed behind me, I could no longer hear the screams and sounds of battle from inside the cafeteria at all. Were the cafeteria doors actually soundproof or something? That was odd, if convenient for my purposes.

Regardless, I quickly made my way down the hallway, following the Map of the Dome that Joe had gotten for me earlier. According to the Map, the entrance to Top Secret was just past our old cell, which was surprisingly close by.

As I walked, I did not run into any Prison Guards, Drones, or anyone else who could get me in trouble. For that matter, I didn't see any Prisoners in their cells, either, although that made sense. Everyone in Maximum Security should be in the cafeteria at the moment, including the Prison Guards, so there was no point in having Prison Guards in the halls outside when there was no one to keep an eye on.

No one to keep an eye on, that is, except for me, of course.

I didn't delay, however, knowing that time was of the essence. Although the few surprises I left for Old Sparky should keep him busy for a while, I knew that it wouldn't keep him distracted forever.

Soon I reached the very end of Sub-Floor 10, which ended in a blank concrete wall in front of me, to the right of me, and to the left of me. I knew the wall to my right hid the entrance to the Emergency Access Stairs, but I didn't see the entrance to Top Secret.

Glancing at the Map, I muttered to myself, "This can't be right. Is the Map wrong? Am I in the right place?"

Then the Ghost's faint voice said in my ear, "You are, Maelstrom. You are."

I started and looked around, but as usual, I didn't see the Ghost anywhere. "I am?"

"Yes …" The Ghost's voice sounded stronger now. "Touch the wall before you with the key card."

Frowning, I stepped forward, pulled the key card out of my jumpsuit pocket, and pressed it against the wall in front of me.

At first, nothing happened, which just left me feeling silly.

Then a clean line appeared in the center of the wall, right where I'd touched the key, and the wall slowly split open. Taking a step back, I watched as both halves of the wall slid to the side, revealing a staircase that descended into darkness well beyond my view.

"Go down the staircase," said the Ghost. "And find the truth."

A part of me was still unsure if I should listen to the Ghost's words, but I'd already come this far. This staircase must lead to Top Secret.

Taking a deep breath, I walked down the stairs, each step echoing slightly off the walls.

And then the walls behind me closed shut with a *slam*, plunging the staircase into pure darkness and making me start.

A second later, however, LED lights flickered into existence on either side of the stairs. The lights were actually built into the stairs, giving it an almost ethereal look that filled me with more than a bit of dread.

But again, I had no choice. Bracing myself for whatever was down there, I resumed walking down the steps, taking them one at a time.

And feeling like I was descending into the heart of pure evil itself.

―――

It didn't take me long to reach the bottom of the stairs, which ended, rather anticlimactically, in front of a simple metal door that looked like the metal doors of the rest of the Dome. Only this one seemed much older than the others, partially covered in rust.

Still, it unlocked when I applied the Top Secret key to the sensor box beside it. Gripping the cold iron door handle, I twisted it and pushed open the door, which squeaked on its hinges loudly. Stepping through the door, I gaped at the sight before me.

A massive, round stone door, with the numeral "1" carved into its surface, towered before me. Easily three times as tall as me and four times as wide, the door was covered in layers of thick, crisscrossing steel chains, with at least half a dozen locks keeping the chains from falling off. The steel chains themselves glowed with energy and when I tried to Scan them, I didn't get any Scan information.

But Scanning the door itself did reveal this interesting tidbit to me:

Stone Door
Materials: *Stone [enhanced]*
Description: *Unknown. You sense a great evil hidden behind there, but that is all.*

No sooner had I finished reading the door's description than this notification popped into view:

Level up! Scan is now Level 2. You can now see the Weak Points of enemies when you Scan them. Continue to level up Scan to gain access to greater knowledge of others and the world around you!

Dismissing that notification, I had to admit that the description of the stone door was odd. Unlike the descriptions of other objects I'd seen in-game, the Stone Door seemed to be describing my own reaction to it.

And honestly, I did feel … *something* behind there. I wasn't sure "evil" was the right word for it, exactly, but at the same time, I struggled to find a better one for it.

Whatever was behind there deserved to *stay* behind there.

Of that, I was absolutely sure.

Although a small part of my mind, the part I associated with my Big Bad self, was already considering the possibilities of what might happen if I opened the Stone Door and let out whatever was inside. Surely I could control it …

"I wouldn't touch that if I were you," said a deep, rumbling voice to my left. "That is how it gets you."

Startled, I looked down at my hand and saw that I was already reaching out to the Stone Door and I hadn't even realized it.

Lowering my hand to my side, I said, "Who said that? Are you the Ghost?"

"I'm behind you," said the deep, rumbling voice.

Turning around, I saw a cell—with rusted bars—set in the wall behind me. In fact, there was an entire hallway to my right, which went down into the darkness well past my vision. I could tell, however, that there was a row of similar cells beyond this one, meaning I was probably talking to one of the Prisoners.

But the cell was too dark for me to see who was speaking, so I stepped forward and said, "Who are you?"

"The better question is, who are you?" said the voice inside the cell. "You do not look like the Warden. You look like someone who should not be here."

I grimaced. I doubted this Prisoner, whoever he was, would have ratted me out to Old Sparky, but I still couldn't risk letting him know my real identity yet. "Uh, the Warden sent me down to check on you guys while he deals with a riot on the upper Floors."

A snort. "Your lies are as transparent as they are unbelievable. Tell me who you really are and I will tell you who I really am."

I gulped. "Okay, well, I guess I was going to have to tell you anyway. I'm another Prisoner, just like you, but I'm in Maximum Security. I managed to steal a card off of Old Sparky and use it to get here. There really is a riot and Old Sparky really is dealing with it, but he definitely did not send me down here to check you."

I didn't know why all of that truth just came spilling out of me like that. Something about the Prisoner's voice compelled me not to leave anything out.

Silence for a moment, then the Prisoner said, "That sounds more like the truth."

"It does?" I said. "It sounds like a poor excuse for a lie to me."

The Prisoner chuckled. "The truth is often stranger than any lie that the mind can conjure."

I shook my head. "Whatever, man. Now I told you who I am. Tell me who you are."

"But you didn't even tell me your name," said the Prisoner. "That doesn't seem fair."

I scowled. "Fine. Call me Maelstrom. You?"

I saw movement in the shadows of the cell, followed by the cracking of bones as the Prisoner inside moved. A vaguely humanoid shape appeared in the darkness, drawing closer to the light in the hallway outside of his cell, until two bony hands wrapped around the bars and pulled a skeletal face into view.

The best way to describe the figure hovering before me was "buff grim reaper." He was a tall, powerfully built skeleton clad in a flowing black robe that hid his legs. He did not have a scythe or any other weapons I could see, but he did have glowing red eyes that gazed down upon me with interest, and a glowing metal collar locked around his neck. The only hint to his identity was the name tag floating above his head, which read [Prisoner #2X].

"Hello, Maelstrom," said the skeletal figure, cracking a grin at me. "I am Fas Alamat, or, as I was known on the surface before my imprisonment, Death Ax."

CHAPTER 33

"Your name is Death Ax?" I said, cocking my head to the side. "Never heard of you."

Death Ax gaze me a confused look. "How could you have not heard of me? My Legion of Villains ravaged the entire world before I was defeated and locked away down here. Has the memory of my name been forgotten already?"

I narrowed my eyes. "Er, well, I am kind of a newer Villain, so I don't know my history of the world all that well yet."

Death Ax nodded. "I see. A new player, right?"

My eyes widened in shock. "Are you a player, too?"

Death Ax shook his head. "No. I'm what you players call an 'NPC,' as derogatory as I consider that name. I exist solely within the confines of this video game called Capes Online and always will, for I cannot leave it."

This was weird. Death Ax was the first NPC I met who actually knew he was in a video game. I didn't quite know how to react to that, or if I even should.

Death Ax sighed, his breath showing in the cold air of the hallway. "Unfortunately, I will likely never leave this prison, either. I am destined to spend the rest of eternity down here, all because I only did what my creators designed me to do."

"Uh-huh," I said, still processing this revelation. "So, uh, Mr. Death Ax, when did you become aware that you were in a video game? And what exactly were you designed to do?"

Death Ax gazed at me, as if he had forgotten I was standing in front of him. "I will answer the second question first. Ten years ago—or however long ago it was, as time is difficult to keep track of down here—an event known as the Rise of Death Ax rocked the world of Capes Online. I was created by the designers of Capes Online to act as the final boss, so to speak, of the event. Players could either oppose me as a Hero or join me as a Villain, which allowed me to create a Legion of Villains known as the Diabolicools."

I gave Death Ax a dry look. "Diabolicools."

Death Ax glared at me. "Is there a … problem with that name, Maelstrom?"

Although Death Ax was probably as powerless as any other Prisoner in here, I had a feeling that openly mocking him to his face would not be wise. Especially if I wanted to get him on my side.

Folding my arms behind my back, I said, "Of course not. Go on with your story. What did the Rise of Death Ax event entail?"

Death Ax tapped the bars of his cage. "It started in Egypt, where I was unintentionally awakened from my magic-induced slumber by a team of archaeologists exploring the tombs of the Pharaohs. Seeing a world in need of conquering, I gathered a Legion of Villains and sought to take over the whole planet. The goal of the event was to kill me to prevent me from turning the world into hell."

I nodded. "I take it the Heroes were successful."

Death Ax's eyes glowed. "Not exactly. The designers made me too powerful. None of the Heroes could defeat me, although many tried. That is, until a Team of Heroes, calling themselves the Order of Light, reached me in my lair beneath the Pyramids and killed me, but only after a long and grueling battle during which I killed several of their members."

I cocked my head to the side. "The Order of Light, huh? That's an odd name for a Hero Team."

"It was quite appropriate," said Death Ax. "Many of their members specialized in Light-based Powers, which proved effective against my own Shadow-based Powers."

"I see," I said. "What happened to you after that?"

Death Ax gestured at the bars of his cell. "To the world, I seemingly exploded in a burst of holy light, my atoms scattered to the winds, and the rewards of killing me granted to the Heroes who slew me. But from my point of view, I woke up not a moment later in this jail cell, locked away from the surface world, in an even worse situation than I had been back in Egypt when I first awakened in the modern world."

"And you've been stuck down here ever since," I said. "Right?"

Death Ax nodded again. "That is correct. The only people I have seen since then are the Warden and the occasional Prison Guard allowed to come down here. You are the first Villain I have seen since my imprisonment. And I must say, I am impressed you got this far, although I question why you have not escaped already if you can get down here."

I pursed my lips. "Because I can't. The Dome is practically inescapable, at least Maximum Security is. I need help from powerful Villains like you and the other Prisoners in Top Secret to free everyone in the Dome. That is why I risked getting fried by Old Sparky just to get down here."

Death Ax tapped his chin. "I see. An ambitious goal, freeing everyone in the Dome. To my knowledge, no one has ever successfully done it."

"Because of Old Sparky," I said. "Everyone says it's impossible, but I have no choice. If I don't … well, the consequences would be very bad for me personally, and not just because I'd be locked up in the Dome forever."

"You speak with much conviction, Maelstrom," said Death Ax. "You remind me of myself in many ways when I was your age, back when I was … alive."

I frowned. "You mean you aren't alive?"

Death Ax shrugged. "I was once an ancient Egyptian king who tricked Anubis into granting me immortality. Unfortunately, the immortality he gave me was this body, which can neither feel, nor taste, nor do much of anything pleasurable."

"I take it you don't like it very much, then," I said. "Perhaps you would like that curse lifted?"

Death Ax looked offended. "Why would I want to lift the curse? I wanted to live forever and I got it. Who cares what I had to sacrifice in order to achieve that goal? I will outlive everyone else, anyway. Time truly is on my side, no matter how much of it passes. It is the world's problem that it fears me, not my problem that I scare the weak."

Right. I had forgotten that Death Ax was a Villain and that all Villains in Capes Online were unrepentant bastards who didn't care about anything except their own self-interest.

"Sure," I said. I looked down the hallway, frowning. "So what is the Top Secret Floor, exactly? Is this where the most dangerous Villains go?"

"In a way," said Death Ax. "In truth, it is where the designers put the final bosses of different events when they are no longer needed. We are caged like animals in case the designers want to reuse us again for some reason, although in my experience, I've never seen any of my fellow inmates leave here for any reason."

That explained why everyone on this Floor was so strong. Raid bosses in video games were typically stronger than normal bosses, often requiring multiple players to team up with each other to take down. If Death Ax was correct, then every single Prisoner down here was basically a raid boss.

Which made me even more eager to free them.

"I see," I said, trying to hide my glee. "How many Prisoners are down here?"

"Ten," said Death Ax. "I was the second final boss put down here, which is why I am labeled 2X."

"What does the 'X' stand for, anyway?" I said. "I was wondering about that."

Death Ax glanced at his name tag. "It stands for 'secret,' I believe, because technically speaking, we do not exist. We are the banished, the forgotten, the old. Our existence is not even acknowledged by the rest of the world. Hence the X."

I pointed at the Stone Door. "And who is behind that Stone Door?"

Death Ax shrugged. "I do not know. In all my time here, I have never seen it open, nor have I ever seen anyone enter or exit it. One thing I do know, however, is that the first Prisoner of Top Secret is locked behind there."

"How do you know that?" I asked.

"Simple deduction," said Death Ax. He gestured at his name tag. "When I got here, I was assigned the number 2X. Since my arrival, I have seen the other Prisoners get the numbers following mine, but I have never seen a 1X. But the Stone Door … it was here when I was first jailed. Plus, the number 1 carved into its surface is a rather dead giveaway, if I do say so myself."

I gazed at the Stone Door again, this time with more interest. "If Top Secret is reserved for high-level raid bosses like you and the others, then logically, Prisoner Number 1X must be Capes Online's earliest raid boss, if not the first."

Death Ax breathed out. "You are a smart one, aren't you? Even I hadn't figured that out yet, but it makes sense now that you mention it."

I shrugged. "Honestly, it's actually very simple. Anyone can do it."

Death Ax pointed at me. "And humble … hmm. Humility is a very rare attribute to find in any Villain. You are certainly a different one, that is for sure."

I scratched the back of my head. "Um, thanks? I try to be humble."

"You shouldn't," Death Ax growled. "Humility, kindness, patience, trust … all of those merely make you weak, Maelstrom. If you wish to be a true Villain, then you must rid yourself of those weaknesses. Become strong. Become so strong that you will never end up down here like me."

I grimaced. "You think you're imprisoned because you are weak?"

"Not exactly," said Death Ax. "Although I doubt they could ever lock you down here. You are a player. You can simply log off whenever you want. You are free in a way I never will be. This is all just a game to you, after all."

Death Ax almost sounded jealous when he said that, prompting me to say, "Maybe so, but trust me, I am invested in this world. I'm not planning to stop playing until I achieve my goal and break everyone out of here. Including you."

Death Ax stared at me. "I don't know if I should feel touched that you want to save me or scold you for sounding more like a Hero than a proper Villain right now."

"You don't have to like me or even think I am a great Villain if you don't want to," I said. "But I know you want out of here as much as anyone else. So does everyone else on this Floor. No one else is offering to bust you out and I doubt you have any realistic escape plans of your own, although I'm open to ideas if you happen to have any."

Death Ax was silent.

"Just what I thought," I said. "So what will it be? Do you want to help me or not?"

Death Ax was still silent. I could tell that the Villain was carefully weighing his options.

Finally, he nodded once. "However odd a Villain you might be, I must admit, you have persuaded me to join you. Although I have my doubts that you will succeed, I also cannot deny I have nothing to lose by joining you."

As soon as Death Ax said that, this notification popped up in my view:

Congratulations! You learned the Persuasion Skill [Level 1], making you both more charismatic and more likely to persuade even the most hostile skeptics to rally to your cause. Level up Persuasion further to gain even more benefits!

Swiping the notification to the side, I said, "Great. But I gotta go. That riot will only distract Old Sparky for so long. I imagine he's probably killing the last of the rioters even as we speak."

"Interesting," said Death Ax. "Despite your obvious confidence in the Warden's ability to put down a riot comprised of Villains much stronger than you are, you seem equally confident you will pull off the impossible and escape here, even though the Warden will undoubtedly be your single biggest obstacle."

I frowned. "I know. Old Sparky is going to be a huge pain in the ass to deal with once I put my plan into action. Doesn't help that I don't know what weak points he has, if any."

"None that I am aware of," said Death Ax. "I suppose you could try starving him to death, but given his immense bulk, that might take a while."

I chuckled before a question occurred to me. "Death Ax, does Old Sparky know he's in a video game like you do?"

Death Ax shook his head. "No. He thinks this is the real world, like most of us. He is a true believer in keeping us Prisoners locked up tightly behind bars, a true believer in justice and in keeping society 'safe' and stable. I doubt he would enjoy being told that none of this is real."

I nodded in agreement, but Death Ax's words got my mind whirring. A potential plan to defeat Old Sparky vaguely took shape in my mind, but I needed more time to hash it out before I felt confident it would work.

With a respectful bow, I said to Death Ax, "Thanks for talking to me. Wish I could talk to the others, but—"

"Worry not about my fellow inmates, Maelstrom," said Death Ax. "We talk to each other often, so I will make sure to spread the news of your plan to them. I will see if I can … persuade them to give you a chance."

I gave Death Ax a surprised look. "That's awfully kind of you. Are you sure you're actually a Villain yourself?"

Death Ax scowled at me. "Let it be known that I am doing this entirely out of my own self-interest, player. And nothing else."

I tried not to smirk at Death Ax. Instead, I turned and left Top Secret as quickly as I could, hoping to reach my cell before Old Sparky or the Prison Guards noticed I was gone.

At the same time, however, I could not feel prouder of myself. Not only did I now have access to Top Secret, but I'd even established a relationship with one of the Prisoners down here.

My plan was coming along and the future looked a lot brighter for me than it had even just half an hour ago.

CHAPTER 34

Getting back to my cell unseen was easier than you might think.

Using the Emergency Access Key, I bypassed the entire Teleportation System and avoided running into any Prison Guards, Drones, security cameras, or even Old Sparky himself by using the stairs. A simple solution to a seemingly complicated problem, but in my experience, complicated problems often did have simple solutions if one looked hard enough.

And since they left the cell doors unlocked during mealtimes, I didn't even need a key to get back into my cell.

As a result, I got back to our cell before either Dinoczar or Joe, although I expected to see them soon enough. When I entered the cell, I heard footsteps in the hallway outside and immediately used Secret Identity again, this time taking on Joe's identity. Again, I looked the same to myself, but I now knew that Secret Identity made me look different to other people.

My transformation wasn't a second too soon, either, because in the next instant, two burly Prison Guards—Ike and Jorge again—walked up to my cell, with Dinoczar and Joe in tow. Joe, of course, looked exactly like me, having used Secret Identity to copy my identity. Even knowing that, however, didn't make seeing myself on the other side of the bars feel any less surreal.

"Finally!" I said in my best impression of Joe's whiny, high-pitched voice, standing up from the cot. "I was wonderin' when youse two would show up."

Joe glared at me. "I do not sound like—I mean, shut up, uh, stupid idiot. At least I didn't get killed."

"God, you guys are annoying," said Ike. "Just go into your cell. We're missing *our* lunch because you idiots decided to fight during *your* lunch."

Jorge opened the door to our cell and Ike tossed both Dinoczar and Joe inside. Then the Prison Guards locked our cell door again and walked away, although I could still hear them quite clearly bitching to each other about how much of a pain we were.

As soon as the Prison Guards were out of sight, Joe's physical form shimmered and vanished, showing his normal self. He sat up, rubbing his back as he said, "They didn't have to *throw* us in here."

Dismissing my own Secret Identity, I said, "Stop whining. Your impression of me was really terrible."

"So was yours," Joe snapped. "You made me sound like a stereotypical Brooklyn mobster or something. I kept expecting you to say 'Hey! I'm walkin' here!' or something equally overused."

"Master is safe!" said Dinoczar, hopping to his feet with a smile on his face. "Dinoczar was worried that master might not have made it to Top Secret."

I folded my arms in front of my chest. "Thanks, but the mission was successful. First, though, tell me what happened in the cafeteria. Did Old Sparky kill everyone like I thought?"

"Surprisingly, no," said Joe, shaking his head as he stood up. "He instead used some new Power to stun the Prisoners. Guess he must have been in a good mood or something today."

I furrowed my brows. "That does seem rather merciful of him. Did anyone fight back?"

"Abaddon did, along with a few of the other higher-level ones," said Joe. "But they didn't last too long."

I nodded. "I think Abaddon is on our side. He helped me escape the cafeteria, which is why I expanded the Emerald Heart's protective field to him."

"I was wondering how he was using his Powers without the Emerald Heart," said Joe. "Although I don't know if I'd trust the infamous 'King of Evil' to help us. The stories I heard about him on the outside made him sound like the most diabolical motherfucker in the world."

I shrugged. "Pretty much everyone here is some level of untrustworthy. It's not like we have much of a choice. The Prisoners are all we have to work with. And fortunately, I managed to make some new friends in Top Secret."

I recounted my conversation with Death Ax to Joe and Dinoczar, the two listening with interest as I explained the alliance I'd made.

"And he said he would convince the other Top Secret inmates to help us," I concluded.

Joe shook his head again. "Wow. I can't believe you got to meet the *real* Death Ax. That is so cool."

"It is?" I said.

Joe nodded eagerly. "Yeah! I'm a huge fan of Death Ax. He was such a badass Villain, a true trailblazer. Did you know he invented the evil laugh?"

"He did?" I said.

Joe nodded again. "Of course! You should have asked him to show it off. I've only ever seen his evil laugh on video. I'd love to hear it in person."

"Are you jerking my chain?" I said. "Because fanboying over someone seems … very out of character for you."

Joe gave me a withering look. "Just because I'm a snarky bastard with *you* doesn't mean I am that way all the time. Because unlike you, Death Ax is a true Big Bad. I'm just jealous I didn't get to meet him myself."

"Dinoczar has never met this Death Ax person, but Dinoczar doubts he is as cool as Joe says he is," said Dinoczar, trying—and failing—to fold his tiny arms. "Dinoczar thinks master is the coolest."

Joe snorted. "Really? You think Maelstrom is the coolest Villain? You clearly need to get out more if you think that."

"But Dinoczar cannot get out more, because Dinoczar is locked up in a prison cell," said Dinoczar, gesturing at our cell.

Joe sighed in frustration. "That's not what I—never mind. You're just wrong."

Dinoczar scowled. "Dinoczar isn't wrong. Dinoczar says *you* are wrong."

As usual, the two started bickering with each other, although it was mostly childish insults along the lines of "You're a doodie head" and "You're a dum-dum."

Their squabbling made it difficult for me to think, so I snapped, "Would you two just stop?"

To my absolute surprise, both Joe and Dinoczar stopped speaking. In fact, they seemed to literally freeze in place, their mouths open, glaring at each other, like they'd taken my command a little *too* literally.

Wait a second … they didn't freeze. The world had frozen. Just like when—

"Hello, Robby, my boy," said a familiar elderly man's voice outside of our cell. "I think it's time for another talk."

I looked to my right and saw, standing just outside the bars of my cell, Grandpa's Digital Double, looking at me with a cold smile.

CHAPTER 35

"Grandpa," I said. "Although I'm still not sure I should call you that."

Grandpa tilted his head to the side. "Why not? For all intents and purposes, I am a perfect copy of Professor Robert J. Baker's mind. Does that not make me, in effect, *him*, especially since your 'real' Grandpa is dead in the physical world?"

I bit my lower lip. "I haven't gotten to that part of your book yet. Sounds like a philosophical question."

Grandpa smiled, a genuine, warm expression that made me feel at ease. "You're reading my book? Wonderful! I wish you had read it while I was still alive. I dedicated it to you and your brother, you know."

"Yes, I know," I said. "It's been an interesting read so far. I'm on Chapter Two."

Grandpa smile grew even wider. "One of my favorites. And very prescient, wouldn't you say? With digital immortality now a fully realized idea, I can say I was right."

I shrugged. "I suppose. I'm surprised you remember what you wrote. It was a long time ago."

Grandpa tapped the side of his head. "Ah, but I have all of my memories. Writing that book was one of my fondest. That book kick-started the VR revolution that turned our whole world upside-down."

"Was that your goal when you wrote it?" I said. "To change society's views on virtual reality?"

Grandpa shook his head. "Not exactly. I was merely a humble philosophy professor at the time who happened to be fascinated with the concept of virtual reality and digital immortality. When I first wrote it, I wasn't expecting it to sell as well as it did, nor to have the influence that it eventually ended up having."

I nodded. "Well, don't spoil anything, because I'm still reading through it myself."

"Yes, yes, of course," said Grandpa with a little wave of his hand. "Please do. It is a very important book, and I don't say that just because I'm the author."

I shook my head. "Sure thing, Grandpa. Anyway, Mom told me that you cheated on Grandma. Is that true?"

Grandpa's smile disappeared, replaced by a frown. "She told you that, did she?" He sighed. "Of course she would."

"Is it true?" I said. "You still haven't denied it."

Grandpa spread his arms wide. "I suppose I forgot to tell you that mental illness runs in the family. And I am not just referring to Daniel. Your grandmother and your mom both have the same mental illness where they make up things in their head to 'explain' the actions of other people they don't like."

I frowned. "I've been to tons of Mom's medical appointments and her doctor hasn't mentioned any mental illnesses on her part even once. And how do you know about Daniel? He didn't lose his mind until after you died."

"I am pretty sure you mentioned Daniel at one point during a previous conversation with me," said Grandpa. "As for your mother, she's undiagnosed. I tried to get her to go to therapy when I was alive, but she always refused. Same thing with your grandmother, who had a similar problem. That's why their medical records don't mention their history of mental illness."

"So you think they're crazy, then," I said.

Grandpa shook his head. "'Crazy' is a harsh term. It's more like they have an untreated illness they refuse to get help for. I wouldn't mention it to your mother, however. She will be very upset if you do so."

I pursed my lips. I'd done some online research which indicated that Grandpa had been accused of sleeping with his students, but truthfully none of the accusations had provided any proof. Maybe Grandpa was right and Mom had just been lying.

Relief spreading across my body, I said, "Good to know. I mean, it's not 'good' in the sense that I now know that mental illness is apparently genetic in our family, but I'm glad you're not as bad as Mom said you were."

Grandpa sighed. "Your mom probably didn't mention all the times I tried to help her and your mother get help. She grew bitter and jealous of my success, especially since she married a man who wasn't anywhere near as successful as I was. Bitter, petty people often do irrational things to protect their psyches, even if they are your own family."

I nodded. Grandpa's explanation made a lot of sense and put me at ease, taking a huge burden off my shoulders. It did make me feel sorry for Mom, though. Knowing that she had an undiagnosed mental condition explained her bitterness toward Grandpa quite well.

"But that is something for you to worry about later, Robby," said Grandpa with a wave of his hand. "In my current state, there is nothing I can do for your mother. But armed with this knowledge, you just might be able to help her where I wasn't able to."

"Hope so," I said. "Anyway, I suspect you didn't show up just to talk to me about Mom."

Grandpa nodded. "As always, Robby, you are quite the observant one. Yes, I decided to speak with you again because I have finished investigating the strange voice you heard in your head."

"That's okay, Grandpa," I said, tapping the side of my head. "I already know who it is. It's the Ghost of the Dome. We're Linked."

Grandpa furrowed his brow. "No, it isn't."

I tilted my head to the side. "It isn't? Then who is it?"

Grandpa gulped. "I have no idea, but I do know that you should not associate with her anymore."

"What?" I said. "Why? Even if we don't know who she is, she's still been helping me. You don't know how many times her Power has helped me—"

"I do, Robby," said Grandpa, "because I've been carefully

watching you this entire time. And I still think you should avoid becoming reliant on her help."

I had forgotten that Grandpa was watching me pretty much all the time, at least while I was in-game. Or rather, it was more like I hadn't even realized it. Then again, what else was Grandpa supposed to do all day? Read philosophy textbooks?

Folding my arms in front of my chest, I said, "You still haven't given me a good reason to distrust her."

Grandpa raised an eyebrow. "Other than the fact that she is a disembodied voice who refuses to actually identify herself or explain her reasoning for helping you? That doesn't seem the slightest bit suspicious to you? Come now, Robby. You're smarter than that."

I shook my head. "Okay, so maybe you've got a point. But what else am I supposed to do? I'm only Level Five, Grandpa, meaning I am extremely weak in comparison to the other Maxies. I need all the help I can get at this point."

"I understand your desperation, but there's no need to take shortcuts, Robby," said Grandpa. "It's not like my wealth is going anywhere. You can take your time—"

"No, Grandpa, I can't," I interrupted him. "Mom's hospital debt is growing even as we speak. We may not have a hard time deadline, but if I don't solve your Riddle as quickly as I can, then I won't be able to pay for Mom's health care. You have to understand that."

Grandpa stroked his beard. "I do understand it, Robby, I do, but—"

"Besides, what's the difference between her and you, anyway?" I continued. "Both of you are guiding me through Capes Online without anyone else noticing. Both of you obviously have your own agendas. There really aren't that many differences between you two when it comes down to it, other than she's more direct with her help than you are."

"The difference, Robby, is that you know me and I know you," said Grandpa, "whereas neither of us know who this woman is. If she's even a woman at all and not merely pretending to be one, that is. In this digital age, verifying someone's sex can be challenging sometimes."

I closed my mouth. Grandpa had an excellent argument, but at the same time, I couldn't give up my Link with the mystery woman. Whether she was the Ghost or a woman or even a man pretending to be a woman, I still needed her power.

So I said, "All right. I'm not going to cut off all contact with her, but maybe I'll be less willing to accept her help going forward."

"That's not enough and you know it, Robby," said Grandpa. "You must cut off all contact with her immediately. Otherwise, the consequences will be severe. I might even consider this cheating."

I scowled at Grandpa. "This isn't cheating. You never specified that I *couldn't* get help for solving your Riddle, or where that help might come from if I do decide I need or want it."

Grandpa opened his mouth, closed it, and opened it again before closing it one last time. Clearly, I'd stumped Grandpa. And despite feeling a little bad about speaking so harshly to him, I also felt rather proud of myself because I'd rarely stumped Grandpa in the real world. He was a lot smarter than me.

Finally, Grandpa nodded. "Fine. Continue to accept her help if you so desire. I will continue to dig into her real identity and see what I can come up with. In the meantime, how has your progress on the Riddle been going?"

"Quickly," I replied. "Although I think you'd know that already, given how you are watching me pretty much all the time."

Grandpa smiled at me. "I just like hearing your updates from you personally, Robby. Plus, it helps me see how you are looking at things, which is always … fascinating."

I quirked an eyebrow. "In what way?"

Grandpa waved off my question. "Never you mind that. But I am disappointed that you have yet to take advantage of that other clue I left for you during our last talk."

"You mean the one about me not being the only person here who wants to be free?" I said. "Yeah, I'm still trying to make sense of that."

"Good," said Grandpa. "I was worried that I might need to spell things out more clearly for you, but as long as you keep thinking about it, I won't utter a word."

I nodded. "That's fine, Grandpa. I don't want or need any hints or help from you. I've gotten this far on my own. You can just sit back and watch and get the money ready to transfer to my bank account, because I am going to solve this Riddle very soon."

Grandpa nodded in response. "If you insist. My only word of caution is not to let your ego get the best of you. Pride cometh before the fall, as the old books say."

"I know, Grandpa, I know," I said. "But I can still be confident in myself, can't I?"

Grandpa smiled mysteriously. "Yes, you most certainly can, Robby. See you later."

With that, Grandpa blinked out of existence and the world started moving again. Behind me, I heard Joe and Dinoczar resume arguing with each other, although I paid no attention to them. I was thinking about my conversation with Grandpa.

On one hand, it was a relief to know that Grandpa wasn't as bad as Mom made him out to be. While I knew Grandpa was no saint, it was nice to know that he wasn't a devil, either.

On the other hand, I now apparently had a clear reason for Daniel's descent into madness. He'd likely inherited whatever mental illness Mom had, or some variation of it at least. That meant that he was probably always destined to lose his grasp on reality and it was just a coincidence that it had happened while he was playing Capes Online.

Such a thought might not have been very encouraging to most people, but to me, it meant that maybe Capes Online was safer than it seemed. Maybe I didn't have to worry about losing my own grasp on reality. Of course, I guess I could have inherited Mom's mental illness, too, but given how I'd maintained my grasp on reality so far, I didn't think so.

That thought was freeing, in a way.

Up until now, I'd been holding back with regard to playing Capes Online. I'd been trying to avoid getting too invested in the game, avoid blurring the lines between reality and game. And I still would always do that to some degree, if only to be careful.

But now … now I could approach Capes Online in an entirely different manner. I could plunge fully into the game, learn all its quirks and mechanics by heart, and truly make my mark on the game itself. It meant I could go even deeper in my quest to solve

Grandpa's Riddle and get the money I needed for myself and my family.

Somewhere in the back of my mind, a tiny voice warned me that I was dancing dangerously close to the same line that Daniel had fallen over. But I ignored the voice—I needed to if I was going to pull this thing off and succeed.

"Master!" Dinoczar's voice snapped me out of my thoughts. "Master! We need your input."

Turning around to face Dinoczar and Joe again, I said, "My input? For what?"

Dinoczar pointed at Joe. "We are trying to find out if Dinoczar is a poopy head or if Joe is a poopy head. Dinoczar suggests that the evidence clearly points to Joe as the poopy head."

"And I'm sayin' that you're ignoring the single biggest piece of evidence pointing to you being the poopy head," Joe said, stuffing his hands into the pockets of his jumpsuit. "Namely, your entire existence."

I sighed. I wondered if this was how Mom felt whenever Daniel and I fought as small kids. If so, I was starting to feel a lot of respect for her. "Enough bickering, you two. We have more important things to talk about."

"Yeah?" said Joe. "Like what?"

I smiled. "Why, our plan for breaking out of the Dome, of course."

"Is master ready to try?" said Dinoczar, eagerly wagging his tail back and forth.

I stroked my chin. "Yes. Now that I have gotten the Top Secret Prisoners on my side, I think we should have enough support to stage a breakout."

"Are you sure, boss?" said Joe. "I know that the Top Secret guys are supposed to be raid bosses and all, but I'm not sure it will be that easy to do. Old Sparky is still around, in case you forgot."

I frowned. "I haven't forgotten about Old Sparky, nor am I saying it will be a walk in the park. But I think the odds are in our favor. We just need to do it, really."

"But Old Sparky is still super strong," said Joe. "I'm just sayin' you still haven't figured out how to neutralize him yet."

I sighed. "Old Sparky may be incredibly strong, but he's not nearly as smart as he thinks he is. We don't actually need to beat him. Just outsmart him, which I can definitely do."

"Well, Dinoczar is in favor of whatever master decides," said Dinoczar with a nod. "Master always knows what is best."

"Not like I have much choice in the matter," said Joe with a shrug. "Shoot."

I rubbed my hands together eagerly. "Okay, so here is the plan …"

CHAPTER 36

As usual, Dinoczar thought my plan was brilliant while Joe thought it was suicidal. In the end, however, I was the Big Bad, so the buck ultimately stopped with me.

And, coincidentally, I thought it was a brilliant plan.

But before we put the plan into action, I decided it was time to take a real-life break. More importantly, however, was the realization that I needed to visit Daniel today, because it was the weekend and I usually spent every other weekend visiting Daniel in the nursing home. We liked to play board games, with our favorite being *Knights and Dragons*, a medieval board game with role-playing game elements.

Given the orders we received from Daniel's doctors telling us not to play games with him, you might wonder why we played board games every other weekend.

The answer is that Daniel's gaming restriction only applied to video games, which were inherently more immersive than board games. The doctors had even told me that board games were fine due to their lack of immersion in comparison to hyper-realistic video games like Capes Online. Even board games with role-playing elements, like *Knights and Dragons*, were allowed.

Given how insistent I'd been with Grandpa about how I needed to solve the Riddle right away, you might wonder why I didn't stay in the game to pull off my plan.

That was because I needed a break. Capes Online's hyper-realism, while immersive, was also exhausting. And despite the realization I'd had about my family's history of mental illness, I still didn't want to risk losing my mind by playing the game for too long. Plus, I needed to do some out-of-game research to make sure that I could pull off certain parts of my plan and to clarify some things for myself.

On the bus ride to Daniel's nursing home, I pulled out my phone and did some research on the early days of Capes Online. What sparked this interest in the first days of Capes Online was my conversation with Death Ax, especially his mention of the mysterious Prisoner #1X. I hoped to get to the bottom of that prisoner's identity. If Death Ax was correct, then Prisoner #1X was either the first raid boss or first event boss that Capes Online featured, which meant I just needed to look at the earliest days of the game to figure out the Prisoner's identity.

Such information might not be available to in-game NPCs like Death Ax, but to real-life players like me with our access to the Internet, finding out Capes Online's secrets ought to be easy.

My research soon turned up something called Launch Day. Apparently, when the Capes Online: VRMMORPG edition first launched in 2027, the game had opened with a world mission called Launch Day. The basic plot of Launch Day, according to the summaries I read online, focused on an alien race known as the Rothlons attacking Earth, forcing the Heroes and Villains to team up to defeat this new threat.

The raid boss of the event was the Rothlon Queen, a gigantic, slug-like monster that acted as the progenitor of the entire Rothlon race. The websites I consulted made Launch Day sound like everyone had been trying to find out who was and was not possessed by these slug-like aliens, with the Rothlon Queen being the final boss of the event.

But I sincerely doubted that the Rothlon Queen was Prisoner #1X. The summaries indicated that the Rothlon Queen, upon her defeat, was driven off to the depths of space, vowing to one day return to get her revenge on the "earthlings" who killed so many of her "babies." Seemed like that plot line had been forgotten, though, because there had been no updates to the Rothlons since then and it wasn't until the Rise of Death Ax event in 2028 that the game truly took off.

So if the Rothlon Queen wasn't Prisoner #1X, then who was?

Guess I was about to find out.

Out of curiosity, I did an online search about Top Secret, but I just got a bunch of conspiracy websites about alleged top-secret government programs and activities. It seemed like even in real life, Top Secret was unknown to anyone outside of SI Games or Maximum Security. Which made sense, seeing as players weren't supposed to end up in Maximum Security anyway, so why would anyone know or care about the secret fourth Floor of the Dome?

My research was cut short when my bus pulled up to the nursing home where Daniel was living. I signed in at the front desk and made my way to Daniel's room, passing by many of the workers and other residents. Most of the other residents of Green Acres Nursing Home were much older than Daniel, which just added to the depressing atmosphere of the place.

Reaching the door to Daniel's room, I raised my fist to knock, only to hear voices on the other side of the door. I briefly paused before realizing that it was lunchtime, meaning that the other voice probably belonged to Daniel's orderly bringing him lunch for the day.

Knocking on the door at the same time I opened it, I said, "Hey, Daniel. Ready to play some—"

I stopped speaking when I saw that Daniel was not alone. A middle-aged man in a gaming T-shirt and jeans sat in a chair across from Daniel, who was sitting in his usual position on his bed. The two were laughing and joking with each other, but stopped when I entered the room.

"Hey, bro!" said Daniel, waving at me. "What are you doing here?"

I lifted up the box of *Knights and Dragons*, though I found it hard to pay attention to Daniel with the stranger in the room. "I'm here to play our weekend board games, remember?"

Daniel slapped his forehead. "Oops! I forgot. Haven't been keeping track of the time recently."

"You play board games with your brother every weekend?" said the middle-aged man, his voice unnaturally high-pitched. He smiled at me. "That's nice."

"Uh, thanks," I said. "And you are—?"

The middle-aged man put a hand on his chest. "Excuse me for not introducing myself. I'm Andrew Mason, a friend of Daniel's. You must be Robby, his younger brother. Pleased to meet you at last."

Andrew held out a hand to me, which I shook. Although his hand was big like the hand of a man, his grip felt oddly … feminine? I wasn't sure how to put it. He was a slim guy, even skinnier than me, which was saying something because I was pretty thin myself.

Letting go of Andrew's hand, I said, "Nice to meet you, too, Andrew, but I don't think Daniel's ever mentioned you to me before."

Daniel looked at me in surprise. "What are you talking about, bro? I mentioned him to you at least once. He was one of my Capes Online friends."

I tensed, although tried not to show it.

One of the doctor's orders had been to limit Daniel's contact with any of his Capes Online friends. Daniel's psychologist had told us that Daniel's breakdown had partly been encouraged by his friends, who were just as terminally online and addicted to Capes Online as he was.

And indeed, Mom and I had done a good job of making sure that none of Daniel's friends knew where he lived or how to get in contact with him. We'd even told his friends, using Daniel's Capes Online account, that he was quitting the game and would never return or talk to any of them ever again.

We also told Daniel that his friends were not allowed to visit him in the nursing home because they were only his friends because of their video game connection. It helped that Daniel hadn't actually met any of his in-game friends in real life before, so it wasn't like he had reason to believe their friendship with him extended into the real world.

Harsh, maybe, but necessary.

Yet here was Andrew, one of Daniel's old Capes Online friends, sitting in front of him like they visited each other like this all the time.

At the same time, however, I didn't know how to communicate that to Andrew without upsetting Daniel or causing a scene. I wished the nursing home staff had kept Andrew out, but how could I have expected them to do that when we didn't give them a list of people who were and were not approved to see Daniel?

I would have to make that list later.

Pushing that thought out of my mind for now, I pulled up another chair and sat down on it, still clutching the *Knights and Dragons* box in my hands. "Well, this is a weird coincidence for sure. Where are you from, Andrew?"

"California," said Andrew. "I'm in town visiting my grandmother, who also lives in this same facility. I ran into Daniel one day on my way out. Then we started chatting and ... how long has it been, Daniel?"

Daniel shrugged. "No idea, honestly. Time's just been flying by ever since you walked in here. It's been great. Just like the old days, except we don't look like buff superheroes."

I pursed my lips. This was a crazy coincidence for sure. How could I have known that one of Daniel's online friends—from California, of all places—had a grandma living in this very same facility as Daniel himself? Maybe God really did have a sick sense of humor after all.

"So what have you guys been talking about?" I said. "Just catching up?"

"For the most part, yeah," said Andrew with a nod. "But I've also been giving Daniel updates on Capes Online."

I bit my lower lip. "Oh, you have, huh?"

Daniel nodded quickly. "Yeah! Sounds like a lot has changed since I last played. That New Future campaign sounded really interesting."

Andrew rolled his eyes. "It was just SI Games' way of trying to salvage their reputation after the Blackouts. Honestly, no one actually likes it, aside from the New Future players who think Capes Online is their new home now or whatever."

"It does sound pretty stupid," said Daniel. He looked at me. "What do you think about it, Robby? You started playing Capes Online recently. What do you think about the New Future campaign?"

Andrew turned toward me, an interested expression on his face now. "You play Capes Online, too? I didn't know that. I thought that only Daniel played. When did you start playing?"

I gulped. "Erm, just a few days ago. I've barely gotten out of the starting area and haven't devoted that much time to it what with my streaming career and everything."

Daniel's shoulders slumped. "Oh. I guess that makes sense. You are a professional streamer. I bet you don't have a lot of time for other games unrelated to your career."

"Can you give me your Capes Online ID?" said Andrew. "Perhaps we can become Friends. I can show you the ropes if you want."

Ugh. I really didn't want to give Andrew my Capes Online ID, but at the same time, I also didn't want to be rude and tell him no. Especially in front of Daniel, who I don't want to upset accidentally.

"Why don't you tell me your Capes Online ID first?" I said.

Andrew smiled. "Sure. I'm player Six Two Four Nine Eight Zero … but you can also just search Capeman and I should come up."

CHAPTER 37

My heart throbbed in my chest. "Your Capes Online username is … Capeman?"

Capeman was the guy who put me in the Dome in the first place, the self-righteous asshole who punched me in the face and treated me like, well, a Villain. Daniel had told me that Capeman had been a friend of his, but I hadn't even considered this Andrew guy could be Capeman.

"Sure," said Andrew. "I'm the only player with that name. Should come up in the game's search engine when you put in it."

Daniel clapped his hands together excitedly. "Oh, this is fun! Robby, didn't you mention that you had run into Capeman when you first started playing Capes Online?"

Crap. I'd forgotten that I mentioned Capeman to Daniel before. Fortunately, I'd kept the details of my encounter with Capeman vague, but I still didn't want Daniel to mention it to Andrew. Otherwise, I risked having my secret identity revealed, and right now I did not want to deal with the fallout from that. I didn't want to see what Daniel would do if he found out that his younger brother was a Villain in Capes Online.

Andrew quirked an eyebrow. "I think I would remember if I ran into my best friend's younger brother. When did we meet, exactly?"

I gulped. "Er, we technically didn't actually *meet*. I, er, just saw you punch out a purse thief who murdered a widow."

"You were there?" Andrew said in confusion. "Strange. I don't remember there being any witnesses to that particular crime."

"A purse thief murdered a widow?" said Daniel. He shook his head. "It sounds like the game has gone downhill since I left."

Andrew sighed. "That's not even the worst of it. The Blackouts led to hundreds of thousands of players logging off permanently, including most of the Hero players. But it's attracted a new wave of Villain players seeking to take advantage of the lack of Heroes to create chaos and harm innocents freely."

"It has?" I said.

Andrew nodded. "One of the things a lot of people don't understand about Capes Online is how the Alignment System is supposed to balance things out. Pre-Blackout, the Alignment System balanced out the numbers of Hero players versus Villain players. There were always slightly more Heroes than Villains due to the nature of things, but generally speaking, a balance existed that allowed for order and stability to be maintained even in the face of true evil."

"But then the Blackouts happened and … well, lots of people decided to log off permanently. People didn't want to risk getting trapped in a video game again. Even a lot of our friends logged off."

Daniel gasped. "Including Master Pig?"

Andrew nodded again. "He was the first. There aren't too many of us left now. As a result, the number of Villain players has increased, meaning there is far more chaos and general anarchy than before. It's becoming harder and harder to maintain law and order in the face of so much crime and evil."

Gulping nervously, I said, "But it's just a game, right? Does it really matter if people are causing 'chaos' in a video game that isn't even real in the first place?"

Andrew gave me a polite but withering look. "It's not just that Villain players are breaking the rules set by SI Games or exploiting bugs or whatever. A lot of real-life criminals are using Capes Online for things like money laundering, sex trafficking, and various other things. In fact, a lot of real-life criminals are even taking advantage of the mind-to-game upload process to avoid going to jail for the crimes they committed in the real world."

I felt like an idiot. "Oh. Really?"

"It's bad," said Andrew. "And I've been working with law enforcement in the real world to deal with it. But it's going to get a lot worse before it gets better, I'm afraid."

Huh. Having spent ninety-nine percent of my time in Capes Online in the Dome, I knew very little about the world outside of the Dome. As far as I was concerned, the Dome *was* my world.

But I had forgotten that Capes Online was much bigger than the Dome. There were cities and towns and tons of other places out there that I didn't even know about.

Grandpa had said that staging a mass breakout of the Dome's prisoners was only the *first* Riddle. Did the next two Riddles include going out into the wider world?

I had no idea. But maybe I should avoid getting ahead of myself. After all, I hadn't finished the first Riddle. No need to psyche myself out if I didn't have to. It was still something to think about, at least.

"That's absolutely horrible," said Daniel. His hands balled into fists in his lap. "Wish I could go back into the game and help. I feel so useless."

"You're recovering, Daniel," I reminded him. "Remember, Capes Online isn't real. It's not your duty to police it."

"Your little brother is right, Daniel," said Andrew. "You should stay here. Your mental health is a lot more important than any video game."

That statement, coming from Andrew, surprised me. I had been sure that Andrew would have encouraged Daniel to get back into the game, yet instead, Andrew seemed to understand exactly why Daniel was here. It made me respect Andrew a lot more. Maybe not everyone who played Capes Online seriously was as detached from reality as Daniel was.

Daniel still looked upset, but he nodded. "I guess you have a point. But Andrew, give those Villains hell for me. Especially that guy who murdered that widow. He sounds like the worst."

Andrew shook his head. "He was a bad one for sure. Fortunately, I sent him to the Dome, although given how easy it is to break out of Minimum Security, I bet he's back on the streets of Adventure City already."

I gulped again. "Heh, heh, yeah. That guy sure deserved getting punched in the face."

Andrew gave me an odd look. "How did you know I punched him in the face?"

"I was a witness, remember?" I said quickly. "I was watching. From the alley. Where you couldn't see me."

Andrew frowned before saying, "Right. The alley. I forgot you mentioned that already."

I had the distinct feeling that Andrew did not entirely believe my story about me watching his assault of the "murderer" from a nearby alleyway. At the same time, however, he did not seem inclined to push any further on the issue, which was good, because the more we talked about this incident, the more likely my secret identity was to come out.

Then Andrew narrowed his eyes and leaned in closer to me. "You look very familiar to me for some reason, even though I'm pretty sure this is the first time we've met."

"You probably recognize him from all of the family photos I sent you over the years," Daniel said. He laughed. "He hasn't changed much since then."

Thank you, Daniel, for coming to my rescue, because I certainly wasn't.

Then Andrew shrugged and leaned away from me, turning his attention back to Daniel. "Probably so. You did send me a lot of pictures of your family back when you played the game. How's your mom, by the way?"

"Fine," I said before Daniel could say anything. "She's fine. Now, do you guys want to play *Knights and Dragons*?"

Andrew rubbed his hands together and glanced at the clock on the wall above Daniel's TV. "I'd love to play, but unfortunately, I promised to have lunch with another friend of mine in the area and it's getting close to noon."

Daniel's shoulders slumped. "You mean you're leaving already? But you just got here."

"I know," said Andrew, "but I hadn't planned to stop in at all, so it's not like I had set aside time to hang out with you."

"How long are you planning to stay in town?" I asked Andrew.

"I'm actually leaving tomorrow," said Andrew. "Early flight. Why?"

I shrugged. "No reason. Just curious."

Actually, the real reason I asked was because I was afraid he might try to visit Daniel again. Yet if Andrew was leaving already, then I would not need to keep him from seeing Daniel again. At least not right away. That would make my life a lot easier.

"Okay," said Daniel, disappointment clearly filling his voice. "But it was nice seeing you again, Andrew. Tell everyone else I said hi."

"Will do, Daniel," said Andrew. He nodded at me. "Nice meeting you for the first time as well, Robert. Perhaps we will run into each other again in Capes Online at some point, if you don't add me to your Friends List."

I gulped once more, but said, in a tone that was calmer and cooler than I actually felt, "Sure thing, man. Safe travels."

With that, Andrew stood up and left the room, closing the door behind him on his way out.

As soon as Andrew left, Daniel sighed and looked at the comic books on his bed scattered around him, prompting me to ask, "You okay, bro?"

Daniel began flipping through a random issue. "I just miss my friends. I know I'm not allowed to see them, but talking to Andrew really did remind me of the good old days. I almost felt like we were back in Capes Online together again, fighting Villains, protecting Civilians, and ensuring that truth and justice won the day."

"I'm sorry," I said. "Maybe you'll get a chance to see Andrew again the next time he visits his grandma. Haven't you made any other friends in the nursing home?"

Daniel gave me a sour look. "No. Everyone else is too old."

I grimaced. I had known that Daniel struggled to make friends among the other residents of his nursing home, but I had hoped he would have made at least one friend by now. It sounded like their age differences were simply too big a gap for Daniel to cross.

Not wanting Daniel to be sad or to dwell on his own misfortune, I lifted up the *Knights and Dragons* box and said, "Well, how's about you set up the board and we can get started on our game? I can order a pizza if you're hungry."

Daniel smiled brightly at me and took the box from my hands. "Sure! Make sure to have them add extra pepperoni. That's my favorite."

While Daniel set up the *Knights and Dragons* board, I opened my phone and went to the website of a nearby pizza place to place a delivery order.

Even as I did that, however, I barely paid attention to what I was doing. Partly because I knew what Daniel wanted, but also partly because of my encounter with Andrew.

That had been super risky. If the conversation had gone in even a slightly different direction, I would have had to fess up about being the Villain who murdered that widow. That would have shocked Andrew, but I knew it would have absolutely destroyed Daniel.

Although Daniel had made great strides in detaching himself from Capes Online, the truth was that he still hadn't entirely recovered yet. Daniel clearly still felt a strong emotional connection to the game. Just look at how he had reacted when Andrew told him about the increase in criminal activity in Capes Online.

What would Daniel do if he found out that I was a Villain? Even if I explained why I was a Villain, I didn't want to deal with that. I didn't want to ruin the progress we'd made on my brother's mental health and possibly set him back to where he started.

At the same time, however, I knew I wouldn't be able to keep lying to Daniel forever. Once I solved Grandpa's Riddles, I would have to explain to Daniel and Mom where the money came from. Perhaps by then, Daniel would be so overjoyed at me getting the money to pay Mom's medical bills that he wouldn't hate me for being a Villain in-game.

That would have to do for now.

As for the other news Andrew shared about the Villains beyond the Dome, that was concerning. I hadn't known about the real-life criminal element that was using Capes Online to break the law, but I suppose it made sense. If I was a criminal in the real world who wanted to avoid going to jail for my crimes, what better way to escape justice than to upload my mind to a video game world where the police couldn't get me?

I was starting to worry about what would happen once I escaped from the Dome and who I would encounter on the outside. The Villains in the Dome, after all, were NPCs who mostly acted according to their programming.

The Villains outside of the Dome, however ... well, I guessed I would cross that bridge when I got there.

In any case, that news did not deter me from wanting to enter Capes Online again and finish the Riddle. I couldn't control how other people used Capes Online, after all. It wasn't my responsibility how they used it.

All I could do was control how I used it.

More than ever, I was determined to start the breakout and get out of the Dome. That way, I'd be able to help Mom and Daniel and set us financially for life.

"Robby!" said Daniel's voice, which snapped me out of my thoughts. "Are you ready to play?"

Looking up from my phone, I saw Daniel sitting across from me, the *Knights and Dragons* board game set up between us. Daniel wore his usual big goofy smile, making him look almost like a child.

I nodded and tapped my screen a few more times. "I am now. Just placed the pizza order. Says it should be here in half an hour."

Daniel smirked. "Will you even last against me that long?"

I smirked back. "Who is the current reigning champion of *Knights and Dragons*, bro?"

Daniel picked up the dice and shook them in his hand. "We'll see who is still standing and who isn't by the end of this quest, brother!"

I chuckled as Daniel tossed the dice across the board, knowing this would be my last chance to relax and have fun before the breakout.

And I was determined to enjoy every second of it.

CHAPTER 38

A week after I logged back in, something flew past my face and crash into the wall opposite me. Startled, I sat up in my cot and looked down to find the remains of an empty ceramic bowl on my bed, partially stained with something red that smelled vaguely like the Dome's [Slop].

"Boss!" Joe screamed. "Get this wild animal away from me! He's trying to kill me!"

I looked over to see Joe cowering in the corner, waving a pillow at Dinoczar, who was snapping at him with his jaws.

"Dinoczar isn't trying to kill you," Dinoczar said in between snaps of his jaws. "Dinoczar is merely trying to remove your other hand for disrespecting master!"

Swinging my legs over the side of my bed, I stood up and said, "Dinoczar, what the hell is going on? Why are you attacking Joe? What do you mean he 'disrespected' me?"

Dinoczar stopped and looked over his shoulder at me. "Joe said your plan will fail. Said that there is no reason for us to risk our lives for little gain. Dinoczar was trying to teach him a lesson."

I sighed. "As entertaining as it is to watch Joe cower before you, I must ask you to leave him alone, Dinoczar. I will need both of your help to pull off our plan, and it won't work if you two are constantly trying to kill each other."

Dinoczar huffed, but stepped away from Joe and bowed his head toward me. "Dinoczar asks for your forgiveness, master. Dinoczar was merely trying to defend your honor."

Rubbing my forehead, I said, "It's fine. By the way, how long have you been doing this?"

Dinoczar thought about it for a second. "An hour. Maybe two. Dinoczar loses track of the time whenever he gets too excited and hungry."

"I'm in hell," Joe muttered. "I'm in hell, I'm in hell."

Ignoring Joe's mutterings, I said, "Well, no more fighting. Because tonight is the night we are going to finally do it."

Both Dinoczar and Joe looked at me in shock.

"Do it?" said Joe. "You don't mean—?"

"We are finally going to cook Joe on a spit roast, season his body with delicious spices, and feast on his flesh?" Dinoczar said excitedly.

I gave Dinoczar a weird look. "No. We're … we're not going to do that, Dinoczar."

Dinoczar's shoulders slumped and he lowered his head again. "Oh. Dinoczar is very sad now."

"You shouldn't be," I said. I punched my fist in my other hand. "Because tonight is the night we are going to finally pull off our breakout."

"Seriously?" said Joe. He slowly rose to his feet, keeping a careful eye on a downtrodden Dinoczar at the same time. "We're finally doing it? No more planning? No more talking?"

I shook my head. "No more planning. Between all the planning and research we've done, I think we're ready to give it a try."

Joe rubbed the back of his neck. "Finally. I was getting bored with the endless planning sessions. I thought you just had a planning fetish or something."

"No, but breaking out of Maximum Security isn't something you can just go and do," I said. "That's why we spent so much time planning and why I spent so much time researching."

That was true. Ever since my last visit with Daniel back in the real world, I'd doubled down on my efforts to break out of the Dome. I'd spent the last week or so with Dinoczar and Joe going over the details of the plan, as well as researching the parts that I knew little about.

I hadn't spent much time thinking about Andrew. Aside from the fact that Capeman was outside of the Dome while I was inside the Dome, I just didn't see any point in worrying about him. I needed to be hyper-focused if I was going to pull this off, and if there was one thing I excelled at, it was being hyper-focused on whatever was in front of me.

And now, we had a plan, a plan I was confident would work.

Putting my hands together, I said, "Before we put the plan into action, do either of you have any questions, objections, problems—?"

Dinoczar raised one of his tiny hands. "Yes. Dinoczar does not remember the plan."

Joe gave Dinoczar a disbelieving look. "How can you not remember the plan? We've gone over it ad nauseam. I could recite it in my sleep at this point. Heck, I'm pretty sure I do."

Folding my arms in front of my chest, I said, "If that's the case, Joe, then why don't you explain it to Dinoczar and I can chime in and correct you if you get any of the details wrong?"

Joe shot me an ugly scowl. "What is this, school? You're acting like my least favorite high school teacher right now. And you aren't even half as hot as she was."

"Explain, Joe," I said.

Joe sighed. "Fine. So, Dinoczar, the plan, summed up, goes like this: Maelstrom will go down to Top Secret, where he will free the raid and event bosses. He will then lead the Top Secret Prisoners to Maximum Security to create maximum chaos and destruction. At the same time, I will sneak into the Warden's office, gain access to the Dome's security system, and open all of the Maximum Security cells. Between the Toppies and the Maxies—"

"Toppies?" I repeated.

"If you think I am going to call those guys Top Secret Prisoners *every* time, you're out of your mind," Joe replied. "Anyway, between the Toppies and the Maxies, the prison administration will get too overwhelmed to deal with it, and then we will go and open the portal between Maximum and Medium Security. This will allow the Maxies and Toppies to escape to Medium and, eventually, Minimum Security, as the upper Floors are simply unequipped to deal with Prisoners as strong as the typical Maxie or Toppie."

I gave Joe the thumbs-up. "Excellent summary, Joe. I will make sure to put a gold star on your report card so your parents will know how good a student you have been."

Joe smirked at me. "Joke's on you, pal. My parents forced me to drop out of school so I could help them deal drugs when I was seven."

"Right," I said. "I forgot that you have a comically evil backstory."

"Dinoczar thinks he understands the plan now," says Dinoczar, "but Dinoczar doesn't understand how master intends to deal with the Warden."

I walked over to the bars of our cell and gazed into the hallway on the other side. I didn't see the Warden or the Prison Guards, but I could imagine Old Sparky in his office right now, no doubt eating a donut and thinking that tonight was just going to be a normal night for him. "A good question, Dinoczar, one I've already given a great deal of thought to."

I turned around to face Dinoczar and Joe, my arms folded behind me. "We know that Old Sparky is basically invincible as long as he is on Maximum Security. His level scaling ability means that he will always be a match for even the strongest Prisoner. We know that even Toppies can't survive against him in a straight fight for very long. Therefore, dealing with Old Sparky will require choosing the battlefield."

Dinoczar cocked his head to the side. "Dinoczar does not understand that concept."

"What the boss means, dino-brains, is that we're gonna lure Old Sparky up to Minimum Security and deal with him there," Joe said. He gestured at me. "And boss here is gonna be the bait."

Dinoczar gaped. "But master can't be bait! Master is too important."

"No, it makes sense," I said. "Old Sparky will know that I instigated the breakout and will feel like I betrayed his trust, so he will probably want to kill me more than killing the other Prisoners. If I can lure Old Sparky up to Minimum, or even Medium, Security, then he will be much weaker than he is on Maximum Security. After all, while his power scales with each Floor, our Levels stay exactly the same."

Dinoczar's eyes lit up with understanding. "Ah, now Dinoczar sees. Yes, that makes much more sense. But Dinoczar is still worried about master's safety."

I waved a hand. "Don't worry. I'm planning to have a few of the stronger Toppies and Maxies with me when the fight happens. That way, they can do most of the heavy lifting while I just stand back and watch."

Dinoczar nodded. "Dinoczar now understands the plan, except for Dinoczar's role."

"You'll come with me to Top Secret and be my bodyguard," I told him. "Once the Dome's Security Systems are done, things will get crazy. Especially once I use this bad boy to give the other Prisoners their Powers back."

I tapped the Emerald Heart hanging off of my neck. It glowed warmly under my touch.

Dinoczar stood up straight, or as straight as a miniature T-Rex could, anyway. "Dinoczar will be the best bodyguard master has ever had! And if necessary, Dinoczar will even sacrifice Joe's life to protect your own."

Joe rolled his eyes. "Did I mention how much I love being an expendable Minion? Because I really do."

I clapped my hands together. "Regardless, we all have a role to play in this plan. Dinoczar, I am going to head out to Top Secret right now. Joe, you know where the Warden's office is, right?"

Joe snapped his fingers and a holographic version of the Map of the Dome appeared in front of him, casting a soft blue glow over his form. A blinking red dot appeared over a portion of the Map near our cell. "Yep. And I'm confident I can break into it, although I am a bit worried about whether Old Sparky will be there or not."

"I don't think he should be there right now," I said. "I know I often joke about Old Sparky living in the Dome, but I'm pretty sure that he doesn't actually sleep in his office. We can even see him on the Map right over here."

I pointed at a yellow dot on MD-SF#5. "See? He's on Medium Security right now. He's nowhere near his office. That means you should be able to sneak in without anyone noticing you."

Joe bit his lower lip. "All right, but I'm not going to stay in there any longer than necessary."

"That's fine," I said. "You can meet Dinoczar and me back here after we've made it through the Prison Guards. In fact …"

I tapped the Map a few times and hundreds of red dots appeared near MX-SF#10, with less than a dozen red dots scattered across the other Sub-Floors. "Most of the Prison Guards are in the locker room, probably sleeping."

That was probably true. Over the past week, I'd consulted with the Map to analyze the schedule of the Warden and the Prison Guards at different times of day. It would have been more helpful to have direct access to the Dome's full scheduling system, but since I was pretty sure whatever hole Ursal had taken advantage of to hack into the Dome's scheduler had been patched, this was the next best thing.

I'd learned that the biggest concentration of Prison Guards was during the day. While there were always Prison Guards patrolling at all times of day and night, the "night crew," as I dubbed them, were much smaller in number than the day crew. It seemed like the Warden assumed that most of the Prisoners were asleep at night and therefore there was less need for Prison Guards.

Too bad Old Sparky was about to find out the hard way why making assumptions was a terrible thing to do.

"Probably," said Joe, "although I don't know how anyone could sleep in that awful locker room. The smell alone almost killed me."

I patted Joe on the shoulder. "Doesn't matter. This is the perfect time to strike, so let's go. Joe, you know what to do."

Joe sighed and walked over to the door to our cell. With his back to us, Joe fiddled with the lock before I heard a *click* and the door cracked open. "Done."

"How did you unlock the cell door without activating the Dome's security systems?" said Dinoczar in amazement.

Joe held up a key. "Snatched a key off of that big dummy Ike when he hauled us back here after the riot. The Dome's security systems won't activate if you use the right keys to open your cell."

"Excellent," I said. I looked at Joe and Dinoczar. "Okay. This is it. This is the night we've been waiting for. Once we leave this cell and go our separate ways, there will be no going back. We will have to live with the consequences, whatever they may be."

"Dinoczar is ready for whatever the Dome has to throw at us, sir," said Dinoczar, holding his head up high. "No matter what."

"Same," said Joe, cracking his neck. "Although I still think this is a risky plan, I have to say, I am starting to feel a little better about our odds. We just might break out of this place after all."

I nodded. It was strange to hear Joe actually be supportive for once. Perhaps that was a good omen.

"No, we *will* do this," I said, punching my fist into my other hand. "We will pull off the first-ever successful breakout in Maximum Security's history. You can count on that. Now let's go!"

Joe nodded. His form shimmered and was replaced by [PRISON GUARD MIKE], while I activated MINION POWERS in the Command Interface and also took on the form of [PRISON GUARD MIKE]. You might think it risky for us both to be Prison Guard Mike, but since we were going in completely opposite directions, we weren't very likely to run into the same people.

And if we did get caught on security cameras … well, there wouldn't be enough time to stop us.

We left the cell and went our separate ways. Joe went to the left, heading toward the Warden's office, while Dinoczar and I headed toward the Emergency Access Stairs, which we intended to use as a shortcut to Top Secret.

As we separated, I felt anxiety rising up inside me. There were so many things that could go wrong here, but I couldn't afford to think about any of them.

Like I said, there's no going back now. All we could do was go forward, hope for the best, and give Old Sparky the biggest headache he'd have in his whole career.

CHAPTER 39

Between the Emergency Access Stairs and the Map, Dinoczar and I had little trouble circumventing the few Prison Guards who were still out tonight, as well as any security cameras or other traps that could trip us up. I also kept my Command Interface open but minimized in order to have a quick yet reliable communication channel with Joe. That way, he could contact me if needed and vice versa. Much faster than Capes Online's messaging system.

Soon, Dinoczar and I reached MX-SF#10, the final Sub-Floor of Maximum Security. It did strike me as a bit strange how we ran into no Prison Guards, but again, the night crew was much smaller than the day crew, and the Map let us see and avoid them pretty easily. It helped that no one used the Emergency Access Stairs other than ourselves due to the very nature of the stairs being only for, well, emergencies or when the Teleportation System was not working.

When we reached the entrance to Top Secret, I pressed Old Sparky's Top Secret key against the wall. Like before, the wall slid open, revealing the dank, dark stone staircase that spiraled into the shadows out of sight.

You might wonder why Old Sparky apparently still hadn't noticed his missing Top Secret key. I wasn't sure, other than Old Sparky probably had multiple Top Secret keys, so he probably wouldn't realize he was missing one. That, and he didn't strike me as being the most conscientious or organized person around, so I bet he lost keys and stuff like that all the time. I mean, did you see his key ring? He had a million keys on there, easy. Even I couldn't keep track of all of that.

Anyway, Dinoczar and I made our way down the stairs as quickly as we could. We didn't bother with stealth. According to the Map, there were no Prison Guards down here, so the only people who might possibly hear us were the Prisoners, that is, the so-called Toppies, as Joe named them. I smirked thinking about what Death Ax and the other former raid bosses might think if they learned about *that* nickname for them.

And best of all, according to the Map, Old Sparky was still on MD-SF#5. That meant it would take him a while to react to the breakout. And that's without taking into account that I gave Joe orders to shut down the Teleportation System, just to make things more difficult for the fat bastard and his Minions.

"Boss, how are things going on your end?" Joe's voice crackled in my ears, coming from the Command Interface.

"Perfectly," I replied as Dinoczar and I walked down the stairs. "We're walking down to Top Secret even as we speak. Didn't run into any Guards. Have you broken into the Warden's office yet?"

"Yep," said Joe with more than a hint of pride in his voice. "Like taking candy from a baby. Which I should know about, because stealing candy from babies is how I got started in my thieving career."

"Thank you for volunteering that information, Joe," I said. "It's not like I didn't already know how much of a selfish bastard you are."

"A selfish bastard who is helping you break out of this joint, boss," Joe corrected. "But you're welcome."

I sighed as we reached the final door to Top Secret. "Never mind. Just get yourself ready. I will tell you when to shut everything down and let everyone out, okay?"

"Sure," said Joe. "In the meantime, I think I am going to help myself to some of Old Sparky's donuts. Haven't eaten real food in forever and they smell so good."

Soon I heard Joe munching on donuts in my ear, a sound so annoying I muted him. I didn't need to hear him eating donuts directly in my ear. So crude.

But at the same time, it was great knowing that Joe had successfully broken into Old Sparky's office. If he'd failed to make it in there, it would make the rest of the plan much more difficult, if not downright impossible, to pull off.

Everything was going according to plan.

Just how I liked it.

Opening the metal door, its rusty hinges screeching, I walked into Top Secret, Dinoczar right behind me, and said, "Hey, everyone! I'm finally here and ready to break all of you out. Death Ax, you guys awake and ready to go? Death Ax?"

I didn't hear any response, either from Death Ax or the other Toppies. That was weird. Maybe they were all still asleep or something. It *was* pretty late at night, after all.

I walked over to Death Ax's cell while Dinoczar looked around curiously. Tapping on the bars of Death Ax's cell, I said, "Death Ax? Hello? Are you awake? It's go-time, dude. I'm here to break you out, which I can't do if you're sleeping like a baby."

I thought calling Death Ax a baby might annoy him enough to get his attention, but still no response.

"Maybe Death Ax took a lot of melatonin," Dinoczar whispered to me. "Dinoczar knows that melatonin is very helpful for individuals who struggle to get a good night's sleep. It is what those awful Synth Group scientists tested on Dinoczar and his friends, after all."

I gave Dinoczar a quizzical look. "I thought they were performing inhumane experiments on you guys."

"Oh, they were," Dinoczar said with a nod. "But sometimes they gave Dinoczar melatonin. That was the best sleep Dinoczar ever got. In an ironic twist of poetic justice, Dinoczar being well-rested is how Dinoczar ate the scientists and all their families."

I shook my head and put my hands on the bars of Death Ax's cell. "This is ridiculous. Do I have to come in there and wake you up myself or—"

I stopped speaking when I accidentally leaned into the door ... and it flung open. I almost fell onto the floor, but caught myself at the last second. Clinging onto the door, I found myself staring at a completely empty jail cell.

There was no sign of Death Ax anywhere. It was as if he hadn't been in here at all.

"What the—?" I said. "Death Ax—? Where are you?"

"Is Death Ax not in there, sir?" said Dinoczar.

I whipped my head around the small jail cell, noting how it was actually even smaller than our cell up on MX-SF#1. Made me feel a bit less jealous of Death Ax's situation. "I don't see him. Where could he have gone?"

"Dinoczar does not see anyone in the other cells, either, master," says Dinoczar. "Maybe they already escaped on their own."

Uh-oh. I had no idea what was going on here, but every bone in my body was screaming at me that this was a trap.

Then I caught a hint of ozone in the air and Dinoczar suddenly slammed into me from behind, yelling, "Master! Watch—"

Boom.

White light. Searing heat. A force that slammed me into a wall.

And then utter silence.

My heart and head pounding, I raised my head, the white light having faded considerably by now.

I was lying inside Death Ax's empty jail cell, staring at the blackened spot of ash that had once been Dinoczar, the air filled with the stench of ozone and smoke. The only remains of Dinoczar were the burnt remains of his paper crown.

And this notification both confirmed Dinoczar's death and made me feel like I was living my worst nightmare:

[DOME WARDEN OLD SPARKY] killed [SIDEKICK DINOCZAR]!

Through the smoke rising from the crater that had once been Dinoczar, Old Sparky emerged. Electric sparks shot off of his fingers as the Warden strode forward, gazing with disappointment at the crater.

"That was disappointing," Old Sparky remarked. "I'd hoped to get you *and* your annoying Sidekick at the same time, but I guess he was more loyal to you than I thought."

Old Sparky brought his foot down on the burning remains of Dinoczar's crown, smashing it flat before grinding it under his heel for good measure.

"You …" I gulped. "Impossible. The Map—"

Old Sparky laughed. "As if I would let myself be so easily tracked."

Frowning, I made the Map appear before me, still showing the Warden on MD-SF#5. "But it says you're still in Medium Security."

"That Map is wrong," said Old Sparky. He shrugged. "Well, not entirely. It still accurately tracks the movements of my Guards, but it always makes up my current location. That way, you never know where I actually am at any given point."

My eyes widened in shock. "So it's useless …"

"Again, not entirely," said Old Sparky. He wagged a finger at me, sending more sparks flying off of it. "But it just goes to show you that one should never mistake the map for the territory. Although I suspect that is a lesson you aren't going to have time to appreciate."

I struggled to make sense of this turn of events. "You mean you knew … this entire time, you knew …"

Old Sparky nodded. "Of course. When I saw you looking at me during Rock Lord's breakout attempt, I knew you were going to be trouble. Although to be honest, even I didn't expect you to get this far."

"Everything was part of your plan," I said in realization. "Putting us in a cell where we could talk to the Prison Guards … me stealing your card key to Top Secret … everything was part of your plan."

Old Sparky put his hands on his hips. "Not quite everything, but most of it. As I said, you did a few things I didn't expect, but nothing I couldn't work into my plan. I played you like a fiddle."

"But you're …" I struggled to find the words. "You're—"

"Fat?" Old Sparky offered. "Paranoid? Slow-witted? Powerful, but dumb? Sure, I like to project that image to the Prisoners of the Dome. But in truth, it's just another one of the many ways I mess with you guys and give you false hope. This isn't even my true appearance."

Old Sparky snapped his fingers. His whole body became covered in crackling electricity, forcing me to cover my eyes to avoid getting blinded. Once the light faded, however, I lowered my eyes, blinking rapidly to allow them to adjust back to the dim light of Top Secret.

A tall, strapping young man in his mid-twenties stood before me. Old Sparky had ditched the formal Warden outfit for a black-and-yellow spandex suit that revealed his powerfully muscular body. His hair was a short crew cut, his round physical features replaced by sharp cheekbones and a jutting chin that could probably break rock. His eyes glowed blue with electrical energy, the lines in his costume glowing with power.

"This is my *real* form," said Old Sparky, his voice younger, stronger, and deeper. He flexed his muscles. "Not so fat anymore, huh?"

"But …" I stared unblinkingly at Old Sparky. "What … how …"

Old Sparky chuckled. "You remember how I wiped the memories of the Prisoners who saw the Rock Lord incident, yes? Lots of people don't realize this, but I am just as strong with Mind Powers as I am with Electric Powers. In fact, Psychic is my actual Type, not Electric. I simply use a very high-level version of Secret Identity to make myself look like a bumbling, balding overweight middle-aged middle manager, when the truth is, I am the exact opposite."

Suddenly, a lot of things about Old Sparky made sense in my mind. His Mind Powers, his overwhelming strength, how a man seemingly as simpleminded as he was could prevent Prisoners smarter than him from escaping …

Everything made perfect sense.

And that was what made it so scary.

I needed to tell Joe. I reached for the Command Interface and, tapping the unmute button on the mike, shouted, "Joe! Get out of the Warden's office! Now!"

Joe, apparently still munching on Old Sparky's donuts, said, "That's a weird sign to open the cells, but okay."

"No, do *not* open the cells," I said. "It's a trap. Everything. We were set up."

"Set up?" Joe said. "Set up by who—"

I heard a door slam open on Joe's end, followed by what was unmistakably the voice of a Prison Guard shouting, "Drop the donuts!"

Then someone screamed like a little girl, only to be interrupted by gunfire, and then a *thunk*. A second later, this notification popped up in my view:

Connection to [Minion-Joe] has been lost. Reconnect? **Y/N**

I didn't bother trying to reconnect, mostly because I knew that Joe was dead.

Old Sparky cocked his head to the side. "What's the matter? Did your stupid Minion get gunned down by my Prison Guards? I hope so, because that's what I told them to do."

I scowled at Old Sparky. "How did you know we would try to break out tonight?"

Old Sparky shrugged. "Truthfully, I didn't. But when I noticed my Top Secret key was missing, well, I knew you must have been planning to try very soon. Or do you think I don't monitor the Dome's security cameras at all times?"

Old Sparky snapped his fingers again and dozens of holographic screens appeared, floating around him like planets orbiting the sun. The screens showed what looked like live footage of various Floors, including one of Abaddon sleeping like a baby in his cell and one showing my own empty cell. Most frighteningly, there were cameras in the Emergency Access Stairs.

"At any time, I can summon the Dome's camera feeds to me and see what is going on anywhere I want," Old Sparky continued. "The Dome, in many ways, is an extension of my very self, which is why I have so much control over it. In essence, I am as close to the god of this prison as any mortal can hope to be."

Old Sparky balled his right hand into a fist and the screens blinked out of existence. Electricity started flowing around his fist, which he held up before his face, a triumphant grin crossing his lips.

"And just like the gods of old, it is my job to dish out judgment on you sinners," said Old Sparky. "To protect the innocent and avenge those who cannot avenge themselves."

I gulped again but rose to my feet shakily. "What about the Toppies? What did you do with them?"

"I put them in temporary holding cells in another part of the prison tonight so I'd have you all to myself," Old Sparky said. "I will put them back here eventually. But first, I am going to cast judgment on you."

Crap. No way in hell could I fight Old Sparky and hope to win, much less survive. But I also couldn't see a way out of here that didn't end with my instant death by lightning.

Suddenly, I was shaking. Up until now, I hadn't died in Capes Online. I'd been punched, beaten, and suffered other types of pain, but I'd never actually *died* before.

And, even though I knew I would respawn eventually, I realized I didn't want to experience death at all. I didn't want to die.

Taking a deep breath, I said, "So what are you going to do to me? Blast me to ashes, like Dinoczar? Or maybe lock me up here in Top Secret with the other Toppies."

Old Sparky shook his head. "No. If I locked you up, you'd eventually find a way to break out. And killing you, while satisfying, wouldn't accomplish anything in the short term. You'd respawn, regroup with your Minions, and then try again, restarting this whole silly, utterly pointless cycle. I'd rather break you instead."

"Break me?" I said. "What do you mean?"

Old Sparky walked up to the entrance to Death Ax's cell. I backed up against the wall, although Old Sparky did not cross the threshold. He just stood there, arms folded in front of his chest, watching me with obvious disgust in his eyes.

"See, you're a pretty willful type," said Old Sparky. "Always the most annoying type of Villain to deal with. You'll keep getting up, no matter how many times I put you down. Driven by your greed and self-interest, you'll never stop trying to break out of here, never stop trying to regain the freedom to harm innocents. It would be admirable if you were a Hero, but unfortunately, you are not."

Then Old Sparky leaned toward me, sparks dancing in his eyes. "But I can break that will of yours. I've done it to other willful Villains. Just ask any of your fellow Maxies who have been down here for longer than a year. The real secret of the Dome's effectiveness is not my overwhelming power or the strength of our security systems, nor the discipline of our Guards. Do you want to know what it is?"

I said nothing. Just stared blankly at Old Sparky.

Old Sparky tapped his head. "Despair. Depriving the Prisoners of all hope of escape or release. Over the two decades I've run this hellhole, I've learned that if you can break a man's spirit, you break the man, even if you don't lay one finger on him. Unfortunately for you, however, I am going to lay a finger on you ... or, at least, something else is."

Old Sparky snapped his fingers again. I flinched, expecting a lightning bolt to come out of nowhere and fry me instantly.

Instead, a hole in the floor opened up underneath me and I plunged down it, screaming my head off as I fell to my doom.

CHAPTER 40

I plunged down the dark pit for a short eternity before I slammed into the ground hard enough to hear an audible *crack* in my spine. I groaned.

A notification popped up in my view:

Debuff added: *Broken Back. -90% Agility and -3 HP/5 second(s). Duration: 30 seconds.*

Goddamn. My back felt like it had broken into a million pieces.
Goddamn Real Pain.
So stupid. Hated this game.
And where the hell was I? I couldn't see anything. It was completely black in here. Would someone turn on a light?
But then something happened that made me forget all about my pain, about the darkness, about my misery.
A monster in the shadows around me growled … and teeth sharper than any knife sank into my neck, ripping flesh out. I tried to scream, but the monster had ripped out my vocal cords, so all that emerged was a weak, sputtering sound that barely qualified as a scream.
More ripping. More tearing. More blood.
And then … more darkness and I felt nothing at all.

A notification then popped up in my view:

You have died!
Thanks for playing Capes Online!
Respawn timer: *1 second.*

I barely even had time to read the notification before finding myself back in the Black Room. This time, at least my back wasn't broken, but everything was still pitch-black.

Rising to my feet, I said, "Hello? Dinoczar? Joe? Are you guys there? Guys—?"

The only answer I got was another growl.

Then something huge and furry slammed into me and thick claws gouged out my eyes and ripped open my face.

Yet somehow, I still read the following death notification just fine:

You have died!
Thanks for playing Capes Online!
Respawn timer: *1 second.*

And then I respawned again.

This time, I didn't say a word. I just ran in what I assumed was the opposite direction of the monster until I hit a wall. Remembering a door from the video of Ursal in the Black Room, I desperately searched for the door handle, but I felt nothing except smooth concrete under my fingers.

Before I could fully search, however, something slashed my back straight open.

Once again, I cried out in pain and fell down.

And once again, the monster hopped on top of me and killed me. This time, I was pretty sure it tore open my skull and ate my brain.

And then I saw the death notification for the third time:

You have died!
Thanks for playing Capes Online!
Respawn timer: *1 second.*

And then I respawned and found myself in the Black Room yet again.

And then I heard the monster growl behind me and felt its claws once again sink into my flesh …

CHAPTER 41

With a hiss, the lid of my GamePod flew open and I sat up. I hastily undid all of the safety straps and, crawling out of the pod, rushed up the stairs to my room. I slammed the door behind me, locked it tight, and then curled up into my bed.

I couldn't do it.

I couldn't handle the *pain* anymore. The pain from the monster clawing my eyes out, tearing open my chest, smashing my brains in, suffocating me under its bulk … I just couldn't do it.

And I didn't know why I suffered ten more deaths before I realized I needed to log off.

That shit shouldn't be legal. That was legit torture. It was what I imagined the CIA put captured terrorists through, only much worse. After all, when you died in real life, you just died once and that was it.

In Capes Online, however, you respawned … over and over and over again until you couldn't take it anymore or you lost your fucking mind.

I still wasn't sure if Old Sparky knew I was a player or not.

But it didn't matter.

The torture had worked.

Old Sparky had broken me.

Completely and thoroughly.

If I'd stayed in there any longer, I would have ended up like Daniel. No, worse than Daniel.

Much, *much* worse.

But the worst part of it wasn't the torture. It wasn't the thought that I could have ended up as crazy as Daniel, if not crazier.

No, the worst thought was that I'd failed to solve Grandpa's Riddle.

I had completely, totally, and utterly *failed*.

Even if the Black Room torture eventually ended—although I doubted it, knowing how sadistic Old Sparky was—I still wouldn't have been able to escape Maximum Security. Old Sparky proved that he had been in control of the situation during my entire time in the Dome. He'd practically planned out everything for me. I had simply been following a script I didn't even realize I was reading.

What did this say about me? That I was so dumb that I could be manipulated by a very advanced piece of code into walking right into a trap? What would Grandpa think?

He'd be ashamed, no doubt. He'd think I was a quitter. He'd think I was stupid. He'd think I'd lost my edge.

And Grandpa would be absolutely right.

And because I couldn't solve the Riddle, I couldn't pay for Mom's hospital bills. I couldn't pay for Daniel's nursing home. I couldn't help anyone.

I couldn't even help myself.

I punched my pillow. I thought about talking to Mom, but I knew she was probably asleep. She wouldn't understand, anyway. Nor would Daniel, for that matter. I couldn't let either of them know about what I was doing. It was pointless at this point, anyway, seeing as there was no chance I would get the money needed to pay for their medical bills now.

"What's wrong, Robby?" said Grandpa's voice suddenly. "You seem upset."

Startled, I looked up to see Grandpa sitting in my gaming chair across from my bed. With his legs crossed and his arms resting on the chair's armrests, Grandpa looked very, well, real. For a moment, I even thought he had come back from the dead.

But then I realized it was just the holo-projector, which I'd left on my chair. Somehow, it had activated on its own or maybe I had forgotten to turn it off or something, letting me see the same

Grandpa recording that had sent me on this stupid quest in the first place.

Wiping the tears out of my eyes, I said, "No shit, Sherlock. I failed."

Grandpa raised an eyebrow. "Failed? Failed what?"

Scowling, I sat up and gestured toward the door to my room. "The Riddle. I failed to solve the stupid fucking Riddle you gave me. I quit."

"You quit?" Grandpa repeated. "So easily?"

My hands balled tightly into fists. "I didn't quit easily. I quit because I tried my best and it still wasn't enough. I'm not smart enough to solve the Riddle. I failed."

Grandpa cocked his head to the side. "You only fail if you think you have."

I scowled even more at Grandpa. "Why the hell am I even talking to you, anyway? You're not the real Grandpa. You're not even his Digital Double. You're just a recording. I am talking to a literal recording of my actual Grandpa. What even is my life at this point?"

Grandpa shrugged. "Do you have anyone else to talk to?"

I pursed my lips. "No, I don't."

Grandpa put both of his feet on the floor and leaned toward me. "Then just believe, for a moment, that I am your actual grandfather and not merely a highly advanced recording of him. What harm does it do? Even if it's false, it isn't like I will be telling you to do something bad."

I rose to my feet, glaring at Grandpa. "Like when you handed me that gun and told me to shoot that widow in the head?"

Grandpa smirked. "I thought it was just a game, Robby. Isn't that what you always tell yourself? None of those people are real. Even the widow you murdered was just a bit of code. You didn't actually murder anyone. Your guilt is highly irrational."

I really, really hated it when Grandpa used logic when I was really emotional.

And I really, really hated it when he was right.

My shoulders slumping, I sat back down on my bed. "Then what am I supposed to do? I clearly failed the challenge. Old Sparky was aware of my movements the entire time. He took out my only two allies and put me into an endless loop of torture specifically designed to break me mentally. That's about as close to game over as it gets for real people like me."

Grandpa leaned back, a thoughtful expression on his face. "That does sound like a sticky situation to find oneself in. I wouldn't want to face that fate myself."

"Thanks for the empathy," I said with a snort. "Even though I know you're just a recording and can't feel actual empathy like real human beings can."

"I don't need to feel empathy to tell that you need help," said Grandpa. "Or, for that matter, to offer it to you."

"What sort of help could *you* possibly give *me*?" I said. I pointed at Grandpa. "The real Grandpa never even played Capes Online. I doubt you have anything useful to tell me."

"True, my original self wasn't much of a gamer despite his fascination with digital immortality," Grandpa replied. "But I don't need to be a pro gamer to tell you that you have been approaching this game wrongly from the very start."

I felt like Grandpa had slapped me in the face. "What are you talking about? I've just been following your instructions."

Grandpa shook his head. "Not quite. For the most part, you've been doing things your own way. You've held the entire game world at arm's length, afraid to treat it as anything other than a game, looking at the game's characters as if their lives do not matter."

"Because they don't," I said. "And I don't want to lose my mind like Daniel."

Grandpa cocked his head to the side again. "Do you want your mother and Daniel to continue to suffer? Because they will, if you continue to sulk like this. Then again, thinking about your own well-being *is* rather villainous, so perhaps you are more integrated into the game than even you realize."

"I can't take care of my family if I lose my mind," I said.

"You won't need to if you can get my wealth," said Grandpa. "But really, you have been hesitant to go all-in ever since you first accepted my challenge. You don't want to lose your sense of self or your grip on reality, so you treat everyone around you in-game as pawns to be used and abused as needed. You don't want to risk sacrificing yourself."

"They're not real," I insisted. "Their feelings don't matter."

Grandpa smirked. "Did I say that it was *wrong* to treat them that way? No. I am merely saying that you have had everything you needed to solve the Riddle all along, but your unwillingness to empathize with the game's characters means you will never see the forest for the trees."

"How do you empathize with video game characters?" I said. "That doesn't make sense."

"Empathy is simply another word for understanding, Robby," Grandpa said. "If you understand what Old Sparky wants, what the Prison Guards want, what your fellow Prisoners want … then you can use that to your advantage and control them far more efficiently without them even being aware."

I frowned. "You sound like a Villain yourself right now, Grandpa."

Grandpa smiled. "Is that a bad thing, given the context of this discussion? Your in-game Class is Big Bad, but you haven't truly been acting like one yet."

"And in order to do so, I need to start understanding my enemies better, to know what they want and …" My voice trailed off as things started to click in my mind. "Oh. *Oh*."

Grandpa smiled even more. "I know that expression. Everything I just told you is starting to make sense, isn't it?"

I nodded quickly. "Yes. Yes, I think I see what you mean. But … I can't handle the pain. It's too real."

Grandpa frowned. "Again, you're forgetting your resources. There is still one trump card you have yet to use, the one that will almost, by itself, guarantee your victory. You know what it is. You just need to use it."

I did. I knew exactly what I needed to know now, although I wondered how Grandpa knew about it. Or this version of Grandpa, anyway, who wasn't even connected to Capes Online and therefore shouldn't know anything about how I had played it so far.

But truthfully, it didn't matter how he knew it.

What mattered was that I now knew what I needed to do to solve the Riddle.

Rising to my feet, I said to Grandpa, "Thanks. I know you're not my real Grandpa and never will be, but like you said, no harm in treating you like you are. You're more helpful than some real people I know, anyway."

Grandpa smiled at me. "I am glad I could be of service, Robby. But tell me, what are you going to do now?"

I looked Grandpa straight in the eyes. "I am going back into Capes Online. I am going to free every damn prisoner in the Dome. And I am going to make that donut-munching psycho pay for what he did to me."

CHAPTER 42

When I logged back into Capes Online a moment later, I did not appear back in my cot in my cell. Instead, I found myself lying on the cold, bloodstained concrete floor of the Black Room, seemingly all by myself.

Of course, I knew I wasn't by myself this time. There was a monster in here, one I couldn't see and knew nothing about.

But I did know it was here. It was somewhere nearby, even if I couldn't see, hear, or even smell it.

But I suspected it couldn't see me, either.

It was a realization that had occurred to me while I spoke to the recording of Grandpa in the real world. The Black Room, per its name, was always pitch-black. Why would a monster need working eyes in a room without light? It was like how most fish in the deepest parts of the ocean in the real world had no working eyes because there was no need for them.

If my theory was correct, the monster relied primarily upon sound to find and kill its prey. Possibly scent, too, but I doubted scent was as reliable a sound for tracking living prey than sound.

So my plan was simple:

Lie as quietly on the floor as possible until I got the power necessary to defeat the monster.

And so far, the plan was working. Even though I'd been logged in for approximately thirty seconds now, I didn't hear or feel the monster nearby. The only thing I heard was my own heartbeat and the only thing I felt was the freezing concrete floor underneath me, stained with my blood and the blood of previous victims of the monster.

Then I felt the monster's hot breath on the back of my neck. I froze, thinking that my plan had failed already, that I had gotten the monster's senses completely wrong, and that I was going to die again. My heart raced at the thought of restarting the endless cycle of dying and respawning in this hellhole.

A second later, however, I heard the *click-clack* of the monster's claws against the floor followed by the sound of something heavy landing on the floor with a *grunt*. A moment later, I heard soft snoring coming from the darkness around me. It sounded like it came from behind me, but I couldn't tell for sure due to how dark it was.

I breathed a silent sigh of relief. It looked like my theory was correct. The creature relied on movement and sound to detect prey. It might not have even been able to distinguish between corpses and still living beings.

Regardless, I wasn't going to push my luck.

It was time to get help.

I opened my menu and navigated over to LINKS. Finding [???], I clicked her name, causing this screen to pop up in front of me:

Would you like to Link with [???]? **Y/N**

I hit "Y," causing another notification to appear:

Linking with [???] … Linking with [???] …

I frowned. This was the first time I'd tried to actively Link with the Ghost of the Dome, so I had no idea if this would actually work or not.

Suddenly, I heard the voice of the Ghost in my ear, like a cold winter breeze. "You are back. I thought you'd quit."

"I didn't," I whispered, keeping my voice as low as possible to avoid waking the sleeping beast. "It was a strategic retreat."

"Interesting euphemism for 'running away and crying like a little boy,'" said the Ghost. "Perhaps I should deny your Link request. You clearly aren't strong enough to handle my power or worthy of its use."

My hands balled into tight fists. "Shut up. I don't need your snark. I need your power. It's the only way I am going to get out of the Black Room and teach Old Sparky a lesson."

The Ghost purred in my ear. "Ah … vengeance. Such a powerful motivation. It is what motivates me, too. Yet it will take far more than the desire for vengeance against our common enemies to convince me to Link with you again. How do I know you won't simply end up getting curb stomped by that silly old Warden again?"

I scowled. "Because this time, I won't hold back. I want *all* of your power."

The Ghost seemed taken aback by my demand. "All of it?"

"Yes," I said. "I'm done sneaking around. I'm done planning. I'm ready to turn this entire prison upside down. And I need your power to do it."

"My, my," said the Ghost. "I didn't realize you had such … *conviction* inside you. You've never been this bold with your requests before."

"That's because this isn't a request," I said. "This is a demand. And I won't take no for an answer."

I waited for the Ghost's response. During my talk with Grandpa back in the real world, I'd realized that he was right.

I *had* been holding back. I'd been afraid of immersing myself too deeply in Capes Online. I'd been worried about losing my grip on reality, about falling into the same traps that ruined Daniel's mind.

But the truth was, I couldn't win unless I stopped holding back. Unless I did everything I possibly could to succeed.

Until I put my very sanity on the line, just to ensure my victory.

And that included Linking with the Ghost and using every Power and Skill she had. The Ghost was the only being who might possibly be able to match Old Sparky's power level in this place. If I could get her strength, then I might be able to defeat Old Sparky and break everyone out of the Dome.

In other words, in order to defeat Old Sparky, I truly needed to become the Big Bad my character sheet said I was.

No matter the cost.

Finally, the Ghost said, "You drive a hard bargain, Maelstrom. But it was this inner strength that attracted me to you in the first place. I accept."

Even as the Ghost said those words, this notification flashed into view:

Link activated! You are now Linked with [???]. You now have access to [???]'s Powers, Skills, Levels, and more for the next 1 hour(s)!

"Don't make me regret this, Maelstrom," said the Ghost, her voice now becoming more and more distant. "And, next time you see him, give the Warden a hello from the Ghost of the Dome …"

The Ghost's voice faded into absolute silence, leaving me lying there on the floor of the Black Room by myself, listening to the soft snoring of the sleeping monster nearby.

Despite having Linked with the Ghost, I didn't feel all that different from how I normally did. So I opened my menu and swiped through it, deciding to see exactly what Powers I now had at my command.

Unfortunately, when I checked my character sheet, I got this notification:

ERROR. [???] has not allowed you to view her character sheet.

That seemed like bull to me. How else was I supposed to take advantage of our Link if I didn't even know what she could do?

Not that it mattered. I remember from the last few times I'd Linked with her how I'd taken down Bi-Clops and Ursal easily using her strength.

It was time to put our Link to the test.

Rising to my feet, I turned in what I assumed was the general direction of the monster and shouted, "Hey, monster! Let's try this again. Round Two!"

The monster stopped snoring. I heard it rise slowly to its feet, a low growl emitting from its throat.

That was when this notification popped up in my view:

[???] is offering you access to her Night Vision! **Accept? Y/N**

Naturally, I accepted the offer, which I found interesting. Linking hadn't worked like this before. Then again, before I hadn't actually used any of the Ghost's Powers or Skills. It made me wish I'd done more research into Linking before I jumped back into the game.

Regardless, as soon as I accepted her offer, I found I could suddenly … *see* again. In fact, I could see the Black Room as clear as day, allowing me to see the monster for the first time.

It was huge. The beast resembled a cross between a lion and a bear, with a bit of gorilla thrown in for good measure. With the bulk of a bear and the mane of a lion, the creature looked like an unnatural abomination. And like I thought, it had no eyes. It only had bangs that partially covered patches of skin and fur where its eyes would normally be.

I Scanned the creature and got this information:

Name: *Chimera [Lion-Bear-Gorilla Hybrid]*
Level: *300*
Weak Point: *Nose*
Description: *Created by the scientists from Synth Group, Chimeras^{TM} are scientific experiments as a result of heavy genetic manipulation. Chimeras^{TM} come in an endless variety of different types based on the combination of animals involved. This particular Chimera seems to have been designed according to the specifications of Old Sparky.*

Synth Group even trademarked their genetic abominations? Truly, Capes Online was wild. It made me wonder if the Chimeras were from the same experiment that created Dinoczar and his people.

I didn't have time to think about that, however, before the Chimera roared like a lion and leaped toward me. Claws longer than swords erupted from its paws, its whole body glowing a shining red color that gave it a terrifying appearance.

But this time, I fought back.

Pulling my fist back, I aimed squarely for the Chimera's nose.

Time seemed to slow down as the Chimera flew toward me, maw open, screaming at the top of its lungs.

Another notification from the Ghost:

[???] is offering Destructive Punch! **Accept? Y/N**

Without even thinking, I accepted. Dark power suddenly flowed through my body and shadow energy crackled around my fist.

Just in time, because the Chimera's claws were less than an inch away from my fist.

I shot forward, past the Chimera's claws and slammed my fist squarely into its nose.

The Chimera flew backward from the blow. It crashed into the floor, bounced several times, and then slammed into the wall on the other side of the room. The impact of the chimera shook the entire Black Room, sending dust raining down on my head.

But the Chimera did not get back up. It just lay there, as unmoving as the grave.

Shaking my fist, I turned away from the Chimera. Although it wasn't dead, I had no reason to kill it. Killing it would just waste time. I knew Old Sparky had cameras in the Black Room. It was only a matter of time before he or one of the other Prison Guards noticed my defeat of the Chimera.

I needed to move fast.

But then I heard a low growl behind me and, sighing, looked over my shoulder.

The Chimera was back on its feet. But just barely. I'd smashed the creature's nose into its face, making its growls sound weak and pathetic. Its mane was matted with blood, while one of its legs had clearly been dislocated from its shoulder. It "stared" at me, which was the only word I could use to describe the blind beast turning its face toward me.

I narrowed my eyes and cracked my knuckles. "Want to rumble again, kitty? That's fine. I could do this all—"

A notification interrupted me:

Chimera wants to become your Minion! **Accept? Y/N**

I raised an eyebrow. "The Chimera wants to become my Minion—? What the—?"

"You defeated it in combat," said the Ghost in my ear. "Consider this creature's genetic makeup. It comes from three species where the weak naturally obey the strong. This beast views you as the alpha male that it must submit to. It recognizes your authority, in other words."

I cocked my head to the side. "That's interesting. Wasn't planning on obtaining more Minions, but I suppose it never hurts to have more."

I hit "Y" and got the following notification:

Congratulations! Chimera has become your second Minion! Go over to the MINIONS tab in your menu to see his Stats, Powers, Equipment, and more!

NOTE: *Big Bads can only control up to a certain number of Minions at a time. Your limit is currently 5 Minions. To increase your Minion count, keep leveling up your character.*

As soon as I accepted Chimera's offer to become my Minion, the beast stood up. It bowed its head toward me, a clear sign that the Chimera had submitted to my authority.

"That's nice and all, but he's still very injured," I said. "Doubt he will be of much use to me in his current state."

"I can help with that," said the Ghost.

Yet another notification popped up in my view:

[???] is offering you Heal! **Accept? Y/N**

Accepting it again, I pointed my hand toward the Chimera and activated my new Power.

A golden wave suddenly washed over the Chimera's body. A second later, the Chimera was good as new, its HP back to full, all of its injuries healed up.

"That's convenient," I said. "I didn't know you had a healing Power."

"I have many varied and useful Powers, Maelstrom," said the Ghost. "And they are yours to use as needed."

I grinned. "You know, it would be very helpful if I could view your entire character sheet."

"Knowledge is power, Maelstrom," said the Ghost. "Do you think I'd really give up that power to you?"

I scowled. "If we are going to work together to get out of here, then yeah, I think you should."

"I will give you the Powers and Skills you need when you need them," said the Ghost. "Not a moment later, not a moment sooner."

I scowled even deeper, but realized that I didn't have the time to argue with the Ghost about her lack of communication with me. Guess I'd just have to trust the secretive ghost of a dead witch whose real name I didn't even know at this point to help me when I needed it.

"Now are we going to leave the Black Room or not?" said the Ghost. "I expect Old Sparky and the Prison Guards will be on their way shortly, especially once they realize you are back."

"We will," I said. "But first, I need to contact a couple of people and get some things in order."

The Ghost huffed. "Do we even have time for that?"

Opening the Command Interface, I said, "Don't worry. It shouldn't take long for me to get everything in order."

"In order?" the Ghost repeated. "In order for what?"

I grinned again as I clicked Joe's name on the Command Interface. "In order to stage the biggest breakout in the history of the Dome, of course."

CHAPTER 43

After quickly communicating my victory over the Chimera to Joe and Dinoczar and working out another plan, I kicked open the door to the Black Room and immediately found myself facing down well over a hundred Prison Guards in the hallway before me. As soon as the Prison Guards saw me, they raised their guns and fired.

However, I'd been anticipating this. With a wave of my hand, I used Energy Barrier—another one of the Ghost's Powers—to form a thick, purple Barrier made of pure Energy before me.

And not a moment too soon, because the Barrier caught all of the hundreds of bullets that the Prison Guards had shot at me.

Instead of bouncing the bullets off of the Barrier, however, the Barrier actually dissolved them into nothingness. In the corner of my eye, I saw my Energy meter—which was way bigger than it normally was, at 1,000 Energy thanks to my Link with the Ghost—refill as the Barrier turned each bullet into 1 point of Energy.

In seconds, all of the bullets were gone and my Energy was back to full. On the other side of the Barrier, I saw the Prison Guards lowering their guns, disbelief etched on their faces.

Cracking my neck, I said, "This Energy Barrier thing is really useful. It practically pays for itself."

"Indeed," said the Ghost. "But perhaps you can be amazed by my Powers some other time. There are enemies about."

Of course, the Ghost was referring to the Prison Guards. They looked like they were at a loss for how to deal with me or were maybe just confused that I was using a Power when I was clearly not supposed to be able to use Powers in the Dome. Thank Snow for the Emerald Heart, which I still had in my possession even after dying multiple times in the Black Room. Turned out it had just been lying on the floor of the Black Room the entire time while Chimera was killing me. I'd been worried that Old Sparky might have taken it or something after I died and logged off for a while.

I didn't know where in the Dome I was, exactly. The Map said I was somewhere between Maximum Security and Top Secret, with MX-SF#10 being just down the hall. The Map also showed that the Black Room was close to the Prison Guards' locker room, which explained where all of these Prison Guards had come from.

"What are you waiting for?" the Ghost hissed in my ear. "Kill them all before they reload their guns and shoot us again!"

I shook my head. "I have a much better idea. Watch."

I stepped forward. In response, the Prison Guards raised their guns, even though they had to know by now that their puny weapons didn't stand a chance against me.

Yet I showed no fear, no hesitation. I could tell the Prison Guards were Intimidated, afflicted by the same Skill that Dinoczar used on Joe what seemed like an eternity ago, a Skill that the Ghost just so happened to have (although at a much higher Level, let me tell you). They did not seem to be frozen with fear, necessarily, but they were significantly weaker and less likely to attack me immediately.

"Prison Guards of the Dome," I said, raising my voice. "I am Maelstrom, a Prisoner of the Dome."

"We know that already," one of the Prison Guards, who I recognized as Ike, snapped. "That's why we're here. We saw you take down the Chimera in the Black Room. We're here to make sure you don't go any farther than this hallway, per the Warden's orders."

I cracked my neck. "You all saw how easily I stopped your bullets. You know how I defeated the Chimera. What makes you think that any of you won't suffer a cruel, painful, and utterly humiliating death at my hands?"

"Because you're a monster!" another Prison Guard, this one

apparently named Lenny according to his name tag, shouted. "Die, Villain!"

Lenny rushed forward, two guns in hand, screaming obscenities at the top of his lungs.

I let him make it three steps before I decided he would make an excellent example to the other Prison Guards of what not to do in life.

Raising my hand toward Lenny, I activated another one of the Ghost's Powers, Dehydration.

In seconds, Lenny's skin turned dryer than dust. He gasped for breath, dropping both of his guns onto the floor. He himself collapsed a moment later, panting and breathing hard. Lenny reached out toward me with one shaking hand before his skin turned to dust, leaving his fully clothed skeleton lying on the ground between us.

You killed [PRISON GUARD LENNY]!

I gave the other Prison Guards an unimpressed look. "Does anyone wish to join Lenny in whatever counts as the afterlife in this place or do you want to talk?"

"Talk?" Ike repeated. He pointed his gun at me again. "We don't talk with Prisoners. If you think we're going to negotiate your release—"

"Of course not," I said. "I'm not naive enough to think that you will be open to listening to why you should let me walk out of this place. For that matter, I know that only Old Sparky can release a Prisoner from the Dome. Even if you wanted to let me go, you couldn't because the Warden wouldn't allow it."

"Then … what do you want to talk about?" said Ike, confusion evident in his voice.

In fact, confusion was clearly written on the faces of the other Prison Guards. That was good. It meant they were willing to hear me out.

I spread my arms. "It's no secret in the Dome that damn near every Prisoner wants out. From Minimum Security to Top Secret, absolutely no one likes this place. That is the nature of prisoners and not just the ones in the Dome, either. Humans hate being locked up and will do anything we can to get our freedom back."

Another Prison Guard, named Adam, snorted. "That's like saying the sky is blue. What's your point?"

I pointed at the Prison Guards. "My point, my slow-witted friend, is that we Prisoners aren't the only ones who want out of this place. You Prison Guards are just as trapped in this hellhole as we are, if not even more so."

"What are you talking about?" Ike demanded. "We're not locked up behind bars like you guys or closely watched during our mealtimes. We have far more freedom than you Prisoners."

I smiled. "But you can't actually *leave* this place, can you? You and all of your fellow Prison Guards must live here twenty-four hours a day, seven days a week, just to make sure none of us Prisoners escape. These walls imprison you guys as much as they imprison me and my fellow inmates. We are trapped by walls and bars, but you are trapped by obligation and contracts."

"We're keeping society safe," said Ike, although I caught a hint of doubt in his voice. "The Warden says we're the only thing standing between order and chaos. If that means sacrificing our personal lives for the greater good, then so be it."

I tilted my head to the side. "Are you protecting society from chaos, though? Are you really? Or is that just Old Sparky's way of keeping you in line? He is very manipulative, you know. He might just be saying that in order to keep you from leaving the Dome and discovering a life outside of work."

"But why would the Warden do that?" asked Jorge. "That don't make sense."

I tapped the side of my head. "Power. The Warden simply enjoys controlling people. Prisoners or Prison Guards, it doesn't matter. In the end, as long as he can attach his strings to you, the Warden is happy. High on his own ego and lacking the ability to respect others' free will, the Warden is as tyrannical as any dictator, except on a much smaller and much pettier scale."

"You can't just say that about the Warden," Ike said. "He'll—"

"He'll what?" I interrupted him. "Kill me? Torture me? Lock me up even tighter than he already has? And what do you think he will do to any of you who ask to go outside of the Dome and have a life beyond these walls?"

Uncomfortable looks were traded between the Prison Guards, which meant I'd hit closer to home than any of them were willing to admit.

"Maybe if we just ask, we can convince him to let us leave the Dome," said Adam. He glanced around at his fellow Prison Guards. "I mean, has anyone even tried talking to the boss about our working conditions?"

"And if you do, what do you think Old Sparky will say?" I said. "Do you think he'll approve even one day off a week for you guys? Or do you think he'll zap you to hell just for daring to even think about that? I know that many of you want a life outside of the Dome but cannot due to Old Sparky's tyranny. I'm simply voicing thoughts you already have."

"Even if you're right, so what?" said Ike. "It's not like any of us can stand up to Old Sparky. He's too strong."

I held out a hand toward Ike. "You're right. But *I* can. I can defeat Old Sparky. I can end his reign of terror. I just need you to step aside and let me do it."

"You want *us* to work for *you*?" Adam repeated with a snort. "Yeah. Like we'd ever work for a Villain like you."

I quirked an eyebrow. "Even if I offered you freedom? Even if I gave you the chance to see your families and develop a life outside of your job? I'm not even asking you to become my Minions. I'm just asking for your cooperation until we can get rid of Old Sparky. You don't have to do anything else for me, other than get out of my way and let me have a crack at him. What do you say?"

None of the Prison Guards responded at first, but I could tell that each one of them was thinking through my words. They were probably thinking harder than they had ever been asked to think before in their lives, but I wasn't expecting a quick or immediate response.

I was, however, expecting the best response for me.

Finally, Ike stepped forward. He raised his gun ... and fired it at me again.

Startled, I deflected the bullet with another Energy Barrier, sending it flying into the wall to my right. I stared in disbelief at Ike, whose grip on his gun never wavered.

"Why did you try to shoot me?" I said. "I am offering you freedom."

Ike snorted. "No, you're not. You're just asking to exchange one set of chains for another. Even if we're sick of being stuck in this place like the Prisoners, we still aren't going to ignore our duties and just let you leave."

"I told you you should have just killed them all," the Ghost whispered in my ear. "It would have saved you a lot of time."

I scowled. "I don't need another snarky sidekick commenting on my mistakes."

The Ghost growled. "If you think I am a sidekick, then you are gravely mistaken."

"Doesn't matter," I muttered. "I've got a backup plan. We'll be fine."

"Who are you talking to, Prisoner?" Ike demanded.

I looked at Ike and the Prison Guards again. "None of your business. And if I were you, Ike, I'd be more focused on surviving against me than whatever I might be saying to myself."

Ike reloaded his gun and pointed it at me again. "We still outnumber you. Even if you somehow got a boost in absolute power, that doesn't change a damn thing. We can still kill you."

Jorge suddenly raised a walkie-talkie in the air. "Plus, I just told the Warden you're back. He'll be here any minute, and then you'll really be sorry."

I sighed. "That would be a very sticky pickle for me indeed … but fortunately, I have an army of my own, just waiting to help."

"Army?" Ike repeated. "What army?"

Grinning like a maniac, I raised my hand and snapped my fingers.

A second later, a loud alarm suddenly blared in the hallways, followed by a computerized voice saying, "ALERT! ALERT! EVERY SINGLE PRISON CELL IN MAXIMUM SECURITY HAS BEEN OPENED AND EVERY PRISONER IN MAXIMUM SECURITY IS FREE! ALL PRISON GUARDS *MUST* REPORT TO DUTY ASAP!"

"What the hell?" said Ike, looking around in alarm along with the other Prison Guards. He whipped his head toward me in disbelief. "How did you do—"

The walkie-talkie hanging off his belt suddenly crackled and a voice I did not recognize but figured was probably another Prison Guard shouted from it, "Ike! This is Bill. Someone released the Maxies. My men are on MX-SF Number Four trying to keep them from advancing, but there's just too damn many of them and they keep respawning!"

Swiping the walkie-talkie off his belt, Ike shouted into it, "Respawning? How?"

"They keep respawning in their cells," said Bill frantically. "But the worst part isn't the respawning. It's their Powers. They are using their Powers in the—"

A sound like roaring fire abruptly interrupted Bill and we heard his screams of terror before his walkie-talkie suddenly went silent.

"Bill?" Ike shouted into the walkie-talkie again. "Bill, this is Ike. Do you read me? Bill?"

No response.

"Did Bill say that some of the Prisoners were using their Powers?" said Jorge with a gulp. "Please tell me that Bill did not just say what I thought he said."

"He did," said Ike, "but that doesn't make sense. The Dome's Power Negation Field should still be—"

A notification suddenly appeared in my vision, and based on the shocked expressions of the Prison Guards before me, it had clearly appeared in theirs, too. And, if I could hazard a guess, I would think that every single Prison Guard and Prisoner in the Dome probably saw it right now, too.

It simply said this:

WARNING: *Power Negation Field has been nullified. All Prisoners on all Floors can now freely use their Powers within the walls of the Dome.*

CHAPTER 44

"What the hell?" Ike said, clearly reading the notification. "Who—? How—?"

I cocked my head to the side. "Deary me, this definitely makes things more complicated for you guys, doesn't it?"

Ike swiped the air like he was getting rid of the notification and glared at me. "This is your doing somehow. How did you turn off the Dome's Power Negation Field?"

I shrugged. "I don't know. Why don't you ask my pet? He would be happy to tell you. She's very personable once you get to know her."

Ike frowned in confusion. "Your pet—?"

Chimera suddenly flew out from the Black Room behind me and bounded straight into the hallway full of Prison Guards. Roaring loudly, Chimera ripped through the first wave of Prison Guards like toilet paper, aside from Ike, who managed to dive out of the way in the nick of time.

His fellow Prison Guards, however, were considerably less fortunate. They all fell underneath the Chimera's sudden attack, crying out and screaming obscenities as my new Minion ripped and tore through them like the monster she was.

That's right. I forgot to mention that the Chimera was actually female. Not that you could tell after whatever those Synth Group guys did to her, but the Chimera's character sheet listed her sex as female. Interesting things you learn about your Minions when you read their character sheets.

Hearing a *beep* in my ear, I switched over to my Command Interface, where I saw I could now toggle between Joe's and the Chimera's points of view. The *beep* had been a notification from Joe, so I toggled over to his view to find Joe sitting in front of the mirror in our cell. His face was bruised and beaten but he otherwise looked normal.

"How did it go, Joe?" I asked.

Joe smirked. "Perfectly. The Warden honestly didn't think we'd try the same thing twice. And finding the Dome's control system to turn off all of the security settings was easier than stealing candy from a baby."

I nodded. "Did you make sure that Old Sparky couldn't turn the Power Negation Field back on?"

Joe nodded in response. "Yep. I smashed everything I could. It will probably take that fat bastard a while to fix everything, although given the general chaos going on outside at the moment, I think he will have more pressing concerns than fixing his stuff at the moment."

I smiled. "Excellent work, Joe. And where are you right now?"

"Hiding in our cell," said Joe. He glanced to the right like he was looking at something off-screen. "Like I said, right, it's pretty chaotic outside. There's practically an all-out war raging between the Prisoners and the Prison Guards, something you told me wouldn't happen."

I scowled. "It's not my fault. Turns out that Old Sparky has these idiots more brainwashed than I realized. But no matter. I'm sure this breakout will still be a success regardless of whether we win over the Prison Guards or not."

Dinoczar suddenly appeared above Joe's head in the mirror, wagging his tail behind him like an excited dog. "And Dinoczar helped! Dinoczar is very good at smashing things with his tail and big feet. Dinoczar also ate a lot of the Warden's donuts, so Dinoczar is also on a big sugar high at the moment."

"Thanks, Dinoczar," I said. "Right now, Chimera is making short work of the Prison Guards who greeted me at the Black Room, but we will be making our way up to higher Sub-Floors shortly. Wait for me there."

"Don't need to tell *us* twice," Joe said with a shake of his head. "Even though everything is going according to plan, I still feel like this is a terrible plan."

"It's our *only* plan," I replied. "And if it works out, then all of us will get our freedom. Do you know where Old Sparky is, per chance?"

"No, sir, we do not," Dinoczar said. "He was not in his office when Joe and Dinoczar broke in again."

"Rumor has it that he's on the higher Floors again," said Joe, "but we aren't sure."

I licked my lips. "Well, if you do see him, shoot me a message. See ya."

I muted and minimized the Command Interface before sighing. With the revelation that the Map was useless in tracking Old Sparky, that meant I couldn't keep track of his movements in the Dome. My hope was that the mass breakout would distract Old Sparky long enough for me to pull off the next phase of my plan, but I didn't know for sure how much the breakout would slow down Old Sparky, if at all.

Regardless of where Old Sparky was and what he was doing now, I knew I needed to get to Top Secret. It was necessary for the next phase of my plan.

So I ran down the hallway, past the scores of fallen Prison Guards, and past Chimera, who was locked in combat with the remaining Prison Guards. A handful of the Prison Guards tried to break off from the group to attack me, but thanks to Linking with the Ghost, I was much faster than them.

And it turned out that turning your back on a giant, merciless monster just to go after one Prisoner was a good way to get killed by said monster. Who'd a thunk it?

Reaching the end of the hallway, I kicked open the doors and found myself on MX-SF#10 again. But I stopped, gazing in astonishment at the scene playing out before me.

Joe hadn't been kidding. There really *was* an all-out war playing out in the Dome. Prisoners poured out from the open prison cells in droves, attacking the Prison Guards, who shot, beat, and killed the Prisoners as quickly as they could. Just as Bill the Prison Guard had reported, however, dead Prisoners would simply respawn in their cells and jump out, ready for Round Two.

That had been another part of the plan. One of the features of the Dome was that Prisoners were locked to respawn in their respective cells. Normally, this proved an excellent deterrent for any would-be escapee, because it meant that anyone who tried to escape would not only be killed, but end up right back where they started, locked up behind bars.

But with every cell in Maximum Security—and probably in Medium and Minimum Securities, too—now open, all it meant was that killed Prisoners could get back into the fight in fairly short order.

By contrast, the Prison Guards, as far as I could tell, did not respawn. Or if they did, they probably respawned in the Locker Room, which just so happened to be situated under MX-SF#10. This meant that any Prison Guard who died on one of the higher Sub-Floors would, by necessity, be forced to climb back up to the surface, which would in turn lower the number of active Prison Guards on the higher Sub-Floors, which in turn would make it much easier for the Prisoners on the higher Sub-Floors to escape.

All in all, it was a wonderful cycle that all but assured the success of our breakout.

Unfortunately, I probably shouldn't have paused to reflect on my own brilliance, because I heard the sounds of guns being loaded nearby. Looking around, I saw well over a dozen more Prison Guards pointing their guns at me.

"Stop right there, Prisoner," said the lead Prison Guard, whose name was Frank. "Take one more step forward and we'll riddle your corpse with bullets."

I cocked my head to the side. "Do you honestly think your little toys will actually do anything to me? That's pretty rich."

Frank scowled. "We'll see whose laughing when—"

Frank was interrupted when the wall to our left exploded open. Chunks of concrete flew outward in a wave, striking several of the

Prison Guards who were currently menacing me. Their armor and helmets, however, seemed to protect them from most of the debris, but they still turned their weapons toward the smoking wall. Even I had to turn my attention to it, wondering who had just come to my rescue.

"Who's there?" Frank demanded. "Show yourself!"

No response.

And then, without warning, the various Prison Guards who had been attacking me started to collapse and scream. Their skin turned a pale purple shade as they struggled against whatever force was clearly killing them, but it was obvious they were fighting a losing battle. I watched, in both horror and fascination, as strange wisps of purple and white energy shot out of their heads and disappeared into thin air.

A second later, the dozen Prison Guards who had been attacking me now lay dead at my feet. I knew they were dead primarily thanks to this notification, which also told me the identity of their killer:

[Prisoner #2X] killed [Prison Guard] x12!

"What pathetic souls these Prison Guards have," came the familiar guttural growl of Death Ax from the smoky opening in the wall. "I have eaten the souls of animals with more passion than these fools."

From out of the smoke emerged Death Ax, scythe in hand, looking very pissed off. Nor was he alone. Walking behind him I counted eight other Top Secret inmates, most of whom I didn't recognize, although I figured they all had to be at least as powerful as Death Ax. The only other Top Secret inmate I recognized was Rock Lord, who cracked his knuckles and glared at the dead Prison Guards.

"Death Ax," I said with a nod. "Good to see you again."

Death Ax returned my nod with one of his own. "Maelstrom. I must say, I am impressed you managed to do what you said you would do. When the Warden hid us from you, I assumed that your plan had been foiled and that you would be tortured forever in the Black Room."

I chuckled. "Nope. My plan just getting started. How did you guys get out of your cells?"

Rock Lord cracked his neck from side to side. "The Dome's security systems went down, which caused our cells to open." He looked at me closely. "So you are this Maelstrom that Death Ax has been telling us about. You are smaller than I expected, although I feel like I have seen you somewhere before."

I tapped the side of my head. "Probably during your own little breakout a couple of weeks ago."

Rock Lord narrowed his eyes. "Ah, yes. I do remember nearly crushing you and your cellmates to death. Perhaps it was good I did not, seeing as you have saved us."

Then Rock Lord looked out across the sea of fighting Prisoners and Prison Guards, an eager smile appearing on his lips. "Either way, we are busting out of this joint."

"What about Old Sparky?" Death Ax asked. "Is he still around?"

"I don't know where he is," I said with a shake of my head. I pointed down the hall. "But that's why we need to get a move on. He's probably still on the upper Floors dealing with the Maxies. If we move fast enough, we might even be able to escape before he can stop us."

"No need to tell us twice," Rock Lord grunted. He cracked his knuckles again. "I still owe that bastard a knuckle sandwich for humiliating me in front of the other Prisoners."

"Then what are we waiting for?" I pointed at the Toppies. "Before you guys leave, however, why are there only nine of you? I thought there were ten."

Death Ax frowned. "Number One's cell is apparently not connected to the Dome's Security System. We considered trying to help, but decided that time is of the essence, and if Number One cannot escape on his or her own, then there is no reason for us to waste time trying to help them."

I shook my head. "Sounds like real Villain logic there, but fine. I'm sure the nine of you will be enough."

"And where are you going?" Rock Lord demanded. "Are you going to join us?"

"No," I said. "I've still got another part of the plan to put into action. You guys go on ahead. I'll join you later."

Death Ax and Rock Lord exchanged puzzled looks with each

other before shrugging and resuming their march into battle along with the other seven Toppies. I stepped aside to let them pass, watching as nine of the most powerful Villains in Capes Online went to back up their fellow Prisoners.

"How kind of you to help them escape," said the Ghost in my ear. "I so wish I could be a part of them."

"You will be soon," I said, turning toward the entrance to the Emergency Access Stairs. "I just need to get to the surface and—"

Bang.

The floor under my feet shook with the force of a bomb, causing me to stagger and almost trip. Leaning against the nearby wall for support, I looked around in alarm, wondering if Old Sparky had made it down here already and, if so, where he was.

But I didn't see or smell the Warden. Instead, I heard screams coming down the hall, screams that seemed to be mostly coming from the Prisoners. Turning my gaze in that direction, I squinted my eyes, not sure exactly what I was seeing.

It looked like a wave of wind was knocking down the Prisoners. Everywhere I looked, I saw Prisoner after Prisoner fall, while the Prison Guards, oddly enough, remained unharmed. Even the Toppies were forced to stop, with Death Ax forming some kind of protective Energy Barrier around them to prevent them from being hit by whatever was taking down the Maxies.

That was when a yellow and blue blur shot through the air and slammed into the Energy Barrier around the Toppies. The barrier briefly cracked under the impact before the cracks reformed, leaving the barrier as smooth as ever.

"What the hell was that?" I said, staring at the Energy Barrier in astonishment.

Death Ax grunted. "It looks like we have a visitor."

Cocking my head to the side, I wasn't sure what Death Ax meant until the blue and yellow blur stopped. Standing amid the piles of fallen Prisoners and Prison Guards scattered everywhere, I realized I recognized that guy, although I really didn't want to.

Evidently, however, I was the only one who did, because Death Ax said, "Who the hell are you? Never seen you before."

"That's because I came long after your time, Death Ax," said the Hero. He put his fists on his hips and thrust out the "C" emblazoned on his chest. "I am Capeman. And I am here to stop you from leaving the Dome and terrorizing society."

CHAPTER 45

CRAP. I HADN'T EXPECTED CAPEMAN, OF ALL PEOPLE, TO SHOW UP AND help Old Sparky stop the breakout. I hadn't even realized that was possible.

Capeman, as you might remember, was the guy who put me in the Dome in the first place. You might also recall he was Daniel's best friend, who didn't know that I was a Villain.

"Capeman?" Death Ax repeated, like he was tasting that name. "What an ... interesting name."

Rock Lord pointed at Capeman. "I remember you! You're the moron who took me out and put me in here in the first place."

Capeman raised an eyebrow. "Amazing. So it looks like the rumors about the raid bosses being locked up in a secret hidden Floor in the Dome were true, after all."

I gasped. Capeman had defeated Rock Lord before? That didn't bode well for me. I hadn't known how powerful Capeman was until now, and truth be told, I really didn't want to know his exact Level now. If he could defeat Rock Lord, then it was no surprise he took me down the first time we met. I just had to hope he would be too distracted by the Toppies to pay attention to me.

"Do not lose your confidence, Maelstrom," said the Ghost. "Remember your goal. We must get to the surface."

I nodded shakily. "R-Right. I'm just having Vietnam flashbacks to when Capeman punched me out. It was very traumatizing."

Before I could move, however, Capeman's eyes darted past the Toppies and widened. He pointed at me. "I remember you! You are Villain Robert, the widow-murderer purse thief I put here. You really are the mastermind behind the breakout, after all, just as the Warden said."

I cringed. "Actually, I'm going by Maelstrom now. It's more, you know, Villain-like than Villain Robert."

Capeman scowled. "I don't know how you fooled me into thinking you were some Level One newbie before, Villain Robert, but clearly, I underestimated you. A mistake I shall correct in due time, once I deal with your new friends here."

Capeman gestured at the Toppies when he said that, prompting Rock Lord to say, "Technically, we're not his friends. More like … allies of convenience."

"How did you even get into the Dome?" I said to Capeman, gesturing at the hallway. "You're not a Prison Guard. You don't even work here."

"True, but Old Sparky is an old friend of mine," said Capeman. "I was dropping off some more Villains I'd caught when he told me about the breakout from Top Secret. He asked me to go down here and provide backup to the Guards, a decision that seems very wise, given the threat I am up against."

"And where is Old Sparky right now?" I said.

Capeman pointed at the ceiling. "He's heading to Maximum Security's first Sub-Floor, preventing the 'Maxies,' as he calls them, from escaping."

Double-crap. I had assumed that, between the Toppies and the Maxies, the Warden would have his attention too divided to put up a decent resistance against me. After all, Old Sparky, for all his power, did not seem to be able to be in two places in the Dome at once.

And evidently, Old Sparky thought the same thing, which was why he brought in Capeman. And given how the Warden clearly knew about my history with Capeman, this was probably a deliberate move on his part to mess with me even more.

I hated that donut-eating bastard. I really did.

Even if I could also respect his ability to think ahead and exploit the weaknesses of others to throw them off their game.

"Move aside, Hero," Death Ax said, the blade of his scythe glowing purple. "You think you can stand against us? Then you must be even more foolish than you appear."

"Don't underestimate the kid," Rock Lord warned Death Ax. "He's tougher than he looks."

"Even so, Death Ax has a point," said another Toppie, a man who looked a bit like Dracula but whose name tag currently read [PRISONER #5X]. "Nine against one seems like excellent odds in our favor, if you ask me."

"I won't let a single one of you evil Villains go," said Capeman, raising his fists again. "I would rather die than let any of you Villains escape into the world and hurt innocent people."

Death Ax smirked. "If that is your wish, then I am sure that my colleagues and I could accommodate you."

Death Ax suddenly looked over his shoulder at me. "Get out of here, kid. We will hold off Capeman. You need to make it to the surface."

Taken aback, I asked, "But what about you guys?"

Death Ax shook his head. "What happens to *us* doesn't matter. You are, after all, the brains behind this breakout. I assume you have a plan for dealing with Old Sparky?"

I pursed my lips. "Yeah, but—"

"Then that is good enough for us," said Death Ax as the other Toppies nodded in agreement with him.

Rock Lord nodded. "Yeah. We'll keep Mr. Boy Scout here busy. You go on ahead and do what you need to do to get all of us out of here."

I pursed my lips even more. It felt weird to see and hear these super powerful Villains treating me with such respect. Especially given how selfless they were acting, which seemed entirely out of character for Villains as evil as they were. It was probably more out of self-interest than anything, given how necessary I was for the breakout to be successful.

On the other hand, I couldn't deny that they were correct. I did have a plan for dealing with Old Sparky and, while Capeman was certainly a big obstacle, he actually wasn't the biggest obstacle. After all, Capeman, despite working with Old Sparky, was still not the

Warden nor associated with the Dome in any way. Defeating him would be nice, but not necessary.

But the Warden ... we had to defeat him. If we did not, then this entire breakout would be for absolutely nothing. Old Sparky and Old Sparky alone held the keys to getting out of here, literally and figuratively. He was really the only person in this entire place who we needed to defeat.

Like I said a long time ago, Old Sparky was the final boss.

And I was going to defeat him.

With another nod, I ran to the Emergency Access Stairs, deciding I would just take the stairs instead of trying to get past Capeman to one of the Teleportation Pads. Even as I ran, I heard Capeman yell and rush toward the Toppies. A *boom* echoed behind me, no doubt the sound of Capeman colliding with Death Ax's barrier. I could only hope that the Toppies kept Capeman distracted.

But I didn't look back to see how they were doing. I just kept running up the stairs, already thinking about my final confrontation with Old Sparky, and how that would play out.

CHAPTER 46

Surprisingly, the Emergency Access Stairs were empty. Although I supposed that wasn't *that* surprising. The Emergency Access Stairs could only be, well, accessed by someone who had the Emergency Access Key. And since none of the Prisoners other than yours truly had the Key, that meant their only option was to use the Dome's Teleportation System to make it to the higher Floors. The Prison Guards, of course, could have accessed the Stairs, but if there were no Prisoners in here and the Teleportation System was still working (just like I told Joe to make sure it was), then they had no reason to be down here, either.

As a result, I made good time climbing the stairs. Actually, I didn't even have to walk. Turned out that the Ghost had Flight as one of her Powers. Since we were in such a hurry, the Ghost gave me Flight, allowing me to fly straight up through the stairwell, all the way to MX-SF#1. Landing on the plateau, I opened the door to MX-SF#1 and peered outside.

The hallway of MX-SF#1, like the other Sub-Floors, was full of clashing Prisoners and Prison Guards. Unlike MX-SF#10, where I had just been, there were far fewer Prison Guards up here than down there. That most likely had to do with the fact that the Maxies could respawn in their cells and return quickly, while any Prison Guard who died up here would respawn in the Locker Room on MX-SF#10. And I already explained that virtuous cycle, of course.

Even as I watched, the Maxies attacked the remaining Prison Guards with gusto, ripping through them like a hungry tiger eating a dead deer. The Prison Guards, to their credit, put up a pretty good fight, but overall it was clear to any objective observer that they were losing and losing badly, that it was only a matter of time before the Maxies overwhelmed them entirely. The Maxies wouldn't even need my help to defeat their captors at this rate.

That was good. I needed the Maxies to keep the Guards distracted while I made my way to the exit.

Activating Stealth—another Skill boosted much higher than it normally was thanks to my Link with the Ghost—I made my way along the walls of MX-SF#1, doing my best not to draw attention to myself. Fortunately, no one seemed to notice me, as everyone was too busy fighting each other to pay attention to me. It felt weird because I didn't *feel* hidden, yet clearly, I was. Capes Online could be pretty weird sometimes

But when I got to Cell 3, I heard a familiar roar and looked around until I spotted the source of it.

Dinoczar was lying on the floor right in front of the entrance to our Cell, with a particularly burly Prison Guard named Brick standing over him. Poor Dinoczar's face was bloodied from the beating Brick had given him, a handful of his teeth having apparently been busted out of his mouth.

"Stupid dino," said Brick, pointing his gun at Dinoczar's head. "Time to make you extinct again."

I narrowed my eyes and rushed toward Brick faster than I normally could. Reaching the Guard, I touched his shoulder and activated another one of the Ghost's Powers, Life Drain.

Brick gasped and went still under my touch. He tried to scream, but no words came out of his mouth. In the corner of my eye, I saw Brick's Health bar drop like a rock the longer I stayed in contact with him. That was what Life Drain did. It allowed the user to absorb the Health of a given target until they died while converting the Health into either HP or Energy Points for themselves, depending on what you needed. As I needed Energy, that was what I converted his Health into.

And because the Ghost's Life Drain was Level 10, the draining time was less than a second.

Brick's colorless corpse collapsed at my feet. Stepping over the lifeless husk that had once been Brick, I bent over Dinoczar, saying, "Are you okay, Dinoczar?"

Dinoczar grunted and tried to rise to his feet. "Dinoczar has suffered worse injuries before. Dinoczar will be—"

Dinoczar abruptly collapsed onto the floor again. With a sigh, I cast Healing on Dinoczar, instantly refilling his Health bar, removing the countless debuffs on him and healing his injuries.

Dinoczar then sat up and looked at his short arms in amazement. "How did you do that, sir? Dinoczar did not know that master could heal."

"I'll explain later," I said, looking around the hallway. "Where's Joe?"

Dinoczar also stood up, not even needing my help. "Joe is where you asked him to go and is ready when you are."

I nodded. "Good. The Toppies are free now as well, although they are currently being distracted by Capeman."

"Capeman?" Dinoczar repeated. He scowled. "Wasn't that the name of the Hero who put you in here in the first place?"

"Yes, but that doesn't matter right now," I said with a wave. I glanced toward the end of the hall, past the fighting Maxies and Prison Guards, and to the Teleportation Pad at the end. "What matters is that we need to get out of here now. Old Sparky will probably be here any minute, and once he is, that's when things will get really ugly."

Dinoczar cocked his head to the side. "What do you mean, master? It looks like our side is winning."

Dinoczar wasn't exactly wrong. The Maxies had driven the remaining Prison Guards—only about six left now—to the end of the hall, right in front of the Teleportation Pad that connected Maximum Security to Medium Security. The Prison Guards shot their guns and waved their batons at the Maxies, but even as I watched, one of the Maxies, who I recognized as Snow, lashed out with her sharp claws and beheaded a Prison Guard who got a little too close to her. That left only five Prison Guards to defend the Teleportation Pad from the Maxies.

Dinoczar continued speaking. "Look at how few Prison Guards there are left. Once the last of them are dead, then all of us will be able to go up to Medium Security and beyond. Dinoczar does not see how any of this could go wrong."

Fate must have laughed at those words, because just then something *did* go wrong.

The Teleportation Pad behind the Prison Guards suddenly glowed blue. Electricity crackled along its surface as a humanoid form came into existence over it. This was the first time I'd seen the Teleportation Pad work from the outside, and I had to say, it was kind of weird to see.

First came the feet, then the legs, the torso, arms ... and finally the head of Old Sparky, who still hadn't reverted to his middle-aged self. Instead, Old Sparky looked like how he had when he confronted me in Top Secret earlier, the lines on his costume glowing with electricity.

And Old Sparky looked *pissed*. He gazed over the entire crowd of Maxies with the sort of judgmental look God probably reserved for the worst of sinners. His mere presence alone caused all of the rioting Maxies to stop what they were doing and stare at him in surprise, fear, and confusion.

The Prison Guards had also stopped fighting the Maxies, and when they looked at Old Sparky, it was with hope in their eyes.

"The Warden is here!" said one of the Prison Guards joyfully, a female one named Amber. "Finally!"

One of her fellow Prison Guards, named Howard, looked out at the Maxies with a grin. "That's right. Now that Old Sparky is here, this breakout is officially over."

The Maxies all exchanged worried looks with each other. That was understandable. Old Sparky was easily the single strongest individual in the entire Dome. I didn't Scan him to see what his Level currently was, but given how his power scaling ability worked, I could guess he was close to the Level cap for the game. He didn't even need to use Intimidation or some other Skill to weaken or scare the Prisoners. He was just *that* powerful.

But I wasn't scared.

I had a plan.

A plan that Old Sparky definitely wouldn't see coming.

Cracking his neck, Old Sparky said, "That's right. But this breakout isn't *just* over. Once I am done with all of you, not a single one of you criminal scum will *ever* even *think* about breaking out of here for the rest of your sorry lives."

With that, Old Sparky raised his hand and snapped his fingers, causing this notification to appear in our vision:

[Dome Warden Old Sparky] is using **Thunderous Destruction***!*

Before I could comprehend the fact that Old Sparky had *two* Ultimate Powers, a wave of lightning exploded from his body toward the Maxies.

But it wasn't just the Maxies who got fried. The remaining Prison Guards also perished as the lightning wave consumed them in its wake, not even giving them time to react. Only Amber had enough sense in her to try to run, but she simply wasn't fast enough to escape the lightning wave.

She did, however, catch my eye for a second, allowing me to see a single emotion in her gaze:

Betrayal.

Then Amber was gone, vaporized by Old Sparky's lightning wave.

Which kept coming to us.

"Run, master!" Dinoczar yelled. "Back into our cell where it is safe!"

But I grabbed the collar of Dinoczar's jumpsuit and said, "No! Stay here. That's exactly what he wants us to do. Here!"

I thrust my hand forward and created an Energy Barrier around me and Dinoczar. I would have extended it to the other Maxies, but they were too far away for my Barrier to reach them, plus my Energy Barrier wasn't nearly fast enough to form around them even if I could have.

And I wasn't a moment too soon, because the lightning wave

slammed into the Maxies the very next instant after I summoned the Energy Barrier.

Again, my whole world became whiteness.

The screams of terror from my fellow Maxies were consumed by the roar of the lightning.

The Energy Barrier cracked and nearly buckled under the strain of the attack, forcing both me and the Ghost to focus intently on keeping it up. It took nearly all of the Ghost's considerable Energy reserves just to keep the Barrier from falling apart under the attack, much less absorb any of it to convert into Energy for our own use.

But then the lightning wave passed, the light faded, and I could finally see again, although the sight before me and Dinoczar was almost too gruesome for words.

The entire hallway had been blackened to a crisp by Old Sparky's attack, and the air was filled with the odor of burnt concrete and human flesh. Every single Maxie other than ourselves had been obliterated, leaving nothing behind, not even their ashes, to indicate that they had once been standing there. Even the Prison Guards were gone, having been caught in the same wave of destruction as the Maxies.

Thus, only three people were left standing in MX-SF#1:

Me, Dinoczar, and Old Sparky.

Sparks dancing along his fingers, Old Sparky lowered his hand to his side and scowled at me. "Damn it. I was aiming for you."

Returning the scowl, I lowered the Energy Barrier around us and said, "Looks like you missed."

"Indeed!" said Dinoczar triumphantly. "Not only did you miss, but you didn't even stop the breakout entirely. Once the Maxies respawn in their cells, then you will have to face our army again, this time by yourself."

Old Sparky cocked his head to the side. "Good point. I should deal with that."

Old Sparky placed one hand on the wall to his side. A jolt of electricity shot through his arm into the concrete wall, the electricity flashing through the wires in the wall. As the electricity passed through each cell, their doors swung closed with a *bang*, the sound echoing up and down the hallway as the doors slammed shut.

"There," said Old Sparky, taking his hand off the wall. "I overrode the Dome's Security Systems to lock every damn cell on this Sub-Floor. Should prevent your 'reinforcements' from making an appearance anytime soon. And if any of the losers on the lower Sub-Floors make it this far, I will crush them, too."

Dinoczar gulped and looked at me. "Um, what do we do now, master?"

I held up a hand. "Be quiet, Dinoczar. I've got a plan. Just trust me."

Dinoczar gulped again but nodded and said nothing. He was probably wondering what my plan was, but no way was I going to spoil my plan to Old Sparky. It hinged on Old Sparky's ignorance and I having the element of surprise.

Old Sparky raised an eyebrow. "I am impressed that you came back, Maelstrom, and even staged a full-fledged breakout. I thought I had thoroughly broken you."

I turned my attention back to Old Sparky. "I thought so, too. But then I realized, I don't break that easily."

Old Sparky frowned. "I can't say I understand how you managed to hide your real Level from me this whole time, but it doesn't matter. You should know by now that in the Dome, I am as close to all-powerful as it gets. No matter how strong you get, I will be stronger still."

I nodded. "I am very aware of that fact, Old Sparky. Doesn't change the fact that I am going to kick your ass and make you sorry you ever chose to pick a fight with me in the first place."

The Warden laughed. "You just saw me take out over a hundred of your fellow Maxies in the blink of an eye. I acknowledge your cleverness, but no amount of cleverness in the world can save you from raw, brutal power like the kind I wield. Nature itself is at my fingertips."

I shrugged. "Maybe. But at least I didn't kill a couple of my own Minions just to get at my enemies. Seems pretty *villainous*, if you ask me."

Old Sparky growled. "They were collateral. They have probably already respawned by now. Those Guards I killed will be fine. Their sacrifice will not be in vain."

I laughed. "Sacrifice? You make it sound like they *chose* to get vaporized by your lightning, when the fact is, you murdered them without a second thought, if you even thought about them at all, that is. I saw how betrayed they looked. I could tell how much that hurt them, and not just physically, either. They really thought you were going to save them."

Old Sparky sneered at me. "Who cares what those simpleminded Guards thought? Their needs don't matter. My needs don't matter. Their *lives* don't matter. Mine does, because I am the only thing—literally the only thing—standing between scum like you and the innocent people who walk on the streets of Adventure City every day. In the grand scheme of things, they don't matter."

"They don't, huh?" I said. I scratched the back of my neck. "I wonder what your Prison Guards would say about that."

Old Sparky chuckled darkly. "They will say nothing because they weren't around to hear it. None of them are. They will simply respawn and go back to killing your fellow inmates to make sure none of them leave this place alive."

"But I heard it ... sir."

Old Sparky froze. His eyes darted past me and, despite knowing how dangerous Old Sparky was, I risked a look over my shoulder as well.

Prison Guard Ike stood about halfway down the corridor, gun in hand, a look of disbelief on his face as he gazed at Old Sparky. Even I hadn't heard him sneak up behind me, though to be fair, I was a bit distracted myself.

"What—?" Old Sparky sputtered. "When did you get here?"

Ike pursed his lips. "I followed Maelstrom up here when he escaped from MX-SF Number Ten. I wanted to catch him because I knew he was the mastermind behind the breakout. I heard everything."

Wow. I hadn't planned for Ike to follow me, but this was good.

It certainly seemed to unnerve Old Sparky, who pointed at Ike and snapped, "Don't repeat *anything* I just said to anyone else. Or you'll spend the next six months in the Black Room. Got it?"

I chuckled. "Ike doesn't need to tell anyone anything, because every person in this prison heard everything you just said."

Old Sparky whipped his gaze back to me. "What? How? There's no one else around other than us."

I gestured at the corner of the ceiling behind Old Sparky. "You might want to smile. You're on camera."

Old Sparky glanced over his shoulder at the security camera hanging in the corner of the ceiling …

Pointed directly at his face, the red light blinking, indicating that it was on and recording everything.

"What?" said Old Sparky incredulously. "The security camera—? When—?"

"It's been recording your ramblings this entire time, asshole," I said. "And not only that, but it's also been streaming your confession to every Floor and Sub-Floor in the Dome. That means everyone, Prison Guard and Prisoner alike, heard you explain just how *worthless* your Guards' lives are compared to yours."

"Impossible," said Old Sparky, looking at me again. "You must be lying. The cameras are under *our* control."

At that moment, I heard a *ping* in my ear. Opening the Command Interface, I saw myself staring at a computer screen from Joe's point of view, Joe's face barely reflected on the screen itself.

"Good news, boss," said Joe. "I'm in the Warden's office again, just like you asked."

I nodded. "Did you hack into the camera system and stream our Sub-Floor's feed onto the other Floors and Sub-Floors?"

"Yep," said Joe. "Even as we talk, everyone in the Dome is watching you, from Top Secret all the way to Minimum Security."

Giving Joe another nod, I minimized the Command Interface and looked at Old Sparky. "My Minion, Joe, broke into your office and hacked the Dome's Security System. That's how we managed to take control of your cameras, but if you don't believe me, look for yourself."

Old Sparky raised his hands. Over a dozen holographic screens flashed into existence around him, each one showing a different Floor or Sub-Floor of the Dome.

And they all showed the various Prisoners and Prison Guards in different stages of disbelief, staring at the holo-screens on the walls nearby. The holo-screens in question showed Old Sparky watching them on his holo-screens, which created a kind of dizzying phenomenon that hurt my brain just to think about it.

But not a single Prison Guard was fighting any Prisoner. Even Capeman and the Toppies on MX-SF#1 had stopped fighting long enough to watch the feed, surprised looks on their faces.

I looked directly into the camera myself. "Prison Guards of the Dome, you heard what Old Sparky said about you. This is no trick. This is not the result of some edited video. This is a raw, unfiltered live feed of what Old Sparky is doing, saying, and thinking right this very instant.

"You now know that Old Sparky hates you, that he sees your lives as less than worthless. You now know that Old Sparky sees himself as being more important than any of you, that your lives matter only insofar as he can use them to his advantage."

I gestured at Old Sparky. "Notice how he didn't talk much about justice, about how much he appreciated the hard work you guys put in to maintaining the prison and making sure us mean old Prisoners stay behind bars. Seems like he's taking all of you for granted. And, as a Big Bad myself, I gotta say, that is pretty bad.

"I'm not going to tell you what to do next or how to react. That's your choice. But if you want my opinion, I think you should respect yourselves and do what's best for *you*, not what's best for this donut-eating bastard. Choose wisely."

With that, I stopped talking. I'd done all I could at this point to make the Prison Guards see reason. The ball was now firmly in their court ... and their reaction would decide the fate of not merely themselves, but the Dome itself, even if they didn't realize it themselves just yet.

A few seconds of silence filled the hallway. I doubted the Dome had been this silent since the day it was built. Even the other Prisoners had gone silent, staring intently at the Prison Guards, waiting for them to respond.

Clunk.

I looked over my shoulder to see Ike still standing where he'd been standing before, only now his gun lay at his feet.

And he was looking at Old Sparky with absolute betrayal.

"You ... you bastard," said Ike. "You betrayed us."

Old Sparky's holo-screens showed the other Prison Guards, on every Floor and Sub-Floor, repeating Ike's action. They dropped their guns onto the floor or threw their batons away, still staring at the holo-screens, wearing similarly betrayed expressions on their faces.

By my count, it looked like every single Prison Guard in the Dome had voluntarily disarmed themselves.

All except for Old Sparky, who watched the holo-screens with utter disbelief on his features.

"Did you hear me, Warden?" said Ike, stepping forward. "I said, you betrayed—"

Bang.

A pile of ash was all that remained of Ike. Old Sparky's right index finger crackled with electricity, still pointing at the smoking ashy remains of Ike.

My eyes widened in surprise. "Wow. I didn't expect you to kill him on the spot like that."

Old Sparky growled. "That is the fate that *traitors* like him—and every other Prison Guard who fell for your malicious lies—deserve."

"You mean like yourself?" I said. "You sure seem like a traitor to them."

Old Sparky's eye twitched. "I see what you're doing, Maelstrom. You're trying to foment a rebellion against me. You're trying to turn my own men against me."

I cocked my head to the side. "And what if I am? Doesn't that seem like the sort of thing an icky *Villain* like me would do?"

Old Sparky's hands balled into fists. "In my day, boy, I've come face to face with some of the evilest people who have ever lived. Villains who take absolute joy in torturing and harming innocent people. But you ... you are the only one who I *really* want to kill and make you sorry your mother didn't end your sorry life before you left the womb."

I rolled my shoulders. "Then what are you waiting for, old man? Are you going to fight me or not?"

Old Sparky growled. "You little—!"

I, of course, didn't give Old Sparky the opportunity to finish his sentence.

Activating Flight, I flew straight toward Old Sparky. The Warden raised his hand, probably planning to shoot me with one of his signature lightning bolts, but he never got the chance.

Because I tackled Old Sparky onto the Teleportation Pad, knocking us both down as I shouted, "Joe! Now!"

And in the blink of an eye, Old Sparky and I disappeared.

CHAPTER 47

In the next instant, Old Sparky and I reappeared, but in a completely different place. Before I could get a bearing on my surroundings, Old Sparky shoved me off of him and I went rolling across the dome-like floor. Digging my fingers into the tiles of the rooftop, I looked up to see Old Sparky sitting up on the Teleportation Pad, rubbing the back of his head.

"Ow," said Old Sparky. He glared at me. "What was that about? Where did you … teleport us …"

Old Sparky's words trailed off as he looked around at our new environment. I did the same, even though I already knew where we were. Just had to be sure.

We were on the roof of the Dome, the very same roof I'd seen from the ground during my Origin Story what felt like an eternity ago. It gave us an excellent view of Adventure City, the mega metropolis that spilled out in every direction for miles. It actually reminded me a bit of Oklahoma City in real life, only much, much larger.

Because we were so high up, the winds whipped through our hair fiercely, hitting us cold and hard. Rising to my feet, I felt my balance wobble slightly, because the curved surface of the Dome's roof was not exactly the most stable ground upon which to stand.

Old Sparky had also risen to his feet, but he was not looking at me. He was pressing a holographic control panel on his right arm, muttering under his breath, "Stupid Pad ... I want to get *back* into the prison ... damn it ..."

Yet no matter how many times Old Sparky pressed what I assumed was the teleport button on his control panel, the Teleportation Pad did not take him anywhere. In fact, the Pad kept blinking red every time he pressed the button, as if it was broken, although I knew it definitely wasn't.

I shook my head. "It's not going to work, Warden. You have been locked out of the Dome's Teleportation System."

Old Sparky whipped his head toward me, his eyes narrowing with anger. "Impossible. I *own* the Dome. I can't be locked out of its Teleportation System."

"Wrong," I said. "I had my Minion Joe hack into the Dome's various Systems and told him to lock us out of the Teleportation System as soon as I got you where I wanted you. He's also the reason why we ended up out here. The Map of the Dome showed me a forgotten Teleportation Pad on the roof of the Dome, which is fortunately still functional."

Old Sparky scowled. "If I'm stuck out here, then clearly, you must be, as well."

I nodded. "That is the unfortunate side effect of Joe's efforts. Technically speaking, he only turned off the Pad on the roof. That means I can't get back inside, either."

Old Sparky cracked his knuckles. "Then I guess that means it's just you and me, pal. You are going to regret this."

"I already am," I replied, "mostly because I don't know when was the last time you showered."

Old Sparky growled. "Quip all you like, boy. It won't save you from my Lightning Donut!"

Old Sparky thrust his hands forward and, despite knowing what was going to happen next, I winced.

Nothing happened.

Old Sparky raised an eyebrow in confusion. He thrust his hands forward again, this time with more gusto.

Again, nothing happened.

"What the—?" Old Sparky thrust his hands once more, but still nada. He looked down at his hands. "Why isn't Lightning Donut working—?"

I punched Old Sparky in the face as hard as I could, sending him staggering backward from the blow. He tripped and fell onto the roof, sliding a few feet before catching himself. Standing up again, Old Sparky rubbed his nose where I'd punched him and looked at his hand. "You made me bleed!"

Cracking my own bloody knuckles, I said, "Yep. And just to even things out a bit …"

I went into my menu, toggled over to LINKS, and clicked DISABLE on my Link with [???]. Instantly, I felt myself weaken, although having been expecting that, it didn't hit me as hard as it could have.

"What did you just do?" said Old Sparky, looking at me again.

I rolled my shoulders. "I evened the playing field between us."

Old Sparky narrowed his eyes. "That annoying Minion of yours. He must have somehow figured out how to expand the Power Negation System outside of the Dome. It's the only explanation that makes sense."

I sighed. "Wrong. The Power Negation works only within the walls of the Dome. Outside, it has no effect on anyone. Think again. What else could possibly affect your Powers and make it possible for me to hurt you? To put us on truly equal footing?"

I could tell that the gears in Old Sparky's brain were turning hard as he considered my question. I knew it would take him a minute to figure it out because, despite his electric Powers, Old Sparky wasn't exactly a fast thinker himself.

Then it clearly hit him like a sledgehammer. "You … bastard."

I grinned. "Figured it out, did you? Maybe you're smarter than you look."

Electricity sparked up and down Old Sparky's body, although it was noticeably weaker. "You … *bastard*."

"What?" I said. "Too angry to speak? Perhaps you're offended that I used your own damn power against you?"

Old Sparky roared and rushed toward me. That would have been scary under any other circumstances, but since Old Sparky was currently about as weak as a normal human being, he just looked silly.

I let him think he was going to punch me before I deftly dodged his punch, grabbed his arm, and slammed him down onto his back. Old Sparky gasped and struggled to get up, but I slammed my foot down on his chest and gazed directly into his eyes.

"That's right," I said, speaking just low enough that Old Sparky could hear me even over the roaring of the winds around us. "I didn't do anything to you. Your own power worked against you."

Old Sparky ground his teeth together. "How—?"

I shrugged. "I suppose, since I *am* a Big Bad, I might as well explain my devious plan to you. It's what any good Big Bad would do, I'm sure."

I dug the heel of my boot deeper into Old Sparky's chest, making him groan, but I ignored his pain. "See, when you were ranting and rambling back in the prison about how much more important you are than the Prison Guards, you weren't wrong. You are singlehandedly the most dangerous person in the Dome, probably the only reason why there has never been a successful breakout in its history. Anytime anyone even thinks about escaping, you zap them, torture them, make sure that even the thought of breaking out causes them unbearable psychological pain. It's brilliant, really."

Old Sparky groaned again but said nothing.

Good. I liked him better when he was silent, anyway.

Leaning in closer to Old Sparky's face, I said, "And that's because of your ability to scale your Level—and therefore your power—against whoever you are fighting against. Whether it's against a Minimum Security newbie or a Top Secret raid boss, your unique power lets you take on any Prisoner, no matter how strong they might be. It's a brilliant way to ensure that the Maxies and Toppies don't escape while giving the Medies and Minnies a fair chance to escape. Perfect game design, really."

"Game design …?" Old Sparky muttered. "The hell are you talking—"

I smashed my foot down on his right hand, making Old Sparky scream in pain. "I'm not done talking. Anyway, I realized that, as long as you were in the Dome, there was no way in hell I'd ever be able to beat you. No matter how strong I got, you'd get stronger still. I bet you could probably even grow past the Level cap if necessary.

"But that's when I realized: What if I could get you *out* of the Dome, instead? What would happen then? Would your level scaling ability still work or would it fail? And if it didn't work, exactly how strong would you be? What is your base Level, in other words?"

Old Sparky grunted. "You … bastard …"

I cocked my head to the side. "Come up with something a little less cliché next time and I might feel insulted. Anyway, it was a gamble, seeing as it may have turned out you had a much higher base Level than me. But now … well …"

I Scanned Old Sparky:

Name: *Dome Warden Old Sparky*
Level: *1*
Weak Point: *Belly*
Description: *The all-powerful Warden of the Dome, Old Sparky is feared among its inmates for his ruthlessness, intense sense of justice, and single-minded focus on making sure no one escapes its walls. Rumor has it that he has a sweet tooth, although that doesn't make him any less powerful or frightening for Villains to deal with.*

"Level One," I said with a nod. "Makes sense. The developers wouldn't have any reason to give you a high base Level if you could automatically adjust it based on who you are fighting at any given time. After all, you most likely aren't even supposed to be outside of the Dome anyway, so they probably didn't think it was necessary to give you anything but the most basic Stats when your ability wasn't in play. It was a scenario, in other words, that they didn't plan for."

I leaned in even closer to Old Sparky. "And now, you are even weaker than me without my own power boost. Pretty ironic, isn't it?"

Old Sparky coughed. "Developers …? What are you going on about, kid? You make it sound like … sound like we're in some kind of video game or something …"

I grinned. "You're close, Old Sparky. Very close."

Old Sparky coughed again. "Doesn't matter. You play dirty. You cheated."

I laughed. "Old Sparky, I am a *Villain*. We cheat. We play dirty. We bend and break the rules as we see fit. In that sense, we're almost like gods ourselves. Isn't that what you called yourself? The god of the Dome? Then I guess that makes me the devil."

"You won't ... you won't get away with this," Old Sparky said. "Not as long as I live. I don't need my Powers to kill you."

"Actually, you probably do at this point," I said. "But see, Old Sparky, I'm not just interested in killing you. That would be boring. Instead ... I think I am going to *break* you."

Old Sparky gulped. "Break me ...? How?"

I took my foot off of Old Sparky's chest. Grabbing the collar of his costume, I lifted Old Sparky off his feet, gazing directly into his eyes the whole time.

"By telling you the truth," I said. I gestured at our surroundings. "The reason I made it sound like we're in a video game, old man, is because we *are*."

Old Sparky's eyes widened even more. "Huh? What do you mean?"

I pulled Old Sparky up to my face. "This entire world is one giant video game, the most advanced video game that ever existed. I am one of the players in this video game, while you are nothing more than an exceptionally annoying NPC who gets in my way far too often for my liking."

Old Sparky trembled in my grasp. "No way. You're lying. You're a Villain. Villains always lie."

I shook my head. "Not this time. Not right now. Every word I say to you is the unmitigated truth. You are an NPC in a video game. You have no free will. Your every decision is decided by a complex algorithm that even I barely understand."

Old Sparky trembled even harder under my grasp. "Im-Impossible. You have no proof."

I grinned. "True, I can't *prove* it, but deep down, you know it to be true. Everything you have worked for—protecting the innocent, defending the weak, keeping Villains such as myself locked up tightly behind bars—is for nothing. It is nothing more than simple entertainment, bits and bytes that go together to entertain *real* people like me."

Old Sparky gulped. "I ... I am real. I'm a real person."

I cocked my head to the side. "No, you're not. You were never real. You never will be real. Justice, as you envision it, isn't real, either. Unleashing the Dome's Prisoners on the city doesn't matter."

"But innocent people will be hurt," Old Sparky protested. "You've seen some of your fellow inmates. They will hurt good people."

I laughed and gestured at the city sprawled out below us. "None of the people in those buildings are *real*. None of them are actual flesh-and-blood human beings, no matter how much they might look or act like them. Just like you, they are advanced playthings designed purely to add some spice to this otherwise boring game."

Old Sparky was sweating now and panting hard. "But ... but ..."

"So who cares if they get hurt or die?" I said. I grinned evilly. "Just like that old widow I murdered and stole from, they're not real. Morality, then, doesn't apply to them. And therefore, your entire existence is utterly, *utterly* pointless."

Old Sparky gulped again. He looked so small and weak now. He probably couldn't handle the revelation I'd just dropped on him.

Which was exactly the reaction I'd been hoping for from him. I'd been betting that Old Sparky, being an NPC unaware of his real status as a video game character, was psychologically fragile. Given how much he loved psychologically torturing others, it only made logical sense to me that he, in turn, was a psychological weakling, however physically powerful he might appear on the outside.

Therefore, instead of taking him down through brute force or overwhelming power, I opted to strike at the very foundation of his worldview and his very sense of self. I gambled that getting Old Sparky to doubt his own existence—and the purpose thereof—would be more than enough to cripple him.

And it looked like my gamble paid off handsomely.

"But don't worry, old man," I continued. "There is some good news to be had, after all."

A puzzled expression crossed Old Sparky's face. "What is that?"

I grinned. "Unlike you, I don't take pleasure in torture. I like offing my enemies quick and easy."

With that, I shoved Old Sparky backward as hard as I could. The Warden stumbled back, windmilling his arms, attempting to get his balance.

And he did. For the briefest of moments, Old Sparky found his footing.

Then I raised my leg and kicked him, *hard*, in the stomach.

Old Sparky gasped as he went falling over the edge of the Dome's roof. He reached out toward empty air, desperately clawing for anything that could save him from his inevitable doom.

But Old Sparky caught nothing ... and plunged to his death below.

I did not see Old Sparky's body—as that would have required risking my own balance—but I did receive this notification a few seconds later:

You have killed [DOME WARDEN OLD SPARKY]! +2,000 EXP!
Level up! You are now Level 6. +2 PP and +4 SP.

CHAPTER 48

I frowned at the notification. I only leveled up once? I'd been expecting to get a lot more experience points as a result of killing the final boss of the Dome. Then again, Old Sparky had only been a measly Level 1 when I killed him, so maybe that explained why I didn't get nearly as much experience as I'd been hoping.

Regardless, I dismissed the notification and turned around. I intended to get Joe to teleport me back into the Dome so I could resume the breakout, because killing Old Sparky wasn't actually the winning condition for solving Grandpa's Riddle.

But before I could open the Command Interface, a new notification popped up in front of me:

> **SECRET MISSION:** *Kill the Warden*
> **STATUS:** *Completed*
> **Description:** *Congratulations! By killing Old Sparky, you completed the Secret Villain Mission called 'Kill the Warden'! You are the first-ever Villain player to accomplish that feat. By doing so, you have sent a message to the world that you are a rising star in the Villain world, signaling to Heroes and Villains alike not to underestimate you or your growing power.*
> **REWARDS:** *+10,000 EXP, +40 SP, +20 PP, Reputation raised to 'Infamous.'*

Another couple of notifications quickly popped into my vision before I could comprehend that one:

Level up! You are now Level 15. +36 SP and +18 PP. Level up further to continue to strengthen your character!

Your Reputation has now risen from 'Unknown' to 'Infamous'! Your name and face will be known to the world over as the Villain who killed the Warden of the Dome. This will affect your relations with Heroes, Villains, Sidekicks, and Civilians alike, closing some doors while simultaneously opening new opportunities hitherto unknown to you.

Those two notifications were definitely worth investigating, but it was the third and final notification that really got my attention and shook my world:

You Conquered the Dome!

By killing the Warden of the Dome, you have officially Conquered the Dome and made it your own! The Dome has now been converted to your Villain Hideout. Check your BASES tab to see the Dome's current Level, Stats, Powers, and more!

You have also earned your first Title: Dome Warden! You now own and control the Dome and can determine who is imprisoned and who is not, among other privileges and perks of being the big man in town. Go to the TITLES tab for further information on that.

My jaw dropped when I read those notifications.

Not only had I defeated Old Sparky, but by killing him, I somehow "Conquered" the Dome. I wasn't entirely sure what that meant, but it sounded like I owned the Dome now and that it was actually my Hideout. That was good, because I didn't have a Hideout of my own yet, although I certainly wasn't sure what I'd do with a Hideout *this* big.

The Title, on the other hand, was odd. It was clearly some kind of mechanic that probably gave you certain bonuses and specials, but beyond that, the notifications weren't that helpful. I would have to ask Dinoczar or Joe about it later, or possibly do some of my own research.

Before I could fully delve into these mechanics, I heard a *ping* in my ear from the Command Interface. Switching over to the Command Interface, I found myself looking through Joe's eyes at the mirror in our cell in the Dome. Dinoczar was right next to him, an eager expression on my Sidekick's face.

"Sir!" said Dinoczar joyfully. "Everyone saw the notification about you killing the Warden! Is it true, sir? Did you really kill Old Sparky?"

I nodded. "Yep. He died crying like a bitch."

"Ouch," said Joe with a wince. "I didn't like the bastard and even I think that is harsh, although probably deserving, all things considered."

"He was weak," I said dismissively. "Anyway, Dinoczar, I leveled up a bunch of times and got a lot of SPs and PPs just now because I completed a Secret Mission. Did you level up, too?"

Dinoczar nodded eagerly. "Yes! Dinoczar is now Level Seven and feels stronger than ever."

"Good," I said. I glanced over my shoulder at the skyline of Adventure City behind me. "Now that we are free, we're going to need to be strong to deal with whoever we run into outside of the Dome."

"That's nice and all, er, boss, but we've run into a bit of a problem," said Joe, scratching the back of his head.

I frowned deeply. "What problem? I killed Old Sparky. I control the Dome now. There should be *no* problems."

"Actually, Maelstrom, killing Old Sparky didn't solve all your problems," said the familiar voice of Death Ax just off-screen. "It has merely given you new ones."

Joe suddenly turned around, allowing me to see Death Ax and the other free Toppies standing behind him. Death Ax was the only one inside the cell, but I could see the other Toppies in the hallway behind him, along with what appeared to be hundreds of Maxies and even Prison Guards.

"Death Ax," I said. "What do you want?"

Death Ax cocked his head to the side. "What do *we* want, you mean, because I've been elected to speak on behalf of both the Toppies and Maxies of the Dome."

Prison Guard Ike suddenly squeezed into the cell, panting as he dusted his pants off. "And the other Prison Guards chose me to represent the Prison Guards and staff of the Dome in order to enter negotiations with you."

I folded my arms in front of my chest. "Negotiations? For what?"

"For what the Prisoners and Prison Guards of the Dome want, of course," said Death Ax. "Freedom."

I quirked an eyebrow. "Okay. Old Sparky is dead and Medium and Minimum Security are a walk in the park, so you guys can leave now if you want."

"It's not that simple," said Ike with a shake of his head. "You're the Warden of the Dome now, which means you and you alone can free us. The Teleportation Pad connecting MX-SF Number One and MD-SF Number Ten became locked when Old Sparky died and ownership of the Dome transferred over to you."

"And the Emergency Access Stairs are also blocked off, by the way," Joe said, his voice off-screen. "We tried."

"Weird," I said. I glanced at the BASES tab in my character sheet. "But whatever. I'm still pretty new to owning the Dome, but I'm sure I could figure out how to turn the Teleportation Pad Network back on from here. Then you guys can go wherever you want."

Death Ax, however, leaned toward me, his dark eyes gleaming under his hood. "Freedom isn't the only thing we want, Maelstrom. We also want something more: Power and security."

"I don't understand."

Death Ax put his hands together. "While you and Old Sparky fought on the roof of the Dome, I and the rest of the Toppies discussed what our next moves would be once we escaped this place. Many of the Maxies chimed in with their own thoughts, including your own Sidekick, Dinoczar, who can be rather persuasive when he wants to be."

"Dinoczar credits that to Dinoczar's friendly demeanor and outgoing personality," Dinoczar said, "along with Dinoczar's blind, fanatical devotion to master."

Death Ax cleared his throat. "Yes, well, after some discussions, we decided that we are not interested in merely escaping. We want to form a Legion ... and we want *you* to lead it."

I felt my eyebrows shoot up into my hair. "You want to form a Legion? And you want me to be its leader?"

"Captain, actually," Death Ax said, "which is technically the same thing as being the leader, but is the proper Title of any Villain Legion leader."

I put my hands on my head. "What would I even *do* with a Legion? I just wanted to stage a mass breakout."

Death Ax tapped the side of his head. "Think this through carefully, Maelstrom. Releasing the Prisoners of the Dome, while an admirable goal in itself, will change the world as we know it. You are too new to realize this, but the Dome has a reputation for being inescapable. You will attract the attention of many Heroes, Hero Teams, and Hero Leagues who will seek to stop us. It is simply the nature of things. Heroes like Capeman, who will do everything in their power to oppose us."

I considered Death Ax's point. Up until recently, I had given the world outside of the Dome very little thought. I'd been so focused on escaping the Dome that I hadn't thought about much else.

But the mention of Capeman made me realize that Death Ax was probably correct. Capes Online, after all, was a superhero game, and what was a superhero game without Heroes to oppose the Villains?

Even so, the thought of running my own Legion felt overwhelming. I didn't know how many of the Prisoners would even sign up for it, much less how effective it would be. And plus, it felt like I was being distracted from my actual goal of solving Grandpa's Riddles and getting his money.

Yet I suspected it would be even harder for me to focus on solving Grandpa's Riddles if every Hero in Capes Online was out for my blood. And despite having leveled up so many times, I was still fairly weak and vulnerable. Having an army—no, a Legion—of high-level Villains to protect me and my fortress might be just the ticket, even if it was a hassle to lead and organize.

First, though ...

"What happened to Capeman?" I said.

Rock Lord, who stood over Death Ax's shoulder, shrugged. "He somehow disappeared while we were fighting him. Seemed to happen around the same time you defeated Old Sparky, now that I think about it."

I scowled. Darn. I'd been hoping that the Toppies would kill Capeman, but apparently he was still out there somewhere. Perhaps the Dome had kicked him out when I took over or something. I would definitely need a Legion to protect me from him, if nothing else.

So I said to Death Ax, "All right. I'll start a Legion. How do you do that?"

"It's pretty simple, master," said Dinoczar. "Go to your Team's tab on your character sheet and send out an invite to all of the Prisoners of the Dome to join. Once over a hundred have joined, our Team will automatically upgrade to a Legion, which will then give you access to all of the perks of running a Legion."

I did as Dinoczar said. I wasn't sure how I was going to invite everyone in the Dome until I saw, under Team Maelstrom, a button that said SEND INVITE TO ALL IN THE DOME.

I clicked the button and got this notification:

An invite has been sent to all of the Prisoners of the Dome to join Team Maelstrom! You will be automatically notified when Team Maelstrom has hit the 100-member limit.

"Okay," I said, lowering my hand. "That should do it. What do I do next—"

I was interrupted by another notification rudely popping up in my view, which said:

Congratulations! You now have over 100 members on your Team!

Team Maelstrom has automatically upgraded to the Maelstrom Legion! Check out the status of the Maelstrom Legion by going to your character sheet and clicking on the LEAGUES & TEAMS tab!

"Wow," I said. "I thought it was going to take a lot longer for that many people to sign up."

"Dinoczar is not surprised," said Dinoczar proudly. "Dinoczar knows how awesome master is and is glad that other people clearly see your awesomeness, too."

Death Ax smirked at me. "Did you think I was joking when I said that everyone was eager to serve under your command? You have done the impossible. We believe, based on the evidence, that joining you would be well worth our time."

I frowned again. "Does that mean that everyone is going to join our Legion?"

Death Ax shook his head. "No. And that, perhaps, is the problem. What do you intend to do with the ones who refuse to join?"

"Easy," I said. "I'm going to let them go."

I went into the Dome's settings and, after messing around with some of the options, finally found the one I was looking for: RELEASE.

Pressing the button, I immediately got this notification:

WARNING! You have released all of the Prisoners on all Floors of the Dome. All Dome security systems are shut down and Prisoners of the Dome can come and go as they please.

"You're just letting everyone go?" said Joe in disbelief. "Not, like, you know, holding some of them hostage until they agree to serve you?"

I shook my head. "My goal was never to amass a Legion, although it is pretty cool. My goal was always to stage a mass breakout. If that means letting some of the Prisoners go their own way, then so be it. Besides, it doesn't seem to have affected recruitment numbers at all. People are still joining at an insane rate."

That was true. A glance at the stat sheet for the Maelstrom Legion showed the number of members ticking steadily upward. I didn't know when it would finally stop, but for now, it was satisfying to see so many of the Prisoners eagerly joining my Legion. Almost made me feel like a real Big Bad.

"Indeed," said Death Ax, tapping his chin. "An unusual move from a Villain, but then again, Maelstrom, you have proved yourself to be a very unusual Villain in many ways."

I shrugged. "I just do what I want regardless of what anyone else thinks."

"Quite," said Death Ax. "By the way, if you ever feel overwhelmed by managing the Legion, you can set up a Vice-Captain and Officers to manage the day-to-day affairs for you while you focus on other things."

That sounded like a good deal to me. I didn't trust anyone enough yet to set up Officers, but I already knew who I wanted to make my Vice-Captain. "Sounds like you want to be the Vice-Captain yourself, Death Ax."

"I would happily accept the role, if you offered it to me," said Death Ax.

I didn't even hesitate. I toggled over to the LEAGUES & TEAMS menu, added Death Ax as Vice-Captain, and said, "There. You can deal with the boring admin stuff."

Death Ax smiled. "Of course. You will definitely not regret giving me this power, Maelstrom. Of that, I can assure you."

I nodded. I did trust Death Ax, if only because he had been one of my strongest supporters. Until I could vet the rest of the Legion, I had to rely on those who I knew already.

"Speaking of the Legion," said Joe, "are we really going with the Maelstrom Legion? That's such a boring name."

"What else should I call it?" I said. "Why does it need a fancy name when I didn't even want it in the first place?"

"Because it will strike fear into the hearts of our enemies more easily, of course," said Death Ax. "I agree with Joe that the default name of the Legion is not the best it could be."

I sighed. "Fine. What do you guys think we should call it, then? Because I'm not going to waste time coming up with names."

"How about the Maelstrom Mongers?" Dinoczar suggested. "That would be a cool name."

"For once, I actually agree with Dinoczar on something," said Joe. "Maelstrom Mongers *would* be cool."

"I also think it is appropriate, given the origin of our Legion," said Death Ax. "That is three votes in favor. What do you think, Maelstrom?"

I pursed my lips thoughtfully. "Not bad. It does sound pretty badass. And, dare I say it, villainous. Let's go with that."

Clicking back to the LEGIONS & TEAMS tab, I clicked on the name of the Maelstrom Legion and changed it to the Maelstrom Mongers. There was a lot of other information about the Legion, too, but I would worry about that later. "There. We are now officially the Maelstrom Mongers."

"Yay!" Dinoczar cried out. "Watch out, world! The Maelstrom Mongers are in the house!"

"Please stop talking, Dinoczar," said Joe. "You're just embarrassing yourself."

I chuckled. "Anyway, guys, I will be back in the Dome shortly to meet up with you guys. I have one last thing I need to deal with up here before I can come back down."

"Sounds good, sir," said Dinoczar. "Dinoczar will make sure to get the chefs of the Dome to throw a huge feast in your honor. The cafeteria shall be overflowing with delicious Slop!"

I made a mental note to improve the cafeteria's food later, only to remember something else and look at Ike. "How do the Prison Guards relate to the Mongers?"

Ike scratched his head. "You are now the Warden of the Dome, which means that all Prison Guards, Drones, and staff are forced to obey your every command. Theoretically, I suppose you could merge the Mongers with the Guards, but—"

"But that would probably be complicated," I said. "Right?"

Ike nodded. "Yes. We will have to obey you no matter what, so there is not much reason in make us part of your Legion. We ask only that you give us more freedom to leave the Dome than Old Sparky did and find lives outside of work, and we will be happy to serve you."

That seemed like a reasonable request to me. After all, the Prison Guards *had* sided with me precisely because of Old Sparky's treatment of them. They joined me under the impression that I would treat them a lot better than Old Sparky ever had. Giving them more freedom to do as they saw fit seemed like a good thing to me.

But then I considered what that might do for the Dome. Although I, as the Warden of the Dome, ran it, the truth was that I needed the

Prison Guards for maintenance and other jobs like that. Although I had no desire whatsoever to imprison people, there was a possibility I would need to do that at some point, so having the Prison Guards around might be useful.

Besides, the Prison Guards weren't real people. Technically, they didn't *need* time off. And as a Villain, who said I needed to keep my end of the deal? Wouldn't having an army of mindless slaves be more useful to me than a team of well-paid employees?

So I looked Ike straight in the eyes and laughed. "Sorry, pal, but no thanks. I'm in charge now. You didn't honestly think that I would give you guys more time off or whatever than Old Sparky did, did you?"

Shock appeared on Ike's face. "But—"

"The answer's no," I said. I waved at Ike. "Go back to work, you and your fellow Prison Guards. I will have more work for you guys later."

Ike looked even more betrayed than before, but I didn't care. I simply closed the Command Interface and turned around to face the person I knew was already standing there. "Was that villainous enough for you ... Grandpa?"

CHAPTER 49

Grandpa was indeed standing behind me on the other side of the Teleportation Pad. His arms folded behind his back, Grandpa wore an impressed expression on his face, one eyebrow raised.

"How did you know I was standing here?" said Grandpa. "I didn't even say anything."

I put my hands on my hips. "I just freed all of the Prisoners in the Dome. That means I solved your Riddle, which in turn means I get the stuff you said I would get. I honestly would have been surprised —and a little embarrassed—if you hadn't shown up right now."

Grandpa chuckled. "You know me too well, Robby. But yes, I did come to congratulate you on solving the Riddle. Before I give you the rewards you deserve, however, I wanted to ask you how."

I frowned. "How? How what?"

Grandpa gestured at the Dome under our feet. "How did you orchestrate the breakout? Not in the physical sense, I mean, because I already know how you organized your allies to pull this off. But how you solved the Riddle."

I put my hands in the pockets of my orange jumpsuit. "You mean how I defeated an enemy way stronger than me. How I defeated Old Sparky, in other words."

Grandpa rubbed his hands together eagerly. "Yes, I'm interested in hearing how you did that."

I shrugged. "I had to stop thinking of Old Sparky as just a video game character and think of him instead as a real person, for one. As you know, that was pretty hard for me because I know this is all just a game. But I also knew, from our conversation in the real world, that I couldn't beat Old Sparky just by getting stronger than him or treating him like a random video game boss."

"Excellent," said Grandpa. "But why could you not defeat him the normal way? You could have overpowered him through sheer brute force and strength, thanks to your Link to that mysterious woman. Once you got Old Sparky outside of the Dome—a brilliant way of dealing with him, by the way—he was completely at your mercy."

I raised a hand and balled it into a fist. "True. I could have crushed him like an ant. That would have been the most efficient way of dealing with him. But I don't think it would have been the *best* way of dealing with him."

"The *best* way, eh?" said Grandpa. "Elaborate."

I tapped the side of my head. "Because, even though this is just a game and none of this is real, the NPCs in Capes Online are far more advanced than the NPCs in any video game I've played before. They are so realistic that you can easily forget you're not talking to real people if you're not careful when interacting with them sometimes. And they're not just physically real, either, but psychologically real as well."

"Explain what you mean by 'psychologically real,' Robby," said Grandpa. "I would love to hear your definition."

I started pacing back and forth. "I mean that the NPCs of Capes Online, with a rare few exceptions, don't know that they are in a video game. To them, this *is* their world, in the same way that the real world is our world. What do you think the average person would do if they found out that the real world was just a fancy simulation, a glorified video game designed for the enjoyment of whoever built it? That their lives, ultimately, are meaningless, existing solely to provide the game's players with enjoyment and depth?"

Grandpa pursed his lips. "That would destroy the average person, I think."

I stopped and pointed at Grandpa. "Exactly. I gambled that the NPCs of Capes Online—specifically, Old Sparky—would react the same way, despite not being real. How much would knowledge of the true nature of their world change them? Was Old Sparky even psychologically ready to handle such a revelation?"

Grandpa glanced over the edge of the roof. "Obviously not."

"Precisely," I said. I spread my arms wide. "Old Sparky's belief in justice, in fairness, in right and wrong, really only makes sense in a real world, with real consequences, where true morality can exist. In a game, however, it's as nonsensical as the idea of leveling up and collecting points in the real world. His entire worldview—and, by extension, his very identity, which he based on his worldview—is irrational.

"And because it was so irrational, it was fragile. All it needed was just the right touch at just the right time to shatter it entirely, precisely because it was fake and, in the final analysis, based on falsehood."

Grandpa raised another eyebrow. "And do you think that shattering Old Sparky's psyche will have any long-lasting or even permanent effects on his psychology?"

I laughed. "I hope so, and given how realistic Capes Online is, probably. At this point, it won't matter if he gets control of the Dome again and gets his power back. He'll be too broken by the true knowledge of the nature of the world to care about anything anymore."

Then I cracked a grin. "And on a more personal level, this is my way of avenging Daniel. Capes Online broke my brother's brain. The least I can do, in return, is break this game's NPCs."

Grandpa clapped. "Bravo, Robby, bravo! Not only did you solve the physical aspect of the Riddle—that is, staging a mass breakout—but you went beyond the surface level and dove deep into the *true* purpose of the Riddle. I cannot be more proud of you than I already am. I am almost literally bursting with pride. I will be more than happy to give you the rewards you so rightly deserve. You—"

Grandpa did not get to finish his sentence because I socked him in the face.

Grandpa's glasses flew from his face and disappeared over the edge of the roof as he staggered backward from the blow. Rubbing his cheek, Grandpa looked at me in horror and confusion. "Robby … why did you punch me?"

My left eye twitched. "Why did I punch you? Why *wouldn't* I punch you? Do you know how close I came to psychologically *snap-*

ping while playing this damn game? How often I had to ignore my own conscience to do some evil, vile things I never would have even *considered* doing under other circumstances?"

"But none of this is real," said Grandpa. "You didn't actually hurt or kill anyone."

I pointed at my head. "But my *brain* thinks it's real! The human brain is terrible at telling the difference between fiction and reality. As far as my brain is concerned, I killed a widow and did all sorts of other horrible things just the same. And to what end?"

"For my money, of course," said Grandpa slowly, speaking to me like I was a tiger about to pounce on him. "So you can support your mother and brother."

I shook my head. "That's why *I* did it. But Grandpa, I still can't figure out why *you* set up these Riddles. If you really cared about me and my mother and brother, then why not just leave us the money when you died like a normal grandparent? Why do I have to jump through all these damn hoops just to get your wealth, wealth you can't even use anymore since you're dead? Why all these elaborate safeguards and security measures for something that should be rightfully mine? What is your actual goal here? What?"

I felt a little bad about chewing out Grandpa, but not really. As much as I may have loved and respected him, I couldn't deny the fact that he'd messed with me in ways that could have caused me a lot more harm than they did. Most grandparents didn't force their grandkids to solve morally ambiguous "Riddles" just to get their inheritance, after all.

It was almost like Grandpa didn't actually care about me, my brother, or my mother at all.

But that was silly … right?

Grandpa, still rubbing his face where I'd punched him, was silent. He seemed to be thinking, no doubt carefully considering the exact words he'd use to address my complaints.

Normally, I appreciated that fact about my grandfather, but now, it made me wonder if he was going to tell me the truth … or was simply buying time to think of a convincing lie.

Finally, Grandpa smiled. "I really did underestimate you, Robby. I thought you might be so overjoyed to see me again that you wouldn't ask these questions or think deeply about my real motives. But that mind of yours ... oh, it's nearly as sharp as mine. Certainly sharper than your brother's, by any measurement."

I scowled. "It's not Daniel's fault he lost his mind."

Grandpa wagged a finger at me. "Ah, but in a way, it is. Compared to you, Daniel was always mentally weak. Probably, he shouldn't have played Capes Online in the first place or had any exposure to any hyper-realistic VR game. Some people simply cannot handle it."

"We're getting better about it," I said. "More people are waking up to the dangers of VR. We just didn't know how bad it would get when this technology first came out."

"The general public did not, perhaps," said Grandpa. He smirked. "But then, the masses have always been dull and unable to think ahead longer than a day, if that. Like animals, human beings are too simpleminded and easy to lead astray. Daniel is one such example of an easily manipulated human being."

"No one manipulated Daniel," I said. "Unless you count the game's advertisements as manipulation, which I can't disagree with you on."

Grandpa shook his head. "SI Games didn't tell your brother to play Capes Online. Nor did the game itself, really, do that to him. I did."

CHAPTER 50

I stared at Grandpa. "What? But you're dead. How could you have told Daniel to play Capes Online?"

Grandpa smirked even more. "Did you really think you were the first to discover my holo-will in the attic? Or did you never wonder why Daniel was so obsessed with Capes Online in the first place?"

I bit my lower lip. "I guess I just thought that the game was so immersive that it caused people to lose their grasp on reality sometimes."

"Wrong," said Grandpa. "Or partially right. You see, Capes Online and similar games *are* very immersive and *can* cause or feed an addiction to VR. But the main reason Daniel—who you always knew to be a very studious and careful brother—fell into it is because I told him to."

My eyes widened. "Daniel found your recording in the attic before me. He tried to solve the Riddles."

"And failed," Grandpa said with a shake of his head. "Quite miserably, I might add. Hence why I said he is weak and simple-minded. He could not solve the Riddles, so he decided to reroll his character and become a Hero instead. He became lost in the game as a result."

"But why did he never mention this to me or Mom?" I said. "Daniel hasn't mentioned you to me even once since he had to go to the nursing home."

Grandpa put his hands together. "Because Daniel forgot why he was playing the game in the first place after a while. Realizing he couldn't solve my brilliant riddles, Daniel decided to play the game his way. He told me himself that he did not want my money if it meant violating his moral codes. He was much less pragmatic than you."

My head spun with the revelation, yet I had no reason to believe that Grandpa was lying to me. It made perfect sense. Why Daniel started playing Capes Online, what drove him to keep coming back to the game, what made him eventually lose his mind …

I pointed at Grandpa. "You still haven't answered *why*, though. Why you put me and my brother through this hell. Is it just because you're as bad as Mom says you are? Is it because you enjoy seeing us suffer?"

Grandpa rolled his eyes. "Your mother … such a weak, whiny woman. It is a miracle that she married her husband, a man who was much smarter than her. I assume that is where you got your intelligence. Or perhaps my own genes filtered through her into you."

"You're still avoiding the question," I said. "Why? I demand an answer."

Grandpa spread his arms wide. "You know, of course, from reading my book how fascinated I have been with the concept of digital immortality. Originally, I sought digital immortality for myself so I could live forever, as I did not want to die.

"But when I realized that I would not live long enough to see the technology become a reality, I changed gears. I wanted to see the effects that digital immortality can have on a person's morality."

I frowned. "I don't follow."

Grandpa started pacing in a circle around me, forcing me to turn my head to keep my eye on him. Although I didn't think Grandpa was going to hurt me, I still didn't entirely trust having my back to him.

"It's a social experiment," said Grandpa. "Video games have been around for years now. Although people have often expressed concern over whether those games cause real-life violence, their concerns have always been rebuffed. Players point out that most gamers are perfectly kind, moral individuals in their real lives, even if they play bloodthirsty killers in their games. Without any hard evidence to indicate an impact that games have on a person's morality, such ideas more or less died off in mainstream society long before you were born, aside from the fringes of civilization, though even there, those ideas aren't quite as prevalent as they used to be."

"Because it's stupid," I said. "Video games don't cause violence. Or make people sexist or racist, for that matter."

Grandpa waved a hand dismissively. "Yes, we know that. But such ideas only applied when the divide between the virtual and the physical was stricter than it was now. Back then, you played video games by picking up a controller, sitting in front of a television screen, and mashing buttons. However immersive or entertaining such games might have been, it was still possible to separate your real self from the game character you were playing, even in an RPG."

I nodded, starting to follow Grandpa's logic. "And then VR happened."

Grandpa held up a finger. "Not necessarily. The original VR games were very simple and difficult to truly get immersed in. The real change didn't occur until decades later, when hyper-realistic VR technology was finally perfected in—and then popularized by—games like Capes Online. I foresaw that the ethics debate over the effect that video games have on a person would be reignited by this advance in technology."

Thinking about my own experiences in Capes Online, I said, "You were definitely ahead of your time, then, because it is something I've thought about a lot."

"Of course I was," said Grandpa. "I'm brilliant, so naturally I would be able to see things that other people couldn't even dream about."

I cocked my head to the side. "Does that make you brilliant or insane?"

Grandpa, who was passing me by when I said that, looked at me with a crazy grin. "In the end, what's the difference between brilliance and insanity, other than society's frankly arbitrary standards?"

I folded my arms in front of my chest. "Let me get this straight. You knew, maybe before anyone else, that the advancement of VR technology would reignite debates about the impact of games on peoples' minds and actions. But you clearly did not live long enough to see those debates revive."

Grandpa sighed and looked down at his body. "However brilliant my mind was and still is, my body still succumbed to old age and disease. So I decided to participate in the debate in a different, more indirect way by coming up with these Riddles. I wanted to know: Would having a good person, like yourself, become a Villain in Capes Online have an effect on your sense of morality in the real world?"

I gazed around at my surroundings. "So this—all of this, everything I've been through since I first started playing this game—was just one giant social experiment."

"*Is* one giant social experiment," Grandpa corrected, coming to a stop in front of me. "I did what philosophers rarely do, which is put my ideas to the test. I wanted to see what would happen to a moral person's views and actions if forced to make immoral choices in a video game that is nearly as real as real life."

I scowled. "Well, your experiment is over. I solved your Riddles without becoming as bad in real life as I am in Capes Online. In the real world, I still care about helping people and doing the right thing."

Grandpa smirked again. "For now. After all, there are still two more Riddles to solve. You still have a long way to fall."

"I'm not going to," I said. "And I'm not sure why you want me to fall. I'm your grandson."

Grandpa raised an eyebrow. "I didn't say I *wanted* you to fall. But I also think you have trended closer to the dark side than you, perhaps, realized. I saw how much you enjoyed killing Old Sparky. There appears to be more darkness in your heart than you realize."

I wanted to argue with Grandpa, but I realized he had a point. I had enjoyed—perhaps a little too much—planning and plotting this breakout. I'd taken great pleasure in inflicting pain and punishment on my enemies.

And who were my enemies? For the most part, people—like Old Sparky and the Prison Guards—who were trying to do the right thing, at least within the context of this world. Meanwhile, I'd just freed a bunch of the worst criminal scum in the game.

But again, I shook my head. "So what if I have a dark side?

Everyone does. I'm just channeling it through this game, where I can't actually hurt anyone."

Grandpa shrugged. "So far. We'll see how you continue to develop, as I suspect you aren't going to quit anytime soon."

I raised an eyebrow. "Why would I quit when I've come this far already? I won't get any of the money until I complete the next Riddles, right?"

Grandpa flashed a smile at me. "That's a good way to segue into your rewards. Here you go."

Grandpa waved his hand at me and a new notification suddenly appeared in front of me:

RIDDLE: *Initiate a mass breakout from the Dome*
STATUS: *Solved*

Congratulations! You successfully killed the previous Warden, freed the Prisoners of the Dome, and even have your own Legion now.

But why stop with conquering the Dome? There is a whole world beyond the Dome's walls that is ripe for the picking. Perhaps you have what it takes to become the biggest baddie in all of Capes Online …

REWARDS: *1% of Professor Robert J. Baker's personal wealth.*
BONUS REWARD: *Maelstrom Suit (1) and Dino Armor (1).*

My eyes were glued to the list of rewards at the bottom. "One percent of your wealth—? But that's—"

"A lot," said Grandpa idly, "although not nearly enough to cover all of your mother's or your brother's medical bills, of course. It should, however, be enough to prove to you that I am not lying when I said I put my money in this game before my death. You should receive a DM from me with a link to the page where you can have the money transferred into your checking account."

A *ping* in my ears drew my attention to my inbox, where I did indeed see a link to Grandpa's money. Even though I wanted the money so badly, I refrained from clicking the link immediately.

Instead, I said to Grandpa, "I got the link."

Grandpa smirked. "Good. I hope this helps you decide to keep playing Capes Online and to keep solving my Riddles."

I raised an eyebrow. "What is the next Riddle?"

Grandpa winked at me. "I would tell you right now, but unfortunately, the next Riddle requires a bit more set-up before I feel you are ready to challenge it."

"How long will I have to wait before I can take a crack at it?" I demanded.

Grandpa raised two fingers. "Two weeks minimum. I will message you when the second Riddle is ready. For now, why don't you enjoy the new Equipment I gave you?"

Puzzled, I went over to my item inventory and spotted both the Maelstrom Suit and the Dino Armor. "What are these?"

Grandpa gestured at my clothes. "That jumpsuit of yours just isn't very *villainous*, in my opinion. Plus, you barely have any Powers and you will definitely need more Powers going forward. I designed these Costumes specifically for you and your Sidekick. I think they will make you both look—and feel—far more like the powerful and feared Villains you rightfully are. They are also unique, so you won't have to worry about running into anyone else who has it."

Again, I was tempted to look at the Costume's Stats immediately, but I still wanted to talk to Grandpa. "Thanks. I'll check it out later. In the meantime, did you find out anything about the Ghost of the Dome?"

Grandpa turned away from me, which I did not consider a good sign. "I did not. But in the end, it doesn't matter, I think. The Ghost, whoever she is, clearly seems to be helping you. She does not seem to be in control of you, so I have no qualms with you continuing to Link with her, if you want."

I cocked my head to the side. That did not seem very in character for Grandpa, especially this more manipulative version of him who clearly hated not knowing certain things.

But at the same time, I was grateful, at least, that he'd stopped bitching to me about her. I still didn't know who exactly the Ghost was, but I figured she gave me an advantage I would be stupid to turn down. I'd have to find out the truth about her eventually, but for now, I would just accept her existence and help.

"I believe that is all I wanted to discuss with you, Robby," said Grandpa. He glanced over his shoulder at me and gave me a thumbs-up. "Enjoy your rewards, your new Legion, and, if you dare, your newfound Infamy among the Capes Online player base. I cannot wait to see the full ramifications of your actions unfold before your eyes."

And then Grandpa was gone, vanished into thin air.

Like a ghost.

I shook my head and turned around to look out at the Adventure City skyline again. Grandpa's parting words, as ominous as they might have been, were probably true. My Reputation was now Infamous, which I assumed meant that I was now going to be instantly recognizable to most of the players and NPCs in Capes Online.

I still had no idea what sort of challenges existed beyond the walls of the Dome, but I knew I could—and would—conquer them.

Because I wasn't just Robert Baker, grandson of Professor Robert J. Baker and minor video game streaming personality, anymore.

I was Maelstrom, the Big Bad of Capes Online, and Captain of the Maelstrom Mongers.

And soon, the whole world would hear my name … and tremble.

But more importantly, I couldn't let Grandpa win. I would solve his Riddles and get his wealth without sacrificing my moral character or principles.

Because truthfully, I didn't care about the Heroes and other Villains I might run into out there. I wasn't playing to win.

I was playing to prove Grandpa wrong … and save my family.

No matter the cost.

CHAPTER 51

Joe the purse thief carefully made his way down the stairs to Top Secret. He'd sneaked away during all of the celebrations thrown by the other Prisoners on the higher Floors. Now that everyone was free, Abaddon had convinced the remaining Mongers to throw a huge, prison-wide party. Even the Prison Guards had been invited, although they had seemed less enthusiastic about it than the Mongers did.

Not that I can blame them, Joe thought with a trace of bitterness. *Like me, they're a slave to a young, cocky upstart who thinks he's all that. They may not technically be Minions like me, but they might as well be, given how they're going to be treated once Maelstrom comes down from the roof to grace us with his presence.*

And, of course, not all of the Prisoners had joined the Mongers. While Joe did not know the full statistics, he concluded, based on his own observations, that about seventy percent of the Dome's inmates had become Mongers. The other thirty percent had left to find freedom on the streets of Adventure City independent of the Maelstrom Mongers.

Seventy percent was a pretty good number and meant that the Mongers had a strong enough force to take on the Winter League, which was Adventure City's biggest Hero League at the moment.

Now we just have to wait and see if Maelstrom can make this Legion last or not, Joe thought.

Villain Legions, after all, were known for being terribly unstable, largely due to the selfish and shortsighted nature of most Villains. In his time, Joe had seen many Legions rise and fall, with the most recent being the Paradox Legion that arose during the Blackouts.

In the end, however, Joe didn't care how long the Maelstrom Mongers lasted or if they even lasted at all. He had slipped away from the party for a good reason, because the party acted as an excellent distraction from what he was actually trying to do.

Reaching Top Secret, Joe found it empty and abandoned. The cells stood open, showing just how empty they were, and the place had a dusty, forgotten smell about it. Joe was still not sure if Maelstrom planned to use the empty cells for holding prisoners or not.

They would make for great holding cells for our enemies, Joe thought, grinning to himself.

But there was one cell that was still locked and closed tightly, despite everything that had happened:

The prison cell of Prisoner #1X, the very first Prisoner to be locked up in Top Secret in the first place.

Standing in front of the massive stone door, Joe tugged on the chains and frowned. "Mom? Are you there? It's me, Joe."

A cold sensation washed over Joe just then, making him shiver. It had been a long time since he'd felt *that* particular sensation and it still was as uncomfortable as he remembered.

"Little Joey," said a cool, elderly female voice in his ear. "I see you were successful in infiltrating Maelstrom's group."

Joe scowled. "It wasn't easy. I got killed way too many fucking times."

"Language," said the female voice. "You know how I feel about my children using naughty language around me. It makes me … upset."

Joe gulped. "Uh, sorry, Mom. Been so long since we talked that I forgot about that."

"Just don't let me catch you swearing in front of me again and you should have nothing to worry about," Mom said, her voice practically a whisper. "Can you free me yet?"

Joe narrowed his eyes and looked at the chains and locks again. "Yes, but it will take a while. And given how Maelstrom is probably the most Infamous Villain in the game now, it'll be a struggle to slip down here and work on this without him noticing. He's too smart."

"Don't worry about Maelstrom," said Mom. "I've got an eye on him. I will make sure he doesn't notice what you are doing."

Joe snorted. "So you're the reason he's so much stronger than he should be. Is Maelstrom Linking with you? Is that it? Should've known. Makes me wonder what you still need me for."

"Maelstrom is a useful pawn, but like you said, he is too smart," said Mom. "If he knew the real reason I was helping him, that would complicate our plans immensely."

Joe paused. "So he still doesn't know who you really are?"

"Not yet," said Mom. "Maelstrom will probably figure it out eventually, but for now, he still thinks I am the Ghost of the Dome. And by the time he does figure out who and what I am, it will be too late for him to stop me."

"Old Sparky said the same thing," said Joe. "And look what happened to him. Splat."

Mom growled. "Old Sparky was a fool. Not like me. I may lack his flash and spark, but I am far smarter than that fat idiot ever was. Unlike him, I have to be intelligent about the way I go about dealing with my enemies."

Joe shrugged. "Still not sure I'd be so confident if I were you, but hey, you're Mom. You know best."

"I do, Joe, I do," said Mom. "Now get to work. My influence is extremely limited inside this cell. Until you let me out, I will have to keep working through Maelstrom."

Joe dug through his pockets for his lockpicking tools. "Fine, Mom. I'll be a good son and get you out of here, don't worry. That's the whole reason I put up with that idiot and his even stupider pet dinosaur for as long as I have."

"Yes, I am aware," said Mom. "Fortunately, you will only have to tolerate their existence just a little while longer. Until then, see you later, my son …"

Joe felt Mom's presence leave him, but he had no doubt she was still watching him somehow. She always was. Even after getting defeated by those Heroes and locked up over twenty years ago now, Mom could still somehow use her Powers to reach him and influence others. Granted, her reach was very limited outside of the Dome, but it did amaze Joe whenever he thought about her power.

Then again, she's not just any Villain, Joe thought as he pulled a pick from his pocket and started to work on the first lock. *She's the original. Some called her a disaster. Others said her mere existence is a catastrophe.*

But me ... I always called her Mom, even when everyone else in the world called her Disastrophe.

Villain Town will continue in book two, Arch Enemy!

THANK YOU FOR READING BIG BAD

We hope you enjoyed it as much as we enjoyed bringing it to you. We just wanted to take a moment to encourage you to review the book. Follow this link: **Big Bad** to be directed to the book's Amazon product page to leave your review.

Every review helps further the author's reach and, ultimately, helps them continue writing fantastic books for us all to enjoy.

———

Also in series:

VILLAIN TOWN
Big Bad
Arch Enemy
Villain

Check out the series here! (tap or scan)

Want to discuss our books with other readers and even the authors? Join our Discord server today and be a part of the Aethon community.

Facebook | Instagram | Twitter | Website

You can also join our non-spam mailing list by visiting www.subscribepage.com/AethonReadersGroup and never miss out on future releases. You'll also receive three full books completely Free as our thanks to you.

Looking for more great books?

Everybody wants a second shot at life... Few get that restart. Chosen by roaming angels and sent off to another word full of magic and cultivation, where they can live in ways that could only be dreamed of on earth. Where the only thing that dictated their fate was power. Anyone who met Chance would have agreed that he deserved it more than most. Life isn't that easy. Just like everything else, there are rules and regulations—and Chance didn't make the cut. Not until a lucky encounter gets him a one-way ticket to his future. A world where he can make something of himself. If only he hadn't landed in the middle of an endless maze full of monsters salivating for his life. Isolated and lost, the only thing Chance has to work with is his strange, luck-based magic and his determination to finally live a life worth living. Fortunately, he has a whole lot of good Karma built up. **Don't miss the next hit Progression Fantasy Cultivation series from Actus, bestselling author of** *Blackmist* **&** *Cleaver's Edge*. **Join the adventure of a Karmic Cultivator in a brutal new world who refuses to compromise his values on his quest to grow stronger. Sometimes, luck isn't all it's cracked up to be.**

Get Weaving Virtue Now!

When you steal Time Magic, prepare to run for eternity... Arlan can go back in time by one minute, once per day. Fail a challenge? Say something dumb? He can get a redo as long as he acts fast. And every time he levels up, he can go back a little further. But, even with his growing power, Arlan has never been in more danger. He was left stranded in the middle of a monster-infested forest, nobody to rely on but himself as he fights to build strength. And his time magic wasn't given to him freely. He stole it. And its original owners would go to any lengths to take it back. **Don't miss the start of a new LitRPG Adventure filled with time magic, three-dimensional characters, a crunchy LitRPG System, tactical combat, and power progression where level-ups are hard-earned and bring with them meaningful change in characters' abilities.**

Get Minute Mage Now!

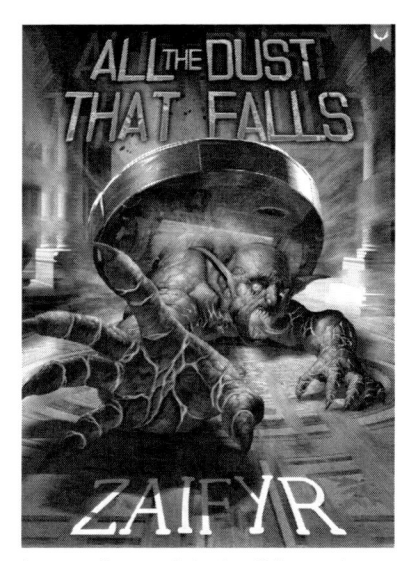

Some seek power. Some seek justice. Others seek to root out the filth lurking in the darkest of corners. Spot was summoned from his comfortable charging pad and familiar floors to a world of magic and intrigue. But after the flight of his new patrons, he is left alone to care for a filthy castle. During his quest to keep this new home clean, Spot will face demons, foreign armies, and his arch nemesis, the dreaded stairs. All those who stand before him will be swept away. Those who follow his spotless trail will find enlightenment, purity, and a world on its knees. **Follow this wholesome vacuum on his quest to power in** *All the Dust that Falls*, **a hilarious new Isekai LitRPG that will make you question what it means to be a hero. Or if heroes even need limbs, or mouths, or... you get it.**

Get All the Dust that Falls Now!

For all our LitRPG books, visit our website.

GET MORE LITRPG

ABOUT THE AUTHOR

Lucas Fliint writes superhero and LitRPG fiction. He is the author of Capes Online, The Superhero's Son, Minimum Wage Sidekick, and The Legacy Superhero, among others. He currently lives in Sherman, Texas with his wife, daughter, rabbit, and guinea pig.

Find links to his books, social media, updates on newest releases, and more by going to his website at www.lucasflint.com.

Newsletter: https://www.lucasflint.com/lucas-flint-super-newsletter-sign-up/

Discord: https://discord.gg/FpWvRqm2md

Made in United States
North Haven, CT
19 November 2023